Saffron Summer

by
Marion Hough

Saffron Summer

Marion Hough

Published by
Russlyn Books
in association with
PB Software
3 Nelson Road
Ashingdon, Rochford
Essex SS4 3EJ

FIRST EDITION
First Printing June 2010

A CIP catalogue record of this book
is available from the British Library

ISBN 978-0-9565891-2-5

Cover by Peter Colloff.

With thanks to my wonderful family,
Bernard, Lynne and Russell
who make my life complete.

ESSEX 1832

"Gawd almighty!" Caleb Jones sank to his knees in the wet sand beside the body of his friend. For days the tides had tossed the dead man across the estuary's turbulent waters. With every wave the sea sucked greedily at the corpse as if trying to reclaim its prize, shifting the lifeless limbs in a mocking imitation of life. Now it lay spreadeagled on the Essex shore, of its once weather beaten and handsome face, only a hideous, lipless grin and empty eye sockets remained. With gentle hands, Caleb cleared away the strands of seaweed from the cold face.

"Is it 'im?" Tom Brewer murmured, unwilling to look too closely.

Caleb nodded. "It's Jack alright. This'll break Mary's 'art. She's been a'prayin' 'e'd been picked up and took over to Kent."

For five days and nights Mary Clay had kept vigil, staring through the cottage window. Knowing in her heart that the evil grey waters must eventually give up their dead. Only a handful of small craft had made it safely through the storm.

Jack Clay's had not been among them.

CHAPTER ONE

Through the open window Saffron stared out across the sullen grey water of the estuary to where a storm-laden sky had bleached colour from the sea and Kent shore beyond. She shivered, hugging her thin shawl closer. Her slender fingers worrying the frayed edges as she leaned to scan the cobbled road to the corner of Horse Hill.

A stiff sea breeze tugged loose a strand of sun-ripened hair and, tucking it firmly back into the knot at her neck, she frowned. Poll was late again, and on her half day. Her sister had changed of late. They had always shared secrets, whispering and giggling in their bed, hushing one another for fear of waking young Tom or their sleeping step-father. But of late Poll had grown up, so unlike the mischievous fifteen year old girl who had begged to take up a position at the big house.

"Come on, Saffy," She had wheedled, "Speak to Pa. There be nothing for me to do here, 'cept work in the boiling sheds or tend young Tom and that be your job. And there's such things go on at the house. That Lady Margaret, she dresses in silk and she give Callie, what's worked there a year or more, a bit of French lace for her bonnet." Bright eyed, she warmed to her argument, artfully delivering a last blow of undeniable reason. "And 'sides, we can do with the money, can't we?"

Saffron had been forced to admit the truth. From the little her stepfather made by fishing, only a few shillings survived its way past the Peter Boat Inn and into her hands. But in the first few short months he had been married to their mother, Jonas Turner had proved to be a good man, doing his best to fill the gap left by the death of their father.

Memories of the night Jack Clay's body had been washed

ashore, after his boat had gone down in the estuary, still haunted her. His bloated corpse, brought home to their cottage by his neighbours, bore no resemblance to the loving man who had filled their days with security and laughter. A good, honest man, he had been well liked and respected. She remembered how she had stood, clutching Poll's hand by the open grave, while Nathan supported their mother

They had managed, with the help of an occasional handout from the Parish and friends and tradesmen, to avoid the poor-house, surviving the following months until Jonas began to call. One night their mother had called them together around the hearth. "Now, listen my dears. You know that we can barely get by." Nathan had made to interrupt. "No, lad. Listen to me. Even with what you bring 'ome and the bit I get from sewin' it's not enough." She paused, looking from one face to the other.

You know that Jonas has been callin' to see us. Well, 'e's asked me to wed 'im."

"You mean you're goin' to marry 'im!" Nathan exploded, jumping to his feet.

"I thought I was 'ead of the 'ouse. What d'you want 'im for?"

"I said I would 'cause 'e's a fine strong man and 'e's willin' and able to keep a roof over our 'eads and food on the table." She looked down at her folded hands. "Your father was the only man I ever loved and I miss 'im still. No one can ever take 'is place but I got to look to tomorrow for you young'uns."

Jonas had indeed proved to be a good husband. Some in the village said he should have waited a full year before courting the young widow. Some said he had had his eye on her long before the accident. But Jonas was an able fisherman with his own pinkie, a trim eighteen-foot craft, bringing home enough to meet the rent for the clapboard cottage and provide a good table.

His joy knew no bounds when he discovered that he was to father a child of his own. His insistence that his wife should rest each day was met with gales of laughter. "D'you think I'm made of glass Jonas? I've borne three already. Another will be no 'ardship." Her pregnancy was without problem, the birth natural and unhurried and for several days both mother and baby thrived. Everything seemed fine until in the small hours of the morning, Jonas shook Saffron from her sleep, urging her to tend to her mother while he fetched a neighbour.

Saffron knelt helplessly beside the fever-ridden woman, unable to do more than dab a cold, wet rag to her sweating face and pray for the Lord's intervention. Within hours the fever had claimed its victim.

The shock of her mother's sudden death only days after the child Tom's birth left Jonas grief stricken and without purpose.

A wet nurse was found for the baby and good neighbours stepped in to make arrangements for the funeral and once again the graveyard at Leigh church saw the young family saddened by the loss of a parent.

In the days that followed, Saffy and her older brother Nathan were made to cope as best they could. Jonas left his boat to ride its moorings while, blank-eyed, he drowned his sorrow in the alehouses along the Strand. Only occasionally would he rouse himself and, on the tide, would join the fleet of fishing boats heading out into the estuary, returning with a modest catch of shrimp. The cost of boiling left barely enough to provide the necessities for a few days at a time.

Saffron's thoughts were cut short by Tom's plaintive voice and she turned to see him squatting on the faded rag rug staring intently into the face of a mewling week-old kitten clutched tightly to his chest.

"Why are her eyes tight shut, Saffy. Is she blind like Sam?"

"No, you goose. Poor Sam lost his eyes fighting old Boney. All kits are born that way." Saffron took the scrap of wriggling fur from her brother's grasp and tucked it back beside its anxious mother in the hearth-warmed box. "You'll see, in a few days she'll be lookin' at the world with eyes as blue as the sky."

"Like mine, Saffy?"

"Aye." She turned to lift the lid of the iron stewpot hung above the fire and to stir the mix of vegetables and meat scraps, returning the ladle to it's hook and wiping her hands on her rough linen apron.

"Tell me, Saffy. Tell me."

"You know Tom." She smiled at the eager child. "I've told you over and over."

"Again." He pleaded, tugging at her skirt.

She sighed, knowing nothing would satisfy his need than to hear the reassuring words he had heard so often. "Your eyes are blue just like your Mother's."

"And?"

"And they were as blue as the deep blue sea."

"And?"

"They sparkled like sun on the waves."

"And?"

"And she was as beautiful as a spring day". She scooped the boy into her arms. "And she loved you Tom and she didn't want to leave us." He struggled, leaning back to look into his sister's face, his sad eyes filled with questions.

"Father said t'was God's will, but..." Her throat tightened with suppressed tears as she held his head to her, stroking soft hair from his face.

"It was her time, Tom. She was tired, too tired to fight the fever. But." She forced a smile. "She gave you to us." She searched the thin heart-shaped face. "And you are so like her." She tweaked her brother's nose. "Now", she set him down on the hard, oak planked floor. "Go and see if you can spy Poll a comin' down the hill."

Tom scampered to the low lintelled doorway and stood, his small frame outlined against the failing light.

"I see her. I see her!" The impatient child hopped from one foot to the other, "Can I go Saffy? Can I?"

"As far as the gate and no further!" She hurried to the door, watching, calling a warning as the child scrambled onto the bars of the gate.

There had been several violent thunderstorms throughout the late spring and into early June and the banks of blue black clouds boiling across the sky heralded yet another. She leaned over the excited child anxiously searching the lane for sight of her sister. The girl's slight figure was bent against the rising wind, her ill-shod feet slipping on the wet cobbles.

"Poll! Poll!" Tom's piping cry was lost in the scream of a gull swooping inland, its wingspread angled above a rapidly rising swell. She scanned the horizon, reminded that Jonas had chosen that day of all days to leave on the morning tide in a half-hearted attempt to bring in a catch.

As Poll reached the gate a vicious crack of lightning lit the foreshore, bathing it in a cold blue light. Saffron grabbed Tom and hurried her sister into the shelter of the cottage, urging her to warm herself by the fire.

"You're late again Poll. What was it kept you this time?" She took her sister's hands into her own, chaffing warmth into the chilled fingers.

"Lady Margaret's come back from Suffolk with some fine

friends, There's a big party goin' on tonight up at the 'ouse and cook said I should 'elp 'er 'afore I left." She offered a weak smile. "But she did give me this to bring 'ome." She held out a paper-wrapped parcel to Saffron. "Go on, open it." She urged, "Cook's always good to me when I 'elp her."

Tom was unable to hide his excitement, while Saffron tore open the wrapping to reveal a large pie, the dish still warm from the oven.

"'Tis filled with good meat and gravy." Poll's tone begged for approval. "And cook said there's more'n enough for all of us."

"She's right there. Will you be sure to thank 'er for me Poll?" Saffron sniffed the crust appreciatively. "I'll rest it on the stove and we'll 'ave it tonight. The stew can wait 'til tomorrow. Now, tell us all the news. What has been going on up there on the hill?"

Poll settled herself by the hearth, slipping her small feet from her shoes and holding out wiggling toes to the warmth. "Well…" She paused. "They've took on a new girl. She's only twelve and they've put her to doin' some of my jobs, clearing out the fire grates and such. She's from the work'ouse, lost both her Mum and Dad two years back to the Cholera. Skinny little thing she is, but Maddie works 'ard, I'll give her that. I sort of look out for her." Poll straightened her shoulders. "I'm older see, and she don't have no one 'cept me."

Saffron sat beside her sister, hoisting Tom onto her lap. "So you're teachin' 'er the ropes then?"

Poll nodded. "The best of it is, when I've laid the fires and such, I get to spend more time 'elping cook, and sometimes I get to peel the 'taters and things." She stared, dreaming into the flames, "I'm going to be lady's maid like Dolly someday".

Saffy smiled at the determined tilt of the firm little chin. "I'm sure you can do anything you set your sights on Poll. You just work 'ard and learn all you can. What about Lady Margaret?" Saffron was eager for confirmation of the latest gossip. "We did hear that she's planning to give the village a fresh water well. We do need one after the sickness took so many a year back."

"Cook said somethin' of the sort." Poll shook her head dismissively. "But you should see the new dress madam's 'ad made for this party. I sneaked a look when I was doin' the fire in 'er room. She were out ridin' with 'er friends. Lovely it is, all pink silk and lace trimmin's. Fit for a Queen." Saffron smiled. As always her sister's head was filled with dreams and fancies.

The afternoon light had all but gone as the first low rumblings of thunder rolled across the bruised sky and, setting Tom down, Saffron hurried to close the window.

"Summer or not, we're in for a bad one tonight." Poll flinched at an angry explosion across the heavens and, as an afterthought. "Where's Pa?"

"Somewhere out there, 'e took the boat out on the tide." Saffron tried to hide her concern, crossing her fingers beneath her shawl. "Don't worry, e'll have tossed a coin to the Sea Witch, e'll turn up like a bad penny." She wrinkled her nose in disgust at the thought of old Mother Watkins who sat on the edge of the quay each day as the men set sail. She would hold out her hand for a coin, promising them a fair wind and good catch and not a man would say her nay and risk her curse. The few who had, returned with empty nets or had been claimed by the sea, leaving their family to face starvation or the workhouse.

Not for the first time that day her thoughts turned to Nathan, her older brother.

If only he had not fought with Tom's father, if only he had not left, if only…. He had been gone more than a year and in all that time there had been no word. As children they had been close and now more than ever she needed him to be there for her and for the family.

"So, what's the news 'ere in the village? Has Sarah 'ad 'er baby yet?" Poll pushed her shoes nearer to the fire to dry. "And what about old Billy Brewer, is 'e still fighting drunk every night?"

Saffron nodded. "Regular as a clock is old Billy. One of these days 'e'll take a wrong turn and pitch into the sea." She shook her head. "Silly old fool. Sarah 'ad a little girl, sweet baby she is. Oh! And I nearly forgot. Juniper Cottage is to 'ave a new tenant. An artist. They say all the way from Brighton."

"What's 'is name?" Poll's curiosity was peaked.

"No idea." Saffron frowned, busying herself with plates and forks. "But I did 'ear 'e's comin' to paint some of the parts 'ereabout. Now come on Tom and you too Poll, get to table and let's 'ave some of that pie. We'll not wait for Pa, the Lord only knows when 'e'll be back."

Tom jumped as a fork of lightning lanced the sky followed immediately by an angry roll of thunder. "Tis alright." Saffy hugged him. "Its right overhead now and if you count between the flash and the thunder you will hear it go away."

"We'll do it together, Tom." Poll caught her sister's eye and nodded. "There it goes again. Now, one, two, three…" Thunder rumbled overhead. "There, see, it's already three miles away." Tom chuckled. "Me now!" He waited for the blue white light to illuminate the cottage. "One, two, three, four, five….. "The child clapped his hands at the reassuringly distant growl in the heavens. But with the evidence of the storm's departure, came the rain, lashing unmercifully at the small cottage and cloaking the village in stygian gloom.

A fist beating frantically at the door brought Saffron to her feet. "Heaven be praised, Pa's 'ome safe." But, as she struggled to hold open the door against the wind's fury, she saw that the pale, pain-wracked face beneath the hooded cloak was that of her brother Nathan. Rain-soaked and bleeding, he stumbled past her to fall groaning at her feet.

CHAPTER TWO

The stunned silence was broken by Poll's scream, as backing away, she clutched a wide-eyed Tom protectively into the circle of her arms. Saffron battled to force shut the cottage door before bending to pull back the sodden hood of the heavy cloak.

"Quiet, Poll! And you Tom." She snapped, glaring at the child whose trembling lip heralded tears. "There's no time for that. 'Elp me get 'im to the fire." Her sister stood, seemingly frozen, unable to hear or respond until Saffron crossed to shake her roughly by the shoulder. "Do you hear me? That's Nathan, your brother, lying there." She brought her face close to Poll's. "Stir your stumps and give me a 'and. I can't move 'im on my own."

Her sister stared into her eyes as if seeing Saffron for the first time. "Is.. is he dead?"

"No, but I think he's bad 'urt." Poll set Tom down and followed her sister, bending to take Nathan's booted feet, while Saffron slid her hands under the young man's arms.

"Tom, drag a blanket from Pa's bed and set it down by the 'earth. Come on, you're a big boy. You can do it." The reassuring compliment stirred the frightened child to do her bidding.

"Now, together Poll, lift. We'll set 'im down by the fire and get these wet things off 'im." Between them they managed to hoist the semi-conscious man away from the door, before stripping his chilled body of its boots and outer clothing and wrapping him in the meagre warmth of the thin woollen blanket.

Saffron tipped hot water from the kettle into a bowl and tore a strip of fabric from a clean rag. "Let's see 'ow bad it is." She bent to bathe the bleeding gash at Nathan's temple. He groaned and, at her touch, his eyes flew open, blank and panic stricken.

"Its alright Nathan. You're 'ome." She murmured. "It's Saffy. Remember?" She brushed the wet hair from his face. "You're safe now. Just lie still while I wipe away some of this blood." She began to dab at the wound. "What 'appened? You been in a fight?"

Poll knelt nervously beside the prone figure, tucking the blanket around him while Tom crept close enough to stroke the back of his brother's grimy hand.

"Saffy?" Nathan's voice was little more than a whisper. He turned his head to stare first at Tom and then at Poll. "I made it then." A brave attempt at a crooked smile touched his mouth. "I lost the bastards!" He winced as Saffron cleaned away the last of the blood. "Not 'afore they 'ad me in their sights." With tender fingers he explored the wound. "'Tis only a graze."

"You mean they shot you?" Saffron sat back on her heels. "Who and why...? Her voice trailed away as she saw the look of horror on Tom and Poll's faces. What trouble had Nathan brought to their door? A sudden thought struck her. What would Jonas have to say on his return?

"I'll tell you later." Nathan raised himself on one elbow. "First a drink and then some food, for the love of God, Saffy, I'm half starved from my ride."

He saw her mouth tighten. "Ride?"

"Aye, I left the poor beast in Westcliff, at the back of one of them fine 'ouses. 'E was all but spent, so I legged it the rest." He bent his head. "I shall miss the Captain. He be a fine 'orse."

"You got a 'orse?" Tom breathed, round-eyed in wonder.

"One of Uncle's pack animals. I sort of borrowed it when the shooting started." Nathan chuckled, ruffling the boy's hair and accepting his small hand to help him rise. "You've grown considerable since I saw you last young Tom. What's Saffy been feedin' you?"

"We're having meat pie this night." Tom made a great show of helping his brother to his feet, and steering him to the table. "And cook told Poll there's enough for all."

"Then let's be at it." Nathan sat heavily on the chair normally occupied by Jason, passing a hand across his head smearing the rapidly clotting blood. Poll was quick to notice that for a moment he paled, swaying before shaking himself and straightening with a grin. "Not so good as I thought I was." He glanced at Saffron. "Looks as if you're stuck with me for the night."

She opened her mouth in protest. "Won't they be after you, whoever they are? Won't they come 'ere first?"

"I'm safe 'ere, at least for the time." He winked, "I'm not known as Nathan Clay." He threw back his head and laughed. "'Twas uncle's notion. Change your name and change your luck he said. So they be scouring the countryside for John Sawyer from Maldon."

"Maldon? Is that where you've been all these months?" Poll stared at her brother open-mouthed. "Why d'you go there? 'Tis miles away."

"Aye, and the further the better. Y'see, I knew Uncle Adam had a fine cod smack in those waters. Our father used to talk about his young brother, remember Saffy?"

She nodded her head "So?"

"So, I went cross country, took me a couple of days, then I goes up to his cottage and knocks at the door bold as brass. ''Ello' I says, I'm Nathan, Jack's boy !" "Well bless my boots, 'e says. Come right in lad and welcome." Then 'e sits me down and I tell 'im me troubles." Nathan leaned back and stretched long arms above his head. "They took me in, 'im and our Aunt and I been sort of working with him ever since."

"Working?" Saffy's eyes narrowed. "What sort of work? I remember Father saying as how his brother Adam was wild, even when he was a young'un."

Nathan threw back his head with a snort of laughter. "Well, 'e's not changed much that I can tell. We brought 'ome a good catch regular, and it weren't fish neither!"

"I knew it!" Saffy groaned. "You've been smuggling. No wonder the Excise are after you. Chelmsford Gaol or deported to the colonies, that's where you'll end. You bring shame on us Nathan and that's the truth." She turned to rest her hands on the table. "If our mother were alive you'd break 'er 'eart. Not once did she ever have to fear the Excise men thundering on the door. Our father, God bless him, would 'ave no truck with smugglin' 'e kept us fed by 'onest fishing," She turned to face him. "Why couldn't you do the same?"

For a moment Nathan bent his head against her tirade, before raising blank eyes to stare beyond her at the darkened cottage window.

"Do you think I wanted to go, to leave you and Poll and Tom? Our precious stepfather said 'e couldn't bear to look at me, I was too like our blessed father. I couldn't do right for doin' wrong. 'E took 'is fists to me once too often, Saffy. That night I gave 'im some of what 'e'd been giving me for a year or more." He ran a hand through thick blond hair, focusing on his sister as if seeing a stranger. "'E said 'e'd see me in front of the magistrates, tell 'em I'd 'it 'im for no reason. It would 'ave been 'is word against mine so you see." He pleaded for understanding. "I 'ad to go."

"I never knew." Saffy breathed, reaching out to touch his arm. "I'm sorry."

"'Ow could you 'ave known? 'E made sure you were never

around when I took a beating. Remember 'ow 'e used to say 'ow clumsy I was, always tripping up, falling on my face and such? I took it as long as I could. I thought if I stuck it out 'e'd keep his hands off you and the young'uns. But if I 'adn't gone then, the time would 'ave come when I think I would 'ave killed 'im.''

Saffy thought back to the night Nathan had left and saw again her stepfather's face, beaten raw and bleeding. He had told her to mind her business and, for more than a week, she had kept Poll and Tom out of his sight while he had staggered home each night too drunk to do more than throw himself on his bed and sleep until morning.

Nathan straightened his shoulders. "Anyway, Uncle Adam and me we got along famous." He caught Saffy's reproving smile. "Well it was that or take to the road. They say you can get rich with a pistol and a good 'orse under you."

Poll gasped. "You an 'ighwayman? Don't you never do that! I did 'ear the mistress sayin' as 'ow one of them 'eld up the London coach not a week since. There be a price on 'is 'ead with Jack Ketch and the gallows at the end of it." She clapped her hand to her mouth as she realised Tom was listening closely to her outburst.

"Who's Jack Ketch?" the child enquired innocently.

Saffron glared at her sister. "Never you mind." Saffron plunged a knife into the piecrust, lifting a chunk dripping with gravy onto the boy's plate. "You just get yourself round that and leave the talking to your elders." Tom shrugged, losing interest, anxious to enjoy a rare treat.

Torn between love for Nathan and the fear of her stepfather, Saffron cut wedges of pie for her brother and sister, thoughts chasing one another around in her mind. "You can't stay 'ere. Although, " she was aware of the storm raging outside, "I can't see Pa making it back to shore tonight. With a westerly blowing, rather than try to make headway into the Estuary, 'e'll likely ride it out on the Maplins 'till morning." She chewed at her lip. "I suppose you can catch an hour or two's sleep upstairs, but you'll best be gone by dawn for fear of being seen."

"So, what of Jonas?" Nathan spat the name with hate. "Does he say my name?"

"Never." Saffron shook her head. "And he won't 'ear it said neither. But I told you, 'e'll not be back this night, and even if 'e were to make it, 'e sleeps down 'ere so you'd ave to be quiet."

"Like the grave !" Nathan promised with a broad wink in Tom's direction. Poll shuddered at the reference, crossing to the window to stare out at the darkened sky, "I best be getting back 'afore long." She muttered, "but I don't fancy the journey. She turned to her sister, "I don't like leavin' you 'ere all alone with Nathan. S'pose they do track 'im down, what'll you do?"

Her brother stood to hug an arm around her. "Don't fret little sister, I've fooled 'em once. I'll do it again. 'Sides, I've 'ad enough of smuggling. I'll be making for Saffron Walden on the morrow. I've a mind to find the family we 'ave up there in the North. Mother used to talk about 'em, her Ma and Pa and her sister Jane. I mind 'ow she used to tell, when she were a child, the whole family grew the crocus flowers, Crokers she said they were called. She used to go on about 'ow the alley-ways were deep in blue petals where they'd been stripped away from the yellow middles. Chives she called 'em that's 'ow they gathered the Saffron. That's where you got your name Saffy." He grinned. "I was only a little'un, but I can 'ear Mother now. The day you were born she took a look at that yellow hair and she would 'ave no other name for you. 'Course the trade died when they started bringing in all the cheap Saffron from foreign lands. The story goes that the family got into brewin'. Most families turned their fields to barley growin' from what I've 'eard. They do say the ale up there is strong enough to make your 'ead spin."

"Do you think they'll take you in? Mother's family, the Porters I mean? We've not 'ad a word from Aunt Jane since Ma died." She frowned. "What'll you do if they turn you away?"

"Don't you fret Saffy, who would turn away a fine strong lad like me, willing to work and earn 'is keep?" He flexed his arm, pinching at the swell of muscle. "They'll take one look at me and say "Come on in lad: and make yourself at 'ome!"

Poll giggled at her brother's conceit. "They'll chase you off more like !"

"Just you wait an' see, Poll my girl. I reckon I'll see if I can find Aunt Jane first. Last I 'eard she were 'ousekeeper or some such at some big 'ouse. I'll come back a rich man, you mark my words." He wiped the back of his hand across his mouth and stretched, yawning widely. "If I'm to be away at the crack of dawn I'd best get some sleep." He bent to plant a kiss on Saffron's cheek. "Thank you." He whispered. She searched his eyes and saw gratitude and fatigue coupled with fear. "I knew you'd not turn me away."

She stretched wide her arms and hugged him impulsively, "Well get away upstairs. But, before you go, you can carry that mite up to 'is bed." She jerked a thumb at Tom who had fallen asleep at the table, his head in Poll's lap.

Gently Nathan lifted the boy and, cradling him, kissed the damp forehead. "If Jonas ever lays a 'and on him." His glance took in both girls. "I'll be back to finish what I started."

They watched him mount the stair. "'E means it," Poll shuddered, moving closer to the fire. "And if he don't, I will!"

"Poll! Don't you let me 'ear you say such things. Pa's never raised 'is fist to none of us," She bit her lip. "Even when 'e's 'ad a drop too much. Now come on, you'd best be away." She crossed to the window, ducking her head to squint up at the sky. "The rain's all but stopped; the storm's cleared, at least for the time bein'. If you go now likely you'll be in the dry 'afore it comes back. 'Ere." She turned to hook a shawl from its peg. "You'd best take this to cover your 'ead."

"But it's yours, Saffy." Poll protested, clutching the soft wool to her chest. "Won't you be needin' it?"

"No." Saffy gave her sister a good-natured push. "You know I never feel the cold. 'Sides, 'tis the first day of June on the morrow. Now off you go or you'll find yourself in trouble. Oh, and give this back to cook." She handed Poll the empty pie dish in its paper wrapping. "And don't forget to thank 'er for 'er kindness. I've set a bit aside for Pa, though I doubt he'll want it."

"Well if he does, I 'ope it chokes 'im after what he did to Nathan."

She hugged Poll to her. "Now no more talk like that. Take care." She whispered, snugging the shawl to frame the thin face. "See you soon."

A thin mist of rain blurred the scattered pattern of lights on the far Kent coastline as Poll paused to wave before disappearing into the gathering gloom.

With a sigh Saffron settled herself by the fire, leaning to ram another log of driftwood into the dying embers. With only a few hours before Nathan had to leave there was little point in seeking the comfort of her bed.

Dancing flames threw shadows on the cottage walls, highlighting the faded curtains, which, when new, had been her mother's pride and joy. A framed sketch of the Billet Alehouse, hung lopsided on one wall while another boasted a rusty sword. She smiled at the memory of the excitement its discovery had caused when it was caught in her father's nets. Nathan had claimed the honour of lovingly cleaning away the barnacles from its tempered blade and displaying it for all to admire.

Little enough to show for a lifetime's labour she mused. Yet there had been more, much more. She dozed, comforted by memories of the years when the timbered cottage, warmed by love, had echoed to the laughter of her parents and siblings.

A board creaking overhead brought Saffron awake and to her feet as Nathan tested each stair tread with bare feet.

"'Tis alright." She went to meet him. "Pa' didn't get back. Come and warm yourself by the fire and break your fast. You didn't sleep for long did you?"

"I didn't sleep at all Saffy. Too much on my mind." He scrubbed a hand over his face. "Far as I know Adam got safe away last night. We'd unloaded on the river bank when the Dragoons came on us. They got the Brandy but Adam and 'is boy reached the boat and pushed off. The last I saw the 'Maggie' was under way. The rest of us made for the dunes." He paused, frowning at a painful memory. "Poor old Bill Ballard caught one I saw 'im go down."

"What about Uncle Adam? Will they catch 'im?" Saffron pushed a wedge of bread and cheese in front of Nathan.

"No. See there was no moon. Pitch black it was and the 'Maggie' stood well off. We'd oiled her planks to stop em creaking, so's they wouldn't 'ave 'eard her slip her moorin'. If they made it, they'll 'ave sailed round to the point. If the Revenue cutter did spy her they'll 'ave given chase, but she's fast. She'll 'ave made it I warrant. If not." He spread his hands. "They'll end up with an 'efty great fine they can't pay and that'll put 'em in Chelmsford jail. The Revenue'll slice the Maggie in 'alf and that'd be a right shame. Sweet little craft she is."

Despite her disapproval Saffy was curious. "Where did the Brandy come from?"

"'T'was brought over from Flushing. They got distilleries there. They can send all we can take, then, 'course, there's the 'baccy what comes in from some place called Ghent. They got craft with false bottoms where they stow the stuff, like the gin. Powerful stuff that were. They rope the barrels together and drop 'em over the side. Then along we come and 'ook 'em out. Simple!"

Saffy sniffed. "Contraband, all of it."

"Look, I know what you say, and I know that over the other side, Kent and Sussex, there be some rough goings on. There were even lives lost. Most of it were down to the Hawkhurst gang or Ruxley's crew out of Howard, but I swear Saffy, we never 'urt no one. Smugglin's a bit of sport, a way to put a few extra guineas in your pocket to 'elp out what's got from fishing." He chuckled, laying an artful finger alongside his nose. "and there be no shortage of buyers among the worthies. There's not a grand 'ouse 'ereabouts without a good, full cellar." Nathan got to his feet. "I suppose it's time, Saffy. God knows when I'll see you and the young'uns. I'll get word to you some'ow once I'm settled. 'Ere." He dug into his pocket. "It's not much." He grinned, closing her fingers over the coins. "I didn't have time to fetch my savings." He put a finger to her lips to silence her protest. "I've kept a few shillin's and you need it more'n I do, you and Poll and young Tom."

"Well at least take a bite with you." Saffron bundled the last of the bread and cheese into a cloth. "You don't know when next you'll fill your belly. 'Ow long will you be on the road?"

"Depends on whether I catch a ride. There's wagons what do a run through Hadleigh and on over the heath to Rayleigh. I reckon I'll make Saffron Walden in about three days."

"As long as that?"

"Well, 'tis forty miles or more, and I'll be staying off the main roads for good reason." He grinned. "Don't worry, Saffy. The good Lord didn't get me this far for nothin'. I'll get there safe enough." Cramming the last crumbs of cheese into his mouth he sat to pull on his boots. "It'll be dawn in an hour and I want to be well away from the village before full light."

Cautiously he twitched the curtain aside. "All clear." He smiled down at Saffy as he turned to hug her one last time. Then she watched him melt into the shadows, the wind tearing at his cloak. "God speed." She whispered, closing the cottage door quietly behind him. She leant against the seasoned wood. With luck Nathan would meet a waggoner on the road and beg a lift at least part of the way to Walden. But if he were to be spotted by the Dragoons.... She pushed herself away from the door with an angry shake of her head. "No" She said aloud. "That won't 'appen. 'E's free and clear. Please God."

CHAPTER THREE

Thin fingers of sea mist hung above the village as a watery sun chased away the night's storm-dark mood. Nathan hugged the shadows, moving cautiously between the cottages. In the stillness the sound of voices alerted him to fishermen rising early, eager to catch the morning tide. The cry of a fractious child disturbed from sleep and the distant barking of a dog urged him to hurry on his way.

At the foot of Horse Hill he lingered for a moment turning to take one last look at the village where, above the chimneys, smoke spiralled from a new day's fires. "God be with you, Saffy." He whispered. "And with the young un's. I'd not be leavin' you with that bastard if I didn't need to."

He set his back to the narrow street and began the climb to where the square church tower stood silhouetted against the dawn sky. The cluster of waterside shacks and shanties quickly gave way to thatched cottages until they too, thinned as Nathan trudged northward, caution and hope his only companions.

Despite the lack of sleep, his determined stride covered the miles through the fields surrounding Hadleigh to where, on the crest of the hill, the castle ruins towered high and proud above the flat marshland.

The sun, climbing through a thin veil of cloud, grew steadily in strength, warming the earth and scenting the air with the sweet fresh smell of wet hay.

The dawn chorus filled the air as keen-eyed birds wheeled overhead, searching for the first meal of the day. Unwary insects fell easy prey to a group of hungry starlings hunting the hedgerows while, over the distant mudflats, a cormorant, its cruel beak open in its hunter's cry, searched for a larger prize.

To Nathan the mingled scent of sea and shore spelt home but he knew if freedom were to be his goal, then he must find it elsewhere. Sobered by his near capture, he vowed with every step to make something of the life he had almost forfieted. The penalties for even the smallest crime were harsh. He paused, shielding his eyes to stare out at the far Kent shore. Although smuggling on a small scale was generally overlooked, those who were caught carrying arms faced the death penalty. Sentences were at the discretion of the Customs or the Magistrate and could result in imprisonment in Springfield or Southampton goal. Many were sentenced to spend the rest of their miserable lives in Western Australia or Tasmania and rumour had it that those who survived the voyage in the overcrowded, fetid and airless prison ships, would not live long with the disease, poor diet, heat exhaustion and violence, that awaited them upon their arrival.

The path he had chosen lay between fields of green wheat, much of it flattened by the storm. A basking adder watched his progress and a lark soared skyward. A field mouse scuttled for cover at the sound of his tread. He stood for a moment, easing the ache in his legs, cramped from the uphill climb. The ruins of Hadleigh castle, its ancient stones looted by generations, now boasted only one defiant tower and a few outcroppings of broken wall. Shrugging out of the heavy cloak, still damp from the night's downpour, he threw himself down and, turning his face to the sun, wearily closed his eyes for a brief rest.

As he relaxed, Nathan's generous mouth curved in a fond smile at an unbidden childhood memory. A sun-drenched summer, when their mother had walked over the same path, taking him and his sisters to gather wild mushrooms. He and Saffy had fashioned knightly swords from stripped branches to defend the castle against imaginary pirates. He remembered how he had scratched his arm on brambles and had sworn straight-faced to their mother that it was an injury sustained in a fearsome battle with a band of cutthroats. "Happier times." He murmured, stretching and clambering to his feet. Turning his face to Leigh he shook his head. "And gone forever. So best put 'em behind you man and get on your way."

Rested, and with his back to the past, Nathan made for the stretch of woodland beyond which lay a few small farms and Daws Heath, a spot notorious as a meeting place for highway-men. A well-trodden footpath wound its way through tall grass studded with buttercups and poppies, their petals wide open to the sun's caress. The sound of wheels on the road behind him saved him from the treacherous desire to stop to rest again, perhaps even to grab an hour's sleep. Scrambling for cover behind a nearby broken wall, he watched, breathing a sigh of relief as a cart came into view.

High-sided and ancient, its boards creaking under the load, it rolled slowly towards him, the horse taking advantage of the dozing waggoner to choose its own pace.

Nathan judged the moment carefully, breaking cover to lope silently alongside the swaying cart. Then, taking hold of the bleached wood, he hoisted himself aboard to sit beside the star-tled driver.

"Mornin'." He smiled broadly. "Lovely day." He held out his hand. "Name's Nathan, Nathan Clay. What's yours?"

His astonished companion sat open-mouthed for a moment or two and then, as if hypnotised by a snake, he mumbled. "Sam Bennett." The sound of his own voice seemed to bring him to his senses. "But, 'ere you can't jus' get up 'ere like that, without a by your leave." He spluttered. "Who d'you think you are?"

"I told you." Nathan took his hand and shook it heartily.

"Nathan Clay, and pleased to meet you I am. Where're you makin' for?"

"None o' your business. You get orf this cart 'afore I throws you orf !"

Nathan shook his head. "Now look, old man, you wouldn't do that, would you? I don't mean you no 'arm. All I want is a bit of 'elp to get where I'm goin' and when I saw you I thinks to meself as you and the 'orse seem to be 'eaded the same way."

"Alright, alright." Blue eyes twinkled from the toothless face, its skin tanned by years of open air toil. "You don't 'ave to talk me to death. I'm taking this 'ere load up to Three Elms Farm, up 'afore the mill by Battlesbridge. Will that do you?"

"It will that, and I thank you kindly and I'm right sorry if I gave you a scare."

The ancient snorted. "Take more than a lad like you to scare the likes of me what's taken the King's shillin'. Where you going anyway?"

"Well, if I make it, I'll be in Saffron Walden in a few days." Nathan liked the look of the waggoner and decided he could trust him. "I've got family up there see." "My mother's kin." He warmed to his story. "She came down with the grand lot she worked for when she were a girl. 'Ousemaid she said. Well they give 'er an hour or so off one mornin'. So she walked over the cliffs to Leigh where she spied my father spreading his nets. 'E were a fisherman." He added unnecessarily. "'E told as 'ow she walked right up to 'im and asked 'im what 'e was a'doin'."

"Sounds like a saucy miss, your mother." The man chuckled. "Bit of an 'andful I should reckon."

"She was that!" Nathan joined in the laughter. "'Ad a mind of her own did Mother. Father said it were love at first sight for 'em both. They tied the knot and I were born within a year."

Nathan turned his head to hide his sadness but the movement did not go unnoticed.

"She gone then?"

Nathan nodded. "Aye, both of 'em. Long gone."

"So who's up in Walden?"

"Mother's sister, Aunt Jane. They both worked for the Benhams. Big landowners they are. When Mother made up 'er mind to stay in Leigh, Aunt Jane went back to Walden. Last I 'eard she were 'ousekeeper to the family."

"Tha's a good job is 'ousekeepin'. She'll be runnin' the place I shouldn't wonder."

"All I 'ope is that she can find a place for me. I'll set me 'and to anythin'. He turned to his companion. "What d'you think?"

"You look strong and if you're family, she'll not turn you away I reckon."

For a while they lapsed into a companionable silence while the sun climbed to blaze from a clear blue sky.

After a while the slow, steady rhythm of hooves threatened to overtake Nathan. He shook himself and for fear of falling asleep, tried again to make conversation.

"So, d'you make this run every day?"

Sam nodded. "I lives over Prittlewell, so I makes an early start to get into Leigh 'afore t'others. Most days I go over Rochford way. 'S'mornin I got a load for further on."

"I've been wondering what you got in the back." Nathan jerked a thumb over his shoulder. "Whatever 'tis it smells real bad from where I'm sittin'."

Sam hooted with laughter. "That be Dacksun lad. A bit ripe for you is it? You gets used to it ar'ter a while." He caught Nathan's puzzled frown. "'Tis what the tide throws up. A bit of seaweed and a few starfish and such. You know, what the little'uns call five fingers. The farmers swear by it. Spread it on the crop, they do, like manure." He thought for a minute. "Tell you what." He glanced sideways at Nathan, "When we gets to the farm you give me a 'and to unload and I'll see you right. Farmer's a mate, see, and there's always a bite and a drop of ale waitin'. What d'you say?"

Nathan flexed his muscled arm. "I say to 'ell with the stink. I'm your man. I'm so 'ungry me belly thinks me throat's been cut!"

The old man's hearty roar of mirth sent a startled flock of starling winging skyward as he flicked the reins in a pointless attempt to speed their progress.

"Well, best pull in your belt, we've a way to go yet. You'll like old George and his missus. They be good folk."

Fields of potatoes, their rich green foliage yet to bloom, but promising a good Autumn harvest, marked their route.

"Good bit o' land up 'ere." Sam broke the silence. "My Pa 'ad a few acres when I were a lad, been in the family for years. He kept a couple of pigs and Ma 'ad 'er own patch for 'taters and the like."

"Sounds like too good a life to leave behind." Nathan shifted to ease the numbness in his buttocks. "So 'ow come you took the King's shillin'?"

"Didn't 'ave no choice lad." Sadly Sam shook his head. "I were a young fool. Poachin' that's what done it. 'T were only a couple of rabbits but I got caught. Magistrate never gave me a chance. Before I knowed it I was on me way to Chelmsford barracks. Hard time that were, those bastards whipped us into shape, I can tell you. One in particular, officer he were, used to yell and carry on somethin' dreadful. Scum of the earth, he called us. I 'ated im but 'e got 'is. I saw him fall, Blown apart 'e were." For a moment he fell silent, savouring the memory.

"Anyhow, from there we were shipped to Lisbon. Wellesley was our commanding officer, him what's now the Duke of Wellington. All through Spain I went wi'out a scratch. Then I gets to France and I caught one. The froggies give me this." He slapped his thigh. "Field 'orspital nigh on finished me orf. Butchers they were but they saved me life, touch and go they said it were." He shook his head. "You don't never want to see nothin'like that lad. They found me in a ditch, spark out by all accounts. First I knew I was laid out on a table with one of them surgeons bending over me. He puts a leather strap between me teeth and says 'Bite on that man." Then he goes to work." He glanced at Nathan. "The pain were that bad I passed out again and when I woke I was laid side by side with some of the frogs I'd been trying to kill only a while before. I kept me mouth shut, I can tell you. When I were strong enough they let me go and it took weeks to find me way back 'ome." He stared into the distance. "Eighteen thirteen that were. Went orf a lad, came back a cripple and there ain't much work for a one- legged bloke what don't know nothin' 'cept killin'. And poachin'." He added with a snigger.

Nathan had no answer. He could only imagine the horror the man had endured on the battlefield. He had heard old soldier's tales before but, for the first time, sitting alongside Sam, it seemed terrifyingly real.

"So 'ow come you're driving a cart?"

"Don't need two good legs, do it? Only a couple o' strong 'ands on the reins. When I come back me Father sold the land and set me up wi' an 'orse and cart. He's dead now, poor bugger. But I took care of 'im 'till the last." He gave a satisfied nod, before lapsing once more into reverie.

As the horse laboured on Nathan respected his companion's silence, content to listen to birdsong and to breathe in the sweet country air. Before long the boarded cottages of Rayleigh came into view and Sam straightened in his seat.

"We'll need the brake when we gets to Crown Hill. A real steep'un it is." Nathan would like to have stopped to slake his thirst at the Spread Eagle or the Crown but Sam ignored the opportunity as he tugged at the reins and, turning the horse's head, the cart began a careful descent down the twisting country lane leading to Rawreth.

They passed the occasional thatched cottage, a parish church and further on a small inn until, after a while, Sam pointed the whip. "That's Rawreth, There she be. We'll bide there while the 'orse has a drink. Us too if you like. There's an alehouse in the village." Nathan nodded his agreement.

For what seemed to Nathan no more than a few minutes they supped their ale, stretching their aching limbs on the bench outside the alehouse. Then, leaving the sleepy hamlet behind, they resumed the journey, through fields of yellow mustard and green eared wheat along the rim of the Crouch valley.

At Three Elms Farm, on the outskirts of Battlesbridge, Sam proved to be as good as his word. With George Makepeaces's help it took less than an hour to unload the cart. Climbing on to the pile of Daksun Sam shovelled the stinking seaweed into waiting barrows for the farmer and Nathan to wheel to the back of the farmhouse. By early afternoon Nathan felt he had earned whatever was to be payment for his labour and was relieved to find himself made welcome by the farmer's wife.

"You can wash your 'ands in the butt by the door. I don't want you bringing that stink in 'ere. Then you come along in an' sit yoursel' down."

Nathan and Sam obediently sluiced their hands, face and neck, ridding themselves of the journey's dust and the evidence of their labours and dried themselves on a rough towel.

Running fingers through his wet hair, Nathan presented himself for her inspection.

"You'll do." She pronounced and, busying herself at the scrubbed oak table, produced a fine joint of cold mutton, home-made bread and a jug of ale. Seating herself along side Sam, she nudged him.

"Well?"

"Well what?" He mumbled, his few remaining teeth working hard to chew the meal.

"Well, what's bin 'appenin' down the hill?"

"What in Leigh?"

She nodded, eagerly leaning forward, her plump forearms encircling a tankard.

"Bin any goin's on?"

Sam gave some consideration to his reply, "Old Ma Wheeler, the butcher's missus, upped and died. Buried her last Tuesday. Then that there Lady Margaret says she's goin' to put a well in the village. They be goin' to run some sort of pipe down the hill from the well up top. 'Bout time too, I says. I did hear there's Cholera up the coast again. They're talkin' 'bout quarantinin' the boats out of London."

"Cholera you say?" The woman crossed herself. "May the good Lord 'elp us all. It took a lot of folk last time."

Sam nodded wisely, easing a lump of chewed gristle loose with a calloused finger.

"An' what 'bout you lad?" She turned to Nathan. "Where be you a goin'?"

He glanced at Sam who shrugged. With a sigh, Nathan reached for another chunk of bread. He would have to tell the tale again.

"Saffon Walden. I've got family there." He added.

"You got a sizeable walk then." She carved into the mutton

leg and heaped his plate, "Best fill your belly with a bit more o' this." She paused, as stamping the muck from his boots, her husband came into the kitchen.

"Now then Missus what's all this talk of belly fillin'? Be 'bout time you was fillin' mine."

"Your belly be big 'nough as 'tis." She laughed, giving her husband a playful push, "I'm talking to the lad. I'll put up a bit of pie and an apple or two for 'im. 'E's got a long way to go."

"She'd feed every beggar what comes to the door." He winked broadly at Nathan. "Best take it lad! She'll not take no for an answer."

"I'll be glad to and I thank you kindly."

"Will you bide for the night?" George reached for a carving knife. "There's the barn."

Nathan was tempted but food and rest had restored him in body and spirit. "'Tis a kindly offer but I'd best be on my way."

"Well, if you walks on past the mill an' over the bridge you'll spy The Hawk tavern at the bottom of the hill. That'll see you on to the turnpike and then it's a bit of a way to Great Baddow."

"That'll do me." Nathan grinned, raising a hand to halt the farmer's words. "I reckon by then I'll be ready to put me 'ead down." He rose from the table and held out a hand first to Sam and then to the farmer. "Thank you both for your kindness, and you Ma'am." He turned to the woman who waved away his thanks.

"No need, lad. No need." She patted him on his shoulder. "Nice young lad like you needs a full belly on a long walk. I wish you well. Mind who you share the road with, there's some out there who'd rob you just for your boots."

"They'd 'ave to be bare foot to want these." He lifted his worn sole to prove his point.

"And there's a lot out there who's not only barefoot but starving' too. The missus is right." George Makepeace raised a warning finger. "Watch out for yourself and don't trust no one."

Nathan nodded and hitching his cloak over his shoulder he started down the farm path to the road beyond. He turned to raise an arm in farewell, before setting his face to the next few miles and whatever might lie ahead.

CHAPTER FOUR

It was earlier that morning that Saffron had watched Nathan disappear from sight, aware that the village was beginning to wake to another day. Closing the door firmly behind her she searched the kitchen for evidence of her brother's visit. "No point in meeting trouble 'alfway when Pa gets back." She murmured, brushing breadcrumbs from the table.

She found herself thinking back to Nathan's words. Leaning her head on her arms against the oak mantle, she stared into the fire's dying embers. How could Jonas have treated her brother so cruelly and how could she not have realised what was happening?

Small half-forgotten incidents began to make sense and to fit the crime. Since her mother's death her stepfather had earned a reputation for brawling, usually when he had taken on too much ale. More than one man had shown physical evidence of his violent outbursts. Harry Thompson came to mind. He had been stupid enough to cross Jonas, sneering at his inability to bring home a catch. Jonas had beaten him unmercifully and it was only the intervention of his friends, who lied to save his skin, that he was not brought before the magistrate. Certainly he had a short temper but he had shown no violence to her or Tom or Poll. At least, she bit her lip, at least so far.

Saffron pushed another piece of driftwood into the fire, watching the grey ash crumble to send a shower of sparks upward into the smoke-grimed chimney. Swinging a small iron pot over the beginnings of a blaze, she scattered a handful of oats into the shallow water. Tom would soon be awake and ready to break his fast. By autumn he would start his first term at the nearby school. Saffron thought with satisfaction, of the few pence she had managed to hide away to pay for Tom's slate and the other things he would need. Lady Margaret's Dame School was yet another example of the woman's generosity and concern for the villagers. Although she was rarely seen in public, she knew what went on in the fishing village and showed her concern for those who lived along the water's edge in many ways.

A thump from the room above followed by the sound of small running feet brought a fond smile to the girl's face. Tom appeared on the stairs, peeping beneath the bannister rail.

"'As 'e gone, Saffy?" His face clearly showed his disappointment.

"'E 'as, and you're not to say a word to Pa about 'im being 'ere." She wagged a warning finger. "D'you promise?"

Tom frowned, his head on one side. "If you say so Saffy, but…"

"There's no but about it. You don't want to get your brother in trouble do you?"

Tom shook his head.

"So, it's our secret. Right?"

Tom's face broke into a smile and he clapped his hands. "I promise." He said, putting a finger to his lips. Tom liked secrets.

"Now you go back up and put on your britches 'afore Pa get back. I'll give you your porridge then we'll walk down the village and fetch a nice hot loaf from Mr.Blake and perhaps…" She paused, deliberately teasing the child. "Perhaps I might find a farthin' for a sugar stick."

As she watched Tom scramble eagerly up the stairs, stumbling on the hem of his nightshirt, Nathan's words again rang loudly in her mind: "If he ever lays an 'and on him, I'll be back to finish what I started."

The sun had begun to warm the cobbled road when Saffron was drawn to the window by the sound of raised voices and raucous laughter. A group of fishermen and their boys were making their way toward the cottage and in their midst strode the burly, swaggering figure of her stepfather, Jonas.

Saffron's sigh of relief for his safe return was short lived as her Stepfather threw wide the door and stamped over the threshold.

"Come you in." He called over his shoulder to the group of men Saffron knew to be his drinking companions. "Saffy." He turned to her. "We're famished, girl. Come," he beckoned expansively again to his friends. "You'll break your fast at my table."

Saffy's mind raced. She had little or nothing to offer except Tom's thin porridge. "Pa." She began. "I've not yet bought food for the day. I've nothing to give you."

She saw Jonas' eyes narrow and his face redden angrily as one of the men sniggered behind his back. "You dare shame me girl in my own 'ome?" He raised a hand as if to strike her.

"S'all right Jonas," Tully Taylor pulled at his sleeve, "The Billet will do. They'll 'ave the makins'." The man winked at Saffy. "Likely we'll wash it down wi' a drop of good ale." Jonas let his arm fall to his side and, with a look of sullen hatred, turned on his heel. He left the cottage without another word, slamming the door behind him.

Tom's voice brought Saffron back to reality. "Was that Pa?" He had appeared at her side, his innocent face turned up in expectation. Saffron reached a trembling hand to stroke the fair hair. "Aye." She managed. "'E'll be back 'afore long." Now, get you to the table or your oats'll get cold."

Tom scrambled onto the chair as Saffron ladled his meal into a bowl. "Get that down you if you want to grow big."

"Like Nathan?" Tom spooned a mouthful of porridge .

Saffron rounded on him, pushing her face close to his. "I told you not to say his name. A secret. Remember?"

Tom shrank from her, his lip beginning to tremble. "Sorry." He muttered. "I forgot".

"Well, don't forget again. Right?" She smiled suddenly, tweaking his nose and hugging him impulsively. "Now eat up and we'll be off." She fingered the coins in her skirt pocket. At least thanks to Nathan there would be food for a few days, whether or not Jonas had brought home a catch.

By the time Tom had finished and was ready to leave, the sun had risen into a clear blue sky. A greedy seagull swooped overhead, wheeling to dive into the shimmering waves. The child ran ahead of his sister stamping and splashing into the few shallow puddles left by the night's downpour. Saffron followed her nose to the smell of newly baked bread wafting from the nearby bakery.

Tom burst through the door ahead of her to stand expectantly in front of the wooden counter. "Morning Mr. Blake." She smiled at the portly baker. "A nice crusty loaf if you please".

"Right you are Saffy. 'Tis good to see you and young Tom". He added, reaching to take a hot loaf from the shelf. "Will this do you?"

"It will that." Saffron passed over the coin in payment. "And 'ow is your good wife?

"She's restin'." A frown wrinkled the man's brow. "She be due any day now, but she says things ain't goin' the way they 'oughter this time." He shook his head. "That there doctor says her time for 'avin' another should be long gone. Says she's too old or some such rubbish."

"Can I do anything to 'elp?" Saffron was concerned for the woman she had known all her life. She had grown up with the

three Blake boys. The two eldest had followed their father into
the bakery, while the youngest had fancied a life on the water
and had been apprenticed to one of the local fishermen aboard
a Pinkie. The kindly woman had once confided to Saffron
that her dearest wish had been to have a daughter but that she
thought that blessing had been denied her.

The baker shrugged. "He says as 'ow she just 'as to rest. '
Says 'e'll come when things start; I just got to call him."

"Well, let me know if you need me." Saffron tucked the hot
bread into her rush basket and, taking Tom by the hand, she
made her goodbyes.

After a visit to the butcher's shop, adding a small parcel of
mutton pieces and potherbs to her purchases, she stopped at
the grocer's. The owner, Widow Ashton, who had no children
of her own, had a soft spot for Tom. While Saffron considered
the cost of a few more items from among the sacks of flour,
dried fruit and barrels of pilchards, the woman lifted the boy
onto the counter and quizzed him about his lessons. Saffron
had already begun to teach him how to read and each time the
willing child spelled a simple word correctly his admirer fed
him a sugared sweet.

"You'll spoil 'im." Saffron warned, laughing at Tom's face,
his cheeks packed and swollen with sweets. "I think that'll be
enough for one day." Widow Ashton screwed the lid back onto
the glass jar. "Mayhap you're right." She chucked Tom under
his chin. "You go on a'learning like that an' you'll do right
well at that school."

The heat of the June morning did little to persuade them to
hurry home. Saffron lifted her face to the warmth of the sun,
planning the rest of the day while Tom ambled along kicking
at stones and calling out to young friends. If Jonas spent the
remainder of the morning drinking at The Billet and she had

no reason to think he would do otherwise, she and Tom might climb the hill to the church. Guiltily she realised that it was a month since she had visited her mother's grave and she felt the raw need for the comfort of memories.

"Tell you what Tom." The boy looked at her expectantly. "What say we go up the 'ill and put a few flowers on Mother's plot?" Tom nodded enthusiastically. He knew that once there his sister could be persuaded to tell him stories of the mother he had never known.

Reaching the cottage, she pushed open the door for Tom to scamper past.

"We'll leave this lot in the kitchen and you can wash your face an' 'ands. Wouldn't do for the vicar to see you in that state, would it?" Tom wasn't sure why the vicar would object to a bit of dirt but he did as he was told knowing it would hasten their departure.

A little later, panting from the climb, Saffron sat on the churchyard wall to get her breath back while Tom threw himself full length on the grass. The view of the village below never ceased to give her a sense of belonging. True not every member of the small community could be called a close friend but the comforting familiarity of those who were was without price. Saffron glanced down at the small prone figure. "Don't stare up at the sun Tom, It'll burn your eyes. Why don't you go and pick a few of those forget-me-nots over there." She pointed to a clump of blue flowers growing wild alongside the footpath. "Mother would like that I reckon."

Tom sat upright and, squinting in the brilliant sunlight, crawled over to look closely at the tiny blooms. Saffron watched as the boy hunted around until he found a sharp stick.

"What are you doing with that?" She stood to see more clearly.

"I'm using it to dig up the flowers, then I can plant 'em proper. If I pick 'em, they'll just die." He pushed a lick of fair hair from his eyes, leaving a smudge of dirt on his flushed cheek. "This way they won't die so quick, will they?"

"No, and you're a clever boy. They won't die so quick." Saffron knelt to help him, and cradling the freshly dug root and blossom, they hurried into the churchyard.

Mary Clay's last resting place lay beside her husband in a shaded corner of the cemetery. It took only minutes to tug out the few weeds surrounding the small headstone and to plant the forget-me-nots. They sat back on their heels to admire their handywork. "That looks real pretty, Tom." Saffron dusted the earth from her skirt. "Now, go get a drop of water from the bucket by the church porch and we'll give it a drink."

As he threaded his way between the graves, Saffron bowed her head. "Oh Mother." She murmured, "I miss you so. Why did the good Lord 'ave to take you? I need you now more than ever. I'm doin' my best but I'm worried about Poll and Nathan. Tom's alright but he's never been strong." Out of the corner of her eye she saw the small figure returning and made a great play of pulling more weeds from around the plot. "May God watch over us." She whispered. "And bless us all."

Tom carefully trickled the cup of water onto the roots then stood to trail his fingers over the headstone. "There, Mother." He said solemnly. "I'll bring some more next time." Saffron put an arm around his thin shoulders conscious of his need for comfort.

"Come Tom, let's be away. We've things to do." The boy straightened, wiping away the suspicion of a tear as together they silently retraced their steps each locked within their own world of regret.

The remainder of the day passed peacefully enough as there

was no sign of Jonas. It was evening and Tom was in bed before he appeared and, having spent the day with his friends, as Saffron expected, he was drunk. The door crashed back on its hinges as Jonas stood swaying in its frame. He staggered into the cottage and slumped onto a chair, glowering at her in the gloom.

Saffron moved quietly around the kitchen, filling a bowl with hot stew and putting it before him on the scrubbed table. She could feel him watching her every move, waiting for her to speak but she knew better. In his mood, she knew from previous experience, a word from her would only serve to open a floodgate of verbal abuse.

Determined to provoke her, Jonas suddenly snatched the steaming bowl from the table and hurled it across the room. "Get this slop away from me." He roared. "A man needs a good meal on his table, not muck fit for dogs!"

Saffron struggled to contain the long suppressed rage, which began somewhere deep inside her. Jonas' smirk of triumph was the last straw and Saffron heard the words burst from her lips in a stream of fury.

"You want a meal fit for a man do you?" She spat out the words. "Well, when you bring 'ome enough to put it on the table, I'll cook it!" She faced him, hands on hips. "But no, you'd rather pour what few pence you make down your own greedy gullet!" She was shaking, not from fear but with pure white hot anger.

For a moment Jonas was stunned by her unexpected outburst, then overturning the chair as he rose unsteadily to his feet, he advanced toward her, beginning to unbuckle his belt.

"You mouthy bitch! You dare talk to me so in my own 'ome?"

"Your 'ome?" Saffron snorted. "You stepped into a dead

man's shoes when you came 'ere. And 'e was a better man than you Jonas Turner!"

"And who's paid the rent – tell me that, slut?"

"Nathan paid it first. Then Poll 'elps with her earnings." She tilted her chin, defying him to argue. "The rest comes from the bit of sewing I do. We've managed without your 'elp for many a day."

"Managed 'ave you?" A crafty, lopsided grin appeared. "Well I'll show you who puts the food on the table this day." He dug deep into his pocket and slammed down a handful of coins, which gleamed dully in the light of the fire.

"Sovereigns !" Saffron gasped. Catching sight of Jonas' satisfied grin her eyes narrowed. "Ow d'you come by them? Not honestly I'll be bound."

Jonas slid the coins around with an appreciative finger. "Well, you'd be wrong, see. Me and the others sort of 'elped a couple of timber barges from the Baltic. Went aground last night on the Maplins. Must 'ave seen our rigging lights and thought they was safe in the channel." He shook with laughter. "Course we 'ad to unload some of the stuff so's they could float off. Fetched a good price too it did." He added with smug satisfaction.

"So you stole it!" Saffron stared at him with disbelief. "You lured them onto the Maplin sands!"

The smile slipped from Jonas' face. "You saying I'm a thief?" He growled.

Saffron straightened, her eyes blazing. "I am! And if you think I'll touch a penny of that." She pointed to the scattered coins. "You can think again!"

Without warning his hand snaked out to trap Saffron's wrist in a vice-like grip, twisting her arm behind her back and pulling her hard against him. "You got too much to say." He brought his face close to hers. "A mite too much. I've a mind to shut you up." He ran his tongue over thick wet lips, his heated gaze travelling slowly over her slim body. Saffron turned her head away from the stink of stale ale and rotting teeth as she struggled against him. "You'll not shut me up." She gasped. "I'll tell the whole village you're a thief and worse." She had the satisfaction of seeing a glimmer of doubt stay his confidence and took the moment to break free. She backed away to the open hearth as Jonas took a step toward her, taking his wide belt between his hands and snapping the leather. The malice in the man's expression warned her that she had gone too far.

"Right girl. "He grunted. "Time you and me 'ad a reckonin'."

"You strike me and I'll shout so loud they'll 'ear me clear to Leigh House. You'll be up 'afore the magistrate before the week's out!" She reached behind her, closing her trembling hand over the heavy poker and raising it on high. "And I'll not go down without marking you. You might have chased Nathan off but I'm standing my ground." The mention of her brother's name stopped Jonas in his tracks. Swaying unsteadily he tried to focus. "What d'you know 'bout that?" He muttered.

"I know you beat him and I know 'e whipped you good and proper." She played her trump card with great pleasure. "And if you lay an 'and on any of us 'e'll be back to finish you, mark my words!"

Fear and anger chased themselves across Jonas' face. His shoulders slumped as the wind went out of him. Without another word or a glance in her direction he scooped the money from the table and slunk to the door, crashing it shut behind him.

Dropping the poker, Saffron buried her face in her hands. By some miracle Tom seemed to have slept through the row. Automatically she knelt and began to wipe the floor, cleaning

away the congealing stew. "Bastard." She whispered bitterly.
"That's right, go back to your fine, thieving friends. Drink
yourself to death for all I care!" With a muted sob she sat back
on her heels to bury her face in her hands. "Oh dear God, if
you're listening I didn't mean that." She sobbed. "Forgive me
for such a wicked thought. Please keep us safe from 'arm."
Dabbing her eyes she got to her feet and crossed to stare from
the window into the clear night sky. "And take care of Nathan
too, wherever 'e may be."

CHAPTER FIVE

It was unlikely that the long arm of the law would reach so far for a small- time smuggler, nonetheless, Nathan intended to skirt around the main towns of Chelmsford and Springfield where lay the new County Gaol. He had no wish to be seen as a stranger and perhaps questioned by an overzealous lawman.

"So far, so good." He thought happily as he turned his face to the sun's rays, taking in the sounds and smells of his newfound bid for freedom.

Open farmland on either side of the winding lane sported a variety of crops. In one field he saw whole families at work. Poorly clad children, no more than six or seven years of age, toiled alongside adults. It seemed that poverty stalked on land as well as along the length of the coast.

By early evening he came to Ford End and Nathan was both tired and hungry. Asking for directions, he was relieved to learn that another couple of miles would take him into Great Dunmow. A sizeable place he was told, yet the last mile seemed more like ten.

As he came to the head of the main street the town was a welcome sight. Dumping his pack he sat beside the road, pulling off his boots to rub his sore feet and count his blisters. The shadows had lengthened and a chill breeze blew in from the North. He winced with pain, as pulling on his boots before drawing his cloak more snugly around him, he stretched his tired limbs. Then, rising and hefting his pack across a shoulder he made his way down the hill.

The sudden rattle of harness and thud of hoof beats bearing down on him, caused him to leap from the path of a liveried coach as it thundered past, narrowly missing him and leaving behind a cloud of choking dust and the mocking laughter of its occupants.

Scrambling to his feet he retrieved his pack and watched the coach disappear beneath the archway of the Saracen's Head, an imposing coaching inn fronting the main street.

"Run me down would you?" His shock turned to anger as he slapped the dust from his shirt and britches. "We'll see how you measure up when you're down off your 'igh seat."

Slinging his cloak over one shoulder he strode toward the inn, then under the arch and into the stable yard beyond. The smell of steaming, sweating horses hit him as he stepped up to the coach and tore open the door only to find it empty.

He spun round as the coach driver appeared. "If you're lookin' for the Squire, you just missed 'im." He grinned. "Gone in there." He jerked a thumb in the direction of the main door. "'Ad a lady with 'im." He winked. "'E won't want disturbin', if you get my meanin'. 'Ere," he sobered suddenly, his eyes narrowed. "you're the lad on the road back there".

"That I am. And you all but killed me. Driving like a madman you were!"

"I'm right sorry." The man put a hand on Nathan's shoulder. "Didn't see you 'til the last minute." He scowled. "Squire, blast 'is eyes, thought it were funny."

"Well, I didn't!" Nathan growled.

"Nor me neither, son. Look, let me make amends. You 'elp me get this lot unharnessed and rubbed down and I'll stand you the price of supper and a pint of the best." He grinned encouragingly. "'Ow'd that be? He held out a strong hand. "Joe Barnes's me name." After a moment's hesitation Nathan took it with a good will.

"Right!" He laughed. "It's a deal."

After an hour of working together Joe was full of praise for

Nathan. "You be good with 'orses, boy. Took to you right off, they did." The four coal black high-spirited animals had indeed gentled under Nathan's hands as he rubbed them down with handfuls of fresh hay.

"They be fine beasts." He admitted, stepping back to appreciate them. "Worth a bit too I shouldn't wonder."

"Squire don't 'ave nothin' but the best." Joe nodded. "Now, 'ow about we go get that dinner?"

They sat in the bar and ate hungrily. "Lamb and 'tater pie 'ere be the best in the county." The coachman smacked his lips.

"Aye." Nathan chuckled. "And the ale's not bad neither." He emptied his tankard in a single gulp and sat back with a wide yawn.

"You look done in, lad." Joe thought for a minute. "Tell you what." He glanced around to make sure he was not overheard. "If you're up and gone by first light, you can 'ave a couple of hours sleep wi' me in the coach."

Nathan looked doubtful.

"Right soft those seats are and there be plenty of room for the two of us."

The offer of a comfortable night's rest was not to be treated lightly and Nathan gratefully agreed.

Joe was right. The plush, well-sprung coach was better than a feather bed and using his pack as a pillow, Nathan was lulled to sleep by the sound of Joe's companionable snoring and the muted champing of the horses.

A few hours later he was roughly jostled from his deep slumber by the swaying of the coach. "'S all right, boy." Joe stretched a hand to brace himself against the door-frame. "Got to piss. Didn't mean to wake you."

Nathan yawned. "'Bout time I was stirring." He stretched his length in the cramped space. In the early morning light he followed Joe into the yard, crossing to dunk his head in the trough. "Bye! That's cold!" He shuddered, shaking the water from his hair. Joe threw him a piece of sacking. "Get yourself dry on that." He laughed. "You look like a drowned rat!"

"I'll give you a 'and to feed the beasts 'afore I go." Nathan offered.

"No need lad. My beauties be well rested. All they'll want is a bag of oats. Squire won't be wanting 'em yet if I know what's what." He shot a knowing grin in Nathan's direction. "He'll be yellin' for his coach and four round about noon I reckon."

"Well, if you don't need me, I'll be on me way. I've a bit to go and a will to get there." He shook the coachman's hand warmly. "I'll not be forgetting your kindness and I wish you well."

"You too lad." Joe walked with him to the archway, watching until Nathan turned the corner to start down the steep road.

Thin, early morning sun glinted on water as Nathan came alongside the village pond. He stopped to watch a bobbing flotilla of ducklings following their parents, a well-ordered regiment, ducking and diving for weed, their first meal of the day.

Thanks to Joe's generosity, he still had the pie and apples given to him by the farmer's wife the previous day and he had promised himself that he would save them until he had covered a few more miles.

The coachman had told him that Thaxted lay a good eight miles to the north, and Nathan would need to walk yet another eight or nine more before he reached Saffron Walden.

"At least the Almighty's smiling on me. 'E's give me a fine day for steppin' out." Nathan settled his pack more comfortably, lengthening his stride and whistling happily. After a while he slowed his pace as the countryside opened up before him, beautiful in its soft, green mantle. A blackbird's song of greeting to the new day lifted his spirits. "I know 'ow you feel." He saluted the songster. "It's going to be a good day. I feel it in me bones."

A group of thatched cottages, a church and a tavern marked the hamlet of Great Easton and as Joe had told him, the halfway point on his journey to Thaxted. Nathan found a shaded spot on the green to sit, before pulling an apple and the wedge of pie from his pack. Leaning back against an oak's stout trunk he bit into the crisp fruit, waving away the fat body of a curious bee. His thoughts returned to Leigh and all he had left behind. Although he knew it had been the wise thing to do, he hated the idea of leaving Saffron and the others to the tender mercy of Jonas. He, above all, knew the unpredictable nature of the man, how violent he could become, particularly when he had had a few drinks. The image of his sister's face swam into his mind and he smiled. Her long, golden hair framing cool, blue eyes and a determined mouth. She was a chip off their mother's block all right, he chuckled to himself. If Jonas tried anything on her he'd find he had a wild cat by the tail, particularly if it threatened the young'uns. Poll was almost a woman grown, he realised, and as for little Tom.... He shook his head. The boy didn't seem strong, for all his cheeky ways. He consoled himself with the knowledge that he had promised to write as soon as he was settled and he knew Saffron would keep him informed of any news in Leigh.

Cuffing the crumbs of pie from his mouth he pulled on his boots, stifling a groan of pain as they squeezed the worsening blisters. "Right." He squared his shoulders. "On to Thaxted. From there I'll be in spittin' distance of Saffron Walden."

Aware that the few coins left in his pocket were the sum total of his worldly wealth, he determined to save them until he reached the next town where he promised himself a draft of ale.

The sun was high by the time Nathan climbed the last rise to overlook the sprawling town, where brightly coloured stalls of the weekly market edged the road winding its way between cottages and shops. The town was crowded, so, without fear of any untoward curiosity cast in his direction, strode down into the packed market square. All around the good-natured banter of the stall owners filled the air, each promising to have wares better than those of their competitors and Nathan would have dearly loved to put their claims to the test. Stalls piled high with fresh fruit stood close to others hung with fresh smoked hams and a variety of cheeses. A few sheep in the care of a young lad wended their way through the throng and all but bowled Nathan over.

By the time he reached the imposing exchange building he was glad to leave the sounds and smells of the market behind and wearily make his way up to the hilltop church and to the welcome sight on the far side of the road, of The Swan Inn..

Nathan fingered the few coins in his pocket before going into the tavern and elbowing his way to the bar. He gulped down the first mouthful of ale appreciatively, turning to cast an eye over the inn's other customers.

"Come far, lad?" a voice at his elbow startled him and he swung round to stare into a walnut face and the blackest eyes he had ever seen.

"Far enough." He grunted.

White teeth flashed in a wide smile. "Only askin'." The man pointed to Nathan's scuffed and dusty boots. "Come a few miles, they 'ave."

Nathan took a moment to size up the stocky figure. Black britches held up by a wide sash were tucked into high tooled-leather boots and a shirt open at the neck to reveal a tanned chest. A red neckerchief matched the sash at his waist, but it was the gold earring, which held Nathan's attention.

"What's wrong, lad? Never seen a Romany 'afore?"

Nathan shook his head. "'eard of 'em though. You from Dengie Marsh?"

The man nodded. "Colom." He said, offering his hand. "Colom du Bois. On your way to the doin's at Walden?"

"Doin's?" Nathan frowned.

"Oh aye, great doin's. They be topping out the church see. All the nobs'll be there. Bands and such too, and a fair."

"Is that where you're headin'?"

"Aye. I've got the gift, see." He saw Nathan's puzzled look. "I tell folk what's a'goin' to 'appen to 'em."

"Oh." Nathan grinned. "You tell fortunes. Load of rubbish if you ask me."

The friendly smile slipped from the gypsy's face. "Rubbish is it? 'Ow d'you reckon that then?

Nathan found himself trapped in the mesmeric depths of the dark eyes, lost for an explanation. "Well, stands to reason." He mumbled. "I'm right sorry if I spoke out of turn."

The smile crept back to flood the weathered face. "S'all right, lad." He clapped Nathan on the shoulder. "Best you come along wi' us." He chuckled "Rosa might learn you a thing or two."

"Rosa?" Nathan shook his head, the ale seemed to have fogged his mind "Who's Rosa?"

"Me daughter." Colom smiled. "Finish your drink if you're comin'." He turned, pushing his way to the door and, seemingly without reason, Nathan willingly followed him into the street.

The fresh air seemed to clear his brain but as he rounded the corner he stopped in his tracks. "What the 'ell is that!" He stared at the brightly painted caravan, its sides hung with pots and barrels.

"That be me Vardo!" Colom's pride was obvious. "And this be Midnight." He moved closer to run a loving hand over the neck of the huge black horse harnessed between the shafts. The animal whinnied at his touch, dropping its great head to nuzzle the gypsy, renewing the strong bond between beast and man.

As Nathan approached, the horse snorted, tossing its head, until Colom spoke softly in a strange language. The animal quietened immediately, warily allowing the stranger to smooth the thick black mane.

"She be a Suffolk Punch ain't she? And a beauty at that" Nathan breathed admiringly.

"Right, lad. It needs a strong 'orse to pull the Vardo, what with all the stuff we got. Ah, there's Rosa." The Vardo swayed slightly as a young girl pushed open the top half of its door to lean upon the sill.

Nathan's first impression was of bare tanned arms contrasting sharply with a white bodice and of tumbling black curls framing an elfin face. "Who be this, Pa?" She stared at Nathan, taking in every detail of his travel-stained appearance. He felt a rush of blood infuse his cheeks, her dark eyes, narrowed with suspicion, seemed to reach the very depths of his soul. His mouth went dry as he felt his normal confidence fade away on a wave of confusion. Never had he beheld such beauty

"'Tis just a lad set on the same road." Nathan saw the broad wink between father and daughter. "Mayhap we'll take him along the way?" After a moment's consideration the girl nodded and, swinging wide the lower half of the door, she stood back, motioning Nathan to join her.

Colom nodded his consent. "Up you go then." He flashed his wide smile. "An' we'll be off."

The inside of the vardo was dim after the sunlight and, as the vehicle lurched into motion, Nathan put out a hand to steady himself only to feel warm flesh beneath his fingers. He leaped back as if stung, his head colliding with something hanging from the roof. A peal of laughter greeted his oath. "You'd best sit 'afore you does yoursel' a mischief." A slim hand led him a few steps and pushed him down onto a narrow bench. As his eyes became accustomed to the gloom he began to see her clearly.

She stood swaying, bare feet braced against the motion of the Vardo, her hands spread on slim hips. "Seen enough?" She asked, her chin tilted aggressively as she tossed back the long, tumbling hair. To his shame Nathan realised that indeed he had been staring at the girl. But she was no ordinary girl. Rosa was different. This was no young maid to be tumbled in the hay. The mere thought of doing so seemed like sagrilege. This creature was a princess. No, his mind insisted, more than that, she was a queen.

"Sorry", he mumbled "didn't mean to anger you."

"You didn't." It was a statement. "Take off your boots."

"Me boots? What for?"

"I seen you limpin'. You got blisters an' I got a cure. So take off your boots."

It was a command, not a request, and slowly Nathan struggled with the task, dropping first one boot and then the other onto the floor of the vardo.

"Now stick your feet in 'ere. They smell like pig's muck." She set a bowl of water in front of him and, with a soft cloth, began to wipe away the grime. A small sigh escaped Nathan's lips as he closed his eyes, allowing the pure pleasure of her attention to wash over him. She knelt before him, her head bowed, as she tenderly dried his feet and began to smooth a pungent balm into the sore skin.

"'Ow's that?"

Nathan's eyes flew open to find her gazing up at him. "Fine." He murmured, painfully aware that she still held his feet cradled to the warmth of her body. Her low cut bodice exposed brown shoulders and the swell of firm, young breasts, but her eyes held a warning. 'Touch me not!' They said.

"You want to go bare foot like I do." She eased his feet to the floor and stood. "Don't get no blisters like that. See?" Nathan swallowed hard as, unselfconsciously she hitched her full skirt up to her thigh, holding out a slender unblemished foot for his inspection. He nodded wordlessly, not trusting himself to speak, or indeed, at that moment, to move, for the effect her display had had upon him was all too evident. He shifted uncomfortably beneath her seemingly innocent gaze. The scent of her body, a mist of a million flowers blended with musk, rocked his senses as she bent to pick up the bowl of water. He wanted to reach out, to caress her sun-warmed olive skin, but as if reading his mind, she stepped out of reach.

"You'd best go sit with Pa. He likes to talk." Disappointment swamped Nathan. She dismissed him from her presence without a backward glance.

Clambering onto the seat beside Colom he was still lost in the girl's provocative aura.

"Put you right, did she? Rosa's good with 'erbs and such." Colom sucked thoughtfully on an old pipe. "O'course, what she does best is dance. Scorches the earth once she gets goin'. She'll be dancin' at the fair and those gents'll come round like bees round a hive." He chuckled. "But she'll have none of it. Right firebrand is Rosa. 'When I picks me man', she says, 'it'll be a Romany. I'll 'ave none other'. And she means it, lad." He wagged the pipe stem at Nathan. "So don't go getting' no ideas."

Nathan shook his head. "What man wouldn't get ideas if he's flesh and blood? But I mind what you say." He added sadly.

"Good lad," Colom approved. "We'll be in Walden 'afore long." He glanced sideways with a knowing grin. "That'll take your mind off Rosa."

But Nathan doubted he would ever forget the beautiful gypsy girl or the strange exciting effect she had had on him.

CHAPTER SIX

Saffron had lain awake until the early hours waiting for the unmistakable sound of her stepfather's return. When she finally heard him stumble, cursing, into the cottage she had listened, every nerve alive, until, after a while, to her relief, it became quiet save for the sound of his snores and she felt safe to assume he had fallen into a drunken sleep.

Tom, as always, had slept the night through and the next day he woke bright and early. Saffron heard him moving overhead and hurried to the foot of the stair, a finger to her lips. "Shh!" She warned. "Pa's still sleeping."

The boy knuckled sleep from his eyes and peered down beneath the banister rail. "Is he poorly?"

"No." She tried to reassure him. "Just a bit tired. Now get yoursel' dressed and come on down. But quietly." She added with a smile. Tom nodded happily and disappeared, exaggerating every tiptoed step.

Behind the dividing wall at the back of the room, the sound of movement alerted Saffron to Jonas' awakening. Holding his head in his hands he emerged, coughing and groaning, cursing as he stumbled over a stool. Viciously kicking it to one side, he raised bloodshot eyes to glower at Saffron "Wot you lookin' at?" He growled.

Saffron looked with contempt at the filthy, stubbled face and crumpled shirt stained with vomit. "I'm lookin' at what used to be a man." She hissed. "You stink. An' if you don't want your son to see you like you are you'll get outside and clean yoursel'."

As he came unsteadily toward her she turned away, her hand hovering above the firedogs. His eyes narrowed as he saw her intention. He came to a halt holding up a shaking hand in surrender. "No need for that." He mumbled. "I'm goin'."

As he crashed through the back door of the cottage Saffron realised that she was trembling. For a moment she remembered Jonas as he had been on the day he had married her mother. He had been a kind and loving man, who, with the loss of his wife, had become disheartened and a drink-sodden monster. As she busied herself with the morning's chores, she began to plan the day ahead. The need to get Tom away from Jonas was uppermost in her mind and a walk along the coastline to the neighbouring town of Westcliff would ensure a full day away from the village.

Tom was excited to hear the promise of a picnic and watched impatiently as she packed bread, cheese and apples into a small basket. Jonas had not reappeared and she guessed, rather than face her again, he had taken the back alley to the home of one of his cronies.

The June sun had already warmed the day as she set out with the child skipping along beside her. Laughing, she called him back as, chasing a seagull, he teetered on the top of the Pilgrim's steps.

Reaching her side he looked up with a puzzeled frown. "Why's the steps called 'Pilgrim's'? What's a Pilgrim?"

"I remember askin' Pa the very same thing when I were about your age." Saffron shielded her eyes against the glare of the sun. "'E said the Pilgrims were folk who were called Puritans. Good folk they were. They 'ad a different way of worshiping God was all." She pulled the boy down to sit beside her on an outcrop of rock, warming to her story. "Seems they wanted to start again, get away from England where they were 'aving some trouble. So they bought themselves a boat and sailed for America. The Mayflower it were called, it were built 'ere in Leigh. Pa said it were an old merchantman, takin' and fetchin' cargoes from all over. A leaky old bucket 'e said it were but it made the journey all the way to America. That were more'n two 'undred years ago."

Tom   frowned.   "But   what   about   the   steps?" "Well, they got the ship ready and then they sailed down from London and moored off the shore right 'ere in Leigh. The Pilgrim's came ashore while they took on food and stuff. Some of them stayed a few days in Leigh. Some of 'em went further inland. Then when everything was ready, they set off. They went down those very steps to board the Mayflower for the rest of the way. Pa said they rested at Plymouth before settin' out for America."

Tom was silent, staring out across the Estuary. "They must 'ave been awful brave." He whispered. "Is America a long way, Saffy?"

She got to her feet, brushing sand from her skirt. "It is. But don't ask me 'ow far, 'cause I don't know. All I know is they got there safe and made an'ome for themselves. Now. Up you get and let's be on our way."

Willingly, Tom scrambled to his feet, slipping his hand into hers. Saffron smiled, the boy was always full of questions. She was glad that on this occasion she had been able to supply the answers and grateful that he would soon be starting school.

The coastal path, bordered by wild yellow Ragwort and Foxgloves, wound eastward to Westcliff. The seasonal Royal patronage of the south end of Prittlewell, or Southend as it had become known, had promoted a migration of wealth to the area. Several imposing houses had been built set back from the coastline. She smiled, wondering which of the owners had been surprised to find Nathan's horse abandoned in his grounds.

Tom had long since shed his boots and stockings and

splashed laughing at the water's edge, running from the waves and skimming pebbles over the surface of the incoming tide.

As the day wore on, the seafront came to life. Seated in the shelter of a breakwater, they watched tall-hatted men escorting elegant women in fine shawls, enjoying the bracing sea air. Tom ran back and forth with handfuls of small treasures, shells and pieces of glass and fragments of china, washed smooth by a thousand tides, piling them beside Saffron in a glistening heap. They sat together enjoying their picnic and throwing crumbs to hungry sparrows gathering to share the feast. Tom squealed with laughter at the antics of the tiny brown birds as their sheer speed and daring foiled the attempts of greedy seagulls to snatch their prize.

The heat of the day was waning as reluctantly, they made their way home. Tom was tired but his sun-freckled face was happier than Saffron had seen it for weeks. Despite her determination to shield him from Jonas' drunken behaviour she knew the boy was aware of his father's ill-tempered outbursts. It was as if she and the boy kept the secret and, by mute agreement, would not share it with one another.

As they came near to the village Saffron shaded her eyes to see a small group of her neighbours clustered around the door of their cottage.

"Come on, Tom." She grabbed the boy's hand. "Summat's up." They ran the last few yards, pushing their way to the front of the crowd.

"Dirty little bitch! I'll learn you!" Jonas' voice was thick with fury as Saffron burst into the room. The first thing she saw was Poll crouched by the hearth, shielding her head against the next blow as Jonas raised his arm to strike again. Saffron pushed Tom behind her skirts. "You touch 'er again and I'll see you pay, so I will!" She screamed. Then, turned furiously to

face the curious onlookers craning their heads for a chance to
relish the shame of a neighbour. "An' what are you lot staring
at? Not one of you man enough to stop 'im?" She accused.
"Cowards, the lot o' you!"

One by one they turned away, avoiding her eyes, muttering
to one another.

She slammed the door on them and faced Jonas. "I warned
you." He heard the icy determination in her voice. "You best
get goin' 'afore I change me mind. Go find one of your fine
friends and tell 'em 'ow you beat a girl. They'll make you
an   'ero!"

Jonas' face, once suffused with fury, paled at her outburst.
"I'll go when I'm ready." He blustered, but his eyes widened
as Saffron reached for the heavy iron poker. "You'll go now!"
She spat, closing her fist around the smooth handle. "An' don't
come back!"

Jonas shuffled sideways round the table. "You'll be sorry,
bitch. You wait "

"I'll be waitin' alright! I'll be waitin' with this in me 'and!"
She hefted the weight of the fire iron, raising it as she threw
wide the door then stepped back to allow him passage before
slamming it behind him.

Tom was kneeling white-faced, his lips trembling as he
looked down at his sister. Poll was sobbing quietly, curled into
a defensive ball. Saffron bent to stroke her hair.

"Come on, Poll, 'e's gone." She helped the shaking girl
onto the settle and, wringing out a rag, she dabbed at the girl's
swollen mouth where a trickle of blood was testimony to
Jonas' brutal treatment.

"What 'appened, Poll?" She asked quietly. "What made 'im
go for you?"

Poll shook her head, her eyes filling with tears as Tom came to pat her arm, "Saffy'll make it better." He promised, biting his lip. Poll winced at his touch, pushing up her sleeve to examine a circle of red finger marks, which would soon blossom into ugly bruises.

"Poll, come on, you got to tell me." Saffron took her sister's hands in hers, "What got 'im so mad?"

"I tried to tell 'im, but 'e said it were my fault." The words were barely above a whisper.

"What was your fault?"

"'E said I was askin' for it! I didn't do nothin'." She raised haunted eyes. "T' were them young men what came down from Oxford with the master's son."

Saffron's mouth went dry. Oh no, dear God, not that! "You mean..,.?" she stopped as Poll nodded. "But how? When?"

Poll palmed the tears from her eyes. "Last night it were. Oh Saffy! It were awful!" Fresh tears began to flow. "I'd just got back to the 'ouse an' was makin' for the back door when Robert, that's the master's son, came round the corner with the other two. 'Ello, he says, nice as pie. I give a little curtsey like cook told me and then he says: 'An' what's your name?' 'Poll', I says. Then one of the others starts capering round me callin' out like the old parrot up at The Billet. 'Pretty Polly, Pretty Polly,' he kept sayin'. Then the other one he grabs me 'ands an' starts to dance me around. They was all laughing and teasin' an' I was gettin' that giddy." She stopped, shaking her head. "I don't know for sure what 'appened next. One of 'em said something to that Robert and he sort of shrugged and nodded. The other two jumped on me an' 'afore I knowed it they dragged me into the stables. I was a yellin' and fightin', Saffy, honest I was." She hung her head. "But they was too strong. They held me down an'…"

Saffron threw her arms around Poll as she began to sob.

"Shh, that's enough." She was suddenly aware of Tom's attention. "We'll talk more later."

"No, I got to tell you now." Poll took a deep breath. "'Twas
Gabriel found me."

"''Im what's the 'ead groom?"

Poll nodded. "'E's a good man. When 'e saw the state I
was in, all torn and bleedin', 'e knew straight off what had
'appened. 'E was all for goin' up to the big 'ouse and sortin' it
out. But I was that shook up an' a'feared they would say I was
lyin' I begged 'im not to. We went back to his little cottage and
I stayed there 'till mornin'."

"What did 'is wife reckon to it?"

"'E 'asn't got a wife any more. She died 'avin' a baby a
couple of years back. The little mite was stillborn. She were
only young. Sort of sad 'e is, but kind. I fell asleep. When I
woke up there 'e was sitting beside me. Been there all night
I reckon. 'Best get back 'ome ,'e says I'll 'ave a word with
Cook. She won't be needin' you for a day or so. So I came
back early. Oh Saffy! Where were you? I was waiting when
Jonas come staggering down the road. 'Wot you doin' 'ere?'
he says. When I tried to tell 'im 'e went into one of 'is rages."
She looked pleadingly at her sister. "It weren't my fault were
it?" She fingered her bruised cheek. "You won't let 'im near
me again will you?"

"Don't you worry 'bout that. Jonas knows what's waitin' for
'im if 'e shows 'is ugly face! Look," Saffron was becoming
increasingly aware of Tom hovering nearby, round-eyed with
concern. "Let's get you tucked up in bed and we'll talk more
later. Tom, swing that pot over the stove and we'll make Poll
a nice cup of broth."

Painfully Poll got to her feet and with Saffron steadying her
she climbed the stair to the narrow rooms above "Now, let's

get your things off." Saffron bustled about turning down the sheet and plumping pillows.

"I want to wash". Poll stammered. "I feel... I feel... dirty, Saffy, filthy dirty. They hurt me so." She threw herself onto the bed, her slender body wracked with heartbreaking sobs.

Saffron hurried to sit beside her, gathering her into her arms and rocking her as if she were a baby. "There, Poll, let it all out." She soothed. After a while the girl's sobs subsided and she allowed Saffron to ease her back onto the pillow. Gently she began to undress her sister, slipping Poll's chemise off her shoulders and down to her waist. With a gasp of horror she saw that Poll's young breasts were scratched and bitten, her thin shoulders badly bruised by brutal misuse.

"Oh my little love, what have they done to you?" Saffron felt her own eyes fill with angry tears.

"Don't cry Saffy," Poll begged. She tried to sit up but the effort caused her to double up with pain. She clutched her stomach. "I think I'm hurt 'ere too." She made an attempt at a faint smile. "But I'll be alright, I'm 'ome now, that's all that matters."

"I'm goin' to send Tom for Doctor Smale." Saffron got to her feet but Poll caught her hand.

"No." She begged, "I don't want no one to know. If them in the village see 'im comin' 'ere, they'll make up all sorts. Promise me Saffy." She hung her head, masking fresh tears. "I can't stand the shame of it and you know what the village is like they'll be pointin' the finger. Me life won't be worth livin'."

Saffron knew the truth of the argument. "We'll see," was all she would agree to. "I'll bring soap and water and we'll see the damage." She wagged a finger at her sister. "But if I think the doctor is needed, then the doctor it will be."

An hour later Poll was washed and tucked into bed, sipping a bowl of broth. Saffron had been appalled at the all too visible evidence of the savage rape but had been persuaded to delay calling the doctor until the next day.

Her sister was right, after the scene earlier, the village gossips needed only to see his visit to the cottage and they would begin to put two and two together. Whatever the sum total they would embroider the truth to suit their own wagging tongues and denial would only add fuel to the fire. There would be no justice, she knew. The young men responsible, were their crime discovered, would get no more than a good-humoured scolding, while Poll would bear the scars of memory for the rest of her life.

A sudden pounding on the door below startled them and Poll shrank into the pillows. "Don't let anyone in, Saffy." She pleaded, her eyes wide with terror.

"I won't, but I must see who 'tis." Saffron ran down in time to stop Tom opening the door and was surprised to see the tall figure of Gabriel Stoneforth standing there, cap in hand.

He touched his forelock. "Sorry to come knocking, Miss Saffron, but I wanted to know if young Poll got 'ome safe. I would'av brung 'er all the way, but master wanted 'is coach, so I 'ad to let 'er come the last bit on 'er own." He paused, shuffling his feet. "'Ow is she? Is she alright?"

Saffron nodded. "You'd best come in. Can't talk on the step." She stood back and beckoned him into the cottage. "Sit yoursel' down. Tom, you go up an' ask Poll if she needs anythin'."

Gabriel nodded understandingly as the boy scampered away. "Don't want the young'un gettin' upset do we?"

Saffron smiled. "Not if I can 'elp it. Now, tell me what Cook said. Poll said as 'ow you were goin' to tell 'er what 'appened."

Gabriel did not meet her gaze, seemingly engrossed in a ragged fingernail. "Well, Cook said I should speak to Master. I chose me time an' he got right mad. 'Little bastards.' He said." He glanced up. "Sorry but that's what 'e said. "Little bastards, I'll take the skin off their backsides.' Then he laughs and says summat about lads 'aving to sow their oats. Lady Margaret's off on her travels again or she'd 'av 'ad more to say. As 'tis the Master give me this for Poll." He held out a small leather pouch. "An' said as 'ow it was a bit extra on what she was owed." He shook his head. "She's not wanted at the 'ouse no more."

Saffron took the pouch, emptying the contents into the palm of her hand. Two gold sovereigns. The price of her sister's innocence.

"An' that's supposed to put things right?" She felt the colour rise in her cheeks. "They think all they need do is throw a bit of money at it and it will go away?"

"Aye, 't'as always been so." He stood, preparing to leave, but turned at the door. "Would it be alright with you Miss Saffron, if I come by now and then to see 'ow she is?" He smiled shyly. "She be a lovely girl an' we've had long talks when cook's sent 'er down to stables with victuals. P'raps I could cheer her up a bit."

Saffron nodded, she liked this giant of a man with his gentle ways. "Aye, but leave it a day or two. She's in no state for callers now."

She closed the door behind him, leaning her head against the seasoned wood.

"Not now." She whispered. "Not for a long time". She thought of the terror Gabriel's knock at the door had caused her sister. There was rape of the body and then there was rape of the mind.

CHAPTER SEVEN

They heard the music before the town of Saffron Walden came into sight, the beat of drums carried faintly on the summer breeze. Midnight, responding to Colom's soft command, brought the Vardo to a halt, his great chest heaving gently from the last hill climb. Rosa came to the door, resting her arms on the painted sill. "Ow far?" she asked.

"Nearly there." Colom sniffed the air. "Smell it?"

Rosa raised her head to the breeze to catch the pungent smell. "The Maltin's," She pointed beyond the trees to the tall chimneys punctuating the skyline. "Local barley makes a good brew. There'll be plenty of ale drunk this night."

Colom laughed aloud. "An' more'n a drop'll go down this gullet."

"So what's all the goin's on you've come 'ere for? Nathan turned to the girl.

"Don't you know nothin'?" Rosa stepped down, squeezing her slim hips between the two men. "'Tis said the worthies." She saw Nathan's frown. "You know the rich folk 'ere about. Well, they 'ave paid to 'ave the church done up. A ruin it were. 'S'evenin' they be goin' to stick the last stone up on the spire." She turned to her father, wriggling impatiently. "An' if we get movin' mayhap we'll be there when it 'appens."

Colom took the hint and urged Midnight to move on. Rounding the last bend in the lane they found themselves looking down the rutted and dusty main street to where cottages, many in a poor state of repair, tradesmen's workshops and taverns edged the market square.

Children, excited by the holiday atmosphere, scampered between the legs of adults, earning a good-natured curse or a well-placed clout. Outside the Rose and Crown several horses were tethered and men in tall hats stood in small groups. Their bonneted ladies at their side daintily lifted their skirts away from the animal dung which seemed to lie everywhere under foot, its stench mingling with a hundred other unidentifiable smells.

One side of the street was sectioned off to house a few pigs and cattle around which clustered a group of farmers examining the animals, assessing their worth.

Nathan called Colom's attention to another dark eyed gypsy, leading a fine mare and wandering through the throng, holding a stick on high in his right hand. "What's 'e up to then?" he asked his companion.

"Why 'e's got that fine creature for sale. That stick is to show folk that 'e's sellin', if 'e 'ad it in 'is left 'and, e'd be buying." He shook his head. "You've got a lot to learn boy."

Above the rooftops flags fluttered in the early evening breeze and, as if obeying an unspoken command, the market square began to empty as the townsfolk began to drift up the hill toward the ancient parish church.

"Come on, father." Rosa urged, jumping from the Vardo and standing impatiently, hands on hips.

"You go Rosa, an' you lad, I got to find a pitch and Midnight needs 'is feed. I'll get there, don't you worry."

Rosa shrugged and beckoned to Nathan. "Comin'?" Nathan eagerly joined her, matching her eager stride as she slipped through the crowd, her head high, the breeze lifting the thick hair away from her wide, excited eyes

Aware of his gaze she turned to reward him with a wide smile. "Ow's your feet?"

"Better." He had been surprised when he pulled on his boots to find the pain had eased. "An' I thank you. Colom said you was good with herbs and such."

The girl acknowledged the compliment with a smile. "Me ma taught me 'afore she died. She were the tribe's 'ealing woman." She bent her head as, for a moment, memory held her silent. "But there was no 'ealing could 'elp 'er when she fell under the wheels of a carriage."

"I'm sorry."

The girl tilted her head defiantly. "Why? 'T'weren't you did it."

"No, but it must have been a terrible way to die. And for you…"

"Aye."

Nathan was glad there was no time for more words as they were caught up in the jostling, happy crowd of visitors and villagers, each with a single purpose. The church awaited its coronation, the placing of the final stone on the imposing newly-built tower. Snatches of conversation from all sides reached their ears.

"They do say it cost three thousand guineas."

"Can't 'ave. "'Tis more than a lifetime's wages"

"Took a year it did."

"'Bout time. Church been closed for thirty year or more. Not safe they said."

The churchyard was packed with laughing townsfolk, their children perched on gravestones to gain a better view. Rosa and Nathan found a good vantage point as a hush of anticipation fell over young and old alike. All eyes turned upward to see a tall figure at the top of the tower directing the laying of the topstone. Then a rousing cheer rose skyward, echoing throughout the village as the band, who had somehow managed to haul their instruments to the tower's summit, struck up a majestic slow melody. Joy filled the hearts of all present. On that fine

June evening Saffron Walden was the place to be. It was a day to remember.

"Best be goin'." Colom, having found and claimed his pitch, had appeared at Nathan's elbow. He beckoned to Rosa. "Folk'll be gathering round the vardo waiting for a show."

"Comin' Pa." She held out a slim hand to Nathan. "'Tis a shame you ain't a Romany." He looked deeply into her dark eyes and for a moment saw a hint of regret. "You be a fine lad." He felt her press something into his palm. "'Tis a charm to keep you safe." She whispered. "Now be off, your future's waitin'." And she was gone, disappearing into the crowd to leave Nathan craning his head to catch one last, precious sight of her.

While many in the crowd made their way back to the market square and to the fairground beyond, some stayed near to the church to enjoy the music which still floated down from the church tower on the warm summer breeze.

"My future?" Nathan smiled, fingering Rosa's gift, a strangely carved stone disc hung on a thin leather tie. "P'raps I should 'ave got Colom to tell me if there were a fortune in me future. Still, what will be will be an' I got to start somewhere, so I'd best find that aunt o'mine."

Mary Clay had told her son many stories of the great house in which she and her sister had worked as girls. It stood, she had said, half a mile to the west of the market town behind stone walls and tall gates.

With thoughts of the wild Romany girl still disturbing his mind Nathan took the road out of town, his shadow following him faithfully as the evening air cooled with the setting of the sun. In less than an hour Nathan reached his goal. The house sat well back from the country lane and through ornate, forged gates he could see a gravel drive bordered by flowering bushes and well-tended lawns leading to the Benham residence. The square, three-story building was plain and unadorned, its windows winking in the last rays of the sun. To his surprise the gate swung open at his touch and for a moment he hesitated. Seeing no sign of life he ventured onto the driveway, each footstep crunching loudly in the silence

Nathan's courage faltered, however, as he came to the imposing main entrance. White marble steps rose from the gravel drive leading to a carved oak door set between imposing pillars. He looked down at his worn boots, smacking the dust from his britches. "Not dressed to go callin." He muttered. "I reckon they'll take one look at me an' set the dogs out. Best see what's round the back." Skirting the corner of the building he was rewarded by the sight of an open door and the sound of voices.

"Well, I say it weren't right we 'ad to stay be'ind. We should'a all gone down the town."

"An' who d'you think would get the master's dinner, an' 'im with all those folk a'coming back to the 'ouse? It's what he does pay us for and he's a good master, not like some as I could mention."

"All the same, I would like to 'ave seen 'em put that stone up and I'd like to 'ave gone to the fair. They do say there be gipsys there an' all sorts."

"Never you mind that, girl, you just take them things through to the dinin' room or we won't never get done."

Nathan edged his way to the door in time to see a girl leave the large kitchen bearing a heavy tray loaded with cakes and tarts. His apologetic cough caught the attention of the plump woman at the long table. Startled, she turned to stare at the intruder. "An' 'oo might you be, and what you doin' 'ere?" Before he could answer she had picked up a heavy rolling pin and advanced toward him. "Whatever you're sellin', we don't want none." She stopped, frowning "Ow did you get in, anyway?"

Nathan smiled. "The gates was open, so I just walked in. I'm right sorry if I scared you and I ain't sellin' nothing."

"Them gates should 'ave been locked. Master'll 'ave summat to say 'bout that. If you ain't sellin nothin' you got no business comin' up on folk like that!" She straightened her voluminous white apron and patted her grey hair into place the meanwhile taking stock of Nathan's travel-worn appearance. "Well, speak up lad!" Her tone had softened. "You'd best come in an' sit. You look 'bout on your last legs"

Gratefully Nathan did as he was bid, sinking onto a stool by the huge black range. "T'as been a long way." He admitted, "An' I'd be glad to rest."

"Ere, get this down you." The woman handed him a mug of cold water and stood watching him closely as he downed it in a single gulp. "That'll settle the dust. Now, tell me what d'you want 'ere?"

Nathan scrubbed his hand through his matted fair hair. "I be lookin' for me Aunt. Porter's 'er name, Jane Porter, or it were last time I 'eard."

The woman's hand flew to her mouth. "Jane Porter? Why she be 'ousekeeper 'ere. You say she's your Aunt?"

Nathan nodded. "Me mother was Mary, 'er sister. She worked 'ere too when she were a girl."

"That must'a been 'afore my time."She stood back to look harder at Nathan. "You got the look of her right enough. She'll be back 'afore long. Master said as 'ow she 'ad to go with 'em to see the church doin's." She sniffed. "Left us to do the last bits. Not that I mind." She straightened her shoulders. I been cook 'ere for six years or more an' she knows I don't leave nothin' to chance. But what she'll say when she sees you I don't know and that's the truth! Might be a good idea if you was to smarten yoursel' up a bit. 'Ere." She held out a small towel, "Get to the sink over there and 'ave a bit of a wash and tidy."

Nathan grinned, stripping off his dusty shirt. "It'll take more than a drop of water to make me sweet after the miles I've come."

The woman cast an appreciative eye over Nathan's half naked body, watching the shift of lean muscle as he sluiced his head under the tap and remembering days gone by when such a sight would have sent her senses racing.

A sudden scream made him turn, spraying water onto the floor as the cook's young assistant came back into the kitchen. "Oh my gawd! Where d'you come from?" She gasped. "Cook, 'e's got no clothes on!"

A bellow of laughter greeted her words. "E's got 'is britches on girl, so shut your noise. Do somethin' useful, make a pot of tea while I dig out one o' the shirts what the footmen wear. They won't miss it and this," she displayed Nathan's ragged shirt for inspection, "won't bear another wash!" Gratefully, he struggled into the shirt she handed him.

The three of them were seated at the scrubbed oak table when they heard the sound of coach wheels on the driveway. Minutes later Jane Porter swept into the kitchen to stand open mouthed at the sight of her nephew. The cook and the girl divorced themselves from responsibility by busying them-selves with unnecessary tasks while, silently, the housekeeper made her way to stand almost toe to toe with Nathan. With narrowed eyes she took in his every feature before nodding decisively. "I don't know what you are doing here, but you must be my sister Mary's eldest". She pronounced. "You are the living image of her."

Nathan was immediately struck by the cultured voice and by the handsome woman's dress and bearing. The dark blue material of her gown, set off by white lace at neck and wrists, clung to the well corsetted figure, accentuating a small waist and the imposing swell of her bosom. Clearly working her way up to the position of housekeeper had necessitated that she improve herself along the way

Nathan said a silent prayer of thanks for the cook's foresight as he held out a clean hand. "Yes, Aunt Jane, I'm Nathan, and right pleased to meet you."

She considered the gesture before taking his hand in her own. "You had best follow me." She glanced at the two servants who were doing their best to hear every word while trying hard to pretend disinterest. "We may talk in my room, but first I must see to the master's guests. You will wait for me there."

Nathan followed his aunt from the kitchen but not without a backward glance and a broad wink at the cook who did her best to smother a smile behind her apron.

The housekeeper's room was comfortable and obviously bore the stamp of its occupant. Beneath the wide bow-fronted window, hung with deep red curtains, was a large desk with books and papers neatly arranged on its polished surface. Between two deep, leather chairs, one on either side of the fireplace, sat a low table and on one wall were arranged shelves containing more books than Nathan could ever have imagined existed. While he waited for his aunt's return he ran his finger along the spines, reading aloud the titles. Essays on household management and accounts were sorted precisely into alphabetical order while the few slim volumes of fiction were squeezed into what little space was left.

The quiet room and the tempting comfort of one of the chairs proved too much for him. He realised that he was more tired that he had imagined and, to his embarrassment, he was found dozing when Jane Porter returned. The quiet swish of the baize-lined door went unheard as, shedding her hat and gloves, she went to stand looking down at the sleeping boy. Her presence alone woke him and he leapt to his feet, flustered with apology, but she reached a slim hand to press him back into the chair.

"Stay where you are, Nathan. I have sent for a tray of tea and something to eat. I take it you are hungry?"

"I am that, Aunt Jane, and I'm right grateful for your kindness."

His Aunt's gentle response to a knock on the door allowed the young girl Nathan had seen in the kitchen to enter with the promised tea and food. She set it down and with a shy smile, bobbed a curtsey and hurried from the room.

"Now, Nathan, you may begin your story." His Aunt began to pour tea into two dainty china cups. She paused, milk jug in hand, looking him straight in the eye. "And mind every word of it is the truth, for I think there is more to your visit than the wish to see your Aunt."

Nathan felt the colour rise in his cheeks. He had come this far and there was no going back. He judged his Aunt to be a strong-minded woman and if he were to win her support he knew he had to tell her everything. And so he began.

He filled in the gaps between the letters, which his mother had written to her sister over the years. He then told her that Poll worked much as she had, in service, and that following her sister's death, Saffron had become a surrogate mother to the five-year-old Tom who had never known the woman who bore him. He told her of Jonas, of his drinking and of the savage beatings he had endured at his hands. And determined to hold nothing back, he told her of his own crimes and the reasons behind his sudden appearance.

Jane Porter sat sipping her tea, her cool blue eyes never leaving his face as he poured out the sorry tale.

"So you see, Aunt, there was nothin' for it but to leg it away from Leigh. I wanted to stay with the young'un's, but t'would serve no purpose with me in jail or worse still in the colonies. Even with a different name they might 've tracked me down. I thought if I could get to Saffron Walden you might put a word in with someone so's I could find work. I don't care what I do, an' I promise you I'm strong and I'd work 'ard for the right master." He glanced anxiously at the woman as she set down her cup on the lace-edged tray cloth.

"I believe you Nathan, and, while I do not approve of," she paused, choosing her words carefully, "your wrongdoing, I am prepared to help you. You are, after all, my dear sister's child and I am your only living relative, for your grandparents are both dead, God rest their souls. For your Mother's sake, I will do my best to find you a position." She appeared to be deep in thought and Nathan held his breath as she steepled her long fingers. "Without a valid character, a reference to your honesty and abilities, I can scarcely speak to Bentley, the butler, and ask him to employ you as a manservant. I can however, speak to the head groom." She raised her head. "Do you have any experience with horses?"

"I 'ave that!" Nathan replied with enthusiasm. "They seem to like me an' I like to be near the beasts."

"Well, I know Bartholemew Jackson, the head groom, is looking for another boy, so I shall speak to him on your behalf." She leaned forward holding up a warning finger. "But understand, I will not be held responsible for your behaviour."

"I understand Aunt, and I'm real pleased that you 'ave enough faith in me to find me a place. I won't let you down, that I won't."

"Very well, that is settled. Finish your tea and we will make our way to the stables. I dare say you will be able to spend the night there until more suitable accommodation becomes available. I have several small duties to perform, but I will return before long."

Left to himself, Nathan had time to think over the day's events. Thoughtfully he fingered Rosa's charm, which hung around his neck. It seemed that yet again he had landed on his feet. The future seemed not only secure but bright beyond belief. And he made a silent vow to make the most of it.

CHAPTER EIGHT

Tom spent the remainder of the day creeping up the stairs and quietly pushing open the bedroom door to reassure himself that Poll was sleeping peacefully. Each time he hurried down to report to Saffron. Unusually quiet, there could be no doubt that his young mind was troubled by what he had seen and heard. Saffron saw his anxious expression, able only to guess at the unspoken questions filling his mind. When he was ready he would voice his fears and she prayed that when that time came she would find the right words of comfort.

Eventually she was able to coax him to bed with promises of a better day to come. She stayed beside him until he fell asleep after listening, with tears in her eyes, to his childlike prayer, an innocent petition to the Lord to 'make Poll stop hurting and get better soon.'

Poll stirred as Saffron tiptoed into the bedroom and she flew to her side as Poll came suddenly awake, aware of her surroundings, her mind flooding with agonising memory. As her eyes focused the tears began to flow.

"There, there. Hush now." Saffron took her hands. "You're safe and I'm here. D'you want the lamp lit?" Poll shook her head miserably, turning to bury her face in the pillow. "Well, could you manage a bite o' supper? You've 'ad nothin' all day."

Poll took a deep breath, pushing herself high in the bed. "Sorry." She whispered, "I gotta stop this, ain't I?" She smiled weakly, wiping her wet cheek on the cuff of her nightgown. "I am a bit empty I s'pose. Could I 'ave a drop of soup or summat?"

"Certainly, madam!" Saffron made an exaggerated curtsey.

"An' would her ladyship like some bread wiv' it?"

"Oh, Saffy!" Poll sniffed back her tears and began to laugh. "You be so funny when you puts on airs all la-de-da like. You sounds just like Cook when she 'as to talk to that there butler up at the 'ouse."

Poll's laughter brought a smile of relief to Saffron's face as she hurried down to the kitchen. Perhaps it would not be too long before she was on the mend.

There had been no sign of Jonas but Saffron dreaded his eventual return. She knew she could put up a fight with words but what would she really be able to do if it looked as if he intended to hurt Poll or Tom? Part of her knew the terror in her heart while a larger part resolved to protect her family no matter what the outcome.

She sat with Poll until she had finished the last mouthful of soup. "Thanks Saffy, I didn't know I was so 'ungry. I feel a sight better wi' that inside me." A sudden thought struck her, stretching her eyes wide with fear. "'Ave you barred the doors? 'E might come back. Don't let 'im in, Saffy. Don't let 'im in!"

"Don't you fret". She patted her sister's hand, "Jonas won't be back this night. Anyway, I've shot the bolts home back an' front an' I'm sleepin' in the kitchen, so you rest easy." She bent to kiss Poll's head. "If you need me you just thump on the floor an' I'll be up. Now." She smoothed the bedcover." Off you go to sleep and I'll see you in the mornin'." She waited long enough to see Poll snuggle down and close her eyes.

The kitchen range still held the heat of the morning's fire but there was no need of its warmth. After the storm, the June night was uncomfortably hot and from the cottage window the sky seemed to be streaked with purple as the sun dipped behind the horizon. Saffron settled herself as comfortably as she could, on the wooden settle, drawing her shawl around her shoulders, alert to Poll's needs but hoping to catch an hour's sleep.

The sun woke her, streaming through the small front window, and she was surprised to realise that she had slept the rest of the night through. She yawned, stretching her arms high above head to ease her aching limbs. A wooden settle, she decided ruefully, was not the best place to seek a comfortable night's rest.

There was no sound of movement from the rooms above, so, sluicing her hands and face and raking fingers through her hair, she rammed a log of driftwood into the grey ash and dimly glowing embers in the range. There was little food in the cottage but she comforted herself that a thin porridge would suffice until she had a moment to go down to the village shop. Leaving the oats to simmer on the stove she climbed the stair to look in on Poll. But Tom had got there before her. Perched in his nightshirt on the end of his sister's bed he was deep in earnest conversation.

Poll was giggling at his account of the 'rich folk' he had seen the day before. "An' their 'ats was this big." He insisted, stretching his arms to an improbable measure. "An' the ladies walked like this." He jumped to the floor and minced up and down, wriggling his bottom in exaggerated mimicry.

Saffron did her best to smother a chuckle. "Tom." She said with mock severity, "'Tis wrong to make fun of folk!" The boy hung his head but as Saffron could hold the pose no longer, she joined them both in uncontrolled laughter.

"Oh, Tom!" She hugged him to her. "You'll end in trouble and that's no mistake." She patted his rear end. "Now put your britches on and go down to break your fast. I'll be there in a minute."

As he scampered away she turned to her sister. "You slept then?"

Poll nodded, "An' I feel a mite better Saffy. I still 'urt a bit 'ere and there but I don't want no doctor. You can see to me needs can't you?"

"I'll 'ave another look at you and then I'll make up me mind". Saffron tucked a strand of hair behind Poll's ear and tilted the defiant chin. "P'raps later we'll get you up and dressed, then we'll know better."

Poll suffered Saffron's attention to her wounds without a murmur. The salve applied the night before had begun to heal the lesser scratches but Saffron was concerned that others were still red and ugly. Poll's slender hips and legs were covered in bruises and, to her concern, Saffron realised that the girl was running a mild fever.

"Your temperature's up, Poll." She laid a hand on the girl's forehead. "'Tis time to call Doc Smale."

Her sister grabbed her arm "No Saffy." She pleaded. "You promised. Don't call 'im, please."

"Well," Saffron frowned, chewing her lip. "There could be another way." She saw the light of hope dawn in Poll's eyes. "I could ask Mother Watkins for one of her brews."

"That old witch!" Poll's nose wrinkled in disgust.

"Witch she may be, but I seen 'er cure more 'n one who's been worse 'n you." She stood decisively. "I'll leave Tom with you while I go find 'er."

"Don't leave me Saffy. S'pose 'e comes back."

"You'll be fine. Tom can bar the door after me an' I won't be gone long." She paused. "It's that or Doctor Smale."

Poll sank back against the pillow, "All right." She mumbled. "But hurry, Saffy. Hurry back."

Saffron did not relish the thought of her visit to Mother Watkins' tumbledown dwelling. She had been there once before and she remembered the stench that greeted her and how it had turned her stomach.

The ancient cottage on the outskirts of the village, sat well back from the main street, its front yard overgrown with tall grass and weeds and strewn with rubbish. Under normal circumstances it was a place to avoid, although many a God-fearing villager was known to have sought help there under cover of darkness. But Saffron could not wait for night to fall. Taking her courage in both hands she rapped on the sagging door. It seemed an eternity before she heard shuffling footsteps and the old woman's querulous voice.

"'Oo's there? 'Oo ever 'tis, you can clear orf!" Saffron was sorely tempted to turn tail but Poll needed the old woman's help.

"It's Saffron Clay. You remember me mother, Mary?" She waited.

"Mary Clay? I 'member 'er. She were a good woman she were. Died 'afore 'er time."

"She did. An' now I got need of your 'elp. Me sister's got a fever an'…"

The door creaked open and Saffron took a step back. It was small wonder the village folk believed the woman to be a witch. The dirt-grimed face was as wizened as a dried plum. The tip of a long pointed nose reached down over a toothless mouth to almost touch the warted chin beneath. She stared suspiciously at Saffron. "What be wrong wi' the girl?"

Saffron glanced over her shoulder. "I'd rather not talk out 'ere," she whispered.

Mother Watkins sniffed loudly. "Like that eh? Well you'd best get inside." Reluctantly, she opened the door a little wider to let Saffron squeeze past her and into the stinking interior. The rag of a curtain at the window all but obscured the light of day and Saffron ducked and shuddered as her head struck something soft, the body of a dead rabbit hanging from the raftered ceiling.

"Best sit." The old woman nudged her toward the hearth, pointing to a low stool. "So what is it that ails 'er?"

"Like I said." Saffron began. "She's poorly. She 'as a fever." She paused, determined to provide as little detail as possible. "An' she 'as some scratches and bruises. She was sort of attacked." She bit her lip. "An' she's a mite upset too."

"Shouldn't wonder." The woman's eyes narrowed. "Attacked you say. 'Oo did it?"

"Don't know," Saffron lied. "She said it were dark."

"Aye, men loves the dark 'cause their deeds is evil." The smile on the ugly face died suddenly. "An' I say as 'ow she'll be worse 'afore she's well."

Saffron shivered, glancing at the wide hearth where bunches of herbs hung above a stewpot suspended over the dead embers of a fire. The words sounded like a prophesy and Mother Watkins was known to be all too accurate with her predictions. "No, not if you 'elps 'er. Can't you give me summat?"

The old woman considered the matter, her milky eyes staring into the distance. "I can stop the fever, but 'tis not the worst of it I'm thinkin'." She turned away to rummage among the pots and bottles lining the mantle shelf.

"What d'you mean?"

"Eh?"

"You said 'tis not the worst of it."

"No, nor 'tis. You tell 'er Mother Watkins can put 'er right." She handed a small stoppered bottle to Saffron. "Give 'er three drops 'o this in warm ale. She'll sleep mostly, so get it down 'er every time she wakes. 'T'will 'eal 'er body for now." She paused, looking long and hard at Saffron. "But that's not the end o' it."

"Why? What d'you mean? Tell me." Saffron pleaded, but the woman's mouth snapped shut. She would say no more and holding out a clawed hand for payment, she pushed Saffron through the sagging door, slamming it behind her.

On the way back to the cottage Saffron called in at the Peter Boat Inn for a jug of ale and purchased a few essential items of food from the village shop.

Reaching the cottage, the reassuring sound of her voice brought Tom to the door.

"Poll and me was frettin." Worry creased his young face. "You was so long."

"I know, love." She ruffled his hair "But I had to get summat for Poll to make her better. An' look, I got some fresh bread and meat and some fruit and stuff. We'll 'ave a feast later." Tom grinned his approval. "First, though I got to give Poll a drop o' this to make her well."

To Poll's disgust Mother Watkins' potion tasted every bit as bad as it smelled.

"It'll do you good." Saffron insisted, watching until Poll finished the last drop.

"Poison me more like." Poll moaned, sinking back against the pillow. "Tastes like it come out the wrong 'end of an 'orse!"

Saffron smothered a smile. "That's as maybe." She said sternly. "But likely the 'orse got well!"

"Oh, Saffy," Poll giggled. "You got an answer for everythin'." Sobering suddenly, she handed the empty cup to her sister. "What'll I do? I don't want to go back. It'll be all round the 'ouse by now."

Saffron looked away. "You ain't goin' back. That Gabriel came while you were sleepin'. They sent 'im with what you was owed." She rested a hand on Poll's shoulder. "They don't want you back 'e said."

Poll's eyes filled with tears. "But it weren't my fault. 'E does know that!"

"Aye, 'e does and right worried 'e is. Said 'e'd call now and then to see 'ow you were mendin'."

"Gabriel's a good man." Poll sniffed. "Always 'ad a kind word when I see 'im. Told me I was real pretty once. Said I'd 'ave all the boys queuing up to walk out wiv me." She raised her head, angrily wiping the tears from her cheek. "But they won't now, will they? Nobody won't want me no more. Not after…" Her voice trailed away as she buried her face in her hands.

Saffy sat beside her, prising her hands apart. "Don't talk that way Poll, this'll all blow over, you'll see. An' Gabriel was right, it won't be long a'fore the lads will be waiting six deep outside the door for one smile from that pretty face o' yours."

Poll raised tear-filled eyes. "P'raps. But what if Jonas tells. You know what 'e's like when 'e 'as a drop too much."

Saffron bent to straighten the bed cover. She knew all too well how spiteful their stepfather could be and, having shamed him in front of his cronies, she was sure he would take any opportunity he could to get his revenge. "Don't you worry about him." She forced herself to sound convincing. "Everyone knows what a liar 'e is. No one will listen to 'im." She brushed a strand of Poll's hair into place. "Now you lie back and rest. Mother Watkin said as'ow that brew would make you sleep. So close your eyes like a good girl. I won't be far away I promise."

Her words of comfort, however, were wasted as, thanks to Mother Watkins, Poll had already fallen into a deep sleep. Saffron smiled as she bent to kiss the smooth forehead.

There was no sign of Jonas throughout the day. It was not until early evening that she had news of him when young Joe, the eldest of the Johnson boys, rapped on the cottage door.

Cautiously, Saffron pulled aside the window curtain to satisfy herself before lifting the latch.

"Me Ma sent me." The lad began, twisting his cap between nervous fingers. "She said I was to say if you needs anythin' she'll come round." He paused. "An' to say Pa says as 'ow Jonas is sleepin' it orf in The Billet."

Saffron let out a sigh of relief. "So 'e won't be back this night then?"

The boy grinned. "Reckon not. Pa said as 'ow 'e put enough away for ten men. Swearing an' goin' on 'e were by all accounts." His grin faded. "Pa said 'e was sayin' some hard things 'bout Poll and said you 'ad no right to keep 'im out." The lad squared his thin shoulders. "But don't you be afeared, me and Pa will be close by if 'e gives you any trouble."

Saffron felt her throat tighten. It seemed that she was not alone. Alice Johnson had been her mother's best friend and she and her family had been aware of all that had happened over the past six years. Jonas' drunken, vile outburst might provide the fuel for gossip for some, but to the dozens of good honest folk in the village it would promote nothing but sympathy for Saffron and the family.

"Thank your mother for 'er concern, Joe. Tell 'er it means a lot. We're well enough for the moment but I'll call on 'er should I 'ave the need."

The boy nodded, pulling his cap on over his untidy hair. "Ma says she'll drop by wi' a cake or summat." He blushed. "An' I could manage a bunch of wild flowers if you think..." He looked hopefully at Saffron.

"I think Poll would like that Joe. She's not well enough for a visit but it would mean a lot to know you're thinkin' 'bout 'er."

The lad beamed. "Right then." He turned to go. "I'll see you on the morrow."

Saffron smiled as she closed and barred the door. It seemed that Poll was not short of admirers, despite everything that had happened. It remained to be seen if, now Jason had opened his mouth, if everyone would prove to be as understanding.

A while later Poll woke and before giving her a second dose of Mother Watkins' unpleasant brew, Saffron managed to persuade her sister to eat a light meal. There was no doubt that the fever had gone and the girl seemed to be more comfortable as she slipped once more into a healing sleep.

Tom had been restless all day. He was not used to being cooped up in the cottage and had spent the time playing with the kittens and generally getting under Saffron's feet. As she cleared away the remains of their meal she felt guilty, having Poll to care for had stolen so much of the time she normally gave to him.

"Tom." She called him to her, putting an arm around his shoulder and looking down into his enquiring face. "Go fetch your slate. Let's do some letters." His eyes sparkled above a wide grin, knowing that he would have all of her attention while she taught him his lessons. Saffron was proud of the fact that at the age of five Tom could already read simple words and could add up and take away. By the time he started at the church school he would be well ahead of some of the other children. She watched him as, tongue out and head bent over the slate, he carefully outlined each letter before holding out the slate for her approval. "Well done! "She wiped the slate clean. "Now, I'll set you some sums. Let's see 'ow you do with those."

She left the boy at the table, sucking the end of his slate chalk and concentrating on the mysteries of addition and subtraction. It was almost dark outside as she lit the overhead lamp to dispel the gathering gloom. On the horizon, the dying sun laid a molten pathway to the shore. The sound of the sea sending the second high tide of the day, rolled its way over the mud, rattling onto the shell strewn beach and peacefully retreating once again into the dark waters of the Estuary. The laughter of a neighbour's child brought a wistful smile to her face. If it were not for the present problems this small village of Leigh would be the only place in the world Saffron thought that she would ever want to live.

"Finished." Tom sat back with a look of satisfaction. "Did I get it right?"

Saffron took the slate from him. "Almost." She pointed. "Try that one again. All the rest are fine." She watched as he counted on his fingers, nodding as he spotted his mistake, using a wet finger to obliterate the error and make the correction. "That's better. Now you've got it." She took the slate as Tom gave a wide yawn. "Time you was asleep my lad, 'tis long past bedtime. Up you go, I'll be there to hear your prayers when I've seen to things down here."

As the boy climbed the stairs Saffron moved around the kitchen tidying away the supper things and damping down the fire but her thoughts were of Nathan. Part of her was glad that he had not been there to see Jonas' behaviour while another part confessed to a longing for her brother's support. Had he heard their stepfather's ranting there might well have been murder done that day. At least, by now, he was safe in Saffron Walden, or so she hoped, with the opportunity to build a new life. "Best he knows nothin' 'bout it." She murmured to herself.

Wearily she climbed the stair, pausing to listen at Poll's door she was rewarded with the sound of her sister's soft and regular breathing, before crossing the narrow landing to keep her promise to Tom.

The boy sat up in bed as she opened the door. "Shall I say

my prayers now, Saffy?" Saffron nodded as she sat beside him. "Aye, and mind you thank God for all the good things he sends us." Tom closed his eyes and bent his head over clasped hands. "Thank you God for our 'ome and for the food we eat and God Bless Saffy, an'Nathan, an' Poll and make her better quick 'cause she's real poorly." He paused, seeming to struggle with the next words, which suddenly came flooding out in a torrent. "And please God keep Pa away!" His eyes flew open and he threw himself into Saffron's arms. She held him fiercely, cradling him tightly to her breast. Jonas' outburst had affected the child more deeply than she had feared. What lasting harm had been done to his young mind?

CHAPTER NINE

Immaculate lawns, where no weed dared to show its head, were bordered by a network of shingle pathways one of which marked Nathan's route to the stable block. The long, low building, fronted by a wide paddock lay beyond a stand of towering firs. Following in his Aunt's wake, he thought fondly of Saffy. She'd be glad to learn of the welcome he had received and he determined to write to her at the first opportunity, entrusting the letter to the first passing waggoner. All thoughts of Leigh were put to one side, however, as the figure of a man appeared at the end of the building. Short and stocky as a bull he stood, legs wide apart, as they approached, dragging off his cap when he recognised the housekeeper.

"Evenin' Miz Porter." Nathan noted with interest the deference in the man's voice.

"Good evening, Bartholemew." His Aunt stood to one side gesturing toward Nathan. "This is my nephew Nathan Clay. He is looking for work and he assures me that he is able to manage horses." Nathan straightened beneath the man's critical appraisal.

"Oh Aye?" The man scrubbed a coarsened hand over his stubbled chin.

Jane Porter nodded. "Yes. I believe you have need of another boy and I should like you to take him." She paused. "On trial of course."

Bartholemew's eyes narrowed. "Nephew, you say?"

"That is what I said." Nathan saw the suspicion of a tinge of angry colour on his Aunt's cheek. "But he is to have no privileges other than those enjoyed by the other stable lads."

"Right! 'E'll earn 'is keep." He turned to Nathan. "Best

come wi' me lad." He raised a knuckle to his forehead. "Boy'll be alright 'ere, Miz Porter."

"Thank you Bartholemew." She laid a hand on Nathan's shoulder. "Mind you work hard Nephew." Briefly her expression softened. "Make your dear mother proud of you."

"I will that Aunt. I ain't afeared of a bit of 'ard work." He watched the tall woman walk away, her full skirts swaying rhythmically with each step, the keys hanging jingling from her wide belt giving a musical accompaniment to her purposeful stride.

Nathan turned as a sharp poke in his back brought him down to earth.

"Well, you comin' or ain't yer?" The groom glowered at the lad as Nathan swung into step beside him. "You'll 'ave to sleep in the 'ay loft 'till I sees about making room wi' the others."

"Others?" Nathan quickened his pace.

"Aye. T'other stable lads." He glanced at Nathan "You think I does the work all by meself? Not that they'll be givin' you a welcome I'm thinkin'."

Nathan caught at the man's sleeve, swinging him round to face him. "An' why not? I'm 'ere to work an' I'm as good as any of 'em." The older man avoided the earnest searching blue eyes. "Well?"

Beligerently, he shook Nathan's hand from his sleeve. "When they knows 'oo you are, kin to Miz Porter, they'll say as 'ow you'll be a tittle-tattling up at the 'ouse."

Bartholemew's jaw dropped at Nathan's shout of laughter. "So you think I'll be carrying tales?" Slowly his smile faded. "If that's what you think, I'll be moving on."

"No need for that." The man grumbled, suddenly aware that he might be left to account for the boy's sudden departure. "Best say nothin'." He attempted a half smile of encouragement. "Tell you what, we'll say you're Nathan Clarke. "Ow about that?"

Nathan frowned, he'd changed his name before and if it was to be the price of peace he could do it again. "Right. Clarke it is. And what do I call you?"

The man beamed at the possible reprieve and pulling himself to his full height he puffed out his barrel chest. "You calls me Mr. Drake and when I says 'op to it, you 'ops! Gottit?"

Nathan grinned. "Wouldn't 'ave no other way!"

"Good. Well get your arse in 'ere and make yoursel' useful."

For a moment Nathan had the ridiculous urge to snap to attention and salute but thought better of it. If the groom was to be won over, subservience had to be the order of the day. At least for the time being.

There were three other lads busy in the stable block. Pete and Jack were cautiously friendly but Patrick Connell was another matter. Big for his age, the raw-boned redhead's sullen acknowledgement, for some unknown reason, seemed to Nathan to herald trouble.

Under Bartholemew's direction carriage horses returning from the nearby town were unharnessed, groomed and fed. Stalls were swept and brasses polished and it was late into the evening before the lads were deemed to have earned a rest and a late supper.

As they trudged across the paddock toward the back of the house the two younger lads were laughing and shoving one another in good nature while Patrick, his mouth set in a mask of disapproval, slunk along behind them.

"'Ungry, lad?" The Groom matched his pace.

Nathan chuckled. "I am that. Not a bite since morning. Mind you." He added with a yawn. "I'm that done in, I doubt I'll 'ave the strength to lift me fork."

"You'll stuff yer face when yer sees what Cook's got for you." The man patted his stomach in anticipation. "I'll say that for Master, ' e don't scrimp on the victuals for them what earns it. A good day's keep for a good day's labour. That's what 'e says." As they crossed the cobbled yard he pointed to where a row of wooden buckets stood side by side on a bench. "Give yersel' a bit of a wash afore you goes in or cook'll 'ave your 'ide."

A sudden thought occurred to Nathan and he drew the groom to one side. "The Cook. She'll know 'oo I am. She were there when me Aunt came back from the village. She'll let on."

The man shook his head. "You leave that to me, lad. Cook and me we 'ave what you might call an understandin'." He winked. "I'll 'ave a word. Not to worry."

The smell of food in the kitchen was enough to make Nathan's mouth water let alone the sight of the large meat pie from which Cook was cutting wedges for the workers around the table.

"Come and sit yoursel' down Bartholemew." She urged. "An' you too lads. There's plenty 'ere. Bring those 'taters over, Sarah, and them carrots. Don't want nothin' goin' to waste."

Nathan watched with interest as the girl carried bowls of food from the range to the table, leaning to set them down on the scrubbed surface. Her dark hair, wound into a knot at the nape of her neck, was covered by a mobcap, her face flushed from the heat of the fire. He found himself fascinated by her graceful movements as she took her seat beside the cook. They bowed their heads at Bartholemew's bidding.

"May the good Lord make us grateful for these 'ere victuals and make us remember as 'ow there's many 'oo don't 'ave nothin' to eat like we does. Amen"

As heads were raised Nathan found himself looking directly

into Sarah's green eyes. For a moment her bold smile took him unaware and then he remembered that she had been in the kitchen when he had arrived earlier that day. They shared the secret of his kinship. He grinned back at her promising himself to improve the relationship at the first opportunity.

As the steaming bowls of food passed around the table Nathan took time to study his companions. Clearly they were all outside workers, grooms, stable lads, gardeners and the like.

"So where's the rest of the workers?" He nudged Pete at his side.

"What, them what works in the 'ouse?" the boy managed around a mouthful of pie. "Oh, they eats afore us in the servant's 'all." He took another bite. "Master first, then them, then us, see?"

"Don't care when I eats." Jack chuckled. "Long as I gets it."

"You gets more than your share. You eat like a pig!" Patrick sneered. "You stinks like a pig an' all."

The laughter died in Jack's throat. "You got no call to say that. You ain't no bunch o'flowers yersel'."

Pete put a hand on his friend's arm. "Don't let 'im get you mad, Jack. 'E ain't worth it."

The exchange had taken only seconds but, not for the first time, Nathan took note of the spite shown at every opportunity by the Irish bully.

When everyone had eaten their fill Cook and Sarah began to clear away the dishes, piling them beside the double sink where the scullery maid began the task of scouring, washing and drying ready for the next meal.

"Can I 'elp?" Nathan strolled over to where Sarah was stacking a tray.

"You can take this if you like." She smiled up at him, offering the heavily laden tray. "Put it over by the sink." She went ahead of him to clear a space in which to set it down.

"Ave you finished yet?" He asked.

"Not for an 'our or more. Why?" She tilted her head enquiringly.

"I thought we'd get a bit of air like." Nathan felt stupidly tongue-tied, trapped in the gaze of those cool green eyes.

"I reckon Cook won't miss me for a couple of minutes." She tucked a stray curl under her cap, raising a warning finger "But mind, I ain't goin' no further than the yard."

The heat of the sun had long gone leaving behind the soft velvet of the summer night as they stood at the open door. For a moment they were silent then both spoke at once.

"Where you from then?"

"'Ow long you been 'ere?"

They laughed. "Sorry, you first."

"No You. Where you from?"

"Leigh Village, down on the coast."

"Got family there?"

"Aye. What about you?"

"I were born in Saffron Walden. Me folk were crokers."

'Ad a nice bit o' land so me Ma said. Then they started getting' all that cheap Saffron in from somewhere or other and they lost the lot. Me Pa works for the master now and we grow a few vegetables. And we got chickens. We manage." The last was added with a defiant edge of pride.

"Are you 'appy 'ere?"

"What at the 'ouse?" Sarah thought for a moment. "I s'pose so. Cook's good and she's teaching me. I made the pie what you 'ad tonight."

"An' very nice it were too!"

Sarah flushed with pleasure. "I s'pose there's only one thing I don't much care for. Or one person more like."

"An' oo might that be." Nathan edged a little closer to her. "Not me I 'ope."

"No, silly." She gave him a gentle push. "It's that Patrick. 'E's always trying to get near me, touchin' me an' saying things."

"What things?" Nathan felt the first stirrings of anger. "If 'e's upsettin' you…" He left the sentence unfinished as she raised a finger to his lips.

"I don't want you getting' into no trouble on my account. 'Sides," she paused, tilting her chin. "'Tis nothin' I can't 'andle."

Nathan caught her hand and, as their eyes met, on the spur of the moment he kissed her work-reddened fingertips. "You say the word Sarah, an' I'll see 'im off. I'll not 'ave 'im makin' you sad."

She laid her cheek against their joined hands. "I know." She whispered. "But I'm alright for the present." She pulled away from him. "I'd best get back or I'll be in Cook's bad books. See you on the morrow?"

"You will." Nathan smiled as she paused, her slender figure silhouetted against the light of the newly lit kitchen lamp. "An' the day after that and the next. You'll be seein' a lot of me Sarah. An' that's for sure."

As he made his way back across the yard toward the stand of firs, his mind full with thoughts of the young kitchen maid, he was ill prepared for the sudden appearance of Patrick Connell. The figure, clearly seen in the twilight, was hunched, ready for attack and as Nathan came to a halt the boy advanced to stand almost toe to toe with him.

"You bin talking to my girl!" The accusation clearly referred to Sarah.

"Your girl?" Nathan stood his ground. "That's not what she

says. She says as 'ow you been pesterin' 'er." He poked the
boy's chest. "An' I says you leaves 'er alone from now - or
else". He added for good measure. He watched as Patrick's
slack mouth dropped open and his mean eyes narrowed.

"Or else what?" He spluttered. "What you goin' t'do about
it then? Think you can best me do yer?" Nathan saw the blow
coming and dodged. Light on his feet, he danced out of reach,
raising his fists as his adversary blundered toward him. "Stand
still will yer!"

Nathan laughed. "What an' let you land one on me? Me
mother didn't 'ave no fools, but if you want a fair fight I'm
your man." He shot out an arm and tapped the bully firmly on
the jaw. "Well, come on then." He taunted. "Let's see what
you got."

Patrick's roar of fury sent a small, unseen animal scurrying
into the underbrush as, fists flailing, he charged like a raging
bull. Aware of the boy's superior size and weight, Nathan
knew he would stand little chance without gaining the advantage early in the fight. Patrick was almost upon him when he
sidestepped and putting all his strength behind the blow he
landed a well-aimed punch to the side of the lad's head. Patrick
went down without a sound, crumpling at Nathan's feet as if
he had been poleaxed. For a moment he lay still and Nathan,
fearing he might have killed him, knelt to turn him over but a
loud groan reassured him as Patrick opened unfocused eyes.

"Ad enough?" Nathan grinned. The boy nodded raising a
hand to his bruised face. "Right, well let's 'ave you up then."
Nathan held out a hand and after a moment the boy grudgingly
accepted his help. For a moment he stood swaying unsteadily.

"'Taint over!" He mumbled as he shambled away. "I'll 'ave
me day."

"Not if I sees you comin'. But you mind what I said. Sarah

don't want you pesterin' 'er, nor me neither." Nathan followed at a distance reaching the stable block just as Bartholemew appeared.

"Alright, lad?"

"Aye."

"Well get yoursel' up to the loft for this night. On the morrow we'll sort out a cot in the livin' quarter. There be room for one more up there." He pointed to the rooms above the stable block. "You'll be sharing with t'other lads." He stretched his arms and yawned. "I'm off to me rest. Early start. G'night lad."

As Nathan climbed the hayloft ladder he thought of the day to come. The head groom was a fair man, young Pete and Jack promised to become good friends and Sarah, he let his mind dwell on the memory of green eyes he could have drowned in, well Sarah promised to be like a shaft of sunlight in a dull day. The only blight in his life was Patrick Connell. As he bunched his coat for a pillow and settled his tired body into the sweet smelling hay, he consoled himself with the thought that he had dealt with the bully once and provided he watched his back, he could do it again.

CHAPTER TEN

A week had passed with no sign of Jonas and Poll's recovery seemed to be going well. She was young and strong and with Saffron's encouragement and Tom's insistence, two days later she ventured down to sit by the kitchen hearth. It took longer, however, to persuade her to show herself outside the cottage.

"'Tis no good, Saffy, I can't face 'em." She hung her head. "They'll all be nudging and pointin'."

"So what?" Saffron demanded "'Twern't your fault, they knows that,'cause they knows you. An' even if they think it were, you'd not be the first. Let them wi'out sin cast the first stone. Jesus said that. It's in the Good Book. She winked. "And there ain't many wi'out sin in Leigh, I can tell you!"

Poll giggled. "Oh, Saffy, you do say some terrible things!"

"Well, 'tis true. There's more'n one who's none too sure of their beginnin's. Tell you what." She took her sister's hand. "'Ow about we go as far as the gate. I'll stay by you." She hastened to reassure her as the fear gathered in Poll's eyes. "We'll stand a while, get a bit of breeze an' if anyone does pass by, we'll smile and say what a nice day we're 'avin".

Poll bit her lip. "You won't leave me?"

"Not for nuthin'. I promise."

Poll nodded. "I'll try, but only for a minute or two."

"Fine." Saffron felt a rush of relief. It was only a small step she knew, but it was a beginning.

Despite the summer warmth, Poll's thin shoulders trembled as, wrapped in a woollen shawl, she stood at the open door. "Come on now, best foot forward," Saffron's firm tone allowed no turning back. "Just as far as the gate."

Poll's step faltered and she would have fallen had it not been for her sister's arm tightly clasped around her waist. "Good girl!" Saffron urged. "Almost there." Poll stumbled the last few paces, stretching her hands to grip the gatepost like a drowning man reaching for a log. "There now, 'twern't so 'ard were it?" Saffron brushed a strand of hair from Poll's cheek. "'Tis a fine warm day, an' look." She pointed. "The tide's full in."

Poll nodded silently, her eyes darting from one end of the street to the other. White-knuckled she gripped the gate as two familiar figures left the bakery and turned in their direction.

"Oh no! 'Tis old Ma Smethwick and that daughter of 'ers. She's never 'ad a good word for me." Poll turned to make her way back to the cottage. "I can't face 'em Saffy, and that's the truth."

"Don't you give me that. You got nothin' to be ashamed of." Saffron's grip on her sister's arm turned her to face the road. "We'll stand 'ere side by side and if they stops to speak we'll say good day like there's nothin' wrong! "Won't we Poll?"

Poll nodded miserably. "If you say so Saffy."

"Right, now head up girl, 'ere they come."

The two women approached, their heads together, slowing as they reached the cottage gate.

"Mornin' dear." Ma Smethick's face was a picture of mock concern. "And 'ows little Poll today? Feeling a mite better?"

Her daughter hung back, a sly smile on her grimy face. "Ain't nothin' catchin' I hope." She smirked.

"Don't you worry your 'ead over that." Saffron smiled. "It's sure you'd not find yoursel' 'avin' to deal with what ails Poll." She looked the girl over from head to toe taking care not to hide her disgust at her unwashed appearance.

Ma Smethick's face flushed as Saffron's inference hit home. "You saying my girl ain't..?" She paused, her eyes narrowed. "Well at least she knows what's what." She lifted her chin triumphantly. "Knows 'ow to keep 'er 'and on 'er 'a'penny, not like some as I could mention!"

Saffron leaned over the gate, her face inches from the woman. "You said enough, you old crone. Now get your foot off my step 'afore I send you arse over 'ead!" Ma Smethick backed away at the unexpected outburst, treading heavily on her daughter's feet and barely regaining her balance.

"If your ma could 'ere you Saffron Clay, she'd turn in 'er grave." She hoisted her ample bosom on folded arms. "Talkin' to me like that, me what's known you since you were born."

"If you've known me and mine for that long then you know better than to make trouble for us." Saffron stood, hands on hips. "I makes a good friend Mrs. Smethick, but I makes a bad enemy. Folks round 'ere best remember that!" She turned to put an arm around her sister. "Come on Poll, you too Tom. I think we've 'ad enough air for one day, specially when it smells so bad." She turned away, leaving the speechless woman spluttering angrily on the cobbled street.

Slamming the door behind them and settling her sister by the hearth, she searched for some way to change the mood. A small pile of folded linen caught her eye. "Look, Poll, I got a bit of sewing to do, you can sit aside of me while I gets it done. That Mrs. Squires over in Westcliff is a fussy old biddy." She glanced at the girl who seemed to be staring into space. "Poll, I'm talking to you. 'Ere 'elp me measure this bit o' trimmin'. She likes a bit o' lace on everything." She thrust the cotton lace into her sister's unresponsive hands.

Poll turned blank eyes in her direction "T'aint right Saffy."

"What d'you mean? You ain't frettin' about what them two 'ad to say are you?"

Poll turned her head away. "I knows it's only spite but t'aint right, I should be puttin' somethin' in the pot. Now Jonas 'as gone an' I 've lost my place." She buried her head in her hands and began to sob. Saffron threw the lace aside and sat, fiercely hugging her sister to her.

"You're not to talk like that Poll. We'll manage. I put a bit by, not a lot but it'll tide us over."

"'Till when?" Poll raised tear-filled eyes. "There be three of us to feed and then the rent, that'll be due and 'ave to be found. No." She wiped her wet cheeks with trembling fingers. "Soon as I'm able I'll find work Saffy, honest I will."

Her reassuring smile was weak as Saffron tenderly brushed away a wayward strand of her hair. "Time enough to think 'bout that when you're full mended. For now you just put your mind to 'elping me in the cottage." She got to her feet. "You can start by peelin' the 'taters for our meal. Tom fetch some of them vegetables and a bowl for Poll." The boy scrambled to his feet eager to be part of a situation he barely understood.

Saffron busied herself slicing the small piece of scrag end of mutton ready for the stewpot, her mind busy with her present problems. Money had never been plentiful but Poll's words rang true. Like it or not they would miss Jonas' grudging con-tribution, meagre though it had been.

Even with the two guineas sent to Poll, the small store of coins she had managed to save over the months would not last long, but her sister was in no condition to find work. Even if she had been, no house would employ her without a charac-ter, that all-important piece of paper from a previous employer, which guaranteed her suitability.

It was possible that there could be an opening in the boiling sheds along the water's edge. The owners got busy when the gipsy cocklers delivered their catch each day. But not yet. Saffron frowned at the deep shadows beneath Poll's eyes showing in dark contrast to the pale face as, head down, the girl slowly peeled the outer skin from the bowl of potatoes. It would be a few weeks at least before her sister would be strong enough to work. Meanwhile, as their mother had always said: "God will provide." Saffron offered a small prayer that indeed He would.

Setting the stewpot on the stove she turned to the small boy at her feet.

"Tom." She drew his attention away from the basket of kittens. "Tom, I want you to be real grown up and look after Poll while I go down to the shop. Can you do that?"

The child was on his feet in seconds, squaring his shoulders with importance. "'Course I can Saffy."

"And you keep the door barred 'til I gets back."

He nodded. "I won't let nobody in, no matter what."

She smiled at the determined set of his jaw. "Good boy." She glanced at Poll, "Don't fret, I'll not be more'n a few minutes. The stew needs salt and there's no bread in the bin."

Poll half rose from the settle. "Sposin' Jonas…?" She bit her lip, leaving her fear unspoken. Saffron took her hand. "Don't you fear, Jonas'll still be sleepin' it off somewhere. Anyway he won't come near or by, not after the scolding I give him. 'Sides, Tom's here and he won't let no one over the step. She took her shawl from the hook, throwing it round her shoulders. "I'll be back 'afore you know I'm gone."

Saffron let herself out of the cottage pausing to listen to the scrape of metal on wood as Tom obediently barred the door behind her. A stiff sea breeze tugged at her skirts as, head down and deep in thought, she hurried toward the bakery where the smell of newly baked bread welcomed her as she entered the shop. Conscious of her need to hurry she was mildly annoyed to see several other customers waiting to be served. As the group thinned she found herself standing beside a tall figure who stepped back with a formal bow, allowing her to take his place at the counter.

"Please, you appear to be in some haste. Make your purchase, I am happy to wait." Startled, she found herself looking up into soft, dark eyes above a wide and generous mouth. The young man held out his hand, the long fingers, olive-tanned against the pure white linen of his shirt cuff. "Jean-Pierre." He said. "Jean-Pierre Howard. And you are?"

"Saffron." She managed through dry lips, ignoring the proffered greeting.. "Saffron Clay."

He dropped his hand. "I am pleased to make your acquaintance Saffron Clay." There was a hint of a faint accent in the deep voice. "I have seen you before, have I not?"

She shrugged. "'Tis likely."

"Well, Saffy, what will it be?" The baker's impatient query broke the spell of the stranger's gaze.

"A small cob, if you please, Mr. Blake." She whispered, aware that her cheeks were burning. Dropping the coins into the baker's waiting hand she picked up the warm bread and made to leave but found her way barred.

"Please wait." The softly spoken request caught her off guard.

"Why. What d'you want?" She backed away as he reached toward her, flinching at the gentle weight of his hand on her arm.

"I want to capture you."

"You what? You ain't goin' to capture me. What d'you think I am?" She raised her head in defiance, shaking herself free from his touch and pushing past him into the sunlit street.

A peal of laughter followed her and she turned to see his tall frame filling the doorway. He sobered suddenly. "I am sorry, Saffron Clay, I did not mean I wished to imprison you. I am an artist and I wish only to capture your beauty."

Despite herself, Saffron was intrigued. "What do you mean?"

Her mistrust was obvious as he came to stand before her. "I wish to paint you Saffron Clay." His gaze seemed to engulf her, taking in every detail from her windswept hair to her shabby shoes. "Do you not know how beautiful you are?"

She shook her head.

Impulsively, he took her hands in his. "Say you will sit for me". He pleaded.

"Sit for you?"

He saw the light of her growing interest. "Just sit still for a while so that I can make some sketches, then an hour or so each day."

`"Oh, no. I couldn't. I got Poll and Tom to see to."

"Your children?"

"No, my brother and sister and she's been poorly so I can't leave her."

"You live here in the village? She nodded. "Well, I am renting Juniper Cottage, so if you were needed you could be home in minutes." He saw her hesitation as she began to warm to the idea. "And of course I would pay you. Shall we say two shillings for every sitting?"

Two shillings! More than she could earn in a week with her bit of sewing. Her mind raced ahead. It would mean a difference to Poll; good food would soon put the flesh back on her sister and Tom's appetite seemed to be growing along with the boy. She looked long and hard at the stranger. The dark eyes beneath arched brows twinkled encouragingly. Thick, black hair curled over the collar of his shirt, which, open at the neck, revealed a broad, tanned chest. Moleskin trousers tucked into polished boots completed the picture of a man well able to pay two shillings a sitting.

"Well, do I pass muster?" He asked softly. "Will you sit for me?"

Saffron realised guiltily that she had been staring at him. "Maybe." She pulled her hands free of his grip. "But that's all." She held his gaze. "I don't do nuthin' but sit!"

He smothered a smile. "Agreed, Miss Saffron Clay. You don't do nuthin' but sit!" Wickedly he mimicked her words. "So I shall see you on the morrow at Juniper Cottage. Shall we say around ten in the morning?"

She nodded. "Aye, I'll be there." Turning on her heel, she left him standing on the cobbled street, conscious that he watched her until she turned into the cottage gate.

Tom was at the window and rushed to let her in. "You was gone a long time, Saffy. I was getting feared."

"No need, Tom, I'm fine and I've got some news." She set the warm bread on the table and hoisted the child into her arms, dancing him round the kitchen. "We're goin' to be rich!"

"Rich, Saffy?" Poll came to take her shawl. "What d'you mean?"

Saffron put the boy down. "Well, you remember I said as 'ow an artist 'ad moved into Juniper Cottage?" They both nodded. "I met 'im and 'e wants me to, what 'e calls, sit for 'im. He wants to paint me picture." She giggled at their open-mouthed astonishment. She paused. "And 'es going to pay me two shillin' every time I go to 'is cottage."

"Ow much?" Poll's hands flew to her face. "Oh, Saffy, are you sure that's all 'e's after? You don't know nuthin' about 'im. 'E might want." She shot a wary glance at Tom. "You know what." She whispered behind her hand.

"I made it plain I'd 'ave none o' that. And 'e's real nice Poll." She frowned. "Different, but real nice. Anyway I can take care of meself. So we'll just 'ave to see what happens on the morrow, won't we?"

CHAPTER ELEVEN

Nathan's daily routine fell quickly into a pattern of early mornings, a long hard day's work and exhausted sleep, his pleasant nature and willingness to learn won Bartholemew's approval and the friendship of both Pete and Jack. Patrick, however, made trouble for him whenever possible, "Watch yourself." The other stable lads warned him. "'E's got it in for you and no mistake." So far Nathan had managed to avoid another confrontation but he knew the time would come when matters had to be settled once and for all. He feared it would be sooner rather than later.

Nathan's knowledge of the house and its staff and structure grew as he and Sarah managed to snatch an hour or so from their duties. With interest he listened to her stories of what she laughingly called the 'goin's on' above and below stairs. It seemed that his aunt's word was law where the maids were concerned, while Bentley, the Butler, ruled the male servants with a rod of iron.

When their duties permitted time in each other's company, they would meet in the wood bordering the estate and out of sight of the house.

"Everyone knows their place." Sarah assured him, pulling him down to sit beside her on the soft grass beneath the trees. "Now, Tim the boot boy, poor little chap, 'e's bottom of the pile. 'E's none too bright but e is willin' and, as Cook says, not every foundlin' gets a place by the fire and a full belly."

Nathan squeezed her hand "You like 'im don't you?"

Sarah nodded. "'E reminds me of the young'uns back 'ome I s'pose. "Anyway." She paused to unwrap the square of linen from a chunk of fresh bread and a slice of cold meat. "Next up there's Connie and Grace; they're the scullery maids. They keep the ovens stoked and cleans up after Cook, scouring pots and such."

"I seen them." Nathan cut a slice from the bread and handed it to Sarah. "That's hard work I reckon."

"It's 'ow I got started." There was a hint of pride in Sarah's voice. "But then Cook took a fancy to me. She's teaching me to cook and sometimes I get to put on a fine cap and apron and help the parlour maids when the Master's got a lot of guests. Bertha and Dorrie think they're better than the rest of us, except Miss Sims. She's Madam's lady's maid and of course, Miss Blake, Miss Sophie's governess. Keeps herself to herself that one. Takes all her meals in the nursery with little master Charles and his old nurse.

"Charles? "Nathan chewed on a mouthful of meat. "I thought there was only Miss Charlotte the Master's daughter."

"No. Charles is six or seven years old, but nobody 'cept Miss Blake or his nurse ever sees 'im. I've been told 'e's sickly and scarcely ever leaves the nursery, poor little scrap."

Nathan compared the boy's life to that of young Tom. "A bit of fresh air would do him a power of good I'd say."

Sarah shrugged,. "They do tell the Mistress 'asn't been right since master Charles was born. Given to losing 'er temper over nuthin'. I've heard 'er shoutin' something awful at Miss Sims. The only one who can deal with her is your Aunt. She runs the house really and most of the time the Master leaves 'er to it."

Nathan shook his head. "All those folk to look after one family. Don't they do nuthin?"

Sarah considered. "Well, the Master's at the Maltin's or the Brewery over in Felsted. Then he likes to visit some of the alehouses he owns. 'E's away from the 'ouse most days. The Mistress 'as visitors sometimes but mostly she just sits and

reads or does some fancy stitching, embroidery she calls it."
She frowned. "It's Miss Charlotte who upsets the house."

"How's that then?" Nathan helped himself to another piece
of bread.

"She orders everyone around with never a please or thank
you and she's wild. Last week she threw 'er water jug at Dorrie,
said as 'ow the water were stale. Broke it she did and blamed it
on the maid. She's a bad 'un and no mistake."

"It's as well she don't 'ave nuthin to do with you then. I can't
see you puttin' up with that sort of thing." Nathan brushed the
last crumbs from his shirt and stretched out, resting his head
in Sarah's lap. "I reckon you'd see her off." He laughed. "You
don't take no nonsense from no one." He reached to stroke the
sun-warmed skin of her arm. "'Cept me, praps?"

"Don't you start that Nathan Clay." Gently she took his
hand away. "I told you, I seen too many girls in trouble to go
lookin' for it." She saw his frustration. "You know 'ow I feel
about you, but I want to take things slow."

Nathan sat up to take her hands. "I know, I've got real feelings for you too, Sarah. I know enough about you to know
you're special. If you want to wait that's alright with me." He
grinned suddenly, pressing her back onto the soft turf. "But
that don't mean I can't have a kiss does it?"

"Just a kiss then?" He nodded, pressing his lips to her yielding
mouth, tasting the virgin sweetness as, trustingly, she returned
his embrace, winding her arms around his neck and lifting her
body to meet his own. Nathan held her to him, bending his
head to bury his face in the warm curve of her neck.

"Sarah." He groaned. "You'll drive me mad 'afore you're
finished." Reluctantly he pulled away, knowing in his heart
that despite his desire he would give his life to protect and preserve that which he hoped one day to possess. He watched her

stand, silhouetted against the glare of the sun as she brushed blades of grass from her skirt and tucked a strand of hair into place. They had known each other for so short a time and yet Nathan knew in a moment of maturity that he had found his soul mate. He stood to take her in his arms. "Sarah." She held her hands to his chest, a warning against further intimacy. "Sarah, if I can fix it with Bartholemew, I want to come over an meet your Ma and Pa on your next half day."

"Well, I'm sure they'd like to meet you." She frowned. "But why so serious?"

Nathan swallowed hard. "I want them to know that I want to marry you. Not yet." He added hastily. "I know it's sudden and they'll tell us we got to wait. And we will." He searched her sweet face for reassurance. "But I want to put my mark on you, like. Let everyone know you're goin' to be mine."

"You're askin' me to be your wife? You know your Aunt won't 'ave that. I'll lose my place at the house. They don't have married folk workin' together."

"I know that. That's why I said we'll 'ave to wait. I won't always be a stable boy. I'll work 'ard and I'll study."He gazed into the distance. "I'll make something of myself." He cupped her face in his hands, staring into her troubled eyes. "You won't 'ave to work Sarah, I'll see to that. We'll 'ave a home and children. You'll see."

"Nathan." Sarah closed her hands over his own. "I know that's what you want, but getting' it is not so easy for folk like us." She paused. "But it's something to think about and work for." She added. "And as for being Mrs Nathan Clay one fine day." She smiled shyly. "I think I'd like that."

Nathan's eyes widened and his whoop of joy sent a star-tled magpie chattering from the branches overhead. He swung Sarah off her feet, dancing her around until she cried out to be released.

"Nathan, will you stop." She pleaded breathlessly. "If we don't get back to the 'ouse we'll both be out on the street and all your fine plans will be in the ditch with us."

"Oh, my dear, sensible Sarah. We'll go after you give me a kiss to seal our bargain." Happily she offered her lips to a kiss, which would bind them together for life.

They gathered the remains of their picnic and hurried down the hill, laughing and skipping over the short turf like children out of school. Within sight of the house they parted, he to the stables and she to the kitchen.

Bartholomew was waiting in the yard. "Where you been lad? He caught sight of Sarah's skirt disappearing beyond the trees. "No, never mind." He grinned. "Just you remember you got work to do. Time and place for everything I say."

"There is that." Nathan agreed. "And I'm sorry if I over-stayed my meal break. I'll work the extra time." He offered no further explanation but followed the groom into the dim interior of the stable block where the smell of fresh straw stung his nostrils as Pete turned the yellow strands with a pitchfork.

"Over 'ere lad." Nathan turned to where the groom stood at the open door of a stall. "Come and tell me what you make of this."

Immediately Nathan recognised the animal. "It's the Master's favourite, Thunder. What's wrong?" He ran a gentling hand over the horse's trembling flank.

"Stepped in a rabbit hole, Master says." Bartholemew pointed to Thunder's right foreleg, raised painfully from contact with the cobbled floor.

Nathan squatted beside the animal taking the swollen fetlock into his caring hands. "I reckon it's a sprain. A couple of days rest'll put it right, and a bit of linament wouldn't come amiss."

Bartholomew signalled his approval with a nod. "Right lad. You're learnin' fast. 'E's a grand horse. Lucky that stumble didn't break 'is leg. Get to it then."

Nathan felt a satisfying degree of pride. Bartholomew acknowledged his knack with horses and obviously trusted him to do a good job. He watched the stocky groom make his way to the next stall, far enough to underline his confidence in Nathan's ability but near enough should his help or advice be called for.

The injury was soon attended to and Thunder was happily chewing on a crisp apple as a reward for his patience when a shrill command broke the silence of the stable.

"I said thee were to have Bright Lady saddled and ready for my morning ride. How dare thee trot out this broken down mare in her place." Nathan heard a mumbled reply and, keeping out of sight, sidled to the open door to see Charlotte, the Master's young daughter, berating Bartholemew.

"Your Father said as'ow Bright Lady were too skittish for you to 'andle, Miss. I'm only doing what the master said." The groom stood his ground.

"My father is not here and I am!" The girl's voice rose angrily. "I will ride Bright Lady today. Thee will saddle her immediately or I will see that thou art without employment by the end of the day." She glanced one way and then the other, her gaze coming to rest on Patrick. "Thee, boy. Do as I say. Saddle the horse or lose thy job."

For a moment Patrick returned her stare, slack-mouthed. Then with a grin he touched his forelock and slunk into the stable. As he passed Nathan he sniggered. "She needs a lesson I reckon." For once Nathan found himself in agreement with the bully but it was not his problem. He watched as the stable lad threw a saddle onto the young filly, savagely tightening the girth.

"You doin' that too tight. You'll hurt the beast." Nathan moved closer to loosen the leather strap but Patrick shoved him out of the way.

"You mind your own business. I been saddlin' horses since a'fore you come along. Anyway." He sneered. "That snotty bitch says she can 'andle Bright Lady, let's see if she can. I ain't forgot when she used that crop on me." He fingered a faint scar on his cheek that Nathan had not noticed before. "Just 'cos she heard me say she was too uppity. Now, get out me way 'afore I land you one." He pushed past Nathan, leading the prancing mare out into the sunlit yard to where Charlotte stood tapping her foot impatiently.

"'Ere you are Miss Charlotte. Bright Lady all saddled and raring to go." Patrick made mockery of a bow. As the girl took the reins and made to mount, the distressed filly skittered sideways, defying her intention. Her face scarlet, she swung her riding crop high, bringing it down viciously across the horse's sleek neck. Nathan flinched at the beast's shrill whinney of pain filled the air.

"Hold her, dolt!" Patrick sprang to the girl's side at her imperious command, trapping the trembling horse against the stable wall.

"'Ere Miss." He cupped a hand to assist her into the saddle but, ignoring his offer, she stepped smartly into the stirrup and swung herself into the saddle.

"Stand away, fool." The horse reared, lunging forward, its flailing hooves narrowly missing Bartholemew but sending him crashing to the ground. Nathan ran to his side, dragging him to safety as horse and rider thundered from the stable yard.

"Stop 'er, lad. Take t'other horse, but for God's sake stop 'er!"

Without a second thought, Nathan threw open the door of

a nearby stall and vaulted onto the bare back of the startled mare within. Digging his heels into her flank he crouched low over the animal's neck, urging her on, shortening the distance between the two horses with every stride. But by the time he reached the tree line Bright Lady had lost her rider and was standing trembling beneath the branches of an oak tree at the foot of which lay the still body of the Master's daughter.

Nathan slid from the saddle to kneel beside the inert figure. "Miss Charlotte, Miss Charlotte, can you hear me?" He was alarmed to see a trickle of blood at the corner of her mouth. "Miss Charlotte!" She stirred, a soft moan escaping her lips. "Lie still Miss. They'll be sendin' help from the house." She opened unfocused eyes and struggled to rise. "No Miss!" Nathan pressed her back gently. "You got to stay still. We don't know 'ow bad you're 'urt and movin' might make it worse." The sound of riders approaching, brought Nathan to his feet in time to see Bartholemew and Pete coming to a slithering halt.

The Groom dismounted and ran to his side. "What 'appened? Is she....?" He didn't dare say more.

"No, but she's bad 'urt and we dares'n't move her. She's got a lump on her 'ead and I think her arm's broke. See?" He pointed to the limb's unnatural angle. It'll need a splint. Send Pete to the house. She'll need a doctor and a litter of some sort."

The stable boy wheeled his horse and was gone. Bartholemew hunkered down beside Nathan. "You say 'er arm's broke. P'raps we'd best leave it. I'd know 'ow to tend it if she were an 'orse." He scrubbed a hand over his bristled chin. "But this be different."

"I seen summat like this back 'ome when Old Rolly Rankin fell off 'is boat. I ain't no doctor but we'll 'ave to splint it, temporary like, afore we move 'er.

Bartholemew got to his feet and backed away. "You'd best not touch 'er, that be the Master's daughter. If anything goes wrong we'll both be for it. Best wait I say."

"Wait? What for? If she wakes she'll try to move. I don't care who she is. It's got to be done." He cast about him. "Give me your knife and pass that bit of deadwood over there." Reluctantly the Groom handed the branch to Nathan who snapped it in half. "Now, while she's still out of it, help me straighten her arm." Together they slit the stitching of the rich brown velvet jacket to expose the broken limb. A soft whimper escaped the girl as, gritting his teeth, Nathan gently realigned the bone, positioning the makeshift splint on either side of her slender arm. "Now, 'old her real still." He warned, as, stripping the shirt from his back, he tore ribbons of coarse linen to bind the branch into place

After a while, he sat back on his heels. "I done all I can for now." He raised his head at the sound of voices. "Thank the Lord, 'ere's 'elp."

Immediately Bentley arrived, flanked by three of the young footmen, he took charge of the situation. Between them they carried a farm gate, hastily padded with rugs and cushions from the house. Nathan ignored the withering stare of the Butler as he cautioned the other footmen to take care of the splinted arm as they lifted the unconscious girl onto the litter.

"You may leave matters to me. The doctor has been summoned." Bentley's sneering disapproval of Nathan's bare chest was obvious. "You may return to your duties now."

Nathan and Bartholemew exchanged glances. "Best get back." Then a sudden thought struck Nathan. "You go on I got something to see to. That Miss Charlotte ain't the only one sufferin'." He watched as, in cautious procession the Groom, Butler and footmen made their way back through the trees before turning his attention to Bright Lady.

The distressed filly snickered nervously at his approach, dancing away from his outstretched hand. "There, girl, there." He crooned. "Nobody ain't gonna 'urt you." She stood wild-eyed with pain but calmed by his gentle tone. "Let's ease that girth so's you can breathe." It took only seconds to loosen the leather strap from its buckle and throw the saddle onto the ground. Bright Lady dropped her head against Nathan's shoulder, nuzzling her gratitude, as he stroked her trembling neck and murmured reassurance. "I seen what Patrick done, and 'e'll pay for it." He told her. "'T'weren't your fault. When you're ready we'll take a slow walk back and I'll give you a good rub down." The filly seemed to nod her agreement and Nathan chuckled. "I reckon you understands every word I says."

It was not until evening that news of Charlotte's accident filtered down to the kitchen. Allowing for floor to floor exaggeration, it seemed that the doctor had set the broken arm, but had insisted that the patient be confined to bed for at least a week. Concussion he called it, due to a bang on the head. There were murmurs of concern from around the table.

"Sounds serious, does that." Cook shook her head. "I don't envy them above stairs. She'll 'ave them run off their feet, fetchin' and carryin'. She ain't easy to care for at the best of times."

"Well, you can't 'elp feelin' a mite sorry for 'er." Sarah frowned. "Master said she weren't to ride Bright Lady, so she'll be in for a tellin' off when 'e gets back, 'urt or not. You know what 'e's like when 'e's crossed. 'Specially as the Mistress 'ad one of 'er turns when she 'eard the news." She set a newly baked apple pie in front of Nathan. "From what I 'eard you deserves a slice o' that."

A movement at the baize door caught her eye and conversation died as Nathan's Aunt entered the kitchen. "I am sorry to interrupt your meal, Cook." She spoke above the heads of the assembled outdoor staff. "But the Master has returned and wishes to see Nathan." She turned a steady gaze toward her nephew. "I am to take you to him immediately."

A murmur of speculation ran around the table as Nathan got to his feet.

"I reckon as 'ow you be in for it now." Patrick sniggered.

Nathan had the satisfaction of seeing the sneer die on the face of the bully as he bent to whisper in his ear. "Truth 'as a way of makin' itself known. And we both know the truth, don't we?"

CHAPTER TWELVE

Saffron rose as the first soft, grey light of dawn filtered through an overcast sky. From the silence overhead she guessed that Tom and Poll were still sleeping and blessed them for the opportunity to enjoy an hour or so of peace. She had tossed and turned into the small hours, her mind filled with thoughts of the day ahead and the young man who had dictated the turn of events. One part of her was eager to see him while into another part crept a small warning voice. As Poll had said, she knew nothing about him other than his name and the fact that he had told her he was an artist. Yet here she was agreeing to spend hours alone with him at Juniper cottage. She shook her head at her own stupidity. She could send word that she was unable to keep the appointment, but the promise of two shillings was too good an offer to turn down. She straightened her shoulders and glanced at the mantle clock, there remained at least four hours before the appointed time and, if she were to look her best, there was much to do.

Saffron poured water, drawn from the village well the day before, into a bowl and reached for the precious sliver of soap, a present to Poll from the Cook when she had worked at the big house. Dowsing her thick hair she began to work a lather into the corn-blonde curls, rinsing away the suds until the long strands squeaked between her hands.

She threw open the cottage door and stood, her fingers spreading apart the thick tumbling mass of damp hair, offering it to the drying breeze.

Seen between the clapboard cottages, along the edge of the estuary, the early tide swept over the gleaming mudflats as if it were alive, sending small boats bobbing and lifting on the incoming waves.

To the west, huddled in the estuary's curve, a dozen or so stall-fronted cockle boiling sheds were already belching steam, their cowled chimneys pouring wood smoke into the fresh morning air. To the east lay the town of Westcliff where the folk in the grand houses still lay abed. Beyond that lay even greater wealth, for Southend, the town in which the Prince Regent had installed his Princess Caroline, had become fashionable. Folk said that it rivalled Brighton or Bath with the recent migration of the upper classes to its shoreline. So far, Saffron thought with comforting satisfaction, little had changed in Leigh. The sea and landscape remained much the same, the two tides each day washed the same shore and the same familiar faces passed the door.

She turned to reach her mother's bone comb from the mantle shelf and began to tease the tangles from her hair before sweeping it into a ribbon at the nape of her neck. She had but one decent outfit of clothes to her name, her 'Sunday go-to-meeting' dress. The original flower print faded from many washings but a good fit for all that.

"It'll 'ave to do." She muttered shaking the folds from the full skirt. The creaking of boards overhead, signalling Tom's stirring from sleep, reminded her that both he and Poll would need to break their fast before she changed her dress.

As she set bowls and mugs onto the table Tom appeared at the head of the stairs. "Mornin' Saffy." He yawned, knuckling the sleep from his eyes.

"Mornin' Tom." Lovingly she watched the small boy slowly make his way down into the kitchen. "Did you sleep well?"

"S'pose so." He turned away. "But I dreams a lot and it sort of wakes me."

Saffron sat and pulled the boy to her. "Is it bad dreams, Tom?"

The boy nodded miserably. "Is it Jonas?" Tom shrugged. "Are you frettin' over Poll?" He shrugged again. "She's on the mend." She ruffled his hair. "And as for Jonas, I won't let 'im 'urt you or Poll."

He raised trusting eyes to her earnest gaze. "Promise Saffy?"

"Promise!" She held him to her. "Now, off you go, get dressed and see if Poll's awake. You got a special job to do today. You're in charge while I go to do this sittin' thing for the artist."

Trusted with responsibility, Tom's mood changed immediately and he scampered away to do his sister's bidding.

Within the hour Poll had emerged, washed and dressed and showing a further, if slight improvement in both her health and her mood.

"I bin thinkin' Saffy." She scraped the last of the oatmeal from her dish. "This sittin' for the artist. It won't last for ever will it?"

Saffron paused, a wet cloth in her hand "I never thought about 'ow long he'd be needin' me." She paused, absentmindedly wiping crumbs from the table. "I s'pose you're right. 'E'll paint my picture and that'll be that I reckon. Still." She brightened, "At least I'll be savin' while 'e's doin' it."

Poll ran a finger around the rim of her empty bowl. "Well I've made up me mind to do my bit." She paused, reluctant to meet her sister's puzzled stare. "I'm goin' cocklin!"

"You ain't!" Saffron's jaw dropped. "You know that's the gypsies' place. They don't let no one near them beds. There's a few who tried it but folks say they ain't alive to tell the tale." She had heard the stories of the gipsy women. Triggers they were called. Armed with knives and guarding the cockle beds while the raked up cockles which were transferred from wooden sleds. Loaded into yoked baskets, they were then taken to be sold to stallholders' sheds where they were boiled. With her own eyes she had seen the women covered in mud, their feet cut and bleeding from broken shells. "You think again Poll, it's not for you."

Poll's head snapped up in defiance. "I got as much right to rake cockles as them gypsies. I'll make meself a sled and, come next week, I'll be out there, you'll see!"

Saffron shook her head. "You must be mad, Poll. I know you got your mind set on 'elpin' out but you're not well enough to work as yet." She put an arm around the girl. "Give it a bit longer 'afore you do somethin' stupid and set yourself back again."

Poll's shoulders sagged as she laid her head against Saffron. "I'll give it some thought." She promised. "But I got to 'elp some way Saffy, I got to."

"I know Poll, but first you got to get strong. Now you just sit while I make up the stove and change my dress. I can't turn up for Mr. Jean-Pierre Howard lookin' like this." Tom's giggle was silenced by a look of mock severity. "You laughin' at me Master Tom?"

"No, Saffy." The boy's wide-eyed innocence belied his words. "But you got a big smudge of soot from the stove on your nose. You look like a Badger."

"A Badger am I?" She swept him into her arms, rubbing her face against his as he squealed with laughter. "There, now you've got the smudge. You looks like a Badger 'stead of me." She set him down, her mood suddenly serious. "I'm leaving you to take care of Poll. You don't let no one in while I'm gone. D'you hear?"

"I know Saffy."

"And while I get dressed you can feed the cat. There's some fish heads I boiled for 'er on the stove." She bent to scoop one of the kittens from the basket, handing it to Tom. "The kits eyes are open now and they need more than their mother's milk."

The boy held the wriggling creature at arms length. "It's got blue eyes like mine Saffy."

"So it has." She smiled. "Put it back in the basket so it don't get trod on. I'll be down presently." It took her only minutes to strip off her apron, grey skirt and bodice and to splash cold water onto her face and arms. Towelling herself dry she slipped the soft fabric of the summer dress over head, smoothing it into place and buttoning it to the neck. The small mirror propped on the pine tallboy showed eyes wide with apprehension. She bit her lips and pinched her cheeks to bring a little colour to her pale face. "That'll 'ave to do." She told her reflection. "If 'e don't like it, Mr. Jean-Pierre Howard'll 'ave to look for someone else to paint."

In the kitchen Tom had mashed the fish into a paste and was feeding morsels to each eager kitten in turn. "Don't give 'em too much." Saffron warned, reaching for her shawl. "You don't want to make 'em sick." She turned to Poll. "I'll be back in an hour or so, and if you needs me you knows where I am."

"Don't fret, Saffy, I can give eye to Poll." His small chin came up "I ain't a baby no more!"

She forced a smile in answer to his confident words. "I know, Tom." She planted a kiss on his nose. "Bar the door like you did 'afore and don't open it for no one 'cept me."

The brilliance of the morning sun almost blinded her as she made her way over the cobbles to Juniper Cottage. It was obvious that Jean-Pierre had been waiting impatiently for her arrival for the door flew open as she raised her hand to the knocker.

"I was afraid you would not come". A half smile played at the corner of his generous mouth as he stood back and motioned her to enter.

She squeezed past him into the narrow passage. "I said I'd be 'ere, didn't I?" She swallowed, uncomfortably aware of his closeness. "I ain't late am I?"

"No, no." He followed her through to the long room at the end of the passage, to where a sunlit terrace beyond jutted out over the shingle beach. "Please, sit for a moment." He indicated a chair by the open window, crouching before her, elbows on knees. "Don't be afraid". He gazed up at her from beneath thick dark lashes. "I only want to make a few sketches." He paused. "Is that all right with you?" She nodded, wordlessly. He got to his feet, head on one side. "But first, we must make loose that magnificent mane."

As he stretched out a hand Saffron jerked her head away. "I'll do it!" With trembling fingers she tugged at the ribbon, leaving her hair to tumble free.

"Please?" It was a gentle request and she allowed him to spread the shining tresses into a golden cape around her shoulders. "Beautiful." He murmured. "But this will never do." He pointed to her dress, buttoned high at her neck. "I wish to see more."

Saffron leapt to her feet, clutching at her throat. "You said you just wanted to draw me." She backed away from him in alarm.

He held his hands high in surrender. "Wait, you misunderstand me. I wish you no harm Saffron." He turned to gather a length of blue silk from a nearby table. "I wish only that you loosen that colourless garment . Just pull it down over your shoulders and drape this around you. Look." He turned away. "I will leave the room if you wish and you may call me when you are ready."

Reluctantly, Saffron took the silk and ran it through her fingers. She had never felt anything so soft, so rich and, she reasoned, the young artist seemed genuinely sincere in his intentions.

"All right, I'll do it. But you wait 'till I call."

"Good." His relief was evident in his smile. "I'll be waiting."

She watched him leave, closing the door carefully behind him. Hurriedly she fumbled with the buttons, tugging the neckline of the faded cotton wide open and down over her shoulders, before settling the blue silk in its place.

She tiptoed to a mirror hung above the stone hearth and was startled to see the transformation. The colour of a summer sky, the silken wrap lit her eyes to a vivid matching shade. Her hair fell softly over smooth skin, which seemed to have taken on a new pearl-like glow. Saffron could not deny herself a smile of satisfaction as she turned first one way and then the other.

Taking a deep breath she turned to the door. "I'm ready." She called, bracing herself for his scrutiny.

Slowly he entered, bending his head to the low doorway. For a moment he paused in his stride, staring open-mouthed in wonder.

"I knew you were beautiful." He came toward her. "But this is more than I dared to hope for." He reached to adjust the silken shawl, staring deep into her eyes. "You are truly…" he struggled, seeking the right words. "You are truly magnificent Saffron Clay. Come." He took her hand. "Sit here by the window, let the sunlight catch you."

Meekly she obeyed him, realising that she was calm and willing, no eager, to please. She sat in silence as, gently, he positioned her, tilting her chin and commanding her to smile. "Wonderful." He whispered. "Stay just like that. Please, do not move."

She watched as he dragged forward an easel upon which sat a stretched canvas. With lightening strokes he began to work, murmuring softly to himself and frowning at his progress as the first lines of the portrait began to take shape.

Saffron took the opportunity to study him more closely. Each time he impatiently brushed a lock of hair away from his brow, he left a streak of charcoal in its place. But it was a good face she thought. A straight nose, if a little long, eyes wide-set and dark as night and a square jaw below a full sensuous mouth. She felt an unexpected shiver of excitement and chided herself for thoughts, which she felt sure had brought a flush to her cheeks. She recalled again the light touch of his long sensitive fingers on her shoulder as he had adjusted the wrap and saw again the depth of wonder in his eyes.

"Can I talk?" She broke the spell deliberately, anxious to return to reality.

He looked startled. "Of course. As long as you do not move. What is it you want to say?"

There were a million questions she longed to ask but she blurted the first thing which came to mind. "Why 'ave you got a Frenchie name?"

He threw back his head and laughed aloud, stepping from behind the easel, spreading his hands wide. "You mean Howard? That is not French surely."

She flushed at his bantering tone. "I mean Jean-Pierre. That's what you said you were called didn't you?"

"Ah, that was my mother's choice. She is a Frenchwoman you see." He paused. "And my father was English. Does that answer your question?"

"You said 'is', so your Mother is alive?"

"Of course, although my Father is dead." He looked beyond her as a seagull wheeled past the open window. "Killed fighting Napoleon. It broke my mother's heart although he left her well provided for. She has a house in Brighton. My father was a fine man, an officer and a gentleman."

"You miss 'im don't you?"

"I hardly knew him. He was away fighting one war or another for most of my childhood." There was a distant sadness in his reply. "But yes, I miss him." He turned back to the easel. "And what of you Saffron, what of your parents?"

"Both gone. First Pa and then Ma five years after."

"So you are an orphan?"

"Sort of. Ma married a second time to Jonas, 'e's Tom's father. But 'e's a bad 'un. I won't let 'im near the cottage no more. I seen 'im off good and proper!"

She heard a chuckle from behind the canvas. "Oh Saffron Clay, you must be a terrifying sight when you are angry. I hope you never see me off proper!"

"You makin' fun of me?" She felt her back stiffen. "'Cause if you are…"

A dark head appeared. "I would never dare to do such a thing. Unless of course, I wanted to rekindle that angry sparkle you have in your eye. If only I could put that on canvas I would become a rich man overnight." He smiled "I was only teasing. Forgive me?"

She felt her rising anger evaporate, knowing she would find it hard to stay out of humour with this man for very long. He stood back, looking first at her and then at his work.

"I think that will be enough for today." He seemed satisfied. "The light has altered. We will continue tomorrow, if that is acceptable to you."

Saffron knew a moment of disappointment, for, as she got to her feet, he threw a cover over the easel, obscuring her view of his sketching. "Can't I see?" She stretched her cramped limbs, wanting to find some reason to prolong the visit but he shook his head.

"You may see your portrait when it is finished. Not before." He dug into his pocket and produced a handful of coins. "We said two shillings did we not?"

Saffron nodded guiltily. "Seems a lot of money for just sittin' 'ere."

"You have earned every penny, I assure you. This will be one of my finest paintings, for never have I had a finer model."

Embarrassed by his words she sought to make light of the compliment, turning away to slip the silken wrap from her shoulders and tug her dress into place.

"There you go again I'm sure I don't know what you mean 'arf the time." She bent her head to hide her confusion. "I'd best be off, Tom and Poll will wonder where I got to. I'll be back in the morning if you want me."

He went with her to the door, watching as she turned away and, without a backward glance, hurried home. Jean-Pierre stood for a moment deep in thought. "Yes Saffron, I want you." He murmured. "If only you knew how much I have wanted you from the moment I first set eyes on you. But I must take my time or you will shy away from me like the beautiful, innocent creature you are."

CHAPTER THIRTEEN

Filled with apprehension, Nathan followed behind his Aunt, the tall ramrod figure giving nothing away as she made her way into the upper regions of the house. At the top of the stairs she paused, turning to face him.

"Are your boots clean, Nathan?" He rubbed the toe of his boot behind the leg of his britches.

"Clean enough Aunt." He grinned. "Cook don't let no one carryin' dirt into the kitchen."

"And your hands?" He held them out for inspection.

"Very Well. Now understand me Nathan. You will speak only when spoken to and you will show respect."

"Am I in trouble?"

"That is for the Master to say. He is waiting for you in the library." She laid a reassuring hand on his shoulder. "For my sake and for your own show yourself in a good light. Remember the family are of the Quaker religion, you may find their manner of speech somewhat different from that to which you are accustomed."

"I will that, Aunt I promise. There's a few Quaker families over Maldon way. Good folk they were, as I remember they were never quick to judge a man for 'is faults."

His Aunt smiled, lifting the hem of her skirt as she swept ahead of him along the richly carpeted corridor. He barely had time to notice the oak panelling or the seemingly disapproving faces glowering down from the gilt, framed portraits before he found himself facing a dark wood door. His Aunt tapped lightly and a distant voice bade them enter.

It seemed to Nathan, at first glance, that every book that had ever been written must be gathered in that room. Three walls were lined with shelving from floor to ceiling and each crammed with leather-bound volumes. On the far wall, behind a massive desk, long windows, hung on either side with sun-faded velvet, overlooked manicured lawns, their perfection broken here and there by sculptured flower beds. Through the glass he could see an avenue of poplars curving away into the distance skirting the still waters of an ornamental lake. Nathan was overcome by the sheer size of the high-ceilinged room and the knowledge of its waiting occupant, but was startled from his sense of wonder by a barked command.

"Well boy, come over here and let me look at thee." Nathan felt as if his feet had taken root in the thick turkey rug.

"Nathan!" His Aunt hissed. "Pull yourself together, the Master wishes to speak to you."

He swallowed hard and walked forward to stand in front of the desk set in the curve of the window. With the sun at his back, the great man who commanded so much respect, was little more than a silhouette, while the boy felt as if he were standing in the revealing glare of the shaft of sunlight.

"Thy Aunt has told me what transpired. I am happy to say that my daughter will make a complete recovery, although she has yet to deal with me!" There was a snort of laughter. "Little madam. I had forbidden her to ride that particular mount. Tell me boy, did thee saddle the horse?"

"No Sir I did not." Without thinking Nathan rose to his own defence. "You don't treat no animal like that. She were in pain, poor thing. It weren't Bright Lady's fault that Miss Charlotte took a tumble."

The man rose to his feet holding out a hand to stem the tide of Nathan's outburst. "And I suppose thee will not tell me the name of the culprit?"

Nathan shook his head miserably. He would deal with

Patrick in his own good time and in his own way. "No, Sir." He mumbled.

"Loyalty to thy fellow workers, eh? When all's said and done that's not a bad thing, but I will discover whether my suspicions are well founded and the wrongdoer will be dismissed from my service." He walked around the desk and seated himself on its edge. "But it's thee I'm interested in. From what I have been told, had it not been for thy quick thinking, young Charlotte's injury could have been far more serious. Your Aunt tells me that thee can read and write and have a good head on thy shoulders. I think perhaps thou art wasted in the stables, so I have spoken to Bentley. I have told him to find a place for thee here in the house. One of the junior footmen has been forced to return home, I understand, so there is a vacancy." He paused, leaning toward Nathan. "How would that suit thee?"

Nathan let out a long breath. "That would suit me real fine, Sir." He felt he must be grinning like an idiot. "And I thank you kindly."

The man strode past him to where his Aunt had been waiting patiently by the door. "So it is settled Mrs Porter. Thee will take the lad away and tell Bentley of my decision. He will see to his apparel and school him in his duties." He turned to face Nathan and, for the first time, the boy could see his Master's face clearly. Thick dark hair, greying at the temples, framed a strong, tanned face. A deep cleft distinguished an aggressive chin, above which sat a long, narrow nose. But it was the eyes that held Nathan's attention for, in that moment, he glimpsed sadness in their brown depths, which took him by surprise. How could a man who owned so much, who had risen to be respected so well, find anything in his life to cause him sorrow?

Urged by his Aunt, Nathan all but stumbled from the room scarcely able to believe his good fortune. "Did he mean it Aunt

Jane? Am I to get to work in the 'ouse?"

"The Master never says anything he does not mean Nathan."
She hurried ahead of him. "And the word is house." She
emphasised the aitch. "If you are to better yourself you must
improve the way in which you speak. For now, however, I shall
take you to meet Bentley. He is the Butler and he will then take
charge of you. You will meet Peacock, the Under Butler and
there are three other junior footmen. Watch your tongue, listen
and learn and you will fit in well I am sure. The Master, Mr.
Benham, is a fair man and if you do your duties you may well
earn advancement." She came to a halt at the end of the corridor and tapped on a narrow door.

There was a muffled response from within. "Mr. Bentley, it
is I, Mrs. Porter. I have a message from Mr. Benham."

The door swung wide to reveal a tall slim man clad in fune-
real black relieved only at throat and cuff by pure, white linen.
His thin, white hair was swept back to show a hawk-like coun-
tenance. He stepped back to allow their entry. "Please come
in Mrs. Porter. I take it this is the young fellow about whom
the Master has already spoken?" He looked long and hard at
Nathan, who shuffled uncomfortably under his narrow-eyed
consideration.

"Yes, Mr. Bentley, this is Nathan. I think you will find him
suitable."

"That remains to be seen, but if the Master wants me to set
him on, then I must. I am told you have been working in the
stables?"

Nathan nodded. "Yes Sir."

"Then you had best collect such belongings as you may have
there and return to the house without delay. You will sleep on
the top floor with the other footmen. Find your way there by
the back stairs, wash and change into the uniform you will find

hanging in the closet and then report to me." He paused. "Is that clear?"

"Yes Sir, perfectly clear."

"Then be off with you. Mrs. Porter, if you would be so kind as to show the lad the way back to the kitchen, I would be pleased if you would join me in a pot of tea upon your return."

"That is most gracious of you Mr. Bentley. I shall be only a moment or two." Nathan was amused to see the flush of pleasure on his Aunt's cheek. There was obviously more to the relationship than the formal exchange had suggested.

Bursting to tell of his good fortune, he was disappointed to find his friends had left the kitchen and returned to work. Sarah, however, hurried to meet him, wiping her hands on her apron. "Well? What 'appened?"

"I bin dismissed!"

"You what?" Cook slammed down the rolling pin she was holding sending a shower of flour into the air. "I don't believe it!"

Nathan burst into laughter at her indignation. "I'm only funnin'." He pulled a chair from the table and sat, his legs spread wide. "The Master said as 'ow I did a good job on Miss Charlotte and, if I wanted, I could work 'ere in the 'ouse as a footman."

"'E never!" Sarah ran to him and threw her arms around his neck. She leaned back searching his face. "You said yes, didn't you?"

"You bet I did. Yes, Sir, I says and I thank you kindly. I gets to start right away, soon as I get me gear from the stables." He thought for a moment. "'Course somebody'll 'ave to show me the way up the back stairs. This place is as big as a palace, I reckon, and Mr. Bentley says I got to change into a uniform and get back to 'im quick as I can."

Sarah giggled. "I reckon I can show you where to go. Mind you, I ain't never been all over the house but I know where the back stairs are. 'Urry back." She called as Nathan made for the door.

Bartholomew was waiting outside the stables as he ran into the yard. "So, what's it to be? Did the Master give you your marchin' orders?"

"Not likely!" Nathan winked, "I'm to be set on at the 'ouse. Nathan, 'e says, you're wasted in the stables, a bright lad like you, I want's you to be a footman, 'e says."

"Just like that?"

"Well, sort of. I 'ad to go and see Mr.Bentley first. 'E's the Butler and by the look of 'im, I reckon 'e's thinks 'e's the next thing to the Almighty."

"You're right there. 'Is word is law and you'll do well to remember that."

The groom fingered his chin, "I'm gonna miss you 'ere though. You got a way with the beasts, and no mistake."

"Ow is Bright Lady? Is she over 'er fright?"

Bartholomew nodded. "She needs to settle. Did you see what 'appened, what made her bolt?"

"I did that! It were Patrick. He tightened her girth so the poor beast couldn't breathe. It were no wonder she bolted when Miss Charlotte stung 'er with the whip. Master said 'e'll get to the truth when the girl's up and about. If you asks me, a touch of the whip wouldn't do Miss Charlotte no 'arm neither." He laughed suddenly, remembering the Master's words. "I reckon she'll feel the length of her Father's tongue when she's able."

"You didn't say nought to the Master, about Patrick I mean?"

"Course not! But 'e's got a good idea what 'appened. Anyway, what d'you take me for? I'll deal with Patrick when the time comes, and in me own way!"

"Good lad! 'Ere, you'd best not stand 'ere talkin'. Get your stuff and cut away back to the 'ouse." Bartholomew laid a hand on Nathan's arm. "Good luck Nathan. Master's right, you be wasted 'ere. I can see a future for a lad like you, so don't waste the chance."

"I won't. And I won't forget it was you who gave me the chance in the first place." He climbed the ladder to the loft and collected the few items of clothing, which were his worldly possessions. He thrust them into a sack and slung it over his shoulder. Below Pete and Jack, who were mucking out the stalls, waylaid him, eager for news as he climbed back down the ladder. Briefly, he explained the reason for his departure, aware that within earshot Patrick had sidled closer and was listening to every word.

"Footman eh?" He crowed. "'Ow long d'you think you'll last up at the 'ouse?"

"A mite longer than you!" Nathan rounded on him. "I get the feelin' Master knows you was behind Miss Charlotte's tumble." He saw the tide of angry colour flood the boy's face. "An' before you say summat you'll be sorry for, it weren't me what give you up. Not that I didn't think about it." He added, relishing the fear in the bully's eyes. "Just you give it mind though, and you stay away from Sarah from now on or I might think again!"

He left Patrick spluttering with rage and, with a jaunty wave to the groom and the other two lads he walked away, whistling, in the direction of the back of the house. At the tree line he halted, looking with fresh interest at the imposing grey stone building, its windows gleaming in the sun and its door open wide, beckoning him to his future.

Sarah had kept her word and was waiting at the kitchen door to show Nathan the way to the back stairs, which led to the upper floors of the house.

"Cook says I'm not to be long, but I can take you 'alf way." She beckoned him to follow, coming to a halt on a narrow landing. "Up two more flights." She pointed high into the poorly lit stairwell. "Then you go off to the right. That's the footmen's rooms. The maids are on the left."

He slid an arm around her slim waist. "So I'm goin' to be sleepin' next door to you am I?"

She wriggled free of his grasp. "No you ain't. An', what's more, if you get caught trying to creep across the way by Mr. Bentley you'll be shown the door an' no mistake. 'E don't miss much and 'e don't allow no goin's on neither."

Nathan put his palms together and raised his eyes to the heavens. "I promise I'll be good." He grinned suddenly. "At least if I ain't, I promise not to get caught!"

Sarah stifled a giggle. "Get on with you! Mr. Bentley'll wonder where you got to and it don't do to be late when e's waitin!"

He saluted smartly, clicking his heels. "Yes, Madam, I'm on me way!" He left Sarah looking after him and shaking her head in despair at his antics.

The footmen's quarters at the top of the house boasted one long room with a small window shedding light on four narrow beds. On the one nearest the door someone had laid a suit of dark green livery, a white shirt and stockings and a pair of buckled shoes. "Well now. Nathan murmured. "Ere's some finery and no mistake." He began to strip, and, looking around for somewhere to leave the discarded clothing, spotted a row of cupboards set under the eaves. The first three were obviously in use while the last contained yet another suit of livery. "This'll do." He dropped his old shirt and britches onto the floor and began to dress himself. He had barely struggled into the jacket when the door opened behind him.

"You'll be the new one then!" He turned to find himself confronted by a dark- haired lad of about his own age. "I'm Tim." Nathan took the proffered hand. "Old Blood and Guts 'as sent me to find you."

"Old Blood and Guts?"

"Bentley. Go and find 'im, 'e says." He mimicked the sour face of the Butler. "'E's probably lorst, 'e says."

Nathan laughed aloud. "You'd best not let 'im catch you taking 'im off like that."

"Not likely. Tim winked. "I know where me bread's buttered. Come on I'll show you the way. You'll soon get the 'ang of it."

They clattered down the uncarpeted stairs together until Tim paused in front of a baize-covered door. "Through 'ere is the main 'ouse. Turn right and it's the first door on your left."

Nathan nodded and squared his shoulders before stepping through the door and onto the richly carpeted corridor beyond. A tap on the Butler's door brought an immediate response and he was once again standing before the man, who he knew could make or break him at will.

CHAPTER FOURTEEN

Rising early the following morning, Nathan made his way down to the kitchen to find Sarah and the cook busy preparing food for the next group of servants ready to break their fast.

"Ah, Nathan, there you are. Be a good lad and take this down to Bartholemew." The cook thrust a package into his hand. "'E's been up all night with one of the mares 'tis a bit of bread and cold meat, but 'is belly'll be empty and I know as 'ow 'e won't leave a new-born foal 'til 'e's ready."

Nathan grinned good naturedly, "'course I will. Don't do a man no good to have an empty belly." Before stepping into the crisp morning air, he winked at Sarah. "I'll be ready to fill my own belly by the time I get back."

As he reached the tree line, fallen pine needles crackled beneath his feet sending a sweet singing lark climbing into the thin air above. The stable door stood open, a lamp within throwing a pathway of light onto the cobbled yard. Bartholemew was kneeling beside the new-born foal, while Pete and Jack stood by, wonder etched on their young faces.

"Is he alright?" Pete frowned. "He's awful little."

"Alright?" Bartholemew chuckled. "I'll say. Little he may be but if I know 'owt, I'd say he's a winner." Gently he wiped the new arrival's glistening coat with a rag. "Just like 'is Ma. Same colour and same bloodline." He looked up fondly at the mare who watched his every move. "You did a good job my beauty. Master'll be mighty pleased with your young 'un."

"He will that." The sound of Nathan's voice brought Bartholemew to his feet. "Allow lad, what you doin' 'ere? Come to see the new foal?"

"No." Nathan laughed. "I've been sent by Cook with this."

He held out the parcel of food. "She says you need something in your belly, you being up all night helping that little fellow into the world." He hunkered down beside the foal as it struggled to stand on shaky legs. It's mother lowered her head to nuzzle and encourage the tiny creature to take its first steps.

"Look at that!" Jack gasped. "'E's up already!"

"'Course he is. I told you 'e's a winner." The groom unwrapped the parcel and took a massive bite from the bread. "Thank Mrs. Rand for me boy. Tell 'er we'll be over soon. Master won't mind if we're late. Not today."

"Well, I'd best get back." Nathan turned to leave the stable. "Old blood and guts will be on my tail and I've not had my vittles yet. See you soon."

To a chorus of goodbyes, he turned his steps towards the house halting as a movement caught his eye. A familiar figure emerged from the side of the long building.

"Patrick?" Nathan narrowed his eyes. "I thought the Master would have sent you packing. What are you doing here?"

The boy advanced menacingly, his hands clenched around the handle of a pitch-fork. "I come to settle what's owin', that's what." He thrust the pitch-fork toward Nathan. "You told on me and I lost me job." He came further into the shaft of light from the stable door. "I was alright 'afore you come. Think you're better 'un me, don't yer?" He came further into the shaft of light from the stable, which illuminated his wild eyes and a mouth twisted with hate. His clothes and hair were thick with mud and leaves. "I bin waitin' all night. Didn't I know you'd be by sooner or later." He bared his teeth in a ghastly rictus of a smile.

Nathan swallowed hard. "Don't be a fool. Put that down afore you hurt someone."

The bully threw back his head with a snort of high-pitched

laughter. "'Urt? I aims to finish you Mister 'igh and mighty! I'm gonna spit you like a pig for roasting" With a roar he lunged, narrowly missing his target as Nathan side stepped the lethal prongs, just as Bartholemew and the two stable lads burst onto the scene.

"Stay back!" Nathan shouted. "He's gone raving mad. Says he's going to kill me. I reckon he means it too!"

"Pete, go fetch someone from the 'ouse!" Bartholemew began to edge around behind the would-be killer, stooping to pick up a fallen branch. "I'll 'old 'im off!"

"You'll 'old me off, old man?" Patrick cuffed away a trickle of saliva from his slack mouth. "When I've finished 'im, I'll do for you, too. You've ordered me 'bout for the last time."

"Put it down, lad." The groom spoke calmly. "Nathan didn't tell on you. None of us did. Miss Charlotte must 'ave told her father what 'appened."

"I'll get 'er too!" Patrick snarled, his mad gaze darting from side-to-side, the pitch fork pointing first one way and then the other.

"You got what was comin' to you." Nathan was suddenly aware of Jack standing by his side. "What you did to Bright Lady was right cruel!"

"You keep your nose out, runt!"

"Who you calling a runt?" The boy took a step forward, his fists balled.

"Leave' im be!" Bartholemew barked. "Get back! Can't you see 'e's queer in the 'ead?" A sneer twisted Patrick's face as he tossed the pitch-fork from one hand to the other, relishing the fear in the eyes of his potential victims.

"So, who wants to be first?" For a split second he turned his head, distracted by the sound of voices as Pete returned with Tim and another footman. Jack seized the opportunity and with a howl of fury, launched himself at the bigger boy.

Patrick swung to meet him, the murderous pitch-fork held at arm's length. Jack didn't stand a chance as the tines pierced his belly. Blood gushed from the fatal wound as with a strangled cry, the impaled boy slumped to his knees.

For a moment, Bartholemew and Nathan were frozen in disbelief, the spell broken by the noisy arrival of the men from the house.

Nathan ran to kneel beside the body of his young friend. "You bastard! You've killed him, you'll swing for this!"

"It were an accident!" Patrick babbled, backing away, aware of the witnesses to his crime closing in around him. "It were an accident! He came at me. You saw it!" Wild eyed, he cast around for way of escape.

"No you don't!" Bartholemew weighed the heavy branch in his hands. "You'll stay and take what's comin'." He turned to the two footmen. "Grab 'im lads. We'll take 'im to the Master. 'E'll know what to do."

"You're not takin' me nowhere!" The terrified boy backed away, turning to run inside the open stable.

"Stop him!" Nathan leaped to his feet, his fury adding speed to the chase. As he burst into the stable, he saw his quarry desperately wrench open the door to one of the stalls, obviously intending to make his getaway on horseback. The boy looked up with a scream of terror as in that moment, there was mutural recognition between boy and beast.

Nathan's blood ran cold. As Bright Lady, her nostrils flaring, emerged with a snort of rage. Time seemed to slow the scene as the filly reared to her full height. Her tormentor turned too late to escape the iron shod hooves. The first struck him on his shoulder, snapping the collar bone with a loud crack. The second, smashed the back of his head to a bloody pulp. Splinters of bone and brain flew from the smashed skull, splattering the ground around the vengeful horse.

As they crowded around the doorway, Bright Lady backed away from the lifeless body to stand trembling against the stable wall. Shaking her head as if in denial, she stared at the pool of blood beneath the dead boy's head which widened rapidly taking with it, fragments of bone and brain.

Pete pushed past them and ran to comfort the filly, murmuring calm words and stroking the soft bowed head. "It's alright, girl, it's all over now."

"It is that!" Bartholemew knelt beside the blood splattered body, staring down into the lifeless eyes. "'E's dead right enough." He raised his head to look at each of them in turn. "But I'll not 'ave Bright Lady blamed. She were only defendin' 'erself."

"What'll we do?" Nathan shook his head. "They'll put her down won't they?"

"No! Not if I can 'elp it." The big groom stood, brushing straw from his britches. "Pete, make sure there's no blood on the filly's hooves. Then wipe 'er down careful like. No one need know what's 'appened 'ere." He paused. "Need they?"

The group of onlookers murmurered their agreement.

"'E got what was comin' to him." Pete nodded. "'Tweren't the Lady's fault. But 'ow you goin' to explain that?" He pointed to the blood stained body.

"We could bury 'im and say nowt." Tim suggested nervously.

Nathan squared his shoulders. "No. We'll stick to the truth as near as we can. Don't forget Jack is laying out there too. We can't bury them both."

"We could say that Patrick killed Jack, then he ran into the stable and sort of fell." Bartholemew finished lamely.

"Not good enough." Nathan shook his head. "Not the way he looks." His gaze came to rest on the ladder leading to the hayloft. "You two, heft that anvil and put it over here. That's it. Put it at the foot of the ladder." He stood back. "If Patrick fell off that and hit his head on this." He nudged the anvil with his foot. "It might work. We'll have to clean up a bit and put him in the right place. What do you think?"

Carefully, Nathan turned the body over. In a face which had all but been destroyed, blank eyes swam in a pool of blood.

"Oh God!" Tim turned away to fall on his knees, his shoulders heaving as he vomited onto the straw covered floor.

Bartholemew slumped, head in hands, onto an upturned bucket. "What'll we tell the Master?" He groaned.

"We'll tell him that Patrick went mad, killed Jack and ran in here to get away." Nathan paused. "He made for the hayloft, got halfway up the ladder and fell back onto the anvil. By the time we got here, he was dead." He looked at each blank face in turn. "Right?" In turn they nodded, glad to be relieved of further responsibility. "That's the story and we all have to tell it the same way. Now come on, help me with him." He jerked a thumb toward a spot at the foot of the ladder.

Reluctantly, the two footmen moved the limp body and repositioned the limbs in what they hoped was a convincing pose.

"Now, fetch the straw from where he fell, and put it around his head." Nathan saw the horror in the boy's eyes. "Alright, I'll do it." He reached for a spade. "You two get some water and wash away the blood, then cover it up with some dry bran and a bit of hay."

Bartholemew watched as Nathan prepared the scene for what was ever after to be referred to as an accident. "Thank you lad, Bright Lady's no killer. She was scared is all. She knew 'im. Must 'ave thought he were goin' to 'urt 'er again."

Nathan patted him on the shoulder. "I know. But see? Pete's calmed her down. She'll be none the worse by the morrow."

"I know, lad. And she's got you to thank for her life. She knows and she'll not forget."

"Right now, I'd best get back to the house. They'll be wondering what's going on. Nathan wiped the blade of the spade and set it against the wall, standing back to survey his work, before washing away the last traces of blood from his hands. "Aye, that should do it." He paused at the door, turning to face the two young footmen. "You had best come back with me, but remember to tell the same tale or old blood and guts will smell a rat. Better let me do the talking."

As they hurried past Jack's pitifully small body spreadeagled in the yard, Pete was draping it with a blanket. "Jack were my friend." He stifled a sob. "We came 'ere from the orphanage together. That bastard were always on at 'im, just 'cause 'e was little. I tried to stop 'im, me bein' older like." He swung back to glare at the stable. "I'm glad 'e's dead. I 'ope he burns in 'ell!"

The three of them hurried back to the kitchen where Nathan left Tim to answer the flood of questions from Mrs. Rand. "I've got to tell Aunt Jane." He whispered in Sarah's ear. "Tim'll tell you what's happened. I'll be back soon."

His aunt listened with growing horror as the story unfolded. "I can scarcely believe that such a dreadful thing can happen. Tell me Nathan, is the other stable lad unhurt?"

"He's real upset, so is Bartholemew and the footmen who came back with Pete. But they'll get over it in time." He saw again in his mind's eye, the killer's smashed skull and the pool of blood. "We all will I suppose."

Jane Porter stood, straightening the skirts of her gown. "You will come with me Nathan. The Master must be told immediately. You will tell him exactly what happened." She raised a warning finger, "Leave nothing out."

Despite the early hour, John Benham was already at his desk in the library. At the housekeeper's knock he bade them enter. "Well?" He glanced up to see Nathan's white face and came immediately to his feet. "What is wrong?"

"There has been," Jane Porter paused, "an accident Sir, Nathan saw the whole thing. I think it is best that he tells you."

Nathan hated himself for having to lie to the man he admired so much but he knew in his heard that he was doing the right thing for all concerned. Haltingly, he told the carefully contrived version of events. John Benham sat back regarding Nathan steadily over steepled fingers. "Thou hast told me everything?"

Nathan nodded. "Yes, Sir. Everything."

"Very well, thee may leave the matter in my hands. I shall send for the Parish Constable. There will be an enquiry and he will wish to speak to thee, I am sure." He waved a dismissive hand. "Until then, thee may return to thy duties."

Nathan realised as he returned to the kitchen that his hands were trembling. He shook his head miserably. "God forgive me," he muttered, "but I couldn't stand by and see them shoot Bright Lady."

For the next few days, the only topic of conversation among the staff was the sad death of the young stable lad who had been well liked and of Patrick, his killer. At the end of the week, they were both quietly laid to rest in the village churchyard and so it seemed, was the whole sad affair, leaving only those involved in the truth to struggle with their consciences.

CHAPTER FIFTEEN

As Saffron neared the cottage, the sight of Gabriel Stoneforth lounging against the gate brought a smile to her face.
He straightened as she approached, turning his cap between
nervous hands.

"Morning Miss Saffy. I bin waiting for you to get back." He
shuffled his feet uncomfortably. "Young Tom said as 'ow you
left orders not to let no one in while you was away."

"Oh Gabriel, I didn't mean you. But Tom's a good boy to
keep the door barred like I told 'im." She bent her head to the
weathered wood. "It's all right Tom, it's me, Saffy. Open the
door, there's a good lad." There was the sound of metal grating
on wood as the door creaked open to reveal the boy's face. "Let
us in lad I got Gabriel with me. 'E's come to see our Poll."

Relief flooded Tom's face as he stood back to allow them
entry. "You said I weren't to let no one in." Frowning, he
looked the big man up and down. "So I didn't!"

"Quite right too!" Gabriel let out a bellow of laughter. "You
do what your sister tells you, young'un. She knows what's
what!" He sobered, turning to look at Poll. "But I don't mean
no one no harm, and that's a promise." He crossed to the hearth
and hunkered down, taking the girl's small hand into his own.
"So 'ow's little Poll today?" Flushed with pleasure at the
attention, Poll returned his smile. "I think I'm mending nicely,
thank you. I get's a bit sort of shaky sometimes." She glanced
at Saffron. "An' I ain't ready to get out yet." She bit her lip.
"Leastwise, not on me own."

"Well now." Gabriel got to his feet. "That can soon be sorted.
'Ow about you take a little walk with me?" He saw the flare
of alarm in her eyes. "Not far, just a few steps to the foot of the

hill and back. It's a grand day to be seen with a pretty girl on me arm. What d'you say?"

"Can I go too, Saffy? Can I?" Tom danced around his sister tugging at her skirt.

"You'd best ask Poll and Gabriel." Saffron chuckled.

"Well I'm not goin' anywhere 'til you've told me all about the sitting you've bin doin'." Poll lifted Tom onto her knee. "So, come on, what 'appened. What's 'e like, this artist?"

"'E's nice." Saffron hung her shawl behind the door. "Talks like a gentleman, looks like one too. 'Is boots must 'ave cost a fortune!"

Poll giggled. "I ain't interested in 'is boots! 'Ow old is 'e? What's 'e look like?"

Jean-Pierre's face swam into Saffron's mind's eye. "Oh, 'bout twenty summat I s'pose. 'E's got dark 'air and ...." Her voice trailed away as she turned away to hide her confusion at the sight of their rapt attention. "And 'e wants me back again on the morrow." She set the handful of coins on the table. "So, there'll be more where that came from. Now if you're done quizzin' me, you can take that walk. A bit of fresh air will put some colour in your cheeks Poll."

Gabriel got to his feet and held out a hand to Poll. "Come on, we'll take the lad to the end of the lane and back." He winked at Tom. With the two of us walking alongside you, there won't be no one who'll dare say a wrong word."

Saffron grabbed a broom from beside the hearth and, laughing, made as if to sweep them to the door. "Out you go, all of you, and let me get straight while you're gone." As Gabriel passed her she caught his arm. "Take care." She whispered. "Jonas may be about and I don't want Poll or Tom upset."

"Don't you fret." Gabriel growled. "Nobody ain't goin' to worry 'em. They got me to deal with if they tries."

Saffron stood for a moment at the open door, watching the big man's confident stride as, with Tom capering at his side, he shepherded her sister gently toward the end of the village street. His manner spoke of more than friendly concern for Poll and, not for the first time, Saffron was aware of the age difference between her sister and the gentle widower.

With a sigh she turned to survey the cluttered table where the evidence of Tom and Poll's hastily made scratch meal still lay. Smiling, she shook her head; the young lad was always hungry but then he had a lot of growing to do.

She was aware that if she were to have the cottage tidy before their return, she would have to change her dress and begin work. She hurried up the stair to her room and, as she slipped the faded dress from her shoulders, she paused, feeling again the warmth of Jean-Pierre's touch as his fingers brushed her skin. For a moment she stood, angling the small mirror to show her near nakedness. He had told her she was beautiful but what did he see? She ran her fingers through her hair, spreading it as he had into a shining cape, imagining the swathe of cool silk that had framed her smooth shoulders. She spanned her waist with small hands, turning one way and then the other. What would he say if he could see her now? With half-closed eyes she let her hands stray upward to cup the young breasts, to feel their firm weight and hardening nipples. Had he wanted to touch her, caress her this way? With a gasp she pulled her thoughts back from temptation, startled at the hitherto undiscovered rush of pleasure that seemed to wash over her.

"Whatever d'you think you're doin' Saffron Clay?" She scolded the mirror image. "You should be ashamed. A nice girl like you 'aving such thoughts. Just 'cos 'e says you're beautiful don't mean nothin'. Best you gets back down to earth."

Hastily she pulled on a skirt and shirtwaist, twisting her hair into a knot and securing it with pins at the nape of her neck before returning to the living room below.

By the time Gabriel and Poll returned, with Tom skipping along ahead, the cottage was tidy and the kettle singing on the range. Poll's cheeks were flushed and Saffron was pleased to see a new light in her eye.

"Seems the walk 'as done you some good." She shot a grateful glance at Gabriel. "An' what's that you got there?"

"'Tis a Cod." Poll beamed. "Gabriel got it from one of the boatmen bringing in their catch. "'Tis for our supper." She looked pleadingly at her sister. "An' there's more n'enough for all of us. I told Gabriel that he could stay and 'ave a bite with us."

"Well, seeing as 'ow it's Gabriel what got it, I'd think it only right. But you must tell me 'ow much it was." She turned to the big man. "We don't take no charity."

"It were coppers. The boatman's a friend o' mine." Gabriel smiled disarmingly. "An' if you'll tend to the cookin' then I thinks that'll make us even."

"That seems fair." Saffron could not resist the man's logic and, taking the parcel of fish from his outstretched hands, thanked him for his generosity.

She took the offering into the back yard to clean and gut and returned to see Poll dozing on the settle, while Gabriel and Tom were huddled, heads together, at the table.

"No, you do it like this." Tom insisted. "I'll show you again."

Curious, Saffron peered over the boy's shoulder to see him carefully outlining letters on his slate.

"Now you do it." He passed the slate pencil to the man who held it awkwardly between his calloused fingers.

"Like this?" A shakey letter A followed by an even shakier letter B appeared on the slate.

"Not bad. Now try a C." Tom put his head on one side and, sensing Saffron's presence, he glanced up. "I'm teaching Gabriel 'is letters Saffy."

Saffron caught Gabriel's wink and smiled gratefully. Tom needed the company of a man. His father was no good she thought bitterly, a lad needed someone to look up to, to learn from, now that Nathan had gone.

By early evening they were ready for their meal. Saffron had cooked the cod to perfection and the appetising aroma brought them eagerly to the table. Even Poll ate well, wiping her plate with the last morsel of bread and sitting back smoothing her dress satisfyingly over her stomach.

"That were the best meal I've 'ad in a twelvemonth." Gabriel got up from the table and began to gather the plates. "Now you ladies 'ave a rest while Tom and me washes this lot." He silenced Saffron's protest with a backward nod at Poll. "You cooked the food, so 'tis only fair. 'Sides I reckon Poll's about ready for 'er bed. All that fresh air 'as tired 'er out."

Poll was certainly heavy-eyed and Saffron agreed, her sister had done enough for one day. "Come on Poll" She held out a hand. "Gabriel's right, let's get you up the stair."

Poll rose wearily from the table. "I reckon so." She yawned widely. "Thank you Gabriel for the walk and for the fish. It were grand." She smiled shyly at the groom. "P'raps I'll see you soon." Her tone implied a question.

Gabriel watched them mount the stair. "You will that Miss Poll. That's for certain."

As Saffron helped Poll to undress, she used the opportunity to examine her sister's ravaged body. The scratches seemed to be healing and the bruises had begun to fade but, aware of her gaze, Poll avoided her eyes, turning her head to stare from the window and into the distance. Saffron reached to tip Poll's chin and was sad to see a tear escape and trickle down her cheek.

"Come on Poll." She wrapped her arms around the girl. "You're on the mend." She leaned back to look at the pinched face. "An' you got an admirer. I reckon Gabriel's more'n a bit smitten. E's a good man. You could do a lot worse. When all this is over p'raps you could start walking out." Her reassuring words were cut short by Poll's broken sobs.

"E won't want me Saffy. Nobody will. Not after what 'appened." With trembling fingers she wiped away her tears.

"But 'e knows all about it an' 'e's still 'ere ain't 'e?"

"Gabriel won't want me I tell you. Not when 'e knows I'm with child."

"You're what? Poll flinched at Saffron's horrified response. "Why d'you say that?"

"I'm late, Saffy. I should 'ave started me monthly's and there's no sign."

"That don't mean nothin' for sure. You 'ad a terrible shock being set on like that. Summat like that can upset things. 'Ow late are you?"

"Only a couple of days I s'pose, but I got this feeling Saffy."

"A couple of days is nothin'. It'll be alright, you'll see." Saffron did her best to reassure her young sister but in her own heart she feared the worst. "Let's get you into bed. What you need is a good night's sleep." She fussed with the covers and plumped the pillows behind the girl's head. "I'll see Gabriel on 'is way and settle Tom, then I'll be back." Poll nodded, her eyes already clouded with sleep. As Gabriel had said she had had a long day. The day to come would, Saffron feared, prove to be even longer.

CHAPTER SIXTEEN

In the weeks that followed, Nathan learned to mould his rebellious nature to a new and disciplined routine. His Aunt insisted that he spent at least one hour of what little leisure time he had each day in her company. To his surprise he found that he had an aptitude for accounting, marvelling at the number of servants employed and the cost involved in the running of such a large household. She also schooled him in the manner of his speech, correcting him at every turn.

"A man is judged by many things Nathan." She constantly reminded him. "Not only by his appearance but by his opinions, his knowledge and the way in which he speaks." She encouraged him to read aloud, nodding with approval at the gradual improvement in his diction.

His training as a manservant, however, was under the watchful and strict eye of Bentley, the Butler. When preparing the table, a fork or spoon marginally out of place, or a wine glass which did not gleam sufficiently, brought down a tirade of fury upon his head. As the days went by he learned to avoid such trouble, even to earn the occasional word of praise until one evening he was summonded to the butler's presence.

"Wot you done now?" Tim nudged him good-naturedly "You been sniffin' round one of the maids again? 'E'll 'ave your 'ide and no mistake."

"I don't sniff round no maids." Nathan rounded on his friend. "Sarah is my girl and don't you think no other." He frowned. "And I don't know as how I've done wrong." He pulled himself to his feet. "I'd best go and see what old Blood and Guts wants me for."

A tap on the dark oak door brought an immediate response.

"Well, lad?"

"You sent for me Mr. Bentley."

The man frowned, his thin lips pursed in judgement. "You're to serve at table tonight. The Master has guests. Make one mistake and you are finished. Understand?"

Nathan's heart missed a beat. He swallowed and nodded eagerly. "Don't you worry, Mr. Bentley, I won't make no errors."

"See that you don't." A thin hand was waved in dismissal as Nathan hurried to find Tim.

"I'm serving tonight. Mr. Bentley said as 'ow the Master 'as guests."

Tim grinned. "You'd best watch me then. I done it lots of times. The best bit is if you listen, see." He winked. "Pick up all the gossip you can. They don't pay us no 'eed, long as it all goes smooth like. That's all they wants."

The afternoon saw a flurry of activity, piles of white table linen, sparkling crystal and polished silver were laid in the long dining room. Wine was decanted and floral arrangements strategically placed, all under the watchful eye of both the Butler and Nathan's Aunt.

The kitchen too was in turmoil, as Nathan knew from a few snatched moments with Sarah.

"Cook's in a fine state." She whispered. "Snappin' at all of us. The Master's borrowed one of the chefs from Audley. Ours for the night 'e is and 'e's throwing 'is weight about and shouting at everyone, cook included."

"Well don't you let 'im upset you, Sarah, or chef or no chef, I'll see 'im off!"

Sarah shook her head. "'E don't bother me. Now get back or you'll be missed." Nathan aimed a kiss at her cheek as she shooed him from the kitchen and he caught a laughing slap in payment.

As the guests began to arrive, Nathan was stationed with Tim in the grand hallway to take cloaks and hats before directing the men and their ladies to the drawing room.

Before dinner could be announced, a last-minute inspection by the Butler was conducted with military precision. Livery was checked for the slightest blemish and white-gloved hands displayed for eagle-eyed inspection as they listened in silence to last minute warnings of unimaginable consequences should the meal be served with anything less than perfection.

Nathan counted twenty guests as they made their way to table, each gentleman resplendent in evening dress and each accompanied by a beautifully gowned lady.

Once seated, and, at a signal from Mr. Bentley, the well-rehearsed army of footmen swung into action. The soup, ladled piping hot from a silver tureen, was met with murmured approval and a smile of satisfaction from the Master. Course followed course: Oysters, pheasant, a roast, a medley of vegetables and sweet confections, each accompanied by complementary wines. Silently and smoothly, each dish was cleared away and the next transported to the waiting diners.

Between the bursts of activity, Nathan stood beside Tim, hands clasped behind his ramrod-straight back. He watched and listened as, under the influence of good food and alcohol, the guests relaxed and tongues began to loosen. Tim was right, for, all the notice the assembled company took of them, they might just as well have been invisible.

It became obvious that the gentlemen were all worthies of the area, landowners in the main, some more vocal than others, yet all cut from the same cloth. Their conversation, he later realised, touched only on generalities, designed to include the ladies who eagerly exchanged gossip behind raised fans, gasping in mock horror or giggling at some neighbour's indiscretion. It was not until the meal was at an end that the ladies left, at the suggestion of Mrs. Benham, to take their coffee in the drawing room. Then Nathan began his education into current affairs.

He and Tim were left on duty when the other footmen were dismissed and, under the watchful eye of the Butler, were directed to offer cigars, brandy and a decanter of fine old port to the remaining guests.

"So, Brownley." The Master sat back, blowing a plume of smoke across the table, "What do'st thou think of the Liberals, eh? Earl Grey got his Great Reform Act passed through Parliament I hear."

The man the Master referred to as Brownley steepled his fingers, "I understand there's to be celebrations in Thaxted, but we won't see the like here in Saffron Walden. They know where their bread is buttered. While we hold the whip hand in this area the poor are well cared for. The new almshouse is all but ready to accommodate the elderly, the cattle market is already open and trading and a healthy stagecoach business makes work for carpenters and wheelwrights." He swirled the brandy in his glass, warming it in a cupped hand. "Then there's all the new building and road repairs needed at the moment. There's work for those who want to work I say." He drew on his cigar. "No, there'll be no trouble here, no trouble at all."

"Could be you're right Brownley." Another joined the conversation. "Though there have been riots and burnings not more than twenty miles away. Confounded incendiaries!" There were emphatic nods and murmurs of assent from all sides.

Nathan caught Tim's eye, raising an expressive eyebrow as another florid-faced worthy joined the discussion. "You're all blind if you can't see that there's trouble brewing. There's a group of reformers right here in the town. Soon every farmer and shopkeeper will have the right to vote. Where will we be then? I ask you."

The Master passed the decanter of port to his neighbour. "Well, the election in December will guage the mood of the county. We're to hold the poll here in Walden. To my mind it will need policing, I can foresee riots among those so disposed to trouble making. Now, what news of the railway?" The Master turned to a man Nathan guessed to be one of the major landowners in the county.

"I've told them they will never cross my land. I'll see them in hell first." The man brought his fist crashing down on the table, overturning his glass. "In hell, I tell you! No need to blight the countryside with rails and great steaming engines. Two good coaches a day take the road from here to London. What more do we need?"

"There are many who can see the advantages." Their host pointed out. "Freight, such as farm produce and sea food from the coast, would reach the markets faster and in better condition thee will have to admit."

It was the first Nathan had heard of the coming of the railway as far north as Saffron Walden, although there had been talk of a line into London along the Essex Estuary coastline. It seemed however that here in Walden there was opposition to the idea and that opposition, backed as it clearly was by Tory wealth, could well delay any further progress. Keen to know more, Nathan made a mental note to discuss the matter with his Aunt at the first opportunity.

It was not long before John Benham decided that as gentlemen, they had left the ladies alone for too long and, by mutual agreement, they made their way to join them in the drawing room. The footmen's work was not over, however, and for the next two hours they were in attendance, ready to cater to the needs and desires of the Master and his guests. By the time Tim and Nathan were relieved of their duties, and the last guest had departed, they were too tired to do more than fall gratefully into their beds in the knowledge that they would be roused before six the next day to begin again their daily round of chores.

"You were right, Tim." Nathan yawned. "You can learn a lot by listenin'. Seems there could be trouble on the way."

"Aye, but we be alright at the 'ouse. It's the poor buggers what work the land as I feel a mite sorry for. Me sister's man don't take 'ome enough to feed 'er and the young'uns and 'e works all the hours God sends 'im."

Nathan stared into the darkness. "Don't seem right. There must 'ave been enough money round that table tonight to make a deal of difference if it were shared out fair like."

"Don't go 'olding your breath waitin' for that to 'appen." Tim snorted. "The rich stays rich and the poor gets poorer my old Ma says."

"Well it sounds as if not everybody thinks the same way."

Tim turned over, dragging the covers up to his chin. "You'd best not side with 'em if you knows what's good for you. The Master does right by us and that's all that matters."

Nathan fell asleep, his mind filled with what he had learned that night, aware of his own security compared with those less fortunate in the world outside the great house.

It seemed that no time had passed before Nathan and Tim were roused to begin carrying coal to light the fires. The kitchen range needed stoking, giving him a few precious moments with Sarah who, out of Cook's watchful eye, blew him a tiny kiss from the tips of her fingers.

It was not until mid morning that he had cause to enter the library in answer to a call for coffee from the Master where he found the man poring over a newspaper.

As he set down the heavy silver tray, John Benham raised his head to focus on the young footman. "Thank thee lad." He rose to cross to the window, staring out across the immaculate lawns. "Thee were serving at dinner last evening were thee not?"

"Yes Sir." Nathan's mouth felt suddenly dry.

The man turned to stare at him. "I noticed that thee were listening closely to every word that was uttered."

"Yes Sir." For some reason Nathan felt that an apology was called for. "I'm sorry Sir if I......."

The Master raised a hand to silence him. "There is no need. Indeed, I wish to ask thee a question."

"Yes Sir?"

"Thee appear to be of above average intelligence, indeed thy Aunt tells me thou art determined to better thyself. I am interested to have thy opinion upon what passed between my guests after dinner; to see the other side of the coin. Understand?"

"My opinion Sir?" Nathan searched his mind for the right words.

"Speak up boy. And don't be afraid to speak the truth."

Nathan swallowed hard, nervously licking his lips. "Well Sir, it seemed to me that there's a sizeable gap between the worthies around your table and the folk outside, some who can hardly survive." Emboldened by John Benham's nod of understanding he raced on. "P'raps the wage for a good day's work should be a bit more. And, as for the railway coming, I think it must be a good thing for everyone. I come from down on the Estuary coast and it takes the better part of a day to get the fish to market by cart."

He saw a frown cross his master's face and wondered if he had gone too far.

"I thank thee boy. We will talk again." Thoughtfully John Benham stroked his chin. "In fact we shall talk later. I have a mind to pay a visit to the brewery. Thee will ride with me on the journey and tend to me on my rounds. Tell Bentley I shall need the carriage within the hour."

The Butler was far from pleased at Nathan's request. "Ride with the master? You've been here but a few days and he chooses you to accompany him? What of Peacock, the Master's own manservant? This is unheard of!"

Nevertheless the carriage was ordered and Nathan instructed to sit high on the box with the driver. John Benham was not alone and spent the journey through the countryside deep in conversation with his land agent, who, Nathan knew from his Aunt managed the Master's estates. Even Bentley knew better than to challenge Jake Barlow, who clearly had a privileged relationship with the master.

Their first port of call was on the outskirts of the village at one of several maltings owned by the Benham family. Nathan's Aunt had explained that the family's wealth came from brewing. They owned the majority of fields where the barley was grown, they owned the maltings where the grain was prepared and they owned the breweries together with a large chain of public houses. "Men will always want ale." She reminded him. "And the master employs a great many men to make it."

It seemed, however, that the building, which housed the malting process was all but deserted. The few workers in evidence were engaged in cleaning the drying racks and maintaining a variety of equipment.

Dutifully Nathan followed the owner around, carrying a satchel of books in his wake. At one point John Benham turned to him. "Well lad, any questions?"

"Yes Sir." Nathan approached the two men. "I was wondering where everyone was. It don't seem as there's much going on."

"Very observant." The Master smiled. "It is the wrong time of year. By October right through to May there will be thirty or more experienced men here and at my other maltings, working long hours and earning a good wage."

"Experienced?" Nathan frowned, eager to prolong the explanation.

"It takes years of knowledge to be able to judge the right moment to arrest the process of germination. The malted barley must be in just the right condition for brewing, see?"

"Why so interested?" The land agent turned to look more closely at Nathan.

Nathan shrugged, determined not to be overawed by the man's steely gaze. "I'm always keen to learn somethin' new. And." He added with a touch of justification. "The master did ask if I 'ad any questions."

"Quite right boy." John Benham nodded approvingly. "How else are thee to learn? He turned to the agent. "Now, if we are done here, I'll take a look at the Hartford End Brewery."

The journey across country gave time for Nathan to think, as, behind him, the conversation between the two men was of crops and yields, harvesting and malting.

In the fields on either side of the lane grew a lush growth of barley, standing tall but yet to ripen in the summer sun. Every now and again, the carriage swept past a group of farm labourers who made way, stepping into the ditch and knuckling their foreheads. Nathan began to realise that John Benham's net was cast wide over the Essex countryside, controlling not only the land but the men and women who worked upon it.

CHAPTER SEVENTEEN

Over the next few weeks it seemed that Jonas had taken Saffron at her word. By all reports he spent his days in the bar of The Smack alehouse. The unsavoury crowd he mixed with were strangers to an honest day's work, preferring to play cat and mouse with the Excise Men on moonless nights.

Many a cargo was smuggled ashore and hidden, awaiting transportation by donkeys, their hooves wrapped in rags to muffle the sound of their passage over the cobbled alleyways. Silk and brandy brought good prices inland, money which, she had been told, Jonas poured down his gullet until he became senseless.

Only once, when Saffron was on the way to Jean-Pierre, had he passed Saffron in the lane. The look of pure hatred he had shot in her direction and the muttered oath "Bitch" all but unnerved her. As angry words threatened to spring from her lips she looked away, determined not to sink to his level.

The effect of the encounter, however, did not go unnoticed by Jean-Pierre. "What is it, Saffron? What is wrong?" He took her gently by the shoulders, turning her to meet his anxious gaze. "You are so pale."

"It's nothin'." She pulled away, sitting to take up the now familiar pose by the open window. "Is this alright?"

"No, Saffron, it is not! How can I paint you when you are clearly so upset?" He paused, searching her face. "What is it I see? Fear? Anger?"

Her shoulders slumped. "A bit of both, I s'pose. It was Jonas." She half smiled at his expression of concern. "You must have heard the village gossip. I threw him out when he went for Poll."

"Tell me." He sat beside her taking her hands into his own. "I've heard tales but tell me what really happened."

She did, encouraged by his concern, the words came tumbling out. Her hatred for Jonas, her present worry for Poll and Nathan and her sense of responsibility for Tom.

Jean-Pierre listened intently until she ran out of words. Then, silently he stood, raising her into the circle of his arms. "Poor Saffron." He whispered against her hair. Spent, she relaxed against him, revelling in the security of his embrace, rubbing her cheek against the sweet smelling linen of his shirt. Reluctantly he held her from him before bending his head to claim her unyielding lips, his mouth firm yet undemanding.

With a bewildered gasp she raised protesting hands to his chest. "No!" She wriggled free, backing away from his outstretched arms. "No, I..I..."

"I know, Saffron Clay." He smiled. "You don't do nothing but sit!" He sobered suddenly. "I meant no harm. But you must know, must have suspected, that you have grown to mean more to me than merely a model, a lovely face for me to paint onto canvas." He turned from her suddenly to stare from the window. "I have a confession. The portrait was finished two days ago." He swung to face her. "I just could not let you go." He hung his head. "I am sorry I have deceived you."

"You say it's finished? "

"I know Saffron, I should have told you before. I believe it is the finest thing I have ever done." He crossed to the shrouded canvass to proudly throw back the cover and beckoned. "Come, see if you agree."

Caught up in his rush of enthusiasm, she ran to his side to stand wide-eyed in disbelief. "It's me." She breathed. "But it's not me. What have you done?"

"But it is you my beautiful girl." He insisted. "I have painted what you are too modest, too innocent to see. You have an inner light, Saffron, a wonderful, iridescent glow which illuminates your whole being. That is what I see."

The face which smiled back at her from the canvas did have a strange glow. It was as if it was lit from within, but there was more, a hint of something in the eyes, which she could not fathom.

She felt the weight of his arm encircle her shoulder and this time she did not move from his side. "What will you do now?"

"I shall take it to London. I have a friend who has a gallery frequented by the wealthy."

"You are goin' away?" Saffron felt a sudden sense of loss. "I shall miss you."

"And I you. I shall be gone no more than three or four days, I promise. When I return we will talk about the future."

She lifted her chin, frowning. "The future?"

"Our future." He corrected, bending his head to kiss the tip of her nose. "For I can think of no future without you Saffron Clay."

She left Juniper cottage, her head spinning from all that had happened, all that Jean-Pierre had implied, knowing that she had for too long been denying her own feelings, finding it impossible to believe that they could be returned. But now, she smiled to herself, perhaps there was to be a break in life's clouds and that at last the sun would find a way to shine through.

The moment of happiness, however, was to be short lived. Her rap on the oak door bought Tom to slide back the bolt, a finger raised to his lips. He nodded to where Poll sat by the range, her head buried in her hands.

"She's bin cryin'." He whispered, struggling to hold a squirming kitten clasped to his chest. "I'm glad you're back Saffy."

Saffron ruffled the boy's hair. "It's alright Tom I'll see to her now. You give that little mite back to it's mum and go wash your 'ands." Tom, happy to be relieved of the responsibility, scampered to do her bidding.

"Poll?" Saffron hung away her shawl and went to kneel beside her sister. "Poll. What's wrong? You were bright enough before I left. What's upset you?"

Poll raised her head, her face a picture of misery, her eyes wet with tears.

"I made up me mind, Saffy. I know what I got to do."

Saffron took Poll's limp hands into her own. "We talked about that. If you're right, it'll not be the first babe born out of wedlock hereabouts, and I wager it won't be the last. "We'll manage. Tongues'll soon stop waggin', you'll see. It won't take 'em long to find someone else to gossip about."

"No Saffy. I've got to get rid of it." She tore her hands from Saffron's grasp. "I've got to get it out of me." She clawed at her belly, her voice rising and tears spilling down her cheek. "Help me Saffy. Help me!"

"How?" Saffron took the hysterical girl into her arms. "How can I help you Poll? What do you want me to do?" She held Poll away the better to hear her muffled reply. "What did you say?"

Poll's response was little more than a whisper. "I wants you to go to Mother Watkins. She can 'elp me."

"Oh no, Poll, not that!" Horrified, Saffron sprang to her feet. She knew of many a child, unwanted in the womb had been denied life by one of the old crone's evil brews. She knew too that it was not without risk. Rumour had it that more than one young maids funeral party had climbed Horse Hill after seeking Mother Watkin's aid.

But Poll was adamant. "If you won't go for me Saffy, I'll go meself'." In the end she agreed to wait out the day and to think more about her decision.

"Sleep on it." Saffron pleaded. "Things'll look different on the morrow."

Poll, worn out by her own emotions, was persuaded to take to her bed for an hour's rest during the afternoon and was unaware of Gabriel's arrival at the cottage.

Reassured by the sound of his voice, Saffron hurried to let him in.

"Poll's restin'." She began. "But I'm glad you've come." She motioned him to sit. "I need to talk to you and it's best she's not 'ere."

Gabriel settled himself, stretching long legs beneath the table. "What is it, Miss Saffy, you looks like it's summat serious."

"It is." Saffron bit her lip not knowing where to start. "You know what happened to Poll up at the big 'ouse?"

"Aye, I know." He growled. "An' if I 'ad me way…."

Saffron laid a hand over the clenched fist that struck the table. "What's done can't be undone and the likes of you and me can't do nothin' to put it right. But that's not the half of it." She took a deep breath, avoiding his eyes, "Poll thinks she is with child." The words fell into a pit of silence, broken at last by Gabriel's quiet response.

"I feared as much." He stood to lean an arm on the mantle. "Who knows?"

"No one 'cept you and me."

"Best it stops that way for the time bein'."

"You don't understand." Saffron shook her head. "She wants to get rid of it. She says if I don't 'elp her she'll go to old Mother Watkins herself."

"No! I'll not 'ave that!"

Startled by his angry words, Saffron hastened to calm him. "I've told her, but she won't listen. I was hopin' you'd 'talk to 'er. You seems to 'ave a way with 'er."

For what seemed an age, Gabriel was silent. One emotion after another chasing its way over his gentle features until at last he seemed to come to a decision.

"Miss Saffy." He began. "I had thought to take things slow, but I got to speak now." He cleared his throat. "I've had it in me mind since I first set eyes on Poll. I wants to marry 'er." Anxiously he searched Saffron's face for her approval. "I love 'er Miss Saffy. She's the sweetest, dearest girl and I wants to take care of 'er." He paused, squaring his broad shoulders. "And the babe too."

Saffron stared open-mouthed at his determination. "But she's so young." She tried to find the right words. "And to take on another man's child…." She left the sentence unfinished.

"I know she's not sixteen 'till next month but I'm sure she has feelings for me, though I ain't much of a catch. If we marries I can 'elp 'er through, and I'll not touch 'er till she's ready, that I can promise." He frowned. "As for the babe, I'll treat it as me own. Folk'll 'ave nothin' to chew over. There's many a young'un born afore time."

Saffron's thoughts were in turmoil. Poll married? And her not much more than a child herself. Yet, she saw a quiet strength in the man before her, a strength that could well be what was needed if Poll were to recover in body and mind.

"You'll 'ave to ask 'er." She put a hand on the rough cloth of his sleeve. "But you 'ave my blessing Gabriel. You're a good man and I know you'll do your best to make Poll 'appy. There's not much to offer but I'd be pleased if you'd stay for a meal, then mayhap you could walk her down to the shore and talk it over."

"Thank you Miss Saffy." His sigh of relief was audible. "I'm obliged to you."

He turned to look around the cottage. "Now where's Tom I said as 'ow I'd give 'im an 'and to finish that boat 'e's been whittlin' away at."

"You'll find 'im out back, in the yard I think, playing with those kittens."

Saffron watched, shaking her head as the big man ducked his head to clear the low doorframe. Gabriel Stoneforth was a giant of a man and had shown that he had a heart to match.

CHAPTER EIGHTEEN

In their few moments of leisure following the evening meal,
Tim had been eager to hear about Nathan's journey with the
Master and Nathan was willing to recount every step of the
way in detail.

"You should see the barley, Tim, acres and acres of it."
He spread his arms wide. "'Course it's not ready for harvest
yet." He was proud to show his knowledge. "Then we went
on to the Maltings. Funny place that were. Only a few men
working, cleaning up and wiping down the racks. Master said
that's where they spread the barley grain and let it do something called 'fermenting'. He said they soak it in water first
then they dries it in a kiln. Tricky business, he said, they has to
stop what's happening at just the right moment if it's to make
good beer."

"I like a good drop of ale." Tim smacked his lips. "So what
'appens then?"

"They carts it off to the brewery, that's where they adds some
other stuff, sugar and such I think." He took a deep breath. "I
didn't get much of a look at everything there but I can tell you
there's some vats, they call 'em, big enough to swim in if you
had the mind, all full of lovely bubbling beer in the making."
He leaned back thoughtfully, staring up at the star studded sky.
"Reckon a bloke could be right happy working in a place like
that."

Tim gave his friend a good-natured nudge. "You count your
blessin's, you got a good place 'ere. Don't you go thinkin' no
daft thoughts 'bout working in no brewery."

"'T'aint daft to want to better meself. 'Sides, if I was to get
put on there or at one of the Master's alehouses somewhere

nearby, I could ask Sarah to marry me." He slanted a sideways look at Tim. "You know they don't allow no married couples to work under the same roof. So if I wants to make Sarah my wife, one of us would have to go and she loves it here."

Tim was silent for a moment. "I'd miss you mate, me an' you 'ave 'ad some good laughs."

"Well, don't go missing me yet, I saw a lot on the road what made me think. I got some studying to do before I can better myself. I saw some what was so poor, the young'uns looked like they was starving." He shook his head. "Someone needs to do a bit of changing to the way things are done."

Tim's sudden roar of laughter shook Nathan from his thoughts. "You'll be tellin' me next you're a going politicin'!" He leaped to his feet and stood offering a mocking bow to his friend. "Pleased to meet you me Lord. An' did you put the world right today or will you be doin' that on the morrow?"

Nathan made a playful swipe at the lad. "No, my man." He affected the tone of the worthies. "I shall leave that sort of thing until after the hunting season. Such a bind you know, such a bind."

Laughing, they made their way back into the brightly lit kitchen where Tim crossed to the range to lift the lid of one of the steaming pots, sniffing the contents appreciatively. Sarah stood with her hands on hips, a frown marring her pretty face. "You two'll be in trouble if you don't get to fillin' the scuttles for the morning fires. Sittin' out there gigglin' like idiots, you should be ashamed."

"I ain't ashamed of nothing!" Nathan took advantage of the Cook's temporary absence from the kitchen to sweep the girl into his arms, swinging her round until she pleaded for him to stop, before kissing her parted lips.

"Put me down, you fool. If Cook comes back we'll both be

dismissed and I'll never speak to you again." She pushed him away but her smile told a different story.

Nathan sat heavily on a stool, spreading his legs to the heat of the range.

"I was just telling Tim how I'm planning to go up in the world." He reached out to pull her to his side. "And I'll be taking you with me my lovely Sarah." He looked long and hard at the girl's face, flushed from the heat of the fire. "I think it's about time you took me home to meet your folk. Next half day. I told you, I've a mind to meet your father, there's something important I want to ask him."

"Oh, and what might that be?"

"Don't you look at me like that, all innocent, you know what I mean, Sarah." Nathan had become suddenly serious. "I wants to ask him if he could see his way to having me as a Son-in-Law."

"You don't know what you're lettin' yourself in for." She chuckled. "I got a big family and they'll all want to look you over." She counted on the fingers of one hand. "There's Matthew, he's my eldest brother, and 'is wife, then there's Luke, 'e's next one down. Then comes Cissy, and Jane and little Bobby but 'e's only a baby. Ma and Pa said six of us was enough for any God fearing family."

"I should think so too!" Nathan grinned. "'Specially if they're all like you. So Matthew's married is he? Are there any little ones?"

"The last I heard there was one on the way. Matthew's got a trade." There was unmistakable pride in her voice. "He was 'prenticed to a carpenter an' now he works for 'imself. Luke's been working with the local blacksmith, big strong lad 'e is. I came next and it won't be long 'afore Cissy is lookin' to be taken on somewhere."

"Sounds like a right nice family. I can't wait to meet them. What about your Ma and Pa, d'you think I'll pass muster?"

"I shouldn't wonder but don't go carryin' on about what you hear at the Master's table or you will set Pa off. 'E goes on fearful strong about somethin' he calls 'inequality'. Once you get him started, there's no stoppin' 'im, and Ma won't thank you for it!"

"Your Pa and me, we seem to have the same thoughts, I reckon we'll get along just fine. So, it's fixed then. Next half day, we'll get things settled."

"P'raps! But you seems to 'ave overlooked somethin'." Sarah pulled away with a swish of her skirts, turning to look at him through lowered lashes. "I ain't said yet as 'ow I'll marry you."

"Well get it said!" Cook's voice from the open doorway startled them. "I can't stand 'ere all night while you two get round to makin' up your minds!"

She bustled over to the range, lifting the lid of one of the pots hanging there. "Make your mind up girl." She turned to smile at Sarah. "You won't get a better catch than young Nathan. 'E'll be going places, you mark my words." She gave Nathan a push. "Go on lad, give 'er a kiss and then get out of my kitchen. You too Tim, I've got things to do."

Nathan felt his cheeks flame with momentary embarrassment and before she could stop him he had aimed a peck on the cheek of the cook. "You're a fine woman, Mrs Rand and I thank you for your words of wisdom." Grabbing Sarah around her waist, he kissed her soundly, releasing her to hold her at arms length. "Marry me woman, or I'll spend the rest of my life wishing you had."

Sarah raised fingers to her tingling lips, her eyes sparkling with joy. "Yes, Nathan, I'll marry you." She paused. "So long as Pa says I can."

"You leave that to me. 'Tis well known, no one can resist my charm. I'll have him eating out of my hand." He caught Cook's eye. "But right now I'd best be seeing to the scuttles for I can see Cook hefting a wicked looking rolling pin and she's coming my way!"

He and Tim ran from the kitchen toward the coal bins in the yard and began to shovel the fuel into the waiting scuttles. "You gone quiet Tim." Nathan panted. "Ain't you got nothing to say?"

Tim leaned on his shovel scratching his head. "I was just thinkin' what a lucky bugger you was. You come 'ere without a seat to your britches, get set on in the stables and, before you knows it, you're workin' in the 'ouse. Then there's Sarah, prettiest maid I ever seen, goes and says yes when you asks 'er to wed. What you got that I ain't? That's what I'd like to know."

"What have I got?" Nathan wiped his sleeve across his forehead. "Let's see. I can read and write and I'm fast learning about accounting. I'm doing my best to talk like the gentry, 'cause it seems to matter to some." He dug his shovel deep into the pile of coal. "And I've got what's called ambition." He threw the load into the nearest scuttle, pausing to stare into the distance. "I remember my father saying to me. 'Listen lad, the man who aims for the stars gets further than the one who aims for the trees'." He bent again to his task. "Didn't know what he meant then but he was right and Tim." He stopped, his loaded shovel poised over the scuttle. "Tim, I reckon I'll be aiming for the stars."

Sleep seemed to escape Nathan that night. He tossed and turned, as thoughts of the future drew pictures on the canvas of his mind. He knew that for the time being, his place in the house, providing he kept to the rules, was secure. But it was not enough. Tim's question had forced him to appraise his situation and to make a plan. Thanks to his Aunt, his education was going ahead by leaps and bounds. Then there was the interest shown in him by the Master and who knew what that could lead to? It was almost dawn before he fell asleep, only to be roused by a bleary-eyed Tim.

"Come on your Lordship." The boy yawned, struggling into his britches. "Time to start serving our betters."

"They ain't our betters." Nathan snorted, reluctantly swinging his legs to the floor. "They're just richer." He yawned, stretching his arms high above his head. "They were born in the right bed is all. They just got to the stars before me." He grinned at his friend. "But if I have my way, I ain't going to be far behind."

CHAPTER NINETEEN

It was several days before Poll gave Gabriel his answer, days during which she veered between hope and despair.

"I know 'e's a good man, Saffy." She reasoned. "But I don't know as 'ow I love 'im, though 'e does make me feel sort of safe and warm inside. And then there's this." She smoothed a hand over her belly. "If we wed soon, 'e says, no one would be a wit wiser. Oh Saffy, what's to do for the best?"

"I can't tell you, Poll." Saffron perched on the edge of her sister's bed running her hand over the sun-dappled patchwork cover. "But layin' 'ere won't give you no answers. All I know is I prayed 'ard for the good Lord to point the way. P'raps 'e sent Gabriel to put things right." She patted her sister's hand. "Now up you get and give me some 'elp. Those sheets need a wash and it's a good day for dryin'." She half closed the door then looked back at Poll. "And it's a good day too for makin' up your mind!"

Gabriel returned later in the day to find Poll waiting at the cottage door. Encouraged by her shy smile he took her arm. "You're lookin' fine this day Miss Polly. That's a right pretty dress."

Poll blushed. "I thought as 'ow we could take a walk as far as the Strand Quay." She lowered her eyes. "That is if you wants to."

"That I do, and proud I'll be to be seen with you." He took her hand, linking her arm with his own.

Saffron watched them go with a prayer on her lips. If her sister accepted Gabriel's proposal, plans for a hasty wedding would have to be made. There was no money for finery or feasting, just a quiet ceremony at the hill top church would have to suffice. But upon their return it became obvious that an elated Gabriel had other ideas.

"I've put a bit by and my Poll is going to 'ave a real fine wedding". He beamed. "We'll get the bans read this Sunday and tell the vicar there's to be a marriage service in three weeks time."

"Three weeks?" Poll found her voice. "But I got no weddin' dress nor no 'ope chest neither."

"You got a dress." Saffron smiled. "Our Mother's weddin' dress has been packed away, just waitin' for this day. An' as for an 'ope chest, I'll wager you won't 'ave need of one, will she Gabriel?"

"There's a home ready and waitin' for you, Poll. 'Tis only small but it's not tied. My Jenny and me, we took a pride in makin' it nice. You'll find all you need there."

"You don't never talk about your wife Jenny." Poll hung her head. "Do you still love 'er Gabriel?"

"I loves her memory Poll." He took her in his arms. "She was a sweet-natured woman and we were happy together for the short time God gave us. I believe if she could speak now she'd say as 'ow I was doin' the right thing." He hugged Poll to his broad chest. "She knows I bin lonely and she'd want us to be 'appy." He held her away to look deep into her eyes. "The two of us, no the three of us, we'll make a new beginnin'." He grinned at Saffron and Tom. "Best spread the news around Miss Saffy. There's going' to be a weddin' here in Leigh."

News of the impending marriage travelled quickly through the fishing village and while there were some who with sly smiles questioned the seemingly hurried arrangements, many more wished the couple every happiness.

The date had been set to coincide with Poll's sixteenth birth-day and Gabriel's daily visits brought about in Poll a welcome change of heart concerning the child she carried.

The following day, Poll bent her head over her sewing. "Gabriel says as 'ow 'e'll treat the baby like 'is own. If it's a boy we're to call it Peter after 'is father, a fine man 'e were by all accounts."

"And if it's a girl?" Saffron held her needle to the light, the better to thread it.

Polly put her head on one side. "I likes the name Jessica. What do you think, Saffy?"

"Jessica Stoneforth. Jessy. Yes it has a nice ring to it. Now up you get and let's try this against you." She held her mother's wedding dress up for inspection. "It'll need taking up a bit, you being shorter than Mother. You'd best slip it on, so's we can see." Saffron gathered the soft sprigged muslin to slip it over Poll's chemise, tugging it into place over the slender body. "We'll still need to take it in a bit more here and there but you made a nice job of the sleeves."

Poll smiled, praise from Saffron was always welcome. "Can I wear some flowers in me 'air? You know like Annie Provost did on 'er wedding day?" She paused. "I wants to look nice for Gabriel. 'E keeps sayin' as 'ow I'm pretty."

"An' so you are, Poll, real pretty. An' you're goin' to be lovely at the weddin'. I reckon Gabriel will be right proud when you walks down the aisle." She held the folds of the dress as Poll struggled free, and saw the girl frown as she smoothed her long hair into place.

"Do you think we'll be 'appy, Saffy?"

Saffron hung the dress over the back of the settle. "That's not for me to say, Poll. All I know is that Gabriel's a good man and I think 'e loves you." She turned to rest an arm along the mantle shelf. "In time you might grow to love 'im the same way. Mother used to say as 'ow marriage were a partnership like. You each got to do what's needed to make the other one 'appy. Gabriel's job is to bring 'ome the money and yours'll be to keep a good 'ouse and bring up the children."

"Children?" Poll's surprise was evident. "What d'you mean?"

Saffron smiled. "You got to know that Gabriel might want some of 'is own as well as the one you're carryin'."

"I s'pose so. I 'ad'nt thought that far." Poll glanced at her sister "I reckon that'll mean we got to, you know." She bit her lip leaving the sentence unfinished.

"Of course." Saffron pulled her sister down onto the settle and took her hands. "But it won't be the same as before, Poll. Gabriel is a gentle man, and 'e'll wait 'till you're ready. It's somethin' wonderful, Mother said, what happens between two people who want to show 'ow much they love each other." For a moment, she saw herself in JeanPierre's arms and knew with certainty, that indeed, it would be a wonderful moment. Dismissing the thought, she got to her feet. "Don't you worry none, Poll. Everythin' will work out, you'll see."

The moment was lost as the door crashed back on its hinges to admit a panting, red-faced Tom. "Saffy, I just seen Pa, 'e tried to grab me." He gasped, glancing nervously over his shoulder, "I got away, but 'e's in a fine rage!"

"I told you not to go near 'im." Saffron hurried to close the door and bent to take the child into her arms. "What got him so riled up?"

Tom hung his head. "I was listenin' to 'im talkin' to that Sam 'oskins. They was sittin' in the Peter Boat and I was 'iding from Colin under one o' the benches. We was playing 'ide and go seek."

"You should'nt 'ave been in no ale 'ouse, you know that." Saffron scolded, "But what was it they said what got 'im so mad."

As he wiped a grubby hand over his face, she saw the fear in the boy's eyes.

"They said there was goin' to be a wreckin' on the Maplins and they was laughin' about what they was goin' to do."

"A wreckin'?" Saffron's hand flew to her mouth. "When? Tom, did they say when?" Regardless of the man's brutal nature, when all was said and done, Jonas was the boy's father and the thought of him being caught and probably hanged, filled her with dread. Since the new Customs House had been built in the village, the Excise men were constantly on the lookout for smugglers; but the crime of wrecking was evil, for it was often accompanied by the murder of the vessel's unfortunate crew.

Tom shook his head miserably. "Soon, I reckon." He muttered. "Soon. What'll we do, Saffy?"

"I don't know Tom, and that's a fact. I'll 'ave to think on it." She glanced toward the small window. "It'll not be for a few nights yet, the moon's on the wain; but they'll have to wait for a dark night or heavy cloud and if I'm any judge, that won't be for a while. I'll tell you what, we'll ask Gabriel, 'e'll know what's best."

Relief spread over Tom's young face. "Aye, Gabriel will know. Will he tell the Excise d'you think?"

"No Tom." Saffron's voice was firm. "That 'e won't do. We'll find a way to stop your Pa but it won't be by tellin' no one from the Custom 'ouse. Now, you keep it to yourself, you understand?"

Relieved of the burden of responsibility, Tom settled at the table for his daily lesson, coached by his elder sister Poll. Head bent in the set task, he was unaware of the look, which passed between the two girls. If Jonas had followed the boy back to the cottage, there could be trouble. Saffron shook her head and put a finger to her lips as, quietly, she closed and slid home the bolt on both back and front doors, which had been open to allow a passage of air.

Fewer and fewer smuggled cargoes had come ashore 'over the wall' since the Custom House had been built in the centre of the village. Sharp-eyed officers missed very little on shore, and, the same could be said of the crew of the fast Revenue Cutter which patrolled the coastline.

Jonas was a fool to take such a risk. Absentmindedly, Saffron began to sweep the cinders from the hearth, only half listening to Tom's recital of his tables. Smuggling had always been common in Leigh, many a night, she had listened to her father tell tales of the trade; of false-bottomed craft and barrels of Gin, roped together and tossed over the side to be grappled and brought ashore at the dead of night. As a small child, she could remember seeing from her window on a sleepless night, the ghostly string of donkeys, the sound of their passage over the cobbles made silent on muffled hooves. Each animal, she later learned, had been laden with smuggled tea and brandy for the eager, wealthy buyers further inland. But, as Nathan had said, unlike the gangs across the Estuary in Kent, the Leigh men were not usually given to violence. Occasionally, though, a few of them would anchor their small craft off the Maplin Sands with their lights riding high on their masts. Lured onto the mudflats, believing the lights marked a passage of deep water, some unfortunate and heavily laden vessel would run aground and be grateful for the willing hands who would offer to unload part of their cargo, to allow the ship to float. Once unloaded, the goods were spirited away, never to be recovered. Harmless enough sport it was said, but on more than one occasion the ship's crew had refused to co-operate. In the fighting, lives had been lost. Of late, she knew from village gossip, the Excise men had tightened their net and penalties had been extreme.

It was almost midday when Saffron glanced at the clock, Jean-Pierre had said he would be back from London that day but he would have to wait. Her place was at the cottage with Tom and Poll, at least, until Gabriel returned and the danger had passed.

CHAPTER TWENTY

Jane Porter's determination to improve her nephew's education was relentless. The hour spent each day under her eagle eye began to pay dividends.

"Your diction has improved considerably Nathan and your accounting skills show a genuine aptitude."

Nathan bathed in the warmth of one of his aunt's rare smiles. "'Tis." He stopped to correct himself. "It is all thanks to you Aunt Jane."

She sat to pour from the china teapot, pushing a plate of fruit-cake toward him. This was his favourite moment, when his lesson over, he could discuss the many events of the day. The housekeeper who was an intelligent woman and was politically well informed, encouraged Nathan to air his growing store of knowledge, playing devil's advocate to his opinions.

After one heated discussion she shook her head. "You must learn to state your viewpoint calmly and clearly Nathan, that way men will listen." She wagged a finger at him. "Bluff and bluster weakens your case."

"I know you're right." He grinned. "I was serving at dinner a couple of nights ago and they were all shouting the odds, then Jack Walker waits until they've all run out of puff and quietly says his piece. You should have seen them. Their mouths just dropped open. They all just sat there not able to think of anything to say." He chuckled. "I could hardly stop myself from giving him a cheer."

"You had best not let the master catching you doing any such thing!"

"As if I would, Aunt. I know when I'm well off." He swallowed a mouthful of cake. "But I don't always want to be a footman." He lifted his cup in a toast. "So, here's to the future, whatever it may be."

"Take care, Nathan. By all means set your sights high but plan your journey well." The woman rose, brushing an imaginary crumb from her skirt. "Now, be on your way and attend to your duties."

Nathan made his way to the kitchen, knowing that Sarah would be helping Mrs Rand to prepare the evening meal. He peered around the door and caught the cook's eye. Raising a finger to his lips he crept over the where Sarah, her back turned to him, was rolling out a slab of pastry. The older woman had grown fond of the lad and smiled knowingly.

Sarah squealed in surprise as, reaching her, he wrapped his arms around her slim waist and bent his head to kiss her neck.

Laughing, she rounded on him. "Nathan, I'll get you!" She threatened him with flour-covered hands, chasing him around the table.

"Now, you two!" The cook flapped her hands, "Nathan, leave the girl alone. I got a job for you, so smarten yourself up and stop playin' the fool."

Nathan sobered immediately. "Sorry, Cook." He winked at Sarah. "What d'you want me to do?"

"The others are all busy, so you'll 'ave to take the tray up to the nursery." She lifted the edge of a napkin, revealing a plate of tiny sandwiches, cake and a jug of milk. "Now listen. You go up the main stairs to the top floor. It's the door on the left. Then you puts the tray on the little table at the side. You knocks and you comes straight back 'ere. Understand?"

"So I just leave it outside? Why can't I can't I carry it in?"

"'Cause nobody goes in there 'cept the nurse, Mrs. Porter." She looked away. "And sometimes the Master." She saw Nathan's puzzled expression. "Don't ask no questions, lad, just do as you're bid."

He shrugged and lifting the tray, made for the door. "If you say so." He said grudgingly. "But it seems a bit funny if you ask me."

"Well you ain't bin asked 'ave you?" The Cook frowned. "And you won't if you know what's good for you."

Curiosity accompanied Nathan's every step as he carried the tray to the top floor of the house. The small table the cook had described stood to one side of a door from behind which, came the unmistakable sound of a child crying. Nathan set the tray onto the table and put his ear to the oak panel. To his surprise the door swung open to reveal the room beyond. Comfortably furnished, a cheerful fire, surrounded by a mesh guard, crackled in the hearth, throwing its light on the polished brass rail. To one side sat a sleeping woman in a deep armchair and at her feet, his body rocking from side to side, sat a small boy, crooning miserably to himself.

Mindful of the cook's warning, Nathan made to close the door but the movement caught the child's eye and scrambling to his feet he made a stumbling run in an attempt to escape through Nathan's legs and out onto the landing beyond.

"No you don't young man!" Nathan caught him and lifted him aloft. "You're not supposed to go out there I'm sure. You'll go head over heels down the stairs." The boy wriggled in his grasp, turning to look into the face of his captor. For a moment Nathan regarded the child with disbelief bordering on pity. The little mite's face was flat, his slanted eyes all but closed and the tip of a fat pink tongue explored a wide mouth distorted in a parody of a smile.

"Well, you're a funny little chap and no mistake." Nathan recovered his good nature as the child wrapped his arms around his neck and planted an enthusiastic wet kiss on his cheek. Pushing the thin fringe of hair from the boy's forehead, Nathan set him gently down, but the child let out a howl of dismay and Nathan found himself unable to move as small yet surprisingly strong arms locked around his knees. The boy's distressed cry woke the sleeping nurse who got hurriedly to her feet, her eyes wide with horror.

"What you doing here? You ain't got no right!" She ran to grab the child. "You get out." She shouted above the boy's screams of protest. Nathan needed no second telling and as he backed away the enraged woman slammed the door in his face. For a moment he stood undecided as to the best course of action. Obviously the child was the responsibility of the woman he assumed was the nurse. Equally, it was obvious that the little lad was in need of comfort for his screams mingled with the woman's pleas for quiet still echoed within the room. At last he shrugged. There was nothing he could do but the boy's misery tugged at his heart.

Trying to make sense of the encounter he made his way back to the kitchen.

"Why lad, you look worried." The cook wiped her hands on her apron. "What's up with you?"

"I saw him." Nathan shook his head. "Poor little bastard."

The cook's sharp intake of breath was audible. "I told you.." She began.

"I know what you said Cook but it wasn't my fault." The heat in the kitchen was oppressive and he loosened the neck of his shirt. Sarah put down the apple she was peeling and hurried to his side, pushing him into a chair.

"What happened Nathan, what are you on about?"

Quietly, he explained how the nursery door had swung open and what had taken place.

"That door should have been locked like it always is." Cook

raised her eyes to heaven. "I said it before and I'll say it again. That there nurse is too old to look after the boy. She'll be in trouble with the Master I can tell you." There was a note of satisfaction in her words. "Wouldn't be surprised if he sent her packing."

"But who is the little chap, and what's he doing shut up like that? It's a right shame." Nathan took Sarah's hand. "He's about the same age as our Tom by my reckoning. A bit of sun wouldn't do him no harm."

"He ain't never been out." The cook sat, resting her elbows on the table "He's not right, see. He what's called a Lammas Lamb." She saw Sarah's puzzled frown. "A babe what's born too late in his mother's childbearing years." She leant forward, lowering her voice. "It's what sent the mistress strange, so they say. She ain't never been the same they say since the day he was born."

"But what's wrong with him?" Sarah was not to be put off.

The cook got to her feet. "All I know is he ain't right up 'ere." She tapped her head. "I was 'ere when 'e was born. There was a lot of rushin' and hushin' that day, I can tell you. I ain't never seen him and you'll wish you 'adn't neither lad." The woman tugged her apron into place. "I s'pose the little mite's luckier than most like im. They usually get shut away in a 'sylum. But the master's bound to find out you seen 'im and then they'll be ructions, you mark my word."

The cook's words proved to be prophetic when a stoney-faced Bentley informed Nathan that he was require to report to the master immediately following dinner that evening.

Later, as he tapped on the library door he waited for the familiar summons to enter. John Benham was slumped in a leather wing-backed chair by the wide hearth and without looking up he beckoned to Nathan to step forward.

"Well, what have thee to say?" Nathan shuffled uncomfortably.

"I'm sorry Sir. The door was open and it sort of swung wide. All I did was lay my head against it."

"And, pray why would thee do that?"

"I heard a child crying Sir."

"And thee thought to make it thy business?" For the first time the master raised his eyes, his expression stern and uncompromising. "I am disappointed in thee boy. I understand thee were told never to enter the nursery and yet thee saw fit to disobey."

"Yes Sir." Nathan squared he shoulders against the unjustified accusation. "All I did was stop the lad running out of the door. His nurse was sleeping, he could have fallen down the stairs and been hurt." He paused, deciding that he might as well be hung for a sheep as a lamb. "And pardon me for saying so, Sir, but I can't blame the poor little chap. Shut up all day by all accounts."

John Benham regarded him steadily. "Take care." He growled. "Thou are in danger of overstepping the mark."

"Then I'm sorry, Sir, but I've got a brother about the same age and he'd go mad if he was shut up like that. Growing young'uns need a bit of sun and God's good air."

The older man got slowly to his feet and crossed to gaze from the window onto the estate, which, if things had been different, would have been a legacy for his only son. "I have no doubt that by now thou knows the story. Five years ago, my dear wife gave birth to the son we had longed for, but within days it became obvious that the child was impaired both mentally and physically." He turned to stare at Nathan. "His mother has never set eyes on him from that day to this."

"But he's a lovely little mite." Nathan protested, throwing caution to the winds. "All he needs is someone to take an interest, give him a bit of love."

Sadly the man shook his head. "Thou cannot understand, the doctors tell me that he is beyond help. He neither speaks nor seems to understand the most simple words. I fear he will not live to reach manhood. Better he spends what time he has secluded from public gaze and ridicule." He sat heavily at the desk, silhouetted against the failing light. "What am I to do with thee? Can I trust thee to say nothing of what thee know? It would be a pity if I had to let thee go."

Nathan saw a rosy future begin to fade. "You can rely on me Sir. I know how to keep my mouth shut. But I've got an idea."

John Benham's mouth twisted into a wry smile. "And what might that be?" He raised a warning finger. "Bear in mind I have not yet arrived at a decision concerning thy present employment."

Nathan swallowed hard. "Well, Sir, I was thinking I could spend some time with the boy. He sort of took to me and it would give the nurse a breather." He added hopefully.

He watched as the man steepled long fingers, pursing his lips in consideration of Nathan's proposal. "To what end?" He said at last. "I have told thee of the doctor's diagnosis."

Nathan studied his shoes. "I think I could sort of get to him somehow. Teach him. I don't know, Sir, it's just a feeling." He shrugged. "I'd like to try, Sir."

"Thou would spend thy free time with my son?"

Nathan smiled. "I would, Sir." He pushed home his advantage. "Perhaps I could take him down the back stairs and into the little walled garden at the rear. We could go when the workers are having their dinner. That way no one need see him." He waited, trying to gauge whether he had gone too far.

The boy's father stood head bowed in thought. "Very well, thee may try just once. If the child is in any way distressed thee will return him to the nursery immediately, and that will be the end of it." He looked up at Nathan. "Remember I hold thee personally responsible. Now, return to thy duties and say nothing to anyone other than thy aunt and Bentley. Dost thou understand?"

"I do Sir, and I thank you."

On his return, Tim was eager to know what had passed between Nathan and the master, but he had to be satisfied with a cautious version of the truth. Mary Clay however, learned the whole story later that night.

"One of these days Nathan." She said. "You will take too much upon yourself and your luck will desert you. When do you start your new duty?"

"On the morrow, Aunt."

"Very well, I will inform Bentley in order that no awkward questions may be asked concerning your absence."

By the time he was relieved of his duties, Nathan was grateful to fall exhausted into bed. The next day would hold a challenge, one that he prayed to God he would be equal to. His last thoughts were of John Benham and his broken hearted wife, of their headstrong privileged daughter Sophie and of the child locked away from sight. He recalled his mother's words. "Money can't buy you happiness." It seemed she was right.

CHAPTER TWENTY ONE

Throughout the day Saffron's impatience had turned to irritability. Gabriel was not due to call on Poll until evening and she was badly in need of someone with whom to share the load.

She paced the small cottage, peering from the window every few minutes, hopefully scanning the cobbled street, yet fearing the appearance of her angry and almost certainly drunken stepfather.

By late afternoon Jean-Pierre was the first to arrive. The reassuring sound of his voice and his urgent knocking brought her to hurriedly slide back the heavy bolt and thrown wide the door. Before she could protest the young man took her into his arms and swung her round before setting her gasping on her feet.

"Oh, Saffy, Saffy." He cupped her startled face with both hands. "Beautiful Saffy. You are going to be famous! Famous!" He repeated, beaming.

She struggled free, aware of Tom and Poll's open-mouthed surprise. Tucking her hair into place and straightening her dress she fought to regain her composure.

"Jean-Pierre Howard, are you mad?" She stared at him. "You're grinnin' like an idiot. What's all this about me being famous?"

"I'm grinning my dear wonderful girl, because not only did I sell your portrait for a fine sum but I have commissions for two more." He rested a gentle hand on her shoulder. "But they must be paintings of the same mysterious, beautiful woman."

"Mysterious? There's nothing mysterious about me!" She felt her cheeks redden at the unmistakable compliment.

"Oh but you are. Everyone wanted to know your identity."

He chuckled. "But I wouldn't tell them. Oh, my dear, you should have heard them." He shook his head. "First they were sure that you were some foreign princess. Then a supposedly knowledgeable art critic decided that no living woman could have such beauty and that you were surely a figment of my imagination."

"What's a figment?" Tom had sidled over to stand hanging on John-Pierre's every word.

The artist bent to lift the boy into his strong arms. "It means something that's not real, something I must have dreamed about."

"Saffy's real." The boy reached out to wind his fingers in his sister's sun-kissed hair. "Feel!" He demanded.

John-Pierre stretched long fingers to stroke Saffron's cheek. "You're right Tom. She is real." His voice softened. "But she is also the stuff that dreams are made of." Gently, he set Tom down to turn and take Saffron's hands. "Say you will sit for me again." His gaze was steady, his dark eyes silently pleading for her agreement.

"If you want." Was all she could utter. The knowledge that she could continue to spend hour after hour with him filled her with a breathless excitement. She swallowed hard. "When do you want to start then?"

"Tomorrow." He smiled eagerly. "As soon as possible."

"Saffy." Poll's quiet words broke the silence. "What 'bout Jonas? 'Addn't you best tell 'im what's bin 'appening?"

Saffron's hand flew to her mouth. "You're right Poll." She felt suddenly ashamed. "I don't know what I was thinking." She took a step back from Jean-Pierre. "I got something I've got to tell you and I need some help."

"Anything, Saffron, anything. Just tell me what is wrong."

"Can I tell 'im Saffy, can I?" Tom ran to hug her skirts.

She bent to brush back a curl from the eager, upturned face. "All right, Tom. But tell it straight, alright?"

The boy nodded, aware of the responsibility as he repeated all he had overheard at the Inn. As he listened, Jean-Pierre's face clouded angrily.

"So you see we don't know what to do for the best." Saffron concluded the boy's tale. "Wrecking is a hanging offence." Miserably, she turned away. "'E might be a wicked man in some ways, but 'e wasn't always. 'Afore Ma died 'e were different. 'E's Tom's Pa when all's said and done." She wrung her hands in despair. "There must be somethin' we can do to stop it."

"There is." Jean-Pierre straightened. "I have a friend at the Custom's House. We have often shared a pleasant hour at the Smack Inn." He raised a hand to prevent Saffron's protest. "I shall mention no names, merely tell him to watch for the next moonless night, for I have heard that there is mischief afoot. It's got to be done. If the Excise Cutter can get to the wreckers before some poor sailor loses his life, then it's something I've got to do." He raised his head, looking at each of them in turn. "You do understand don't you?"

Saffron chewed her lip. "But that'll mean Jonas will be caught."

"Not if we can prevent him from being there. He must be warned." The young man crossed to the sit heavily on the wooden settle. "Do you have paper and pen?" Saffron nodded and hurried to find a piece of wrapping paper and one of Tom's pencil stubs. "I shall write a short note to Jonas and leave it on the bar of the Peter Boat." Jean-Pierre bent his head to the task. "No one will know that it came from me. He can read?" Saffy nodded. "Well, perhaps it will make him see sense."

"An' p'raps it won't'." Poll snorted. "Let im get caught, I say. 'E won't 'ang. 'E'll just go to Chelmsford Jail and be our of our 'air for a while."

"You know that's not so, Poll, and you don't mean what you say." Saffron smiled kindly at her sister. "If he gets the letter it might sober 'im up long enough for 'im to think again about the wrecking."

Poll shrugged and turned away to where Tom huddled miserably by the hearth watching Jean-Pierre make his way to the door where he paused long enough to squeeze Saffron's hand reassuringly.

As the artist reached the gate, Gabriel turned the corner of Horse Hill. The two men met on the cobbled street and Saffron saw them exchange hurried words, which as the artist left, sent the big man running toward the cottage. As he burst into the low-ceilinged room Poll rushed into his arms.

"What's this I hear, girl?" He growled, holding her from him. "Be you alright? You ain't 'urt none?"

"No, Gabriel, I just needed you 'ere." She nestled back into his arms. "'Tis Jonas." She raised a tear stained face to her sister. "You tell 'im Saffy."

"That Jean-Pierre give me the bones of it. You let me get at 'em. Wicked wrecking bastards. I'd make certain sure, that there Jonas ain't in no fit state to join 'em." He sank onto the settle and pulled Poll onto his knee. "Don't you fret yourself, Poll, we'll see to it."

"Now, don't you go tanglin' with Jonas, Gabriel. You leave it to Jean-Pierre." Saffron reached for a cloth. "I've had a pot cooking' slow in the oven since mornin' you'll stay and have a bite with us?"

"I will that, Miss Saffy. I'm not due back 'till eight when the master wants 'is coach. 'Ow about you 'elp your sister, Poll, while Tom and me finishes whittling that boat 'e's been on about?"

Reluctantly Poll rose as Tom scampered across the room to sit at Gabriel's feet, the half-completed craft held out for inspection.

It was dark by the time Jean-Pierre returned. The meal had been eaten, Gabriel had left and both Tom and Poll had gone to bed leaving Saffron to clean the pots and rake the stove ready for the next day.

Reassured by his gentle tapping on the door and her name whispered against the wood, she slid back the bolt to admit him. She raised a finger to her lips.

"Shh! Tom and Poll are sleeping. Worn out they were." Closing the door behind him, he caught her arm.

"Don't walk away from me, Saffron. I only came to tell you that I saw Jonas read the letter. It is up to him now. He has been warned." He tilted her chin, taking in every detail of her face. "You look tired and no wonder." He smiled suddenly and taking a white kerchief from his sleeve, he wiped a streak of chimney soot from her cheek. "That's better, I cannot have my beautiful mysterious lady with a smudge on her face."

Saffron chuckled and would have made fun of him had she not found herself in his arms, held close against his chest. He bent his head, pausing only to register her lack of protest, before gently claiming her lips in a lingering kiss.

Unashamedly she pressed her body closer, feeling the rapid beating of his heart through the thin fabric of her dress. "Don't do this." A small voice warned.

"Why not?" Came the reply. "I know now that I love this man, I want to belong to him, to share my life with him." "Caution." Said the voice. "Take care." But Saffron was not listening, lost in the wonder of his caress, she wanted more. Tom and Poll were sleeping, what could be the harm?

Jean-Pierre sensed her growing passion and as the kiss ended he buried his face in her hair, "No, Saffron, this is not right." He groaned. "I want you, God, how I want you, but not like this." Abruptly, he released her, flinging himself onto a chair by the table. "You mean more to me than that." He buried his head in his hands. "I lie and think of you at night, you are my first thought each waking day." He looked up at her, "I am in love with you Saffron Clay. I will not bruise the blossom that one day I shall have the right to pluck."

She stood open-mouthed at his passionate outburst, robbed of the ability to move until he stood to take her once more into his arms.

"Tell me that you return my love Saffron. I need to know that at least you will consider my proposal."

"Proposal?" Saffron felt her senses spiral. "What is it you're proposing?"

"Why marriage of course! What did you imagine?" Anger clouded his glittering eyes. "That I wanted you to be my mistress?"

She lifted trembling fingers to his lips, silencing his words. "No, No. It's just, just. Oh, Jean-Pierre. It's just that I've wanted to hear you say it." She laid her head against his heart. "An' I do return your love." She tilted her head showing him the truth in her eyes. "I think I've loved you from the first time I sat for you." She smiled shyly. "Remember, when you let loose my 'air and gave me that lovely blue silk wrap?"

"Remember? How could I forget. I could scarcely believe my eyes. You were more lovely at that moment than I had dared to dream, and I am not alone in that belief. As I told you, before long your portrait will hang in some of the finest salons in London. The mysterious lady they are calling you. Some of the titled folk are clamouring for your beauty to adorn the walls of their grand houses." He stroked a finger over her lips. "But you shall remain a mystery to all but me. For I shall be the first and last man to lay claim to all the delicious passion that lies so well hidden beneath the surface of Saffron Clay."

Willingly she lifted her mouth to his, knowing that she was safe, free to give her love to an honourable man, who would wait to claim her only within the sanctity of marriage.

"Now. " He raised his head with a wicked smile. "You have not yet said that you will marry me Miss Clay, and I have no intention of releasing you until you do." He crushed her to him. "Say yes Saffron, or, if needs be, I shall hold you prisoner all night!"

"Jean-Pierre you are breakin' my ribs!" She laughed. "Yes, yes, I will marry you, but not yet!"

"But why?"

"There will be a wedding, but it will be Poll and Gabriel first."

"Little Poll? When did all this happen?"

"While you were in London." She took his hand and led him to the settle where he pulled her down to sit beside him. "I'd best tell you the whole story, seein' as 'ow you're to be one of the family."

He kissed her cheek. "Go on."

Haltingly she told him of Poll's condition and Gabriel's pro-posal. "So you see the wedding 'as to be soon, so's folk'll think the babe is born 'afore time."

"But what of the father?"

"Poll says 'e's the son of the family at the big 'ouse where she worked. 'E won't want nothin' to do with it I reckon." She thought again of the sovereigns, payment for her sister's shame. "Anyway, Gabriel's posted the banns and they are to be wed on Poll's birthday. She'll be sixteen in three weeks."

"I understand. Gabriel's a good man, I'm sure he will make

Poll a good husband, as I will for you." He added taking her hands. "But don't keep me waiting too long, my love for I am impatient for the world to know that you are mine." Gently, he dropped kisses on her eyelids, her nose and her cheek before taking her mouth in a lingering embrace. She laid her head in the hollow of his neck, breathing in the warmth of his masculinity. "Of course, it will give me time to take you to meet my Mother before our wedding. That I must do, or she will never forgive me."

"Your Mother?" Saffron raised her head in alarm. "What's she like? Will she like me?"

"She is French, as I have told you. She is arrogant and thoroughly spoiled, yet I love her dearly. As to whether she will like you my love, I care not." He laughed aloud. "And neither must you, for you are more than capable of returning tenfold any shots she may fire."

"I don't want to shoot her!" Saffron looked astonished. "She can't be as bad as you make out. Can She?"

"We may catch her on one of her good days." Jean-Pierre teased. "I shall write to her tomorrow and give her advance warning of our visit." He stood, raising Saffron into his arms. "But now I must go, and you must get some sleep if you are to be at your most radiant for your sitting in the morning."

Hating to let him go, she watched him turn to wave at the gate, before closing and bolting the door behind him. Unwilling to disturb Poll, she decided to spend the night in the bed space behind the dividing wall, occupied in happier times by her father and mother. As she undressed, her mind raced over the day's events. So much had happened in so short a time that she doubted she would ever be able to rest. Yet with her last waking thought of Jean-Pierre, within moments of laying her head on the pillow she was asleep.

CHAPTER TWENTY TWO

Saffron's letter reached Nathan early one morning, as he sat with the other footmen to break his fast.

"What's it say?" Tim, always eager for news of the world outside the great house, attempted to peer over his shoulder. Nathan held the package out of reach.

"Well, let me read it and I'll tell you." He pushed his chair from the table and crossed to the open kitchen door. Smoothing the folds from the pages he began to read. "Well, bless me!" He laughed. "My little sister Poll's to be wed to Gabriel Stoneforth."

"Who's 'e?" Tim joined him in the thin morning sunlight.

"Gabriel's a good man, Tim. A widower he is." He frowned, "Mind you he's a good bit older than Poll. She's barely sixteen by my reckoning."

"Old enough." Tim grinned, nudging Nathan in the ribs. "If you know what I mean."

"You're talkin' about my sister, Tim. Mind your mouth."

The smile slid from his friend's face. "I didn't mean nothin'. Just joshin'." But Nathan wasn't listening, as lips moving soundlessly, he read the remainder of the letter. Saffron had told him everything and he felt his anger rise as the story unfolded.

"I should have been there." He muttered.

"What?"

"I said I should have been there. My sister's had a bad time and there's me settled here with not a thought in my head for them back home." He folded the letter thoughtfully. Aunt Jane would need to be told but he knew that it was pointless to hope he could be at Poll's wedding. To beg for leave of absence, so early in his employment, would almost certainly mean dismissal and that would upset his plans.

Later in the day, released for an hour from his duties he tapped on the Housekeeper's door. At her bidding he stepped into the now familiar room to find his Aunt at her desk

"Nathan, you are five minutes late." She consulted the silver watch, which hung on a ribbon above her considerable bosom. "Punctuality is considered to be a mark of good manners, remember that. If you are to spend time with the boy, every other spare minute should be fully employed in learning."

"Yes, Aunt."

She looked up to see him frowning. "Why boy, you look as if you have the cares of the world upon your shoulders. What ails you?"

Miserably he handed her Saffron's letter. "Best read this Aunt Jane."

Wordlessly, she took the pages from him and began to read, shaking her head in disbelief. "Poor child." She murmured. "But it seems that Saffron has dealt with matters efficiently. Tell me, is this Gabriel Stoneforth a suitable match?"

Nathan nodded, "He's a fine man Aunt. Head Groom up at the big house. Lost his wife in childbirth, the babe too. I knew him when I was a young'un, he used to whittle away at bits of driftwood, making boats for me and my friend Caleb. Giant of a man he is but real kind, I'd say. Poll could do a lot worse, seeing how things are."

"You realise you will be unable to attend the wedding, Nathan?"

"I do, Aunt but I shall write to Saffy tonight explaining and I'll send Poll my best wishes for a happy life."

"So shall I, Nathan, so shall I. In fact you shall write the letter now, it will prove to be a good exercise." She slid a sheet of paper across the desk. "I shall correct your grammar and spelling before it is sent."

As Nathan bent his head and began to write, he hid a smile. His Aunt never missed an opportunity to improve his education.

The task completed he hurried to the nursery where a disapproving nurse grudgingly allowed him entry. The child, snugly dressed despite the warmth of the day ran eagerly to him, squirming with delight at being lifted aloft in Nathan's strong arms.

"I don't hold with all this nonsense." The elderly woman crossed her arms over her thin chest. "No good will come of it, likely Master Charles will catch his death."

"Don't worry Nurse, I'll take care of him. We won't be gone long this first time." He tickled the child. "We're going to look at the flowers aren't we Charlie?" Plump arms encircled his neck as Nathan winked at the Nurse. "Be back before you know we're gone."

With a snort the woman closed the door on them and together they began the descent down the back stairs to the walled garden. As the sunlight hit them the boy flinched as if struck and Nathan hugged him tightly. "It's alright young'un. I won't let you go. Look I'll walk you round and show you some of the pretty flowers. You'll like that won't you?" The child tightened his grip on Nathan's neck. "Come on now, you'll choke the life out of me." He chuckled, setting off across the close-cropped turf, to stop in front of a standard rose in full bloom. "Here, smell this." He broke the stem of a blossom an held it to the boy's face. "Sniff. That's right. Lovely isn't it?" The boy bent to bury his face in the flower once again, beaming as Nathan wiped the pollen from his button nose. "That's it, now how about we sit for a bit?" Slowly Nathan sank to his knees, gently unwinding the trusting arms from around his neck, and setting the child beside him on the warm grass. Immediately the boy scrambled onto his protector's lap, whimpering and hiding his head against Nathan's chest. Gently but firmly Nathan lifted him away, settling him once again beside him. "Don't be afraid, see I got my arm round you. Nothing is going to hurt you." The trusting smile, which slowly appeared on the boy's face was proof of his ability to understand the spoken word and Nathan began to wonder why no one had noticed or reported it before. Shadows had begun to lengthen in the garden when Nathan scooped the child into his arms, intent on returning him to the nursery. His encouraging words, however, were met with howls of dismay.

"Now, come on Charlie, there's a good lad. If you make a fuss I may not be able to bring you out again." He searched the tearstained face and was relieved to see the child cuff his nose and attempt to silence his sobs. "That's right, you know what I'm saying don't you? If you're good, we'll come here again on the morrow. Would you like that?"

The arms thrown about his neck were answer enough and swinging the boy onto his shoulders Nathan made his way back to the nursery and an anxious, tight-lipped nurse. "You've got him all excited." She accused. "Now he'll never get to sleep, and I won't neither." She added giving weight to her displeasure.

"I reckon you get enough sleep Nurse, from what I saw yesterday." The moment the words were out of his mouth Nathan regretted having spoken so sharply.

The woman's face crumpled as she buried her face in her apron. "I do my best, I have done since the day the poor mistress gave birth to him but he's a handful sometimes."

"I'm sorry Nurse, I shouldn't have spoken to you like that."

Nathan put an arm around the woman's shoulders. "You and me can sort of work together if you like. Give you a bit of a rest if you see what I mean. You can see he's come to no harm today and I don't mind taking Charlie off your hands now and again if the master says I can. How would that be?"

The woman wiped her eyes, considering the offer suspiciously. "You won't tell the master that I need help? If he lets me go I don't know what I'll do. I'm too old to find another position an I've been with the family since before Miss Charlotte was born."

"I'll tell him that I've never known a better or more caring nurse, which is the truth, because you're the only one I've ever met." He laughed aloud. "And you can tell him that you think the hour I spent with Charlie did him a world of good. Is it a deal?"

She nodded, turning to where the child had curled up on the rug in front of the fire and fallen fast asleep. "Give me a hand to get him out of his coat and boots. You can lift him onto his bed too, he's getting to be a bit heavy for me."

As Nathan carried the boy he looked down into the innocent face and smiled. "There's a lot more to you young'un than meets the eye but you and I are going to be friends, you see if we're not."

By the following day, the letters to Saffron had been entrusted to a passing carter bound for Leigh and Nathan had been put to work in the large dining room. It seemed that there was to be another gathering of the wealthy members of society but on this occasion, Bentley informed them, there were to be no ladies present.

"It 'appens sometimes." Tim confided, polishing the tines of a silver fork. "It'll be more of a meeting like. They'll 'ave their dinner, then they'll sit back with their brandy and cigars before they gets down to business."

"What sort of business?" Nathan carefully folded a linen table-napkin. "Like it was last time?"

"No, they gets serious when they've 'ad a few. I've seen 'em get real nasty sometimes."

"They seemed to get along well enough, they're all Dissenters ain't they?"

"So they says but it don't stop 'em 'aving a go!" Tim nudged his friend as he caught sight of Bentley bearing down on them.

"This table should be ready by now." The butler consulted his fob watch. "The guests will be here within the hour." He shot snow-white cuffs from the sleeves of his black tailcoat. "Finish what you are doing and change your livery. You look more like farm hands than footmen!"

Behind the man's departing back Nathan pulled a face. "'Old Blood and Guts' has got it in for us again."

"Like always." Tim grinned. "But e's right, we're runnin' out of time, best get a move on."

Once changed, they presented themselves for inspection and stood ready in the grand entrance hall to receive the guests. Nathan recognised one or two faces from the previous occasion but one man in particular caught his interest. John Walker was a well-known, if controversial figure in Saffron Walden society. Nathan recalled that his Aunt had told him the man, known as Gentleman John Walker, had over the years become accepted among the worthies in recognition of his work in the community. "He came to Saffron Walden as a sickly child, but the country air seemed to do him good and eventually, so I'm told, he served in the Admiralty and also married well." She had looked down her nose disapprovingly, "His wife had a considerable fortune of her own, and they settled back here in the town. For the last decade he has brought about many of the improvements in Saffron Walden."

At dinner, Nathan was pleased to find himself stationed immediately behind Jack Walker. The man appeared taller than average, his dark hair, white-plumed above the ears, was swept back from a high, unlined forehead. But it was the pale, grey eyes that seemed to miss nothing, that had intrigued Nathan. He had felt them search his face as the man handed over his topcoat. To this worthy at least, he realised he was not invisible, a belief underlined by the quietly spoken 'Thank you'.

The Master's wife had taken their daughter, Charlotte to visit relatives and, as course followed course, it became obvious that a different and more relaxed level of conversation could be permitted.

"I hear Richard Cranford will be presiding over the Agricultural Show again, this year." The remark, dropped into a lull in the conversation, came from a mean-faced individual seated across from Nathan. "If you ask me, he thinks he's the Lord Almighty!"

His host snorted with amusement. "I don't know about 'Almighty', but he's certainly a Lord in his own right. As for the show, he's the biggest landowner in the County. He has a right."

Nathan suppressed a smile as he caught his master's eye.

"Quite right, though the way he treats his workers is scandalous and it causes unrest elsewhere. They have jobs for life I'm told and their families too." A florrid- faced man to the right, waved a hand angrily. "He spoils 'em, I say. They get charity handouts, schooling for the children, pensions and a home in their old age, why he even pays for their burial."

"And why not? He treats them well and receives loyalty and a fair day's toil in return." Jack Walker's voice of reason brought all eyes to bear on his quiet, confident smile. "This is eighteen thirty two, Gentlemen. The days when agricultural workers were treated no better than slaves are long gone. Each man has the God-given right to education, good health and a sound roof above his head."

"And what of the cost of all this mollycoddling? I ask you that, Sir!"

Jack Walker regarded the man with mild contempt. "Your income, Sir, would suffer only a little were you to treat your tenants more kindly."

"None of your business, Sir! I suppose you would have us all wasting our time, the way you do." The man blustered. "What's your latest idea? Oh yes!" His words were heavily laden with sarcasm. "A Literary and Scientific Institution or some such rubbish."

Jack Walker remained unruffled. "This is the dawning of an era of progress and invention. If we are to understand, to progress, then we must promote knowledge to those willing to learn."

John Benham nodded. "Quite right, Jack, the world no longer belongs to a handful of men who, due only to wealth and position, have for generations determined the law."

At a discrete signal from the Butler, the group of young footmen moved forward to clear away the last course and shortly afterwards, Nathan and Tim took decanters of port, brandy and a box of fine cigars to the table. For a while, interest revolved around Jack Walker and his proposed National History Society and his plans for a local museum.

"What do we need a museum for?" His portly, adversary was not to be silenced. "Another of your high falluting schemes, I suppose."

"Are you aware?" Jack Walker steepled his long fingers and sat back, his expression one of tolerance. "This area has a rich and colourful history?"

"He has thee there, George!" John Benham slapped his thigh, as the deflated man shrank, muttering, back into his chair.

"That told him!" Tim muttered from the side of his mouth "Silly old Fool!"

Nathan gave an almost imperceptible nod, warming to the quiet dignity of the handsome man.

"It is but two years since Lord Cranford journeyed to Newport Prison to dispose of the 'Swing Rebels'." He continued. "The first lord, thirty years ago, dealt with the labourer's unrest at that time. The high cost of food led good men to rise, to defend their rights. Poor harvests, when his son inherited the title, caused labourers to become incendierists, for their families were starving." He raised an expressive hand. "And now we have the 'Captain Swing Rioters' in search of a fairer wage. They have the courage to find their voice, to demand twelve shillings a week. I say, thank God for Lord Cranford, he is the first of his kind to attempt to address the problem." He raised his glass as if in salute. "It is a wise man, who can see that it is knowledge of the past which determines our future."

"You make him sound like a saint!"

"No, not a saint." Jack walker shook his head. "But a man whom I both respect and admire. And now gentlemen, if you will forgive me, I shall take my leave. I have an early start in the morning for my journey to London on business." He rose from the table and made a small bow to his smiling host. "Thank you John, for your excellent hospitality. I shall see you again, upon my return."

Nathan hurried to open the dining-room door for the departing guest, handing him his topcoat and hat at the main entrance.

"Thank you, Lad."

Momentarily confused, Nathan stared into the grey eyes.

"No, thank you Sir." He managed. "'Tis a privilege."

The man's generous mouth curved into a smile. "A privilege you say?"

"Aye, Sir." Nathan, reassured by the man's interest, swallowed nervously. "I was listening while you were talking and …" He faltered, surprised by his own boldness. "And I admire you, Sir, for what you said about the past being important to the future."

The grey eyes narrowed, speculatively. "What is your name?"

"Nathan, Sir."

"I have a feeling that I shall have need to remember that name." Fleetingly, he placed a hand on Nathan's shoulder. "Good night to you boy, we shall talk again."

As Nathan watched Jack Walker descend the steps to the waiting carriage, something told him that the brief exchange marked a turning point in his life.

CHAPTER TWENTY THREE

The news of Poll's wedding travelled like wildfire. Whenever Saffron ventured into the village, one or another of her neighbours would stop her, eager for details of the coming marriage. Many who had been close friends of Mary Clay offered their help, aware that since her death, Saffron had assumed the role of mother to both Poll and Tom.

Not everyone however was charitable. "Bit sudden ain't it?" Ma Smethwick had barred her way, sniffing suspiciously. "Only a day or so since she were supposed to be like at death's door. Now she's well enough to be getting' wed. Funny goin's on if you ask me."

"Well, I didn't ask you, did I?" Saffron thrust her head forward. "There's nothin' funny about it and you keep your mouth shut or I'll shut it for you."

The woman backed away. "I only said…"

"I know what you said. Gabriel Stoneforth's a good man and he's lucky to be getting our Poll as a wife. Which is something your girl don't never 'ave a chance of bein'."

A tide of fury suffused the woman's face as Saffron pushed past her into the street. The small triumph was short lived however, as she caught sight of the bent figure of Mother Watkins beckoning to her, and prompted by curiosity, Saffron followed the old crone into the dim alleyway.

"Well." She muttered. "What d'you want?"

"'Ow is she, your sister?"

"Well enough. Your brew did the job." She added grudgingly.

"I 'ear she's getting' wed."

"You 'eard right. End of next week."

"So, 'e's takin' it on then?" The woman's sly, knowing grin made further comment unnecessary.

Saffron bridled at the implication. "I don't know what you mean."

"She didn't 'ave to wed." The woman whined. "I could've seen 'er right." She sounded hurt. "Not the first I've got rid of."

Saffron clenched her fists, controlling her mounting anger with great difficulty. "She didn't need that sort of 'elp then and she don't need it now, you old witch." She hissed.

Mother Watkins sucked in her breath, her mean eyes glittering with hate and raising a filthy finger, she pointed at Saffron. "It'll bring her nothing but sorrow and pain." She ranted, spittle dripping from her trembling chin. "Spawned in shame it were and marked for worse." She seemed to shrink, deflated by her own vitriolic outburst as she shuffled away, turning once to glare at Saffron before disappearing into the street beyond.

Saffron determined to say nothing of the encounter to her sister because as the days passed, she watched the young bride to be grow more nervous.

"If you try that dress on one more time it'll look like a dishrag come Sunday." She scolded.

Poll frowned at her reflection in the small mirror. "What blossoms shall I wear in my 'air, Saffy?"

"'Ow about a wreath of wildflowers? There's plenty of pretty colours in the hedgerows this time of year."

Poll nodded. "And what about me 'air? Shall I put it up?" She scooped it away from her neck piling it in a tumbled mass and turning her head from one side to the other. "Or will Gabriel like it all loose like?"

"I don't know what Gabriel would like, but you got lovely 'air Poll, why not just give a good wash and let it fall natural. Now, get out of that dress, do and finish stitching that nightgown. You'll not want to go naked to your marriage bed."

Poll handed the wedding dress to Saffron with trembling fingers. "Oh Saffy, don't remind me. I'm that feared."

Saffron threw an arm around her shoulders. "I told you Gabriel won't look for nothin' 'till you're ready, 'e give me is word on that, so don't you worry no more. Now you get yourself dressed and come down when you're ready."

As she descended the stairs, however, the smile died on her lips. She froze as she saw the figure of her stepfather Jonas swaying by the hearth, clutching his terrified son, Tom to his side.

"I'm sorry, Saffy." The boy sobbed, struggling to free himself. "He tricked me to open the door."

"Let the child go Jonas!" Saffron regarded the man steadily. "You got no reason to scare the boy." She took a step toward the door. "Let 'im go, or I'll be outside screamin' and yellin' to anyone who'll 'ear!"

Jonas' eyes narrowed, weighing her threat. At last he pushed Tom from him. "I didn't mean 'im no 'arm." He mumbled, as the boy ran to bury his head in Saffron's skirt. Without taking her eyes from the unsteady figure she hugged the child to her. "Shh Tom, you're safe now. Run upstairs and tell Poll to stay put, there's a good boy."

Tom edged his way across the room to scramble up the wooden stairway.

"Now, Jonas." Saffron folded her arms. "What d'you want? Get it said, then get out!"

"I'll go when I'm ready." He slumped heavily onto a chair. "I bin told as 'ow Poll's gettin' wed." His words were slurred as he stretched a leg to stuff a hand into his trouser pocket. "I brung 'er this." He slapped some coins onto the table, regarding them with blurry eyes. "Tell 'er Jonas says 'e 'opes she'll be 'appy. And as 'ow 'e's sorry." The last was said with great effort. He glanced up at Saffron. "Don't worry, girl." He growled. "I won't be at the weddin' to shame you."

For a moment Saffron almost weakened. The sad unkempt shell of the man was barely recognisable as her once loving Stepfather, yet it seemed that some small spark of his former, decent self still survived.

"I'll tell 'er." She spoke quietly. "And I thank you Jonas."

"I can spare it." He smirked. "Plenty more where that came from." He laid a knowing finger alongside his nose. "There's ways and means. Ways and means." Getting to his feet, he laughed, full once again with his old drunken bravado.

Armed with the knowledge of the imminent wrecking, his meaning was unmistakeable. Saffron had watch the moon growing smaller and she know that within the next night or two conditions would be ideal for the wrecker's villainy. She felt behind her for the latch, and opening the door, stood to one side.

He paused as he came level with her. "Look after the boy."

She nodded. "An' you look after yourself, Jonas." Briefly, she felt the need to reach out to him, to warn him, to beg him to stop drinking, but the moment passed as, belching he made his way unsteadily to the gate. Nothing she could say would make him change, it was too late, far too late. She leant against the closed door watching Tom and Poll cautiously descend the stair.

"As 'e gone?"

"'E 'as, and 'e left that for you Poll." She gestured toward the coins. "That and 'is good wishes for your weddin'."

"Pa scared me, Saffy." Tom's tear stained face still showed signs of fear.

"'E was drunk, Tom, 'e didn't mean to frighten you. 'E said so."

Poll had stacked the coins into three small piles. "I don't want this Saffy!" She glared angrily at the money. "I know 'ow it's come by and' I ain't 'aving it." She swept the coins from the table, scattering them over the floor and collapsing into a chair. What I want is our own Pa. He should be 'ere Saffy, to handfast me to Gabriel. Even Nathan's gone. 'E could 'ave done it. I know we got 'is letter sayin' Gabriel was a good match and wishin' us well, but it's not the same as 'avin' 'im 'ere."

"Well it seems it'll 'ave to be me what gives you in marriage." Saffron slipped an arm around her sister's slender waist. "Will I do?"

"Oh, Saffy, you know you will." Poll gripped her hand. "It's just I still miss Pa and Ma. She would have liked Gabriel wouldn't she?"

"She would. She'd 'ave said you was doing right, the way things are."

"I like Gabriel too." Tom was not to be left out. "He's a real good whittler."

Saffron and Poll burst into laughter. "Oh Tom, trust you to 'ave an answer!" Poll hugged him to her, her sadness dispelled by the child's innocence.

Saffron sobered, busying herself about the cottage deep in thought. The next few days she knew held not only last minute preparations for Poll's wedding but also the promise of time spent with Jean-Pierre. "We'd both best wash our 'air before bed, Poll. Don't forget I'll be sitting for another picture on the morrow and time's getting short."

"We've done most things." Poll ticked them off on her fingers. "The dress is finished, we've asked all of our friends to be with us at the Church. Most of the food 'as been promised for the wedding picnic and Gabriel says as 'ow the Parson said he can use his pony and trap to carry me up the 'ill." She smiled proudly. "Says it will be all dressed up with flowers and ribbons and such."

"Sounds lovely, Poll."

"Can I ride in it?" Tom's eager face appeared over the table top.

"No, you silly goose." Saffron ruffled his hair. "You will be waitin' with Gabriel in the church for Poll to get there. You got something special to do, can you remember what it is?"

"'Course I can." Tom stood straight to pantomime his task. "I'll be wearing the new britches you made for me won't I Saffy?" She nodded. "Right, well, Gabriel's going to give me the weddin' ring to 'old. Then when he gives me a wink I give it to the Parson who puts on the Holy Book to bless it."

"What then?"

"The Parson gives it to Gabriel who puts it on Poll's finger." He frowned. "Then it makes them married, I think."

Saffron hid a smile. "Quite right, Tom, well done. I'll be takin' Poll to the church in the trap and after they're wed, Gabriel and Poll will be ridin' off in it to their new 'ome."

Tom shivered with excitement. "I never been to a weddin' before Saffy, will there be lots to eat?"

"There will, thanks to some of our friends. A real fine picnic there'll be all spread out on the green alongside the church. Your friend Jake's Ma has said she'll make some of those little cakes you like so much and I 'spect there'll be lots of folk bring fruit pies at this time of year." She smiled as Tom licked his lips in anticipation.

"And there'll be dancin' too. Jack Sloan's promised to bring his fiddle, so there'll be some merry tunes that night."

She turned away to hide the longing in her eyes. How long would it be before she and Jean-Pierre could begin to plan their own wedding? They had vowed to keep quiet until after Poll's big day, agreeing that nothing could be allowed to steal the young bride's thunder. She laid a hand over her heart, it was as if her longing for the artist manifested itself as physical pain and she knew that the cure lay only in the arms of the man she loved.

CHAPTER TWENTY FOUR

It seemed to Nathan that the days flew by. After rising early, he and Tim attended to their various duties, reported for morning prayers and throughout the day answered the various demands of the master and his family. His few brief hours of leisure were either spent in further tuition with his aunt, or with young Charles Benham, the Lammas Lamb with whom he had forged an affectionate bond.

His one half day however, was jealously guarded for he and Sarah had made plans to visit her family.

"So, will I do?" Nathan met Sarah at the kitchen door, turning for her inspection. His new boots, britches and shirt, recently purchased in the nearby town from his first month's wage, met with immediate approval.

"You look like a real gentleman." She pirouetted for his benefit. "And what about me?"

"You always look lovely." Nathan chuckled. "Even in your old work clothes with flour on your nose."

Sarah stamped her foot. "You're supposed to notice I've got a new dress." She paused. "Well, almost new. Chloe, the upstairs maid got it from Miss Sophie, but it didn't fit her, so she passed it on. I trimmed it, 'cause it was a bit plain like, but its good stuff." She smoothed the dove grey folds of the fabric, which clung well to her pouting breasts and tiny waist. The white collar had been adorned with a blue ribbon to match the small bunch of flowers on her hat.

"Now you've both finished admirin' each other, you'd best be on your way." The cook smiled affectionately at the young couple. "I've put up a basket of fruit and such for your Ma, Sarah. With all those mouths to feed a bit more won't come amiss." She waved away the girl's protest. "I know there's money comin' in but your Ma and me, we've been friends a long time so you just give it to her with my good wishes".

"Thanks, Cook, though Ma knows we're coming, so there'll be a fine table waiting." Sarah's chin tilted with pride. "Ma's known for her cookin'"

"I reckon that's who you take after then." The woman nodded. "You still got some learnin' to do but one day you'll be good enough to take over from me."

Nathan smacked his lips. "Cook's right, that pie you made last night was real tasty." He slanted a sideways grin in her direction. "'Cos, I'm only marrying you for your cooking."

"If that's all you want me for Nathan Clark, you can think again!" She turned away in mock dismissal, only to be caught up in his arms and spun to face him. A sparkle of mischief lit her eyes and a smile tugged at the corner of her mouth.

"That's not all." Nathan growled. "And you know it. But it will be all the better for waiting for." He felt a thrill of antici-pation, the thought of possessing the girl he loved was having a disturbing effect upon him. Gently he released her, breaking the tension of the moment with a kiss to the tip of her nose. "Come on." He grabbed her hand pulling her out into the midday sun. "We've a fair walk ahead of us and I'm already fit to eat a horse."

Happy in each other's company, the journey across country took less than half an hour, despite Nathan's insistence that they stop to admire the view and for him to steal a kiss. As finally, they stood at the gate to the isolated dwelling, Nathan let out a low whistle. The sprawling cottage stood in the centre of what he judged to be a closely fenced half-acre. The door, fringed by the climbing tendrils of a heavily blossomed yellow rose, stood open wide to the summer breeze, and from within came the sound of voices raised in laughter.

"Well, they sound a right merry lot, your family." Nathan squared his shoulders. "Though I feel like Daniel going into the lion's den."

"They won't eat you!" Sarah threw back her head, laughing aloud. "Come on, let's get it over with." Taking his hand she led him between beds of flowering potatoes, plants and regimented rows of carrots, onions and cabbage. "Mum grows most of her own vegetables, so they don't want for much. There's chickens round the back too, they've even got their own cow in the field yonder."

Nathan was puzzled at the apparent affluence of Sarah's family. "You never said what your Pa did for a living, Sarah. Does he own this place or what?"

"No, the cottage is tied, but its safe, the master took him on soon after him and Ma were wed. He's gamekeeper to the big house." She saw the frown cross Nathan's face. "What's wrong? You look bothered."

Nathan remembered the kindly carter who had helped him on his way to Saffron Walden and the tale he told of the penalties of poaching which in the end had led to his being left a cripple. "It must take a hard heart to be a gamekeeper." He avoided her eyes. "There's a lot of poor devils been deported for trying to feed their families on a rabbit belonging to some Lord or other."

"You'll not find my Pa to be hard hearted." Sarah shook her head. "He knows when to turn a blind eye. The master knows what goes on and Pa has his blessing, everyone knows that John Benham's a good man, and no one in his care would be left to starve."

Nathan's initial caution was dispelled the moment he met the man who towered above him and took his hand in a crushing grasp. "So you be Nathan we've heard so much about. Come on in lad and welcome." He stood back to allow their passage into the bright interior of the cottage. "Mother". He called. "Sarah's 'ere and she' brought a friend."

From a doorway to the left, from which came the inviting smell of food, tumbled two giggling children, wide eyed with curiosity, followed by a smiling woman, as broad as she was high. She folded Sarah against her ample bosom. "Hello my dear." She kissed her daughter on both cheeks. "And who's this you've brought to share our meal?"

"This is Nathan, Ma. Remember, I wrote to tell you he was comin'."

"So you did, so you did." The woman looked him up and down. "And a fine young fellow he is." She held out a hand to Nathan, which he took willingly. "Make yourself at home lad." She turned to the two children hiding shyly behind her skirt. "Say hello nicely, this is Cissy and the little one is Jane." The two girls smiled shyly and bobbed a curtsey. "Bobby's still sleeping, 'e's had a trouble cutting a tooth, but you'll see him a'fore the day's out."

"Is Matthew coming over with Annie?" Sarah removed her hat and hung it behind the door. "What about Luke, is he still living over the forge in the village?"

"Questions, questions." Sarah's Mother waved them to sit at the scrubbed table in the centre of the room. "I'm sure your friend needs something to quench his thirst, I know your Pa does." She reached for a jug of Cider and poured a generous measure into two drinking pots, before handing them to the men. "Now, Matthew and Annie should be here any minute, and Luke shouldn't be much behind him. They're both doing well, but I'll let them tell you themselves. Pa." She turned to her husband. "Why don't you show Sarah's friend over the place."

The big man caught her meaningful glance and got to his feet. "Aye, come on lad, let's take a walk while the women see to the meal."

Nathan saw Sarah's nod and followed the man out of the cottage and into the well kept garden. "So what d'you think lad? Ma and the young'uns do most of the work out here growing the vegetables and such. I'm out most of the day with me gun looking after the master's estate."

"Your gun?" Nathan stopped in his tracks. "Have you ever shot anyone caught poaching?"

The man regarded him seriously. "Well, you don't waste words do you, lad. Would it upset you if I had?" He asked.

"It would Sir. 'Tis a sad world when a man must lose his life for trying to feed his family." For a moment Nathan wondered whether he had spoiled his chances of making Sarah his bride by speaking his mind and wished he had kept his council.

"You'll do, son. You'll do." The big man clapped him on the shoulder and let out a bellow of laughter. "I'll set your mind to rest. I've blasted a few birds from their nests when I've shot into the air. That's enough to scare any poacher off but it's only the ones I know are makin' a business of it."

Nathan's relief was obvious and he grinned good-naturedly at his companion. "I'm right relieved to hear it, Sir. I got something important to ask you and I wouldn't like to think I might be on the wrong end of that gun."

"Important? I wonder what that could be?" The man's eyes held a knowing twinkle. "It couldn't be sommat to do with our Sarah could it?"

Nathan felt the colour rise to his cheeks. "It could, Sir. You see I want your permission to make Sarah my wife." He paused. "Not right now, but when I can offer her the life she deserves. I can't marry until I can find work away from the big house because they won't have husbands and wives working together, and Sarah is happy where she is."

"Our girl wrote to tell us a bit about you. Said you come from good stock. Your father owned his own fishing boat she says. That right?" Nathan nodded. "Your wanting to marry her don't come as no surprise. She says as how you're going up in the world one day, an that's good." He frowned. "But some say the higher you go, the harder the fall. I wouldn't want to see our Sarah come to sadness."

"Nor more would I. I've made up my mind to get to the top but it will be one step at a time." Nathan held out his hand. "Will you shake my hand, Sir and give me and Sarah your blessing. I love her dearly and I promise you no harm will come to her, not while I live and breathe."

Sarah's father considered the outstretched hand for a moment before taking it. "You seem to be a good lad, you've got your head on straight, I'll give you that. But mind, you're both young, so I want to see you wait a while before you set the date." His grip tightened as their eyes met. "I want your word you'll not go jumping the gun. I think you know what I mean. Sarah's a good girl and we don't want no rushed wedding in the family."

"You have my word, Sir." Nathan grinned. "Sarah has already made that plain and I respect her wishes."

"Then I think we've settled things and I don't know about you but my stomach's rumbling for some of Ma's cooking." They returned to the cottage to find Sarah and her Mother waiting, hope written clearly on each of their faces.

"Well?" Sarah bit her lip impatiently.

"Well what?"

"Oh, Pa, don't tease." She implored, running to her father's side. "Can we?"

"Can you stay for dinner? Of course you can."

"Don't keep the girl waiting Pa." Sarah's mother scolded. "Tell her yes or no."

Nathan however, could contain himself no longer and throwing his arms around Sarah he planted a kiss on her cheek. "Your Pa has said yes but we've to wait a while." He danced her around the room. "But you're to be mine and I want to tell the whole wide world. It's you and me from now on Sarah. We'll work and we'll save." He leaned back to gaze down at her trusting face. "And I'll better myself you'll see. There's things I can set my mind to that before now I didn't know nothing about. Aunt Jane says that opportunity never knocks twice and I plan to be there to throw wide the door when it comes a'knocking the first time. Trust me darling Sarah, I'll see you won't never want for anything."

The sunlight from the door was suddenly blotted out as the figures of a slender woman and a tall man filled the opening. "What's all this about?" His jovial laughter filled the room as Sarah released herself from Nathan's arms and ran to greet him.

"Matthew, you could not have come at a better moment. Pa has given his permission for me to marry Nathan." She turned to beckon Nathan to her side. "Nathan this is my brother Matthew and 'is wife Annie."

He held out his hand. "I'm pleased to meet you Matthew and you too Annie. I've heard lots about you."

"And all of it good, I hope." The man shook his hand vigorously. "If you've passed muster with Pa you must be alright. Welcome to the family Nathan."

"We saw Luke coming down the lane Ma." Matthew's sweet faced wife seemed at home as she helped to set the table for their meal. "He should be here any minute."

With Luke's arrival, the family seemed complete, even the baby woke in time to join in the noisy, happy crowd who sat together to enjoy a hearty meal.

Nathan felt Sarah's hand slip into his as he bowed his head in prayer.

"We thank Thee Lord for the food on our table, for the good health we have and for the blessings showered upon us. We thank Thee too, for sending to us the lad Nathan who, if it is your will, is to be handfast to Sarah. Amen."

Nathan glanced around the table. Here were folk who were the salt of the earth, who worked hard for their living and thanked God for his bounty. The men and women whose labour fed the rich yet who had no say in governing the land of their birth. He thought again of Jack Walker's words. Perhaps in time the pendulum would swing in their favour, and he realised, that is some way he intended to part of that movement.

CHAPTER TWENTY FIVE

After a restless night, Saffron was grateful to see that the day of the wedding dawned bright and clear, the thin veil of cloud having burned away with the rising of the sun. The ceremony was set for midday and it was all she could do to contain Tom's excitement. "No, Tom." She told him for the tenth time, "You wait 'till just a'fore you go to put on your new clothes. I want you to look good and you have a way of makin' the cleanest shirt look grubby in five minutes!" She relented, seeing that Tom looked crestfallen. "Look, go stand at the gate and watch for Jean-Pierre, he said he would look in on the way to the church with a gift for Poll. It's your job to let me know when 'e gets 'ere."

Endowed with the responsibility, Tom brightened and made for the gate, eagerly watching the street where seagulls wheeled overhead, dipping and diving into the incoming tide for their first meal of the day. Through the open door, Saffron saw several of her neighbours stop to speak to the boy, no doubt to reassure him that indeed they would be at his Sister's wedding later that day.

Saffron sighed as she mounted the stair to Poll's room where she found her sister impatiently brushing the tangles from her hair. "Here, give me that brush, you're only makin' it into an 'aystack!" She began to smooth the unruly mop into a thick and shining cascade. "There, now give your cheeks a pinch, you look a mite pale. Then we'll get you into your dress and I'll pin the wreath of flowers onto your hair."

Poll fingered the fresh blossoms, lovingly picked that morning by Tom. "There's lots 'ere Saffy. P'raps I could carry some too." She glimpsed her sister's face in the mirror. "I thought, after the weddin' I could put 'em on Ma's grave."

"She'd like that Poll, I know she'll be watchin' over us today and so will Pa. They'd both be real proud of you."

"Saffy, Saffy, Jean Pierre's comin'." Tom's voice from the foot of the stairs sent her hurrying, her heart leaping with joy, to the bedroom door.

"Ask 'im to come in and tell 'im I'll be down in a minute Tom." She looked back at Poll. "You just stay where you are, I'll be back, we've got an hour yet before we 'ave to leave for the church." Without waiting for a reply she ran lightly down the stairs in time to see Jean-Pierre arrive bearing a small canvas covered frame.

His face lit up as he saw her and setting the gift to one side, he took her in his arms. "I have missed you." He murmured against her hair.

Gently she pushed him away. "'Tis only a few hours since you and me." She paused, blushing at the memory.

He searched her face. "It seems like a lifetime. I shall never want to let you out of my sight once you are truly mine." He bent his dark head to kiss her unaware that Tom had followed him in and was staring open-mouthed at their embrace.

As Jean-Pierre released her Saffron caught sight of the boy. "I think it's time you put those new britches on Tom." She straightened her dress, patting her hair into place. "And try not to get your best shirt dirty, understand?"

Tom nodded, backing away, round-eyed to do as he was bid.

Smiling ruefully, Jean-Pierre watched him go. "I wonder what the little chap will make of that." He turned back to Saffron. "We cannot keep our love secret for long. As soon as Poll and Gabriel are wed, I shall take you to meet my Mother and then I shall delight in shouting to the world that you are to be mine." He took her hands. "Forever my Darling, Forever."

She laid her head against his broad chest, rubbing her cheek over the sweet smelling, crisp white linen of his shirt. "Yes, I know." She looked up into his dark eyes. "But for now you must let me go. I must finish 'elpin' Poll and I've yet to change my own dress."

"You look beautiful just as you are, but I shall go, much as I want to stay." He paused, his hand on the latch. "I shall see you again at the church and as Poll and Gabriel make their vows I shall be dreaming of the moment when we make ours."

He blew her a kiss and was gone.

By the time she returned to Poll's room, Tom had managed to button his britches and was stuffing his shirt into the waistband. "I brushed 'is 'air, Saffy and 'is boots are clean. Will 'e do?"

"I think so." Saffy turned him around approvingly. "Now down you go and wait for Gabriel. He'll be by in a minute to take you up to the church. And mind you stay clean." She called after him as he scuttled from the room.

Her own dress of sprigged muslin hung on the back of the bedroom door together with a fine white woollen shawl, part of her Mother's legacy to her.

"Jean Pierre 's brought you a gift." Her voice was muffled as she slipped the dress over her head. "It looks like one of 'is paintin's." She tugged the soft fabric into place and swept the shawl over her shoulders, settling it in place and securing it with a tiny spray of flowers. "There, that's me ready, now let's wind those blossoms into your hair." She laughed suddenly, pointing to Poll's feet. "I 'ope you ain't going to church barefoot. Where are your shoes?"

"I forgot." Poll giggled. "I'm so excited, I'd forget my 'ead if it wasn't screwed on!" She slipped her feet into the white slippers Saffron had fashioned from the wedding gown trimmings, and stood for inspection. "I'm ready Saffy." She tilted her chin. "And I know now I'm doin' the right thing. I'm goin' to work 'ard to make Gabriel a good wife and with God's 'elp." She ran a hand over her belly. "I'll give 'im children of 'is own as well as this one."

Saffron's eyes filled with tears. Had things been different, Poll would be celebrating her sixteenth birthday not her wedding day. She would still have several years ahead of her to decide her future, but thanks to a few minutes of mindless sport by a man without honour, she had been left with only one option. Not for the first time, she said a silent prayer of thanks for Gabriel and his unmistakable love for her sister.

"You look lovely, Poll." She kissed her sister's cheek. "Now pick up those flowers and off we go. The trap will be at the door and Gabriel will be waitin' to make you his wife."

The pony and trap had, as Gabriel had promised, been hung with flowers and ribbons. The driver, one of the young grooms from the big house, winked as he helped them onto the padded seats. "'Old tight." He grinned. "Next stop Leigh Church!"

The notes of the organ reached them as they neared the church and Poll clutched Saffron's hand. "'E will be there, won't 'e Saffy?"

"'Course 'e will, silly. 'E loves you Poll, 'e ain't goin' to miss the chance now 'e's come this far."

As they stood together at the door of the church Poll's fears were gone. At the altar stood the tall figure of the man who was soon to be her husband. Smiling he turned to watch her slow progress up the aisle, flanked on either side by folk from the village, well wishers, all dressed in their Sunday best.

At the right moment, Saffron handed her to Gabriel and Tom played his part with serious perfection. Once the register had been signed, the bride and groom were showered with petals in the church porch and the festivities began. Jack struck up a gay tune on his fiddle and Gabriel swept Poll off her feet in a lively jig. He had made a hobbyhorse for Tom, which brought a whoop of joy from the child.

"'T'is a thank you for being our ring bearer." He ruffled the boy's hair. "You did a good job lad."

Tom ran his hand over the carved head of the horse. "It's wonderful." He marvelled, fingering the rod and wheel attached to the horse's neck. "Can I ride it now Saffy, can I?"

Saffron smiled. "Aye, but take care while you're a'gallopin', that looks to be a lively animal you have there." Turning, she mouthed a silent 'thank you' to Gabriel, who acknowledged her words with an understanding wink.

The celebrations continued throughout the afternoon. Families sat on the meadow grass in friendly groups, breaking open their picnics and sharing with their neighbours. Poll and Gabriel wandered among them, acknowledging the congratulations and good wishes, thanking folk for attending the ceremony and for their gifts, for many of the villagers who had known Poll from the time she was born brought small tokens for the young bride and groom. A rush basket of vegetables, a cooking pot, a candlestick hand carved from local driftwood and a small rag mat were added to the list and gratefully accepted by the couple, together with Jean-Pierre's painting of a collection of boats moored in Leigh Creek. True to his word, there was no sign of Jonas.

As evening drew near, a chill breeze from the Estuary cooled the sun-warmed gathering as Jean-Pierre drew Saffron to one side. "I have decided to leave for Brighton this evening." He put a finger to her lips to stay her words. "I know, my love, I had intended to write but it is best that I speak to her face to face. I want to make arrangements for you to meet my Mother without further delay. She can be, well," he paused, "a little unpredictable. You may think me mad if you wish, but I can think of nothing else than the desire to make you my wife."

He gripped her shoulders, "Say you understand Saffron. I shall be back in two or three days. I promise."

Saffron nodded sadly. "I shall miss you." She whispered. "Hurry back."

Her heart went with him as she watched him turn and stride away down the hill. His mother was unpredictable he had said. It was another of those big words he was so fond of using and although its true meaning escaped her she had recognised the warning tone in his voice. Surely the woman could not be that bad, she was after all Jean-Pierre's mother, a gentle-woman from what little he had told her. Perhaps he had gone to prepare her for her meeting with someone not of her status. For a moment, suddenly made aware of her own social shortcom-ings, the thought horrified her. Would Jean-Pierre be forced to make excuses for her? For the way she spoke? For her simple dress? No! She shook her head. He would never do that. If his precious Mother chose not to like her he would stand up for her. Wouldn't he? She tilted her chin defiantly, She could stand up for herself, she always had and she always would and there was no point in meeting trouble half way. Jean-Pierre would be back before long and he would lay her fears to rest she felt sure.

Although the wedding party went on into the evening, for Saffron the day had been spoiled by Jean-Pierre's departure. It was not until Poll had left with Gabriel for her new home and she had returned to the cottage to tuck an exhausted Tom into bed that she realised that there was no moon. She hurried down the stair to let herself quietly from the cottage, going to the gate to strain her eyes over the black swell of the Estuary's water.

The night was silent save for the plaintive call of a night bird
and the faint murmur of voices from nearby dwellings, their
windows open to the still, warm air.

"Oh no." She murmured. "Not tonight!" But in her heart
she knew that conditions were ideal for the wreckers and their
intended devilry. She could only hope and pray that Jonas had
seen sense after reading Jean-Pierre's letter and had decided
not to take part in tonight's villainy.

She returned to the cottage, pacing the floor before making
a sudden decision. She ran lightly up the stairs to push open
the door of Tom's bedroom, and was relieved to see him fast
asleep, the precious hobbyhorse propped by the side of his bed.
Worn out by the excitement of the day, his slender young body
lay sprawled above the covers. Gently Saffron lifted the patchwork quilt into place, smiling as the boy turned onto his side
with a muffled sigh. She bent to kiss the smooth cheek. "Sleep
well, Tom." She whispered. "I don't like leavin' you alone but
I won't be long. I just got to be sure Jonas 'asn't gone with
them others."

She stood for a moment looking down at the child. He always
slept soundly, she reasoned and would probably not wake until
daybreak, allowing her to leave the cottage and return long
before he woke.

Saffron closed the door quietly and made her way carefully, plotting her path, so as not to be seen, from one dimly
lit window to the next, avoiding the pools of light, which here
and there spilled onto the cobbles. Clearing the village, and
with only the pale, ever-shifting surf line to guide her, her pace
quickened. Just beyond the last cottage, the cliff path rose,
becoming studded with shrubs and ragged outcrops of black
rock. Behind one of these she crouched down to wait.

She pulled her shawl more closely about her against the

chill fingers of sea mist curling toward her from the blackened waves below. If Jonas had gone with his friends and they had run true to form, they would have stolen the cargo from the unfortunate ship, which would have run aground on the Maplins and they would have gone ashore at Wakering. The loaded donkeys would have then be led along country roads and down into Leigh to be stored in the cellars of one of the alehouses.

She heard the first faint evidence of the wrecker's approach along the beach as, breaking the silence, sand crunched beneath the feet of men and beasts. She strained to hear evidence of Jonas' presence but the distance defied the clarity of whispered speech. As the group grew closer she could just make out the outline of half a dozen men and three heavily laden donkeys.

As they drew level with her, she was startled by a shout from above and a hail of sand and shale tumbling from the cliff top, to rain down on her hiding place. Huddling close to the rockface, she shielded her head against the shower of loose earth and small stones.

And then a shot rang out.

And another.

And another.

The silence of the once calm night, was shattered by the screams of the injured and the triumphant shouts of the excise men as they surrounded the small band of wreckers.

Saffron watched, biting hard on her knuckles to stifle her own cry of horror. Illuminated by the hastily lit Excise lanterns, she could see only three men standing while two others lay at their feet, she assumed either dead or too badly wounded to rise. She breathed a sigh of relief as she realised there was no sign of Jonas.

Saffron waited as the bodies were lifted and captives and

beasts were led away, fervently thanking God that her stepfather was not among them.

At least Tom would be spared the knowledge that his father had gone to the gallows. She stayed crouched against the rock until the last sound of their departure had died away. Then getting stiffly to her feet and preparing to make her way down to the lower path she heard a muffled moan from a nearby patch of scrub. She froze where she stood, every sense alert. She listened again, straining every nerve and was rewarded by an unmistakable muffled groan of pain.

Although her eyes had become adjusted to the dark, Saffron, her feet slipping and sliding, cautiously felt her way along through the loose shale until her fingers came into contact with the thorns of a prickly hawthorn. Kneeling to reach forward she crawled over the dry dune grass until her hands felt the soft material and warmth of a man's arm.

"No." She sat back on her heels. "No, it couldn't be." But as she ran her hands over the figure, she recognised Jonas' wide leather belt with its distinctive and unmistakable heavy buckle. "So you did it." She muttered. "You wicked devil. You deserve all you've got. You can lay there for all I care." She got to her feet but could not suppress her scream as a hand gripped her ankle.

"Don't leave me 'ere girl." The words were barely audible. "Saffy 'ave pity, I'm bad urt."

She crouched beside Jonas. "Ow did you get 'ere? The others got caught." She paused. "Or worse."

"I was laggin' be'ind. I see what 'appened to the others, so I climbed up the cliff but I fell." He paused. "They missed me I s'pose".

"So you ain't shot then?"

"No, but I cracked my head and I think me ankle's broke"

Saffron's mind was racing, leaping from one possibility to another. If she could manage to get Jonas back to the cottage without being seen she could make up a tale to explain his injuries and with luck he might escape the hangman's rope.

"You don't deserve it but if you can make it back to the cottage I'll 'elp you."

"You're a good girl Saffy." His voice broke as he reached to take her hand.

"Don't start that." She dragged her hand away. "Now let's see if we can get you up."

It took several attempts before, leaning heavily on Saffron, Jonas managed to stand. Every step of the journey back to Leigh caused him pain. His broken ankle could not take his weight but it was the blow to his head, which was a greater cause for concern, as he seemed to drift in and out of coherent speech. Saffron had to all but carry the semi-conscious man and by the time they reached home she was exhausted.

With a silent prayer that Tom stayed sleeping in the room above, she lowered Jonas onto the bed that he had once shared with Mary Clay. By lamplight she examined his wounds and thankful that he appeared to have lost consciousness, she straitened and splintered his ankle as she had seen the village doctor do on more than one occasion. Bandaging Jonas' head was difficult and she was alarmed to see that the blood, which continued to seep from the deep wound, had soaked the pillow.

As the first thin light of dawn lit the cottage she bathed away the last of the blood from Jonas' face and neck but still he did not stir other than to mumble words she could not catch.

She crossed to lean on the hearth stooping to push another log of driftwood into the dying embers, planning and dismissing one excuse after another to explain away Jonas' injuries. "He fell off the Strand Quay" was the most convincing story.

"Drunk as usual" she would say and in keeping with his recent behaviour, she felt sure she would be believed. In an hour or so, she would call Dr Hoskin and with luck he would verify the lie. But what of Poll and Tom? Should she tell them the truth or lie to them as well? She shook her head, what could be gained by involving them in the night's happenings? Best they believe the fiction rather than the fact. When Jonas woke she would warn him to stay silent if he wished to cheat Jack Ketch.

A board creaked overhead and Tom peered down over from the top of the stairs.

"Morning Saffy." He knuckled the sleep from his eyes and hitching up the hem of his nightshirt made his way down to the kitchen.

Saffy held out her arms and the boy came willingly into her embrace, his face still flushed from sleep he laid his head against her hip. "Didn't Poll have a lovely day Saffy?"

"She did that Tom."

He climbed onto the settle tucking up his legs and squirming into the corner "There was lots of food wasn't there?"

Saffron nodded. "More'n I've seen of late."

"And music and dancing." Tom hugged his knees. "And best of all was my horse what Gabriel made for me."

"You're a lucky boy Tom and no mistake." She bit her lip. "But today's not going to be as 'appy." She sat at the table and stretched her hand to the boy. "Come 'ere Tom, I've got something to tell you." Obediently Tom clambered from the settle and came to stand at her side his eyes wide with concern.

"What's up Saffy?"

She lifted him up onto her lap. "Well, first of all I don't want you to feel frightened. You're safe Tom, believe me."

"I won't be a'feared I promise." He lent back to gaze at her. "I'm a big boy now. Gabriel says I got to be the man of the 'ouse now Nathan's gone."

"And a fine man you are." Saffron hugged him to her. "Well, it's like this Tom." She took a deep breath. "Your Pa's 'ad an accident and I found 'im by the Strand Quay. E's banged 'is'head and 'urt his ankle so I brought 'im 'ome to get better". She felt the slim body stiffen against her breast.

"'E's here?" Tom struggled from the circle of her arms his eyes wide with terror. "Where Saffy? Where?"

"'Ush now Tom." She held him firmly stroking his back and rocking him gently. "'E's in no state to 'urt no one and you don't 'ave to see him if you don't want. Come on now, man of the 'ouse, up those stairs you go and dress yourself then 'urry back down and you can go fetch Doc Hoskins and tell 'im what's happened." Toms face was pale but Saffron's reassurance seemed to satisfy him and without another word he ran to do her bidding. She waited until Tom had mounted the stair before returning to the bed behind the partition and to Jonas, who seemed not to have moved.

Within minutes Tom was on his way to fetch the village doctor leaving Saffron to rehearse the tale she intended to tell. Doctor Hoskins was not known for wasting his time upon malingers but when summoned to a genuine case he was kindness itself. Tom's urgent knocking had brought him to his door, still wiping the remnants of breakfast from his generous moustache.

Having listened to the boy's frantic pleading, he was quick to follow him through the village to where Saffron waited at the open door of the cottage.

"Now Miss." He stopped to catch his breath. "What's all this I hear about Jonas?"

Saffron stepped aside as he brushed past her. "'E's 'ad a bad fall Doctor."

"A fall? I can't say I'm surprised. I hear he's never sober. Where is he?"

"Over 'ere." Saffron led the way, standing back as the Doctor approached the low bed. She watched as he bent over the still form, taking Jonas' wrist between his fingers. He shook his head and glancing up, saw Tom peeping from behind Saffron's skirts. "Get the lad away." He muttered. "No need for him to be here."

Saffys hand flew to her mouth, the doctors meaning was plain. She turned to put an arm around Tom. "Look, I want you to go see to those kittens and their Ma, they're out in the yard. They ain't had nothin' to eat yet and they'll be real hungry."

Tom frowned, craning his neck to see past her. "But..."

"No buts." She managed to smile. "Off you go now, there's a good boy."

Reluctantly Tom did as he was told leaving Saffron alone with the Doctor. "He's gone then?" Saffron's mind was racing unable to grasp the reality.

"I'm afraid he has. You did a fine job getting him home but no one could have done anything about this." The doctor turned Jonas' head to one side revealing the seeping wound. "Skull fracture. He was a dead man the moment that happened." He eased Jonas' head back onto the pillow. "You say he fell?"

Saffron swallowed nervously. "I didn't see 'im fall, but that's what it looked like when I found 'im. By Strand Quay it were." She added.

The man pulled his nose regarding her steadily for a moment or two. "By Strand Quay?" He repeated. "It's possible, it's a good drop from the quayside and there's a strong smell of rum about him if I'm not mistaken." He laid a gentle hand on her shoulder. "I'll ask Sam Blake, the undertaker, to call by, he'll deal with everything. Best not leave him here."

Saffron bit her lip, a funeral would cost money and Sam
Blake knew how to charge but it would have to be done. She
nodded. "Thank you doctor and I'm much obliged. 'Ow much
do I owe you?"

"Nothing Miss Clay." She met the kind grey eyes. "I believe
you have enough to deal with." He put a hand to her cheek.
"Keep the boy away until Sam has been. Send him on an errand
or ask a neighbour to take him in. And don't go thinking about
keeping the body here." He looked disparagingly around the
small dwelling. "I know it's going against tradition but it's
been proved that the ill humours produced by the body's decay
are injurious to the health of the living. So there'll be no laying
in. Can you deal with that?" Saffron nodded. "I'll pop by later
with a certificate of death which in my opinion was the result
of an unfortunate accident." He turned to lift the thin sheet over
Jonas' face. "May he rest in peace." He spoke quietly before
turning to leave the cottage.

Saffron breathed a sigh of relief, no matter what crime Jonas
had committed, at least his death would record him as a fool
rather than a felon. Somehow she would find the money to pay
Sam Blake if only for the sake of her Mother's memory. There
would be no pauper's grave for Jonas. She shuddered recall-
ing the tales recounted to her stepfather by a carter down from
London. Resurrectionists he had called them.

Body snatching was their trade, supplying fresh corpses for
dissection by medical students.

As far as she knew, the churchyard at Leigh had so far been
untouched by the evil trade but no one could guarantee that it
would remain so. Demand exceeded supply the Carter had said
and not only for the purposes of dissection. She remembered
how her blood had run cold when with obvious enjoyment, he
had told them that the teeth of the dead fetched a high price too,

being made into dentures for those able to afford them.

Each year, he had explained, the corpses of twenty or thirty criminals, together with the bodies of the poor found their way legally to the dissection tables but the resurrectionists still did a satisfying trade in stealing the bodies of the newly dead from their graves. Their wooden shovels made little sound and once the empty graves were refilled, their crime often went unnoticed. Stuffed into sacks and crammed into boxes, the cadavers were delivered under cloak of night to the rear of medical schools, each worth at least twenty guineas. Saffron felt no love for the man but at least she would do her best to save him from that one last unthinkable indignity.

Tom was still sitting on the back step watching the kittens tucking into fish scraps but as he raised his head, Saffron saw that his cheek was wet with tears. He jumped to his feet as the sight of her outstretched arms and ran sobbing to bury his head in her skirt.

"I know Saffy. I know. I was listening at the door. Pa's dead isn't 'e?"

She held the child's shaking body to her. "Yes Tom, Pa's gone. He's in heaven now with Ma." She blinked back her own tears.

"Will he find your Pa there too Saffy?"

She smiled into the upturned face. "More'n likely." She wiped the boys wet cheek with a corner of her apron. "Now I got things to do Tom and I need you to be real grown up."

The child frowned "Course Saffy."

"I need you to go out the back way to Mrs Johnson's place. Tell her what's happened and ask if you can bide a while with her and her boys. You know you likes them."

Tom sniffed cuffing his nose "All right Saffy."

Saffron swung him round and patted his bottom. "Now off

you go. I'll see you later." She watched his reluctant departure, waving him on his way as he glanced over his shoulder one last time. For a few moments she stood raising her face to the early morning sun, yet to add warmth to it's light. She felt a sense of guilt, forced to acknowledge that relief rather than grief was uppermost in her heart.

CHAPTER TWENTY SIX

It was not long before Nathan and Sarah's news had the staff buzzing with excitement.

"So, your Pa said yes did he?" Cook beamed with satisfaction. "And so I should think, that boy's a good catch, you mark my word."

"He did." Sarah nodded. "But we got to wait a while. Ma's set on us doin' it right, so it'll be a year or more before we can wed."

"Quite right too." Cook turned her attention to a pot steaming on the stove. "You know what they say about marrying in haste." She caught sight of Sarah's down turned mouth. "What's up now, girl? You ought to be dancin' with joy."

"I am 'appy, Cook. 'Course I am but it seems so long to 'ave to wait."

"Rubbish girl, the days will go quick you'll see. Now take them 'taters to the table a'fore they gets cold."

Obediently Sarah carried the tureen to set it down in front of Nathan who shifted along the bench seat to make room for her.

"Come on Sweetheart." He whispered, taking her hand. "Sit here with me."

"Here you two. You ain't wed yet." Jake laughed.

"He's a lucky sod." Sam, another of the footmen, joined in the teasing. "'Ad 'is eye on Sarah from the start."

"Long as it's only 'is eye 'e's got on 'er." Sniggered Jake.

"Stop it, all of you!" Cook banged her hand on the table. "Can't you see you're making the girl go red in the face. You're shameful, the lot of you. I won't 'ave no dirty talk in my kitchen. You want to talk like that you go out in the yard and you'll go without your supper!"

"Well, I did hear Miss Charlotte had her eye on our Nathan too." The upstairs maid Bertha took spiteful advantage of the sudden silence. "What d'you think about that Sarah?"

"Well, it's the first I've heard of it." Nathan grinned good-naturedly. "Perhaps I'd best think again." He winked at Sarah. "She is a rich young woman and not bad to look at neither."

"Nathan Clark!" Sarah aimed a slap at his head. "Don't you go even thinkin' of it."

"Well, I've seen her making sheep's eyes at him, so there!" Bertha had no intention of letting Nathan off the hook. "She follows him around like a puppy."

Nathan's good humour began to evaporate. "No, she don't, she's just grateful I helped her when she fell off Bright Lady." He frowned at the housemaid. "You want to watch what you say. Sarah's my intended so that's an end to it!"

Although, as the murmur of general conversation resumed, Nathan reached to squeeze Sarah's hand, the reassuring gesture did nothing to wipe away the misery in her eyes. It was not until later when they had a moment to themselves that Nathan could try to explain.

"Bertha was right in a way, although I'd not given it much mind 'til now."

"What d'you mean Nathan? You're getting' me worried like."

"Well, since Miss Charlotte's been up and about, she seems to be waiting around every corner. She's always got some job that needs doing. Nothing that couldn't wait, things like open or close a window, make up the fire, that sort of thing. It don't amount to much but it makes me sort of uncomfortable."

"Well, you watch 'er." Sarah moved closer to him. "She's trouble, always 'as been."

"Don't you worry about me, my lovely girl. I can take care of myself." He kissed her lightly on her cheek. "Nothing's going to spoil our plans."

She laid her head against his shoulder. "Promise?"

"I promise Sarah, you and me we're meant to be together for life and nothing's going to get in the way of that."

The mood was shattered by Tim's sudden breathless appearance at the kitchen door. "Nathan get off your arse and get in here quick! The Master's got unexpected guests and old Blood and Guts is ranting and roaring for the two of us."

Nathan scrambled to his feet, tugging his neck cloth into place and pausing only to blow a kiss to Sarah, he ran back into the house, hard on the heels of the young footman.

"It's a bit late for visitors." He panted, taking the back stairs two at a time.

"They ain't come for a meal 'parently. Bentley's shown 'em into the library. We got to take 'em Brandy and cigars and 'ang about in case they want summat else."

"How many of them?" The two young men skidded to a halt at the door leading to the main house.

"I dunno." Tim brushed himself down and pushed past his friend into the carpeted hall beyond. Nathan pulled on his white gloves and made his way to the library to find Bentley waiting at the door.

"Where the hell have you been?" He hissed. "The master called for service five minutes since. "Now, get in there and stand silent by the door!"

The Butler followed Tim and Nathan into the library where John Benham sat by the hearth taking in low tones to his visitors. Nathan immediately recognised Jack Walker and two other worthies from an evening earlier in the month when they had dined at the house with their ladies. He sensed however that the mood was far different to that on the previous occasion.

John Benham looked up and beckoned to the Butler who bent his head to listen to his master's quietly spoken command. Nathan saw him nod and turn to scowl in his direction before coming to stand almost toe to toe with him, "The Master wishes you to stay." He managed through gritted teeth. "And you." He turned to Tim. "May go. Now!" He barked as the young footman shot a puzzled glance at his friend. As Tim left, Nathan was surprised to see Bentley follow him, closing he door firmly behind them.

"Now, gentlemen, this is the lad I have been telling thee about." John Benham motioned for Nathan to approach. "This is Nathan." He paused, frowning.

"Nathan Clark, Sir." Nathan supplied, standing stiffly to attention.

"Of course, Nathan Clark." John Benham smiled. "Sit thee down boy, we shall not eat thee."

Nathan edged to the only empty chair by the hearth and perched on the edge of its seat, his mind racing. It was unlikely that he was in trouble as the interested smiles of the assembled company were reassuring but why he wondered was he here? It was a mystery until their host began to explain.

"My friends." He began, indicating Nathan. "This is the young fellow I offer to thee all as a breath of fresh air. A clear headed outlook on the problems of our times, based not on the experience of wealth and status, as are our own, but upon the world in which he lives."

Jack Walker sat forward, extending his hand. "We have met before I believe."

Nathan swallowed, taking the man's outstretched hand. "We have, Sir, and honoured I was to make your acquaintance."

The man sat back, resting his long fingers on the arms of his chair. "You impressed me then and now I shall be interested to hear your views."

"My views, Sir?" Nathan faltered. "What about?"

"What about? What about? I thought you said the lad was smart." The snort of derision came from the florid faced landowner on John Benham's right.

Jack Walker glanced at the man with distaste before returning his attention to Nathan. "Your views upon the state of the country in which you live. How much, for example do you know of the Reform Act passed by Parliament earlier this year in March?" He prompted.

Nathan thought hard for a moment, the views he had so vehemently expressed in the company of his Aunt, may well not be acceptable to the group of worthies gathered together in the master's library. Speak your mind, Jane Porter had told him. Make your arguments clear and well founded. Speak slowly, say nothing in haste and above all remain calm.

"Well Nathan, speak up." John Benham smiled encouragingly.

"Very well, Gentlemen." Nathan cleared his throat, glancing at each face in turn. "In my opinion reform was long overdue." There were murmurs of either assent or dissent, he was unable to make the distinction.

"Go on." Jack Walker sat forward, eyes narrowed with interest.

Nathan searched his mind for the scraps of knowledge he had acquired from his Aunt. "From what I understand the Bill will give a better representation in Parliament than before when most of the seats were taken up by Tories."

"And what else?"

"I know that it gave the right to vote to a lot more people. I think it was only for men, householders who paid a certain level of rent." He paused. "I suppose it makes things fairer but

I can't see why all men should not be able to vote."

"All men?" The one member of the group who until now had remained silent, joined the discussion. "By that do you mean every shopkeeper, farm labourer, every tradesman?"

Nathan looked him in the eye. "I do Sir. For it is those very people who are most affected by the laws passed in Parliament. They should be free to cast their vote for the man who will best represent them." He felt the first twinge of anger at the man's dismissal. "If I may say so, Sir, you live a life of privilege, I doubt that you have ever known hunger or laid shivering in winter in a damp cottage which should have been condemned. Could you work the land seven days a week and hope to keep your family fed on seven shillings?" He struggled to keep the passion he felt from his words. "I grew up in Leigh, a small fishing village on the coast. Men worked hard for the little they brought home to feed their families and if they died, those same families would find themselves in the poorhouse. Even that was better than being evicted from their homes to roam the country begging for food and shelter for the children."

"But what of the lawbreakers?" The man was determined to make his point. "Do you agree with the villains who smash the threshing machines, who burn the hayricks?"

"No Sir, I do not. Violence is not the answer, although to my knowledge that sort of thing took place mostly in the North. Folk here are better treated in the main." He shot an accusing glance at the florid faced landowner. "But there's still things to put right. Perhaps if the right men were responsible for ruling the country things would be different."

For a moment there was complete silence, each man looking speculatively at the young footman. John Benham broke the silence. "Thank thee, Nathan. Thee may leave us now. Ask Bentley to bring coffee, then thee may retire. We shall speak again tomorrow."

Nathan felt a sense of relief and getting to his feet he turned to each address man in turn. "Good night gentlemen." They murmured an acknowledgement as he left the library. For a moment he stood with his back to the closed door, letting out a long sigh. "Thank the Lord that's over." He grinned suddenly. "But I told them." He sobered, mindful of his Aunt's caution. "I just hope I didn't come on too strong. Well, I'll know tomorrow." He pushed himself away from the door with a shrug. "And who knows what tomorrow will hold."

CHAPTER TWENTY SEVEN

There was a great deal of speculation concerning Jonas' death. Those more kindly disposed to Saffron's loss accepted her version of events without question. Many had learned of the apprehension and arrest of the band of wreckers known to be close associates of Jonas and spoke behind their hands of narrow escapes and just deserts.

Sam Blake had been and gone, taking the body with him by the time Gabriel and his young wife, on hearing the news, had hastened back to the cottage, where Poll wasted no time in speaking her mind.

"Good riddance, I say. Wicked Bastard 'e were!"

"Now, now, Poll." Gabriel shook his head. "Don't go talking bad about the dead. T'ain't Christian."

"An' you think 'e were? T'aint Christian to go thieving and murderin' neither."

"Maybe so but 'tis said that the Good Lord forgives the biggest sinner." The big man paused. "So if Jonas repents like, praps 'e'll find a place in 'eaven after all."

"Not likely! It's down to 'ell 'e'll go and serve 'im right!"

Saffron put an arm around her sister's shoulders "Don't carry on so Poll, Tom'll be back soon and I don't want 'im to 'ear such talk."

Poll glanced away. "I'm sorry Saffy but when I think.." She left the sentence unfinished. "Anyway." She straightened her thin shoulders "We came over to help, so what can we do?"

"You can go to the church and set a time for the funeral. Sam Blake took the body away an hour ago. He said day after tomorrow would do."

"Leave it to us Miss Saffy." Gabriel took Poll by the arm.

"We'll be back afore long."

Saffron stared absently from the window. The day after tomorrow she mused, was the day Jean-Pierre had said he'd be back. "Oh, Jean-Pierre, not long but I need you now." She whispered. "I need to feel your arms round me, see the love in your eyes, I need your strength."

She wandered aimlessly through to the rear of the cottage and began to strip the bed gathering the bloodstained sheets into a bundle. "Best boil these." She said aloud. "That's what Ma would do." For a moment as if the words were spoken like a summoning spell, she fancied that Mary Clay had returned to comfort her. She closed her eyes. "Oh Ma." She whispered. "What's to do now? I know I got to get through somehow. Nathan's miles away, Poll's wed and Jonas, God forgive him has gone. There's only Tom and me left." She paused and took a deep breath. "And, Jean-Pierre, God willing." She added.

Saffron took the soiled bedding into the yard and stuffed it into the copper boiler, covering it with water drawn the previous day from the village pump. Resolving to set the fire later she returned to the kitchen and settled down at the table knowing that she must write to her brother without delay.

She wrote quickly, her pencil flying over the page, sparing none of the details of her version of Jonas' supposed accident. She read it over with satisfaction. "He don't need to know the truth. Not now. P'raps I'll tell him one day." It was enough for her to carry the burden.

Poll and Gabriel returned from the church to confirm that the funeral could take place two days later at four in the afternoon. They had already told the undertaker so little remained to be done other than send the letter to Nathan on the first cart out of the village.

Gabriel undertook the errand leaving the sisters together.

"So, 'ow you feelin Poll?" Saffron took a broom to the ash littered hearth, watching her sister from the corner of her eye.

"I s'pose I'm alright Saffy." She faltered, searching for the right words. "I was scared when I got home from the weddin'. You know why, but Gabriel was so kind." She shook her head. "He said as 'ow I'd 'ad a busy day and I needed me rest. He put me to bed Saffy, kissed me gentle like and then took himself off to sleep down in the kitchen. When I woke up this morning 'e 'ad food on the table and a brew of tea waiting." She sat, head bowed, hands clasped together. "Do you think Gabriel really wants me Saffy?"

Saffron threw back her head and laughed aloud. "You silly Goose. 'E wants you and no mistake, 'e loves you Poll." Her voice softened "'E's showing you 'ow much by not rushing you. 'E knows it'll take time." She crossed to tilt her sister's chin to meet her gaze. "But not too much time Poll. Gabriel's a good and gentle man but 'e 'as 'is needs. Trust him, e'll know when the time is right."

Poll smiled. "You always know what's right Saffy and I will be a good wife. I just need a bit of time is all."

The morning of the funeral dawned sweet and clear but it failed to lift Tom's spirits. For two days he had eaten very little and Saffron suspected slept hardly at all.

"I don't 'ave to go Saffy do I?"

Saffron took the child onto her knee. "Not if you don't want to Tom. But 'e was your Pa." She brushed a curl back from his eyes. "I know 'e wasn't always, well the best Pa in the world, but p'raps today's a chance to forgive 'im. And to say goodbye." She added. "You and me we'll walk up the 'ill together. Poll and Gabriel will be there and I dare say some of your Pa's friends. Then everyone'll come back 'ere, for a bite to eat and a drink to wish 'im on his way. Now." She stood him down, straightening his jacket. "You can give me an 'and to tidy up and set the table, there's no knowing 'ow many folk might come back."

Encouraged by her words, Tom set about the small tasks she gave him while Saffron prepared the meagre funeral feast. The baker had donated a dozen or so bread rolls and the grocer some cheese and a few thin slices of ham cut from a newly smoked joint. One of Jonas' cronies, more from guilt than generosity had earlier left a small keg of ale at the door with a muttered explanation "From 'is mates, Miss Saffron."

She had replied frostily "Beggars can't be choosers, so I thank you."

By half past three the small party gathered to follow the horse drawn funeral cart bearing the rough elm coffin up the hill to the church. Tom dragged his heels until with a wink at Saffron, Gabriel lifted the boy onto his broad shoulders.

"Come on lad, we'll make the climb together."

A handful of villagers, those kindly disposed to Saffron, gave their support by walking behind the family taking Jonas to his resting place. With her mind in a turmoil, Saffron relived snatches of memory. Jonas as a good provider and stepfather only six years earlier. Her mother dying so soon after Tom's birth and Jonas' gradual decline into a drunken parody of his former self. The horror of the wrecker's capture and Jonas' plea for help, clawed at her mind, still too recent to be softened by the passage of time.

The grey stone tower of Leigh Church rose square against a clear blue sky. The afternoon sun, beating down on the heads of the mourners, made a mockery of the solemn business in hand.

The plain elm coffin, borne aloft by men from the village was carried into the church to rest on trestles before the altar where the Reverend Parsons stood waiting to conduct the ceremony. Voices raised in praise did justice to the first hymn and the creaking knees of the elderly bent obediently to pray for the departed soul of Jonas Turner.

Little was said by the vicar about the man himself other than that he had been born and spent his life in the village, had married and produced a son. No reference was made to the last few years of his life for which Saffron was thankful. Never speak ill of the dead as Gabriel had said, let Jonas rest in whatever degree of peace he could find.

Once again the coffin was carried high on strong shoulders over the close cropped turf to where the waiting grave's damp black maw yawned wide to receive it's offering. A fat bee settled to lazily explore the bunch of wild flowers resting on the coffin lid and as they grouped around the edge. As the lid began to sink from sight Tom let out a strangled sob.

"Ashes to Ashes."

Saffron squeezed the small hand. "Not long now." She mouthed.

"Dust to Dust."

Gabriel's arms tightened around his white-faced wife.

"In the sure and certain knowledge…"

As the first handful of earth fell to rattle it's death song on the elm coffin below, the mourners threw the sprigs of rosemary they had carried, into the open grave and only the muffled cough of an elderly neighbour broke the silence.

The service came to an end and Saffron tore her thoughts back to the moment in hand. Kind words of condolence were offered by friends as they left the graveside to wend their way between the stone markers of those who had gone before.

Reverend Pearce, the Parson shook hands with Saffron and Poll, crouching to look kindly into Tom's pinched face. "Your father will be with the good Lord now, so no tears boy." He glanced up at the sisters standing side by side. "Come, I will return with you to your home where we will wish Jonas well on his journey."

It was a subdued party that wound its way down the hill, each with their own thoughts, brought starkly to mind of the only sure thing in life. Their own inevitable, unavoidable, date with death.

Only a few of Saffron's closest neighbours stayed to partake of the funeral feast, offering their comfort and speaking to each other in hushed voices. By six o'clock they were gone leaving Poll and Gabriel to help Saffron clear away.

"They didn't leave much." Poll sniffed, sweeping crumbs from the table.

"The ales finished too." Gabriel chuckled as he shook the empty keg above his head. He caught Tom's eye. "You gave your Pa a good send off boy." He set the keg down. "But now I reckon you need to get some sleep, you look wore out." He lifted Tom into strong arms tweaking his nose. "How about I tucks you into bed and tells you a tale or two?" Gabriel saw Saffy's nod of approval and he took the stairs two at a time tickling the giggling child on the way.

"He's good with young'uns." Poll watched wistfully as they disappeared from sight.

"Well, he'll soon have one of his own." Saffron slid plates into the bucket of warm water. "By my reckoning that baby will have the best Pa 'e could wish for." She handed a towel to her sister. "Wipe this lot up and we'll put them away and take care, they're all what's left of Ma's wedding gifts." She held a plate up to the light "See how thin it is? That's good stuff that is. Her sister gave it to her. The one who Nathan's with up in Saffron Waldon."

"Last time I see these was when Ma died." Poll wiped the plate carefully.

"Well let's hope we don't see em again for a while."

The day had drawn to a close, sending a chill breeze from the sea to rob the earth of the sun's warmth. When Gabriel came quietly down the stair he found the two girls sitting in companionable silence each with they own memories of the day.

"We'd best be off Poll." He bent to kiss his wife on the cheek. "Young Tom'll sleep 'til morning, poor little chap."

Poll got to her feet "You be alright Saffy?"

"Course I will. I'll walk Tom over to see you on the morrow. Take 'is mind off today."

"You'll be welcome Miss Saffy." Gabriel held open the door for Poll. "You know where we are if you need us."

As she closed the door behind them, the tension of the day seemed to evaporate suddenly, and she found herself without immediate purpose. Save for Tom sleeping in the room above, the cottage was empty of life but filled with memories. She fancied she could hear her fathers booming laughter, her mothers gentle chiding. Voices from her childhood when she and Nathan and Poll were safe in the warmth of a poor but happy family. She reached to pull together the window curtains and caught her reflection in the darkening glass. "Those happy days are gone forever, never to return." She told the sad young woman was stared back at her. She felt the tears begin and sank heavily onto the settle as head in hands she gave herself up at last to the agonising sobs which all day had threatened to rack her slender body.

The sound of urgent pounding on the cottage door broke through her misery and hastily wiping her eyes she stumbled to answer the summons.

She lifted the latch the door swung open and in that second

she was in his arms.

"Saffy my love." Jean-Pierre held her to him. "I've just returned and met Gabriel and Poll on my way here. Oh my darling, I should have been by your side."

Saffron laid her head against his chest. "You couldn't 'ave done nothin'."

"Maybe, but somehow I'm sure I could have made things easier for you."

"It don't matter it's over now and you're 'ere." She raised her head, feeling a sudden urgency for physical comfort. "Stay with me Jean-Pierre. I don't want to be 'ere alone tonight."

"My sweet lovely girl I will stay for as long as you wish. I have so much to tell you but it can wait." He felt her slender body relax against him and in a moment was all concern. "But you should rest." She laid her head on his shoulder as he lifted her into his arms, and slowly climbed the stair, pushing open the bedroom door and laying her gently on the bed.

Somewhere at the back of her mind Saffron felt she should protest as Jean- Pierre bent to kiss her but the tension of the day now eased by his presence, robbed her of the last remnants of caution. Reaching to wind her arms around his neck she returned his kiss welcoming the firm pressure of his lips.

"'Old me, 'old me tight. Tell me again that you love me Jean-Pierre."

The bed dipped as he lay beside her, taking her into his arms and burying his face in her sweet scented hair.

"I shall never cease to tell you that I love you. I vow I will say it every day my dearest. Now that the way is clear, we have so many plans to make for our own wedding. We have so much to discuss but we will talk about it all in the morning."

But Saffron was not listening, Jean-Pierre smiled, her beautiful eyes were closed, her sweet lips parted in sleep.

"Yes, we will talk tomorrow my love." He murmured tracing a gentle finger over her cheek. "And tomorrow and every tomorrow for eternity. I shall prove to you that I love you more than life itself."

In the days that followed, for Tom's sake, Saffron made every effort to restore a sense of normality in her everyday life. While she sat each morning for Jean-Pierre the boy played with his friends on the beach below and within sight of the window of Juniper Cottage. Now and again, at the end of the day, Saffron caught him staring out to sea, lost in his own private thoughts. Everyone grieves in their own way, her Mother had said. The time would come, she hoped when Tom would find it easier to talk about his father and the unhappy months leading up to his death.

Poll had begun to blossom under Gabriel's tender care and Saffron could not help but to smile at her sister's growing confidence. "So I says to Gabriel as 'ow we'll be needin' a crib 'afore too long." She had smoothed her gown over the now evident bulge of the child growing within her. "I know there's months yet, but he's started on it so it'll be ready." She had frowned. "I found a length of white cotton packed away in a cupboard. Gabriel's wife must 'ave got it. I asked 'im if I could make some sheets for the crib and things and 'e said she would have wanted it so. She had paused, dipping her head shyly. "And Gabriel and me, well we're getting to know each other Saffy. Its just like you said. He knowed when it was right."

All in all Saffron felt she could feel a cautious satisfaction that for the time being at least, things had settled down, even Nathan seemed to be happy in Saffron Walden and Jean-Pierre was anxious to complete the latest commissioned portrait for a buyer in Brighton. "I shall deliver it when we visit my Mother." He had said. "She told me that she cannot wait to meet you, my love."

And now the day had arrived and Poll and Gabriel had been happy to have Tom for a few days.

A stiff, early morning breeze tugged at the skirts of her new gown as Saffron waited nervously on the Strand Quay. She glanced back at the village and for a moment she envied her neighbours as they went about their everyday life. Few of them had ventured more than a mile or so from the small fishing village and here she was on her way to Brighton.

Jean-Pierre had explained their route, the first part to be by water into the Port of London, disembarking at Billingsgate Wharf. Then by Hackney Carriage to Southwark where, he assured her, they would find a coach bound for Brighton.

"I shall be with you, every inch of the way, my love." He had chuckled reassuringly. "Just put your hand in mind, trust me, Brighton is not at the far ends of the earth."

She glanced up at the tall figure shading his eyes to scan the horizon. Jean-Pierre Howard, the young artist who had visited Leigh intending only to paint the surrounding countryside but who, struck by her beauty, had persuaded her to sit for him.

Aware of her gaze, he smiled into her upturned face, encircling her waist with a strong arm and hugging her to his side. "Not long now." He pointed. "See, there's the barge making its way toward the Quay." His smile turned to an expression of concern as he realised that she was trembling. "Are you cold?"

She nodded, "A bit, but the sun will soon be up." She pulled the folds of her woollen cloak closer, forcing a smile. "I'll be alright." Her confident words seemed to satisfy him but she knew it to be a lie. The thought of meeting Madam Louise Howard, Jean-Pierre's aristocratic French mother, filled her with dread, her fear enhanced by his snippets of description of the woman's unpredictable nature. Apparently she lived in style in a large house left to her by Jean-Pierre's English father, where she entertained on a grand scale. Prior to his arrival in Leigh, the man Saffron had agreed to marry had lived with her in Brighton and was used to rubbing shoulders with the artists and writers who were constant visitors to the imposing house. But for Saffron, it represented an alien and frightening world.

The Thames Barge rode gently on the smooth swell of the high tide as under the skilled hand of its master, it came to rest alongside the Quay. Jean-Pierre and Saffron seemed to be the only passengers that morning and once aboard, they settled on deck between a collection of bales and crates, a cargo destined as they were, for the Port of London.

"Mornin' Miss Saffy." Bill Croft's weather beaten face creased into a wide smile, showing tobacco-stained teeth. He had seen Saffron grow from child into woman, sharing many a yarn with her father in the bar of the Smack Inn. He stood swaying with the roll of the barge, curling a mooring line around his bare arm. "'Ow be young Poll? I 'ear she got wed."

"She did, a month or so back. Gabriel Stoneforth will make 'er a good 'usband."

"And that rascal of a brother 'o yourn, young Tom. What is 'e now, four or five?"

"Five, and 'e can already say some of his tables and write a few words." Saffron added proudly. "He'll be startin' at the Church school come September."

"My! 'Ow these young'uns do grow." The man turned to stare at Jean-Pierre.

"An' who be this fine fellow? I ain't bin ashore for a while, but if I ain't mistook you'll be that artist chap what's bin livin' at Juniper Cottage.

Jean-Pierre held out a hand. "I am that artist fellow." He grinned."Jean-Pierre Howard at your service Sir."

Bill Croft took his hand willingly. "Sir, is it? Well now, 'tis a while since I bin called that!"

"Anyone who handles a craft this size with such skill deserves my admiration." Jean-Pierre spread expressive hands to encompass the sixty foot craft. "'T'would be beyond my capabilities, I'm sure."

The barge owner chewed on the stem of an ancient pipe as he considered the compliment. "Well, now, I dare say as 'ow I couldn't draw nothin' worth lookin' at neither. So it makes us sort of even I'd say." The men's roar of laughter cemented a newly formed friendship and once again Saffron marvelled at the ease with which Jean-Pierre seemed to find, in everyone he met, a level of common interest.

"So how much will she carry?" Her companion's genuine show of interest gave Bill Croft the opportunity to talk about The West Wind, his beloved Thames Barge. At times, Saffron had seen the deck loaded with hay to a height of twenty feet or more, so high that the boy, the only other crew member, had to stand on the top of the stack to shout instructions to the skipper, who could not see ahead of the Barge.

"She'll take two hundred and fifty tons, well loaded." Bill Croft's chest swelled with pride. "She b'ain't as fast as some but she can go where most can't. She gets the wind in that spritsail rig and she'll take me anywhere I want's 'course she's flat bottomed see." The man saw Jean-Pierre's puzzled expression. "No keel, so she don't need deep water. She's got leeboards. I lets 'em down on each side when I needs to settle 'er on 'er moorin'."

The early morning chill had begun to give way to the warmth of sun and Saffron was only half listening. She loosened the neck of her cloak and reached to tug the pin from the crown of her cream straw hat, turning the brim to admire the spray of blue flowers stitched to the matching ribbon. She stroked the folds of the cloak. Jean-Pierre had insisted that she allow him to order both the hat and cloak for their visit to his mother, together with a length of blue sprigged muslin from which she had sewn the simple gown. At his suggestion, its full skirt was gathered into a neat waist and sported a bodice which Jean-Pierre had assured her had a fashionably low neckline. Nonetheless, she constantly adjusted it in an effort to preserve her modesty. A wide blue sash and new supple leather shoes completed an outfit, which to Saffron was both unfamiliar and uncomfortable.

"Why do I 'ave to get dressed up?" Earlier, she had stood in front of the mirror in Juniper Cottage. "If you tie a bow on a donkey, it don't make into an 'orse!"

Jean-Pierre had closed his arms around her. "Look at yourself, my love. You are certainly no donkey. Rather I see a thoroughbred, high stepping filly. Just look at the proud lines." He ran a finger over the side of her neck. "And this wonderful mane." He threaded long fingers through her long sun kissed hair, spreading it into a shining cape. "But in this sad world, first impressions are important and I want my mother, who has only a superficial appreciation of all she sees, to recognise the beauty that has held me captive from the moment I saw you."

"But it's not just what she'll see." Saffron bit her lip. "It's what she'll 'ear. I don't talk like you." She smiled. "Though I've 'eard you take off old Ma Hoskins to make Poll and Tom laugh. You've got her voice off to a tee."

"That's mimicry. Anyone can do it." He paused as a thought struck him. "If it worries you so much, why not mimic me?"

"I couldn't."

"You, my darling, could do anything if you tried hard enough."

She smiled at the memory, if that was what he wanted she had made up her mind to do her best to play the part.

"Look, Saffron." His voice broke into her thoughts. "Tilbury Fort." Leaning against the ship's rail, he pointed to the squat red stone building built to guard the Thames against invasion.

She joined him at the rail. "I learned about that in school." She was pleased to display her scant knowledge. "It's got lots of guns to stop attacks from the sea, 'asn't it?"

"That's right." Jean-Pierre looked pleasantly surprised, "It has been there for over a hundred and fifty years. It's still home to a garrison and rumour has it there's enough gunpowder stored within its walls to blow the whole fort sky high." He saw her concern and pressed her to his side. "Don't worry we'll soon be past."

She shaded her eyes against the glare of the sparkling sunlit water. "What's that out there?"

"Where?" He followed the line of her pointing finger. "Oh, those are prison hulks. Old merchant ships and naval vessels, converted into floating prisons."

"You mean there's men on board?"

"Too many of the poor devils, most of them waiting for transportation to Australia. I've heard that the conditions on board are beyond belief." He added angrily. "The men are half starved and ill treated by their jailers who pocket the profit from the food and clothing meant for the prisoners."

Saffron shuddered. But for the grace of God her brother Nathan could have shared the same fate had he not escaped to Saffron Walden. She remembered the night he had fallen, exhausted, through the cottage door, injured and with the Excise men hot on his heels.

To many men along the Essex coast, smuggling was little more than a harmless way to subsidise their income from fishing, but with the building of the new Custom House in Leigh and the fast Revenue Cutter off shore, more and more found their way into custody and deportation.

As if reading her thoughts Jean-Pierre stood away from the rail. "Have you heard from Nathan lately?"

She reached into the small bag on her wrist and found the letter, which had arrived by Tom Carter only the day before. She passed it to him. "I should 'ave told you, but with all the preparation for today, it slipped my mind. "'Ere read it for yourself."

Jean-Pierre smoothed the closely written pages and scanned the content. "It seems he is well settled working at the house. Your Aunt got him a job in the stables and listen to this." He began to read the letter aloud. "When I started I thought in time I'd make a good groom but when the horse, the Master's young daughter was set on riding, bolted, I was in the right place to find her and see to her. Then things began to happen. I was called up to the big house. I thought I was in real trouble, I can tell you, but no." "You be wasted in the stables lad." The Master says. "Your Aunt tells me that you can read and write." "Well I just nods, then he looks me up and down like and says." How would you like to work in the house?" "I just stood there grinning like an idiot. It seems that one of his footmen had been called home to Colchester, where he was needed by his family, and I got the job.

You should see me all dressed up in a smart green coat and britches with white linen and polished shoes. Barthelomew, the head groom, he says I got the luck of the devil. I'm learning my duties as the Butler calls it and I share a room at the top of the house with two other lads and it's a sight more snug than the room over the stables."

"Well, I think you can cease to worry about Nathan's welfare,

he has obviously fallen on his feet." Jean-Pierre folded the
letter and handed it back to Saffron. "Have you written to tell
him about Jonas?"

Saffron nodded. "Our letters must 'ave crossed 'cos he
makes no mention of it." She knew her brother would rejoice
at the news of the death of their stepfather, removing as it did
the threat to her and the others. She thought briefly of the sad
burial party, which had made its way to the churchyard with
only a handful of followers, Tom, Poll and herself to mourn
the passing of the drunken bully who had once been a fine,
honest man.

"You look tired, my love, and we have still a way to go."
Jean-Pierre moved a bale of hay to one side and pulled her
down to sit beside him. She snuggled into the comforting circle
of his arms, resting her head against his chest.

"Where are we now?"

He raised his head to peer over the gunnel. "Just entering the
Woolwich Warren." Saffron knelt to see the maze of workshops, warehouses, wood-yards and foundries slip by as the
barge made its way between the growing number of ships in
the river. "Wait a few minutes and you will see Greenwich
Palace. A beautiful sight that is. In your lessons did you learn
about Henry the Eighth and Elizabeth?" She nodded. "They
were both born there."

She hung her head. "You know so much about everything.
You must think I'm a fool."

He bent his head to kiss the tip of her nose. "How could
you know about things you have never seen. I have travelled
this way several times on my way to Brighton, so the route is
familiar." He got to his feet, offering his hand. "Come, now,
we shall soon be docking at Billingsgate Wharf where I assure
you, you will not wish to tarry. There is a fish market there and

the noise and stench are unbelievable."

Within the hour they were ashore and Jean-Pierre's word were proved to be true. Great quantities of fish were brought both from along the coast and by land and Saffron clapped her hands to her ears as the loud ringing of bells added to the shouts of men and the rumble of carts.

"That's the opening bell." Jean-Pierre shouted to make his voice heard above the din. "The market will stay open now until five, so we'd best find a Hackney carriage before we are trampled under foot."

Once through the market it was easy to hail one of the many carriages plying for custom and lifting the carefully wrapped portrait and their only piece of luggage onto the rack Jean-Pierre settled himself beside a wide-eyed Saffron.

"I've never seen so many folk all in one place." She whispered leaning forward, determined to miss nothing.

He put an arm around her shoulder. "This is London, my love. A wonderful, vibrant city, teeming with life. A bit bigger than Leigh, is it not?"

"And smellier!" Saffron wrinkled her nose. Do we have far to go?"

"Only to Southwark, where I have booked rooms for us at the George Inn. The coach leaves early tomorrow for the journey to Brighton. We should arrive before dark."

The moment when Saffron would come face to face with Madam Louise Howard, had that morning, seemed far away but suddenly it became uncomfortably near and she wondered what the next day would hold.

CHAPTER TWENTY EIGHT

Tim had already fallen asleep by the time Nathan climbed the back stair to the attic he shared with the other footmen. Thankful to have escaped the necessity of explanation, he fell gratefully into his narrow bed, aware that only a few hours remained before his duties began once again.

He woke to find Tim poking a hard finger into his chest. "Come on Nathan, wake up! What 'appened last night after we left?" Reluctantly, he opened his eyes to see his friend struggling into his britches. "Old Blood and Guts was right put out, bein' sent off like that." He laughed. "Went in and slammed his door. I reckon you'll get the rough edge of his tongue this day."

Nathan swung his legs to the floor. "Well, it weren't my fault." He ran his fingers through sleep tousled hair. "I can't help it if the master wanted to ask me things."

"What things?" Tim shrugged into his jacket, the floodgates of his curiosity open wide.

"I suppose mostly what I thought about wages and working conditions. That sort of stuff." Nathan stood yawning and stretching to his full height.

Tim stared at him open mouthed. "What they want to ask you for?"

"They wanted to know what it's like to work for a living." Nathan frowned. "I just hope I said the right things. I did sort of speak my mind."

"Well that's you finished then." Tim sat to pull on his shoes. "I've 'eard you when you gets goin'!"

"We'll see." Nathan shrugged in an attempt to make light of it. "The master said he wants to talk to me again sometime today, so I'll find out then won't I?"

"Most likely you'll get a tickin' off. Mind you the master seems to favour you. God only knows why." Tim dodged Nathan's playful clout and made for the door. "You'd best get a move on or Old Blood and Guts'll flay your 'ide.

It took only minutes for Nathan to sluice his face and hands and to run a comb through his hair. Still tying his neckcloth he clattered down the stairs to push open the door to the main house. Stepping into the richly carpeted corridor beyond he came face to face with Charlotte, the master's young daughter.

He managed a smile. "Morning, Miss Charlotte. How's the arm?" He indicated the sling she still wore.

"Well enough." She looked him up and down. "Which is more than I can say for thy appearance."

Nathan felt the colour flood his cheeks as she took a step forward and ran a hand over his stubbled chin. Startled, he backed away. "I'm sorry Miss Charlotte." He stammered. "I'll see to it later."

"If Old Blood and Guts sees it thee will be in trouble." She smiled at his gasp of surprise. "Oh, I know what thee calls him." She whispered conspiritorily. "I think it fits him perfectly. But he can wait. Thee may tell him that I had a little job for thee." She turned on her heel beckoning him to follow.

Smothering a frustrated curse, Nathan did as she ordered, almost bumping into her as she came to a halt at the door of her bedroom. She stood back. "Well, open the door, boy. Thee can hardly accomplish the task I have for thee from out here in the corridor."

Nathan grasped the brass handle and held the door back to allow her entry. She swept past him with a swish of her skirts and turned to see him step over the threshold.

"Now, close the door and come over here!" Something in

her smile, the way she placed a hand on one hip, twisting her body precociously from side to side, sent a warning signal to Nathan. It was not the first time, he realised, that Charlotte had tried to corner him. This time like a fool, he had become like a fly caught in her web.

"What is it you wish me to do, Miss Charlotte?" He fixed his gaze on middle distance, refusing to meet her eye.

"What would thee like to do, Nathan?" The autocrat had become the coquette as with a single step she closed the gap between them and placed her hands on his chest in an artful pretence of brushing the lapels of his jacket. Against his will, he found himself gazing down into her up-tilted face. Una-shamed lust coloured her cheeks as she ran a wet tongue over her parted lips. "Wouldn't thee like to kiss me, Nathan?" She laid her head against his heart. "I know thee would." She chuckled softly. "I've seen thee watching me, wanting me."

"No, Miss Charlotte." Nathan sprang away from her. "You must not say such things." He raised his hands as if to ward her away. "I could never have such thoughts! You are the mas-ter's daughter!"

She leaned back, the smile left her face, leaving in its place a mask of thin lipped fury. "And what if I were to report to my father that indeed thee had dared to touch me, to kiss me?"

Nathan's mouth was fear dried as he shook his head. "You wouldn't do that Miss, it wouldn't be true and I'd lose my posi-tion."

"Yes, boy, thee would. Thee would be wise to consider that. But thee will not need to be reminded will thee?" She turned away, waving a dismissive hand. "Thee may go now. For the time being." She added glancing over her shoulder.

Nathan needed no second bidding and wrenching open the door, he stood for a moment steadying himself against the wall. "Whew!" He let out a long breath. "I'm lucky to get out of there in one piece." He frowned. "You're going to have to watch your step, Nathan me lad." He muttered. "That filly's got the bit between her teeth and no mistake."

It was fortunate that the butler was busy going over the household account with Nathan's aunt when he finally appeared below stairs.

"Where 'ave you been?" Sarah hurried to his side. "I put something by for you but the others 'ave all broke their fast and gone about their tasks." She urged him to sit at the kitchen table. "Cook and me thought you was ill, but Tim said you was on the way down. So what 'appened?"

Nathan shook his head. Now was not time to go into details. "Miss Charlotte told me she wanted me to open a window in her room, is all."

"You took your time, lad." The Cook gave him a knowing glance. "Little Madam up to her tricks is she?"

"Don't know what you mean, Mrs Rand." Nathan concentrated on the food on his plate, refusing to meet her gaze.

"If you says so." The woman sniffed. "But you wants to watch your back where that one's concerned. She makes mischief any chance she gets. You ain't the first she's set 'er sights on and you won't be the last. There were a young gardener not much older'n you." The cook raised her eyes to heaven. "Miss Charlotte took a shine to 'im too!"

"What 'appened?" Sarah pulled a chair forward to sit beside Nathan.

"Ran 'im ragged, she did. Cutting fresh flowers, pickin' apples and such. Never left 'im alone." The big woman sighed for effect, aware the young couple were hanging on her every word. "Then one day the master caught them together in one of the greenhouses. Poor Robbie, that were 'is name, he tried to explain but that little madam saved 'er own skin by saying' 'e'd been pestering 'er for weeks."

"And of course, the master believed her!" Sarah's snort of indignation brought a troubled frown to Nathan's face.

"She said she'd do as much to me unless I…" He faltered, glancing a Sarah.

"Unless you what?"

"Unless I kissed her and…"

"And what else?"

"I don't know." Nathan shook his head miserably, reaching for Sarah's hand. "It's you I want, no one else. Least of all Miss Charlotte."

Sarah regarded him steadily, searching his face for the truth. "She is awful pretty. And it seems the master thinks a lot of you."

"What are you saying? That he'd think me fit to court his daughter?" Nathan threw back his head and laughed aloud. "He'll make a match for her when the time is right and it won't be with no footman like me."

"Well if you asks me he wants to make it soon." The cook chuckled. "If she were a plum, she'd be ripe for the pickin'!"

Sarah giggled. "Oh, Mrs Rand you do say some dreadful things." She turned to smile at Nathan. "You just make sure it ain't you what harvests the fruit!"

"Come here woman." As Sarah rose Nathan grabbed her arm, pulling her onto his knee, cupping her chin and turning her to face him. "There's only one fruit I want to pick and when the day comes I'll strip the tree bare." He felt her slender body tremble within the circle of his arm as she buried her head against his neck.

"Now you stop that, you both got work to do." The cook lent heavily on the scrubbed pine table. "You'll be missed 'afore long." She wagged a finger at Nathan. "And you Miss, you've got 'taters to peel."

Reluctantly they parted, each to their duties, each warmed by the memory of their embrace.

Tim was in a filthy mood when Nathan appeared. "I 'ates cleaning the silver. T'is a maid's job." He grumbled as Chloe slid another pile of forks toward him.

"Oh, stop your moaning. The job's gotta be done and many 'ands make light work."

"And look what it's doin' to my 'ands." Tim held them out for inspection. "It'll take hours to get 'em clean and Old Blood and Guts will spot it a mile off." He glared at Nathan. "'Bout time you showed up. Here give us a 'and with this lot." He tossed a polishing cloth in his friend's direction. "Where you been anyway?"

Nathan shrugged, "Doing a job for Miss Charlotte and breaking my fast with Sarah."

"Miss Charlotte?" Chloe sneered. "She can't do nothin' for 'erself. Do this, do that girl, she says and never a please or thank you. Yesterday she says "Fetch me that book", and 'er sitting not an arm's length from it."

"I bet you give it to 'er." Tim sniggered.

"I did. And I give 'er a little curtsey like. I know where I'm well off."

"Its not right though, is it?" Nathan reached for another piece of silver, thoughtfully turning it over in his hand. The way I see it is there's three sorts of folk living under this roof. There's us." He indicated his companions. "We're up at dawn working all hours. Then there's those in the middle, the Governess, ladies maid, housekeeper, butler." He ticked them off on the fingers of one hand. "They think there're better than us. And then of course, there's the family." He began to polish a small silver salver. "The Master's a good man, none better to my mind. The mistress is a bit strange if you ask me but nice enough all the same, and little Charles, well he's a lovely little lad. But Miss Charlotte's another kettle of fish altogether." He rubbed savagely at the tray. "Trouble is what she is."

Tim caught his eye. "She up to her tricks again?" Nathan nodded. "You'd best tell the Master." His friend grinned. "Mayhap he'll believe you, you being well in with 'im."

"You think I should?"

The smile faded from Tim's face. "I was only joking."

"No, you could be right." Nathan turned his attention to a silver cream jug.

"If I tell him first it will sort of spike her guns if you know what I mean. She'll have nothing to hold over me."

"Rather you than me." Tim began to sort a handful of cutlery. "Likely as not you'll be out on your ear come nightfall."

"I'm not planning on doing anything hasty. I'll bide my time. Next time the Master asks for me I'll test the water like. If he's in the right mood to listen I'll choose my words and hope for the best." But Nathan knew in his heart that his words were but a thin veneer of bravado overlaid upon a sea of uncertainty.

CHAPTER TWENTY NINE

Arrangements for their overnight stay had been meticulously supervised in advance by Jean-Pierre. Two separate and adequately furnished rooms at the Swan Inn awaited them and after a meal of roast beef served by the Innkeeper's wife, Jean-Pierre suggested they retire. The old staircase creaked as they made their way onto the first landing.

"It has been a long day, my love. Tomorrow we shall be in Brighton. Mother is expecting us and is, I know, eager to meet her future daughter in law."

"I just'ope." She paused, correcting her speech. "I just hope." She repeated. That I shall not let you down."

"You could never do that." He took her in his arms. "When Maman knows you, she will love you as I do." He kissed her softly on her cheek. "Now, get some sleep. I will wake you in the morning."

Reluctantly Saffron let him go, closing the door behind him. Although she was travel weary, at first sleep eluded her. Finally she drifted into an uneasy slumber beset by dreams of dragons in silken gowns.

Good to his word, Jean-Pierre woke her early next day and after a light meal the coach began the last part of the journey to Brighton. As they neared their destination, Saffron became more anxious, while Jean-Pierre became more and more reassuring. At last the coachman reined the horses into the courtyard of the Royal Hotel.

"We can walk from here to Maman's house." Jean-Pierre helped her from the coach. "Would you like that my love?"

"I would certainly like to stretch my legs." Saffron smiled ruefully. "I feel as if I have been sitting in that coach for days."

"Then walk we shall. We'll take the coast road and I shall show you some of the places I remember from my childhood. Are you hungry?"

Saffron shook her head. "A little thirsty perhaps."

"Then we shall find a coffee shop along the way." He squeezed her hand. "I shall sit and enjoy the jealous stares of the other customers when they see your beauty and know that you are mine."

Saffron felt a rush of colour to her cheek. "I'll never get used to the things you say Jean-Pierre." She smiled shyly. "But I do love to hear you say them."

He chuckled, tucking her arm into his own. "Then I shall think of something new to say to you every day of our lives. Now, come, we have much to see."

A fresh summer breeze tugged at Saffron's hat as they set out. "There are so many people." Saffron was bewildered by the crowds of finely dressed men and women, strolling in the afternoon sun. "Do all these folk live here?"

"Many are visitors." He pointed to a stretch of beach. "Those strange contraptions being drawn down into the sea are bathing machines."

Saffron nodded. "I have seen them before on the beach at Westcliff. They look like sheds on wheels. I was told that people change their clothes inside and then walk down to swim."

"That's right. Look there is a lady just emerging from the waves."

Saffron gasped. "Why she is almost naked!"

Jean-Pierre threw back his head and laughed so loudly that a passing couple turned to see the cause of his merriment.

"She is wearing a bathing dress. It is considered to be very respectable I assure you."

Saffron tugged at his sleeve. "Respectable or not, you have no need to stare so." Eager to change the subject she hurried him along the promenade. "Are we almost there?"

"Not far now, we will soon be in sight of the house. At one time Brighton was little more than a village, then about a hundred years ago a doctor proclaimed his belief that bathing in seawater was beneficial to the health. Before long the rich made the place popular. Years later the Prince Regent, as he was then, used to come here to escape from public life. He built the Royal Pavilion, I must show it to you before we leave. And, see over there." He pointed seaward. "That's the Chain Pier. A steamship operates from there between Brighton and France. Perhaps we will go there one day."

He stared across the water. "There are a few of my mother's family still there, I want you to meet them all in time."

"A few left?"

"Those who escaped the Guillotine."

Saffron's hand flew to her mouth. "I have heard tales, but I did not know …" Her voice trailed away.

"How could you? I have told you little of my family's history." He walked in silence for several minutes, his head bent in thought. "My Grandmother fled Paris taking my Mother who was only six years old. They were smuggled from the city hidden in a straw filled cart and crossed the channel by means of a small fishing boat. In common with many émigrés during the revolution, they found friends of their own social standing here in Brighton. Some took them into their homes. My Grandpere stayed behind to protect his estates." Sadness clouded Jean-Pierre's eyes. "He paid the price. Within year he had been denounced and after months in the Bastille, he fol- lowed so many other innocents to the Guillotine."

"And your Grandmother, what happened to her?"

"My Grandmere, although heartbroken at his death was fortunate in time to find a wealthy protector. She was, so I am
told a woman of great beauty, so she and my Mother wanted
for nothing."

Saffron lent her head against his shoulder. "How dreadful for
her." She murmured.

"They were indeed dreadful years. Grandmere died when
Mother was nineteen, fortunately she had just met my father."
He smiled down into her upturned face. "Don't be nervous, my
love. My mother will not eat you. I promise I shall be by your
side every moment."

The Howard residence was set in the centre of a crescent of
imposing, four storied houses. Faced with gleaming marble,
they seemed to loom threateningly above Saffron as together
they mounted the wide steps to the front entrance.

In answer to the bell's summons, the door opened to reveal
the brightly dressed figure of a young man. "Yes?" He raised
eyebrows, which owed more to artistry than to nature. "Can I
help you?"

Jean-Pierre regarded him with distaste. "You can kindly
stand aside, Sir. I am here to see my mother."

The suspicious set of the rouged lips relaxed and broadened
into a simpering smile. "Why didn't you say?" He held out
a limp hand. "Jean-Pierre is it not? Well, do come in." He
stood back to allow them to pass. "Your dear mother is in the
drawing room. One of her little soirees you know."

He went ahead of them to throw open a door at the end of
the wide hallway. A gale of laughter greeted their arrival and
for a moment Saffron's footsteps faltered as all eyes turned
to appraise the new comers. John Pierre squeezed her hand,
leading her confidently through the jostling crowds and
murmurs of curiosity to a grand piano and to the petite woman

seated there.

"Maman." He bent to kiss the pale cheek. "This is Saffron." He drew her forward. "Who as I told you, is soon to be my wife."

Saffron bobbed a curtsey. "I am pleased to meet you Mrs. Howard." She had rehearsed the words so often, yet now they sounded affected and meaningless.

The woman regarded her with disdain. "I am sure you are." She purred, her voice thickly accented. "Saffron, is that how you say it? Surely Saffron is a cooking aid, usually found in the kitchen is it not?"

A titter of laughter from the assembled guests broke the silence.

Jean-Pierre glared angrily over his shoulder. "Had I known, Maman, that you would be entertaining this afternoon, I would have delayed our visit. As it is, perhaps we should depart and leave you to your ill mannered guests." He turned on his heel, tucking Saffron's arm into his own.

"Oh, Jean-Pierre, I'm sure my friends meant no harm." Louise Howard rose to place a small lace mittened hand on his arm. "Please stay." Saffron watched as the tiny birdlike woman smiled up at her son. "I thought you would like to meet again some of the people you grew up with. The musicians, writers and artists who you knew when you were here. She turned to hold out a hand to Saffron. "Come my dear, I shall introduce you to some of the most interesting people in the world."

Saffron glanced at Jean-Pierre, silently begging for his support.

"By all means, Maman, but I shall stay by Saffron's side. As you may remember I do not approve of all of your friends or their lifestyles. I have no wish for her beauty to attract unwelcome attention."

She saw his mother's lips tighten. "Really, Jean-Pierre, you go too far. But this time I shall forgive you."

There began a round of introductions and true to his word Jean-Pierre stayed by Saffron's side. Somehow she managed to keep a smile on her face for the next hour until one by one the guests took their leave.

"Now at last we can talk." Jean-Pierre slipped an arm around Saffron's shoulders. "Come, sit down Maman. We have much to discuss."

"If you say so, Jean-Pierre, but I can think of nothing to say which you would want to hear." She sat, spreading the skirt of her gown daintly around her, arranging the silken folds with exaggerated care. All the earlier public pretence of gaiety gone, she glared at her son.

"Nonetheless, you had best say it, Maman." Jean-Pierre's voice rose angrily. "But I warn you, I am no longer your little boy to be told what I may and may not do."

"No, you are a man. A very stupid man." She spat the words. "You chose for a wife a peasant." She glared at Saffron. "After what her kind did to our family."

"Saffron is no peasant!" Jean-Pierre's face was livid with fury. "You will apologise Maman. Immediament!"

"Apologise?" Louise Howard leapt to her feet. "You expect me to humble myself to this fisherman's spawn?" She pulled herself to her full height. "Noble French blood flows through my veins." She poked her son's chest with a rigid finger. "The same blood which flows through your own!"

"I wish it were otherwise." He growled, brushing her hand away. "Your blood carries with it only arrogance. Thank God I am more like my father."

"You know nothing of your father." She took a lace edged

handkerchief from her sleeve and began to cry. "He would never have spoken to me as you do."

"Then perhaps it would have been better had he done so. And don't pretend, Maman, you can no longer win an argument with false tears." He turned to Saffron who stood by his side, white faced and trembling. "I am sorry, my love, that you should have been forced to witness such a scene." He drew her into the circle of his arms. "I should never have brought you here. We shall return to Leigh tomorrow. To Poll, little Tom and Gabriel. To a better world where we shall forget today and start our life together."

"So, still you will go against my wishes?" His mother had abandoned all pretence of misery, her face a mask of anger and bitterness.

"Yes, Maman. I will." Jean-Pierre's tone was hard and uncompromising. "Saffron and I will be married in her home town as soon as possible." He paused, with a twisted smile. "I assume that you will not be there to offer us your blessing?"

Louise Howard turned her back on them . "I do not wish to see you marry beneath you Jean-Pierre. I would be grateful if you would go now and take your peasant with you."

Saffron had felt an uncontrollable fury building within her until she could contain herself no longer. Reaching out she spun the woman to face her.

"You dare to call me names Madam?" She chose her words with care mimicking the precision of Jean-Pierre's speech. "If I had behaved as you have, my God fearing Mother would have given me cause to remember my manners. My father was a good and honest man, born of good English stock. He worked hard to provide food and a roof over the heads of his family. I have nothing to be ashamed of. I am proud of my roots in good English soil."

Louise Howard took a step back, her mouth hung open at Saffron's onslaught.

"I love your son, Madam. I intend to make him a good wife." She took a deep breath. "With or without your blessing." She turned to face Jean-Pierre. "And now, you will please take me home."

He put an arm around her shoulders and walked with her to the door, pausing to look back at the lonely figure standing in the centre of the over ornate salon. "Perhaps time will heal this wound. Perhaps not. Goodbye Maman."

Once outside into the early evening air, Saffron buried her face in her hands. "Oh, Jean-Pierre, I am so sorry. I should not have spoken to your mother like that."

He gathered her to him. "She deserved every word." He said looking deeply into her eyes. "I am proud of you Saffron Clay. My Mother's behaviour today has reminded me of why I left her in the first place. I have seen her reduce a full-grown man to a shivering wreck. But not you, my love. You have shown yourself to be more than a match for her spiteful tongue." He kissed her softly on the tip of her nose. "Now we will forget her. I shall book rooms at the Inn we passed and we shall dine in splendour overlooking the sea."

"And tomorrow?"

Tomorrow we shall return to make final arrangements for our wedding, for I can wait no longer to make you my bride."

Saffron laid her head against his chest. It seemed that the steady beat of his heart was echoed by her own. Two hearts that beat as one.

CHAPTER THIRTY

Nathan greeted the news of John Benham's departure with mixed feelings. Word had filtered down by means of a conversation overheard by one of the chamber maids. The latest item of household gossip was savoured over the evening meal.

"Gone for about three weeks they said. Visiting 'is alehouses all over the county."

"Looks like you lorst your chance to 'ave a word with 'im." Tim nudged Nathan's shoulder.

"It can wait." Nathan shrugged. "I'll just have to stay out of Miss Charlotte's way until he get back."

"Easier said than done." Muttered his friend. "She's got it in for you and no mistake."

"I'll manage."

"And if you don't, I know someone who'll put 'er straight!" Sarah sat beside him.

"Who?"

"Why your Aunt." She whispered. "That's who."

Nathan glanced around, satisfied that no one had heard. "Clever girl." He smiled. "I'll have a word with her this evening."

Later, once released from his duties, he realised that he looked forward to the hour he spent with Jane Porter and to her approval of his progress. "Well, Nathan, what would you like to read aloud tonight?" She ran a finger along the bookshelf. "Let me see…"

Aunt Jane, if you don't mind I would rather talk."

She turned to stare at her nephew. "I thought there was something on your mind. Come on, out with it. What have you done now?"

"It's nothing I've done." Nathan lent to rest his arm on the desk. "But I am in trouble and I need your advice." He raised his head to gaze appealingly at his aunt.

Her expression softened as she sat down to face him. "Tell me."

Nathan took a deep breath and explained the situation, leaving nothing out. When he had finished the woman was silent for several long minutes. "Have you given Miss Charlotte any reason to behave in this manner?" She raised a warning finger. "I want the truth, Nathan."

"On my honour, aunt. I've kept out of her way as much as possible, but she won't leave me alone."

"Then we must be grateful that for the time being, she cannot run to her father with her lies." She meshed her fingers in thought. "Although it is not my place, I shall have words with her. I have watched her grow from a baby into a wilful young woman." She stood decisively. "I cannot allow her to destroy your future, Nathan. Leave the matter with me. The blame is not hers alone. Her father has indulged her and her mother, poor woman, has taken little notice of her since Charles was born."

The following day it was evident that his aunt had been as good as her word. Charlotte swept past him with her nose in the air and a telltale flush to her cheek. For the next three weeks she rarely crossed his path but Jane Porter refused to tell her nephew what had passed between her and the wayward daughter of the house.

By the time John Benham returned, Nathan had all but put the matter out of his mind. Life returned to the regimented routine of early mornings, daily tasks, an hour or two spent each day with young Charles and further tuition with his aunt, leaving little time to spend with Sarah.

It was not until the master had been back for two days that Nathan found himself on duty in the dining room. The guests were all local worthies, each one Nathan knew to be wealthy and influential. At first the conversation revolved around the Reform Act and upon the impact it would have on rich and poor alike. Nathan had heard similar arguments put forward before and would dearly have loved to air his own opinions. On more than one occasion he was aware of John Benham's critical gaze. The meal seemed to take longer than usual and by the time the last dinner guest had taken his leave both Nathan and Tim were longing for their beds.

Tim stifled a yawn. "By my reckoning we got 'bout four 'ours afore we got to be up again."

"Think yourself lucky you've got a bed to go to. There's many tramping the roads and sleeping in the fields. Didn't you hear what there were saying at dinner?"

"I wasn't listening. I was fightin' to keep me eyes open."

"That was obvious, boy!" Bentley stood in the open doorway. "You'll smarten up or be out on your ear! And you." He turned to Nathan. "The master wants to see you."

"What now? It's past midnight!"

"Yes now! He is in the library."

Reluctantly, dreading what lay ahead, Nathan made his way along the richly carpeted hallway. By now, he felt sure, Charlotte would have reported to her father, embroidering the truth with spiteful lies. He knew as he raised his hand to rap on the oak door that the summons from within could mean his dismissal.

At the curt response, Nathan straightened his shoulders and stepped into the room closing the door behind him. The library was dimly lit by the wavering glow of logs burning in the wide hearth. John Benham was slumped in a wing-backed armchair.

Without raising his head he beckoned Nathan to stand before him.

"Well, what hast thou to say for thyself? My daughter has told me of thy behaviour."

Nathan had rehearsed his defence over and over again during the man's absence but when he needed them most the words deserted him.

"What can I say, Sir? If Miss Charlotte has accused me, then am I not already judged guilty? What father would believe the word of a servant rather that his own daughter?" His bitter tone did not go unnoticed. John Benham raised his head to look long and hard into Nathan's eyes.

"I will hear what thou hast to say Nathan. I shall know if thee speaks the truth." He listened intently as Nathan explained how Charlotte had cornered him on more than occasion.

"I give you my word, Sir. I have never encouraged her behaviour. If for no other reason than that I am engaged to be married to a wonderful girl. There is no room in my heart for any other."

"Engaged you say?" The man sat back with a half smile. "And who may I ask is the fortunate young woman?"

Nathan swallowed, aware that his careless revelation could mean dismissal, but he had gone too far to go back. "Her name is Sarah, Sir. She is one of your kitchen maids." He saw the frown appear on his master's face and held up a defensive hand. "Before you say anything, I know that when we marry, I must leave your employ." He paused. "And that will sadden me but I know that you will not employ both man and wife under the same roof."

"Sadden thee? Dost thee find pleasure in my employ?"

"I do Sir." Nathan warmed to the question. "I have learned a great deal about a world of which before, I had little knowledge."

John Benham's smile widened. "Thee hast learned well and formed opinions which thee are not slow to express." He rose from the chair and crossed to the window to stare out over the gardens beyond. I did not call thee here to punish thee Nathan." He turned to face him. "My daughter's behaviour is a matter for serious concern. She will not avoid correction. However, I have considered the matter and in view of thy relationship with another member of the household, I can see only one course of action open to me. You must leave your position as footman by the end of the week."

Nathan hung his head. It was no more than he had expected but brought his future plans crashing around his ears. "Yes, Sir." He muttered, his inner pride railing against the perceived injustice.

"I called thee here to offer thee alternative employment."

Nathan caught his breath, clutching at the straw of reprieve. "Sir?"

"There is a position at one of the breweries for a trainee. If thee applies thyself, I am sure thee will soon learn the trade. There is also the tenancy of a small tied cottage available for the right man." He came to stand close to Nathan. "Thee look surprised boy." He smiled. "Dost thou not think my plan would solve many problems?"

Nathan gulped trying hard to find the right words of appreciation. "It would, Sir. Oh! indeed it would. And I thank you, Sir, for your kindness." He heard himself laugh aloud. "I shall make a home for Sarah and with her father's blessing, marry her the sooner."

"Slowly, Nathan, slowly." John Benham admonished. "Thee have yet to say thee will accept my offer."

"Accept it Sir? Of course I accept it!" He felt that if his smile widened any further it would split his face in two. "What will I be doing at the brewery, Sir?"

"If thou are to learn anything thee must start at the bottom. The man spread his hands wide. "Thee will learn every step of the process which goes to make a fine ale and the distribution of ale to the alehouses. Your aunt tells me thee have a knowledge of accounting. That too will serve thee well."

Nathan's head was spinning. Only a few months past he had been running cross-country to escape the excise men. Now, here he was facing yet another challenge, one that thanks to his aunt he felt equal to. "I'll work hard, Sir. Honest I will. You will never regret giving me this chance."

"I know that, boy. I have watched thee closely over these past months and have spoken of thee to thy aunt on many occasions. I have plans for thee and I know I shall not be disappointed. Now, off to thy bed. Until the end of the week, thee will continue to attend to thy duties as a footman."

Despite his earlier fatigue, Nathan left the library to sprint happily up to the servant's quarters. His companions were already snoring as he stripped and climbed into the narrow bed. But not to sleep. He was far to busy planning his future which thanks to a turn of fate could now include his beloved Sarah

Nathan and Tim were in high spirits as they burst laughing into the kitchen next day. "Mornin' Mrs. Rand." Tim danced around the cook. "I'm starvin'. Me belly thinks me throat's been cut!"

"Me too." Nathan grinned at Sarah. "Come on girl, feed me before I die from lack of nourishment." He caught her around her waist. Giggling, she struggled from his grip and aimed a playful slap at his head.

"Your meal's been waiting on the stove these last twenty minutes. Where you been? You're late."

"Old Blood and Guts was reading the riot act again. 'Do this and don't do the other'. We had to stand there with our bellies rumbling".

"Well, before you eat, young Nathan, there's Master Charles' tray to take up to the nursery." The cook checked the items. "Warm milk, porridge, tea and toast for the nurse." She wiped her hands on her apron. "Right, off you go lad. Sarah will keep your food warm 'til you get back."

Willingly Nathan lifted the tray and made for the door. "Won't be a tick." He winked at Sarah as he backed through into the corridor. Still smiling, he took the stairs two at a time, expertly balancing the loaded tray, but stopped short at the last landing. "Oh, no!" He murmured as he saw the nursery door wide open.

Slamming down the tray on the small table, he burst into the room. The nurse was snoring in front of the fire. There was no sign of Charles. Roughly, Nathan shook the sleeping woman from sleep. "Wake up! Wake up! Where's the child?"

"What?" She started from the chair. "What d'you mean?" She looked wild-eyed around the room. "He was playing here just now." She wrung her hands. "I only closed my eyes for a minute."

"You left the door unlocked you stupid woman! He's gone!"

"Well find him!" The woman screeched, beside herself with fear. "The master will blame me, I know he will."

"And so he should! Just pray the little chap's come to no harm." With a prayer on his lips, Nathan rushed from the room. He had not passed the child on his way up, so the back-stairs to the garden presented the most likely route, familiar to Charles from Nathan's frequent visits.

He clattered down the three, ill lit flights, scanning each landing for sight of the child but stopped short of the bottom stair. Charles lay huddled against the door. A pitifully small, crumpled figure. One arm flung high as if in silent plea for help.

Nathan sank onto the top stair. "Oh, Charlie!" He stifled a sob. "You were looking for me. I know you were." He straightened, stepping carefully around the child. He bent an ear to the narrow chest. There was no heartbeat. Bending, he lifted the lifeless body into his arms. For a moment he held the child to him, looking into the small face, serene in death. "Poor little chap. Not much of a life was it? Perhaps you're best off in the next world. This one did you no favours that's for sure." As he turned to go, Nathan caught sight of a sheet of paper on the floor, stirred by a draft from beneath the outer door. Balancing his burden, he stooped to retrieve it. It was Charles' last attempt at a picture. He had always been eager to present Nathan with a colourful, wax crayoned scribble. A way of saying thank you, Nathan believed, a gift from one friend to another.

On leaden feet he retraced his steps to the empty nursery. Laying the child's body on the bed and straightening the limbs, he settled a pillow under his head. The nurse had obviously gone the alert the house. Within minutes she returned with John Benham.

Nathan stood back as the man knelt beside the body of his dead son. "Where did you find him?"

"At the foot of the stairs, Sir." Nathan paused. "His neck is broken. He must have been trying to get out into the garden."

"Where thee took him each day?"

"Yes, Sir."

"He was happy there?"

"He was. He loved the colours of the flowers." Nathan's voice broke.

The stricken man bent to kiss the child's cold face. "My poor dear Son. God hath gathered thee in. We must believe that he had a reason for taking thee from us." He got slowly to his feet, aged by sorrow. "I must tell his Mother." He seemed to be speaking to himself. "There are things to be done." He turned to Nathan. "Tell Mr. Bentley and Mrs Porter I wish to speak to them. I shall be in my study." With a last look at the dead boy he left, passing the child's cowering nurse without a glance or a word.

With a heavy heart Nathan followed him. At his knock, his aunt bade him enter, looking up from the household account spread open on her desk. She caught sight of her nephew's ashen face

"Nathan, whatever is the matter?"

"It's Master Charlie." He slumped unbidden into a chair. "He's dead, Aunt!" He buried his head in his hands. "That useless old nurse of his fell asleep and left him to wander." He looked up, his eyes filled with tears. "He fell, Aunt. I found him with his poor little neck broken."

He felt the woman's hand on his shoulder. "I'm so sorry, Nathan. I know how you loved the child."

"The master said you and Mr. Bentley should go to him in his study." She nodded.

"There will be much to be done. Stay here for a few minutes until you feel better."

Nathan got to his feet. "No, I'd best get back to the kitchen. Mrs. Rand will be wondering where I've got to. Will it be alright if I tell her what's happened?"

"Well, they will have to know sooner or later. Warn them to go about their duties quietly and reverently. I imagine the Master will wish to speak to the staff later today." She put a gentle hand to his cheek. "Now, off you go. Tell yourself that master Charles has gone to a better place than this cruel world."

Nathan returned to the kitchen and to a barrage of questions.

"Where you been?" Sarah demanded. "Your meal's spoiled, keeping warm all this time."

He took her hands and led her to sit at the table. "I'm not hungry Sarah."

He looked at the cook. "I think you had best sit down too, Mrs. Rand. I've got some sad news."

When he finished there was a long silence. "Poor little mite." The cook's voice was hushed. "I said as 'ow that nurse was too old. She ought to be 'orsewhipped. Leavin' the door unlocked and letting the little chap fall like that."

"I've been thinking on that." Nathan frowned. "Young Master Charlie must have seen his nurse lock that door a hundred times. He was a bright little lad in some ways. He could have opened the door himself. But you're right, she should have kept an eye on him all the time."

"I s'pose we'll never know." Sarah whispered. "D'you reckon as 'ow we'll all be expected at the funeral?"

"We will." The cook nodded. "I remember when the old master died. I was a kitchen maid then, about your age, Sarah. A Quaker's funeral's not like ours if you know what I mean."

"Not exactly. How is it different?" Nathan's interest prompted the woman to warm to further reminiscence.

"Well, first of all they came from all around, the Quakers that is. We all went down to their meeting house in the village. 'Course we all sat at the back. At first there was some music then they all prayed for the departed. Then it went quiet. Every now and again someone would stand up and say something good about the old master. It wasn't as sad as I thought it would be. The mistress said it was a celebration of life. I remember her words to this day."

Preparations under the guidance of Mary Porter and the Butler went smoothly with the minimum of disturbance. It had been decided that the service preceeding the boy's burial would be held at the Meeting house in the village. Nathan's aunt had told him that John Benham wished him to attend the service with the rest of the staff.

"He knows how much Master Charles meant to you." She explained. "He felt that you would want to be there."

On the morning of the funeral, it was a solumn group who walked together into Saffron Walden. They sat in silence as the hall began to fill and as the mourners arrived on foot or by carriage John Benham stood at the door of the meeting hall acknowledging each arrival with a firm handshake. Nathan watched as Charlotte and her Mother took their places in one of the front pews.

An air of serenity seemed to settle over the congregation as prayers were said for the departed. After a brief silence, some of the Friends stood to pay tribute to the dead child. Their words were well chosen and kind but Nathan felt almost without meaning. None of them had known the boy as he had. He reached into his pocket, closing his fingers over the folded scrap of paper. He pictured the colourful scribble. His last present from Charlie. He fought to keep back the tears. His Aunt was right, the child had gone on to a better place. Surely a soul so innocent, so pure would readily be accepted into Heaven.

Before he realised what he was doing, he found himself getting to his feet.

John Benham turned toward him with an expression of mild surprise. For a moment their eyes met before he nodded his head in Nathan's direction.

"I want to say something." Nathan began, clearing his throat. "Master Charles, Charlie, I called him, was my friend. He loved to touch and smell the flowers. He liked to listen to the birds singing. He would point to the wind turning the leaves on the trees. If I was able to teach him small things then he repaid me by teaching me more. He taught me that the most important thing we can give to one another is love." He glanced at the child's mother. Her head was bent in prayer. Or was it regret? "Charlie had a lot of love to give and I shall be forever grateful that some of it came my way. God Bless and keep the little chap."

As he sat down, he had the satisfaction of catching his Aunt's approving glance.

The burial was brief. One of the Friends signalled the lowering of the small coffin into the waiting grave. He then shook hands with John Benham, which seemed to signal the end of the meeting.

As the mourners made their way back through the burial grounds Nathan noticed the obvious conformity of the marker stones. Each was the same in size and design as its neighbour, allowing no distinction between one person or another.

He felt a sense of sactisfaction that in death Charlie, the Lammas Lamb, would be judged equal to those who had gone before.

CHAPTER THIRTY ONE

Two days later, Tom was playing with a friend on the beach beyond the window of Juniper Cottage. Under Saffron's watchful eye the two boys were engrossed in building a shell-adorned mound in the wet sand. Jean-Pierre put down his brush and crossed to slip an arm around her shoulders.

"What are you thinking my love? You seem so far away." He laid his head against her hair.

"I'm sorry Jean-Pierre, did I move from my pose? I was watching young Tom, he seems to grow more each day, I shall have to make him some new britches before he starts at the school."

"No, my darling, you did not move, you are as always the perfect model." He tilted her chin to meet his gaze. "If only I could capture that wistful smile I saw a moment ago." He shook his head. "If I live to paint a thousand portraits of you, I doubt I shall ever do justice to your beauty." He bent his head to claim her lips, a gentle loving kiss, to which her response left no need for words.

He had barely returned to his canvass when the cottage door shook under a thunder of heavy blows and with an oath he strode to open it.

"Is she here?" Gabriel craned his neck to see past him into the room beyond.

Saffron leaped to her feet. "What's wrong, is it Poll?"

"No, I'm 'ere Saffy." Poll pushed past her husband to run to her sister's side. "But I 'ad to come. I told Gabe you'd know what to do." She wrung her hands and began to pace the room. "They sent for me."

"Who sent for you? Calm yourself Poll, here sit and get your breath back." Pushing her sister into a chair she knelt beside her. "Now, slowly, tell me what's happened."

Gabriel came to stand beside his young wife. "It's Lady Caroline up at the big 'ouse." He began. "She sent a footman down with a message for Poll."

"A message?" Jean-Pierre frowned. "I thought they wanted nothing further to do with you." He met Poll's startled gaze. "Saffy told me." His tone was apologetic. "'Tis family business and will go no further."

Saffron took her sister's hand. "So, tell me, what was the message?"

Poll sniffed miserably. "We're expected at the 'ouse. Her ladyship says me and Gabe must be there at noon today. Oh, Saffy." She buried her head on Saffron's shoulder. "I'm afeared to go there." She glanced again at Jean-Pierre. "What does she want? Why can't she leave us alone?"

Saffron got slowly to her feet. "There's only one way to find out, I suppose. You'll have to go and face her. Gabe will look after you." She shot a smile at the big man.

"We wants you to come too, Saffy. We both do, don't we Gabe?"

He nodded , clearing his throat. "We do. You being sort of 'ead of Poll's family while Nathan's away. 'Sides, you've got the words if you know what I mean."

"That's a certainty!" Jean-Pierre managed a chuckle at the memory of Saffron's encounter with his mother. "She can see off a dozen fine ladies." He wrapped an arm around Saffron's waist. "You must go, my love." He dropped a gentle kiss on her cheek. "Hurry back and tell me what happens."

"If you think I should." The shadow of doubt left her eyes to be replaced by the light of battle. "Right, let me tidy myself and we'll be off. Jean-Pierre will you give eye to Tom? He'll be fine for an hour or so."

"Of course." He glanced out of the window. "He won't even know you're away. Now best hurry, the morning is almost gone."

The steep climb to the top of Horse Hill left Poll breathless.

"I'll 'ave to stop a minute Saffy." She cradled her swollen belly, grateful for Gabriel's strong arm around her.

"Not far now." He murmured angrily, catching sight of Saffron's worried frown. "You should be resting, not climbing 'ills to suit her ladyship!"

"We're almost there, Gabe, don't fret." Poll smiled up at him. "I'm alright now."

The imposing gate opened onto a short drive. Gravel crunched beneath their feet as they approached the main entrance.

"Should we go round the back?" Poll's lips trembled as she moved closer to her husband.

"No we will not!" Saffron's firm reply underlined the proud set of her head. "I am no servant to his house, neither are we tradesmen. We are expected and will begin as we mean to go on." She ran lightly up the three steps and yanked hard on the bell pull.

The door was opened almost immediately by a livered footman.

"Yes?" He seemed to stare into middle distance, his face while impassive held a hint of contempt.

"We have come to see Lady Margaret." Saffron felt an angry colour flood her cheeks. "She knows we are coming, so I'll be obliged if you would step aside and inform her that we are here!"

The man's mouth fell open and for the first time he focused on the young woman facing him. Tight lipped and unblinking, she returned his gaze, motioning to Poll and Gabriel to follow her she swept past the speechless servant. Struggling to regain his composure, he indicated a door to the left of the hall. "Wait in there, I will inform her ladyship of your arrival."

"Yes! Please do!" Saffron snapped at his retreating back.

"Oh, Saffy. You shouldn't talk to 'im like that." Poll giggled nervously.

"Why not?" Saffron tucked a stray curl into the ribbon at her neck. Her hand trembled, but she was determined to display a show of bravado. "He's no better than you or me. If he thinks he can put on airs and graces with his smart coat and britches, he's mistaken! Jean-Pierre taught me that. Beggar or Lord, they're all the same under the skin and don't you forget it Poll."

She looked around her, the room, lit through tall windows by the midday sun was exquisitely furnished. Two cushioned wing back chairs sat either side of a richly coloured rug, which lay by the wide brick hearth, it's deep red tones reflected in the long velvet window drapes. Several upright chairs were grouped around a highly polished table sporting a bowl of freshly cut Roses.

"Keep your chin up, Poll. You too Gabe. Her Laydship's richer than us, but she's still only a woman."

"Am I indeed?" Silently the door behind them had opened to frame the diminutive, straight-backed figure of Lady Margaret.

Her heart pounding, Saffron returned the woman's ice-cold glare. She swallowed. "I had no wish to offend you, but 'tis the truth." She heard Poll's gasp of dismay and turned to smile weakly in her direction. "This is Polly Stoneforth and her husband Gabriel. I am Saffron Clay, Poll's sister. I understand you wish to speak to us. May I ask why we are here?"

For a moment the woman regarded Saffron with a hint of surprise, before taking stock of both Poll and Gabriel. "I wished to meet your sister and her husband to discuss a matter vital to us all." She turned her critical gaze back to Saffron. "I had no idea that you had been invited to accompany them."

"No more I had." Saffron tiled her chin defiantly. "But as you can see Poll is with child and easily upset. Your 'invitation'." She stressed the word. "Sounded like a summons." She paused. "And when Poll was so ill after the shameful treatment she suffered when she was in your service, I am here to make sure that it won't happen again."

"But that is precisely why I wished to see her." The woman's cold smile failed to reach her eyes. "Please be seated." She indicated the group of spindle legged chairs, onto one of which Gabriel cautiously lowered his heavy frame.

"Now." Lady Margaret sank gracefully into one of the winged armchairs, arranging her skirts and steepling slender fingers. "You will not yet be aware, but my husband and I have suffered a terrible loss." She paused, raising a scrap of lace to her cheek as if to blot away a tear. "Our beloved son, our only child, died two days ago on the eve of his bethrothal. A carriage race with some of his university friends, we are told. The funeral will be later this week."

In the shocked silence that followed Saffron realised that for a brief moment she felt sorry for the proud woman. No child should pre-decease their parent, no matter what their station in life. "We are truly sorry, Lady Margaret." She frowned. "But how does the death of your son concern us?"

The woman stood, taking a step toward Poll. "It concerns you, my dear."

"Me? How?" Poll's face was drained of colour.

Because I believe you carry my son's child. The heir to our estates. Is that not so?"

Saffron leaped to her feet, bristling with fury. "If you mean did your son rape my sister, then yes, she carries his child.

And what did you do?" She spun to point at Poll cowering in Gabriel's arms. "You turned her out with a few sovereigns, the price of her innocence!"

"I know. That was unfortunate." The woman waved her hand, dismissing Saffron's outburst. "Now, however, I wish to put matters right. Please hear me out." She motioned to Saffron to resume her seat. There was a long silence broken only by Gabriel's comforting murmurs as he held Poll to him.

My husband left for Cambridge to make the necessary arrangements this morning, and I am anxious to settle certain matters before his return.

Lady Margaret took a deep breath. "We are prepared to settle a considerable sum of money upon you on the understanding that when your time is near, you come here to give birth. It is only fitting that our son's child and our heir should be born under this roof. He or she will be raised in a manner befitting his station in life."

"No! No!" Poll was on her feet, her fists clenched. "You ain't getting my baby. E's not yours. Ee's mine, d'you 'ear, 'e's mine!"

"'Calm down child. I will not tolerate such behaviour!" Unruffled, the woman settled back into her chair. "Think for a moment of the advantages. First to you. You would have more money than you could earn in a lifetime. Then to Gabriel, who may keep his position here at the house. Then to the child, who would have the best care and education throughout his or her life."

"And of course, you will have your heir!" Saffron spat through gritted teeth. "You cannot buy a child. You talk about education? What about love? A mother's love?"

The woman closed her eyes, ignoring Saffron's angry interruption. "The child of course will never know his birth mother.

That is part of our agreement." She continued. "He will be told that his mother, a woman of breeding, died at his birth. No one will dare to question my word. And you." She turned to Poll. "In turn will let it be known that the child you carry also died at birth."

"No!" Gabriel got slowly to his feet, clearing his throat and twisting his cap between nervous fingers. "Beggin' your pardon Lady Margaret, but no." His jaw tightened. "We be man and wife, Poll 'an me. The child is ours." He seemed to grow in stature. "Boy or girl, t'will be raised right by us. We're poor, I'll give you that, but the babe will have all the love it needs. And that." He looked the woman squarely in the eye. "Is something money can't buy."

For a moment she sat, slacked mouthed with surprise, before rising unsteadily to face him. "How dare you speak to me in that way." She hissed, her voice rising on a tide of fury. "Consider yourself dismissed from my service." Her eyes glittered as she pointed a trembling finger at the door. "Now get out, all of you. Get out I say!"

Gabriel helped Poll to her feet, steading her against his broad chest. "Come on now, my darlin'. We're goin' 'ome." He swung suddenly to face the irate woman. "And as for bein' dismissed, that don't be a worry. I can earn our keep, and it won't be as a servant to no man." He added, his head held high in defiance. "You comin' Saffy?"

Saffron had been watching and listening throughout the heated exchange. She saw tears in the eyes of the older woman and realised that to her, Poll's child was the only living link with her dead son. Behind the autocratic demands lay a good woman with a desperate heartache, rooted now in defeat.

Lady Margaret hurried to stand with her back to the door, barring their way. "Wait, please wait." She seemed to be searching for the right words. "Perhaps I should have waited, left things until after the funeral." She faltered. "But the news of our son…" She left the sentence unfinished.

"Wouldn't 'ave made no difference." Gabriel growled. "But we're right sorry about your son."

"Thank you for that, at least." She bit her lip. "Will you allow me to see the child when it is born?" She gazed pleadingly at Poll. "I owe it to my son to see that you and the babe have everything you need. Perhaps when the child is born we will talk again." She moved away from the door.

Poll nodded wordlessly, huddling closer into Gabriel's protective arms. "We'll see." She managed.

"But until the child is born there's to be no more meddling, no more demands." Saffron's decisive tone seemed to startle the woman and for a moment their eyes met.

"Very well, but I wish to be kept informed of your sister's progress. Gabriel," she paused, not meeting his eyes.. "Gabriel you will bring me the news each week when you report for duty."

Saffron saw a half smile curve the man's generous mouth. He knew that her words were a reprieve, the nearest he would get to apology from the proud woman.

They left as they had arrived, through the main door. Not until they had cleared the gate did Poll speak.

"She can't take my baby can she Saffy?"

"How could she?" Saffron looked at Gabriel for support. "Once the little mite is born and you've been churched, we'll arrange the christening. Then short of kidnapping," she chuckled, "and I don't think her Ladyship would stoop to that, your baby will be safe and sound."

"Promise Saffy?"

"Yes, Poll, I promise." Saffron hid her feelings behind a confident smile. Instinct told her that Lady Margaret had given in too quickly. The most powerful family in Leigh would, she felt sure, would not be so easily denied.

CHAPTER THIRTY TWO

The next few days proved to be difficult for Nathan. The news of his impending departure from the big house, was greeted with mixed speculation by the other members of staff.

Tim bristled with indignation when Nathan told him of their master's decision,

"T'aint right, you being the one to get the blame. That little madam needs a good thrashin'. 'Er Pa ought to take his crop to 'er backside. We all know's what she's like."

The cook nodded her head. "I know Master's a good man, but it's not right sending Nathan away like that." She chopped angrily at the pile of vegetables destined for the stew pot. "That little miss needs a good lesson. She'll come to no good you'll see."

"It's no good going on Cook." Sarah shrugged. "And it's not all bad. Nathan and me could never 'ave been wed while both of us worked 'ere at the house." She smiled. "At least now we can start makin' plans." She carried a pile of clean plates from the sink to arrange them on the oak dresser. "We 'ad a long talk this morning. 'E told me what the master said. E's given him the chance for a new start." She bit her lip. "I shall miss 'im though."

"New start?" The Cook stood with knife raised, her curiosity aroused. "Doing what may I ask? Not back in the stables!"

"No." Sarah glanced at the closed door. "Nathan don't want no one to know 'til he's ready to tell them 'imself, so I can't say."

"Well I won't say nothin' will I?" Affronted, the woman hoisted her ample bosom on folded arms. "I don't hold with gossip as well you know." She tucked a stray grey hair into place.

Sarah hid a smile. "Well, I got to tell someone or else I'll burst." She pulled a chair from the table and sat beside the older woman. "It's like this. Master's starting Nathan on at the Maltings. Says he's to learn all about brewing. She leaned forward her eyes sparkling. But the best bit is there's a cottage to go with it. Oh Cook." She got to her feet wrapping her arms around the woman's waist. "I'm so happy!"

The cook returned her hug. "So you should be Miss. You got a good lad there what loves you, that's plain to see. I said he'd go a long way. I did, didn't I?"

Sarah nodded happily. "And I'll make him a good wife. We can live in the cottage when we're wed and I can come to the house every day to work, just like now."

"That'll do 'till you get too near your time."

"What do you mean?"

"Well, Nathan won't wait too long to get you with child if I'm any judge!" She smiled slyly. "And I am when it comes to a man's needs."

Sarah blushed, "I know about all that. Ma 'ad a long talk with me when Nathan asked if 'e could wed me." She straightened her apron. "And I've 'eard the maids talking, saying what they get up to. But I'm waitin' 'till we're wed. Nathan knows that." She hugged herself. "'E loves me. Once we're wed I'll give him as many children as he wants."

The older woman snorted with laughter. "You get the first one over and done with. You might change your mind. I remember Miss Charlotte and Master Charles crying and carrying on. Nearly drove their nurse to the mad'ouse they did."

"Our babies will be angels. Nathan says they will look like me and be smart like 'im."

The woman smiled at the girl's radiant confidence in the

296   *Saffron Summer*

future. "Mayhap you're right. Now fetch me the big stew pan. We'll be in trouble if the meal's not ready on time."

"You will that, Cook!" Nathan and Tim had come unnoticed through the door leading to the yard. "What smells so good, a roast?"

"It is." The woman bent to open the oven door, prodding the joint of beef sizzling in its own juices. "But it ain't for the likes of you. Master's dining with the family tonight. Likes a nice roast, does the master."

"It's lamb stew for supper." Sarah added herbs to the stew pot. "With fruit pie to follow."

Nathan slipped an arm around her shoulder. "You making it?"

"Of course. Cook says I've got a good 'and with pastry."

"You have that Sarah." Tim grinned. "That meat pie you made t'other day was real lip smackin' tasty. Just like you." He added with a wink.

"Here. You watch what you're saying to my intended." Nathan aimed a good-natured slap at his friend's head. But Tim wasn't smiling he was staring open mouthed at the figure framed in the kitchen door. Nathan turned slowly to meet the stoney glare of his aunt.

"Is this a kitchen or a fairground?"

The cook bustled forward wiping her hands on her apron. "I'm sorry Mrs Porter. Can I help you?"

"You can keep these young people under tighter control." She stared directly at Nathan. "I will not tolerate such horse-play."

"We were only funning." Tim muttered. "It won't 'appen again."

"Very well, mind that it does not. Now get about your duties". She held up a hand. "No Nathan, not you. You will accompany me."

Tim shot him a pitying glance before edging past the house-keeper into the main house beyond. With a carefully concealed smile at Sarah, Nathan followed his aunt's stiff back down the corridor to her room. Once inside, she closed the door and turned, thin lipped to face her nephew.

"When did you intend to inform me of your conversation with the master?"

Nathan heard the anger in her voice, "I'm sorry aunt, I thought I would tell you everything when we had our hour together later this evening." He hung his head. "I did not mean to upset you."

"I am not upset Nathan, rather am I hurt." Her voice softened. "I thought we had become friends. Imagine how I felt when the master called me in to tell me that you were leaving." She reached a hand to smooth his sleeve. "I shall miss you boy." Nathan was surprised to see a tear slide down her cheek. "It is however, time to move on and if you apply yourself and work hard, you will make a fine future for yourself.

She straightened, briskly brushing away the telltale tear, "Now, I have received a letter from your sister Saffron." She took the folded page from the pocket of her severe gown. "It contains an invitation for both you and I to attend her wedding. I shall not be able to go, but I will ask the master to delay the commencement of your new position for a few days to enable you to make the journey. Would that please you?"

"Yes Aunt!" Nathan's smile widened. "A chance to see Tom and Poll and to see Saffy wed. I'd walk a hundred miles to be there."

"I trust you will not have to walk that far Nathan." A thought seemed to strike her. "Indeed, I may have a better idea." She turned to look from her window toward the immaculate lawns beyond, preventing further discussion with a dismissive gesture. "The master wishes to see you later this evening. Make sure you present yourself well and immediately after dinner."

Nathan nodded, eager to return to Sarah with the news of Saffron's impending wedding. "I'll be there Aunt Jane, I promise."

He hurried back to the kitchen where Sarah was happily humming to herself . A smile lit her face as he slipped an arm around her waist.

"I've got some good news and some not so good news." He grinned. "Which d'you want to hear first?"

Her smile faded as she pushed him away, searching his face for some telltale hint. "I s'pose the bad news. Let's get it over and done with."

He sobered. "I'm going back to Leigh."

She gasped. "Not for good?"

"No, only for a few days. My aunt's had a letter from Saffy. She's getting wed and she says I should go."

"But what about your new position and how will you get there? You said it took you three days to reach Saffron Walden travelling across country."

Nathan frowned. "So it did, but Aunt Jane said she had an idea. She wouldn't tell me what it was. Anyway I've only got two more days under this roof." Sarah looked away. "Now, come on Sweetheart, we won't be apart for long." He tipped her chin to smile into eyes suspiciously damp with unshed tears. "A few days in Leigh, then I'll be back. I'll have a new job and my own little cottage." He hugged her to him, planting a kiss on her cheek. "I'll work hard to get everything ready in time for our wedding in the New Year."

"So will I." The thought of their life together brought a smile to her face. "I can sew, curtains and such and I know Ma and Pa will not see us go short of a few sticks of furniture." She buried her face against his chest. "Oh, Nathan, we're going to be so happy."

"We are that." Nathan chuckled. "We are that."

The day passed quickly until immediately after dinner that evening he presented himself at the door of the Master's study. In reply to his knock on the dark oak, the familiar voice bade him enter.

John Benham stood silhouetted against the last of the day's sun in the high windowed bay. "Come in, boy." He turned and beckoned to Nathan. "I understand from thy Aunt that there is to be a family wedding in thy home town of Leigh."

"Yes Sir." Nathan was surprised that he should have been informed.

"And thee would wish to attend?"

"Yes, Sir." Nathan fidgeted under the man's steady gaze.

"Thee sound unsure."

"It's the time, Sir." He swallowed nervously. "I want to go, but it would mean almost a week away and I am to take up my new employment in only a few days."

John Benham tugged his ear thoughtfully. "So thee do. Thy aunt has suggested a way in which I think thee could accomplish the journey in far less time than on foot." He paused. "Dost thou think Thunder could make the trip in a day?"

Nathan gasped. "But Sir, he is your favourite. No one else is permitted to mount him. I've heard folk say he's too spirited to allow anyone to ride him save yourself."

"And so he is. I've spoken to Bartholemew and he tells me that thee forged a bond with the creature and that thee often visit him in the stables. Do you think thee could manage him?"

"I think so Sir." Nathan stammered. He straighted his back.

"No, I know so Sir. Thunder is a wonderful animal."

"Then it is settled. Thunder will take thee to thy Sister's wedding and back again in good time. Treat him well." He raised a warning finger. "He is a valuable animal and I expect him to receive the care he deserves."

"I will Sir." Nathan beamed. "I'll treat him like a king, and I thank you for trusting him to me."

"Very well, thee may tell Bartholemew to have him saddled and ready by four tomorrow morning. Take this letter with thee." He folded a sheet of paper and handed it to Nathan. "Should someone wonder why such a young lad should be in possession of a mount like Thunder, it will give thee the right of temporary ownership. With luck thee should reach Leigh by nightfall. Be aware that there are many dangers along the way. In these worrying times many a good man will turn to robbery and violence for the sake of a few shillings. Rest the beast for a day before making the return journey. I hold thee to thy word. Do not give me cause to regret my trust."

"That I would never do Sir. Not now or for ever while I am in your service."

"Go then about thy duties. I wish thee a safe journey and a speedy return." As the door closed behind Nathan John Benham sat wearily in the winged leather chair, "Would that I had a son like thee, boy. A son to carry on all that I have begun." He clasped his hands in prayer. "Can it be Lord that thou hast sent me this young man for reasons that thou alone may know?"

The next day Nathan woke before dawn and took care not to wake his companions. He dressed hurriedly in the clothes which he had worn to visit Sarah's parents. "Can't go to Saffy's wedding in rags." He told his reflection in the small mirror. "She would never forgive me if I turned up looking like a beggar."

Bartholomew, yawning and rubbing sleep from his eyes, came to meet him.

"There you are lad." He clapped Nathan on the shoulder. "I've 'ad word from the master that you are to take Thunder cross country. Is that true?"

"It is. And proud I am to be riding such a beast."

"You make sure you rest 'im." The groom wagged a warning finger. "A king 'mong horses is Thunder. You make sure you treat 'im like one!" He turned, beckoning Nathan to follow. "You get 'im saddled. Give you a chance to tell 'im where he's agoin'. Settle 'im like."

In the stable's dim light, Nathan heard Thunder's soft whinny of recognition. He ran a hand over the noble head and was rewarded with a snort of pleasure.

"We've a few miles to go today, my beauty, so I'd best make you ready." The great beast stood quietly, obedient to Nathan's soft words and gentle touch. Bartholomew watched approvingly as man and horse emerged into the still night air.

"All set lad?" He patted Thunder's gleaming flank. "You bring 'im back in three or four days, fit and healthy, you 'ear?"

Nathan grinned, feeling the horse dance impatiently beneath him. "The sooner we go, the sooner we'll be back." He reached down to clasp the groom's hand. "I'll be obliged if you could see that Sarah gets this note." He passed a folded scrap of paper. "It was too early to wake her to say goodbye, but that'll say it all."

Bartholomew returned the firm grip, standing back as Nathan gave Thunder his head and horse and rider disappeared into the trees.

The village was still asleep, shrouded in the night's last hour of darkness. As they clattered over the cobbles into the main street a stray dog bolted from the path of Thunder's well shod hooves.

His mind filled with memories of the day he had arrived in Saffron Walden and the thought of Rosa the lovely Gypsy brought a guilty smile to his face. "Bye! But she was a beauty." He muttered. Best never tell Sarah about that day, or she'll have my hide!"

The church on the hill stood silhouetted clearly against the moonlit sky, proudly boasting the spire he had watched raised on that day. As the houses gave way to the road South, Nathan settled into the saddle.

"We'll keep going 'till daylight, that should get us to Thaxted. We'll stop there and break our fast." The beast, without breaking his stride, tossed his head as if in agreement. For the next hour man and horse ate up the miles, over rutted roads fringed by low hedges and open farmland. Surefooted, Thunder never faltered, his magnificent body responding to Nathan's gentle mastery, until, cresting a rise, they saw below the lights of the wakening village. Conscious of the thoroughbred's value and anxious to arouse curiosity, Nathan decided to skirt the hamlet and rest beyond the cluster of houses. As he slid from the saddle beneath the canopy of an ancient oak, Thunder butted his shoulder, almost knocking him from his feet.

"All right your Majesty." Nathan laughed and turned to rub his cheek affectionately against the sweat damp muzzle. "I'm hungry too." He rummaged in the saddlebag, producing two apples and a chunk of fresh bread. "This will have to do for now." He held out an apple to the eager animal. "The grass round here is long and sweet, so eat your fill." As Nathan munched on the crisp fruit, he squinted up at the lightening sky. "I reckon our next stop will be in Dunmow." He ran a hand over the animal's flank. "So, after you're rested, we'll be on our way."

By the time the early Autumn sun had begun to warm the land, Nathan had reached the outskirts of Dunmow, reining in his mount at the head of the main street. He leaned forward to stroke the horse's neck. "I made a good friend here. After he'd almost run me down he bought me a fine meal. See that Inn down there? I slept the night in a fine gentleman's coach." He chuckled. "'Course, he didn't know it!"

There's stables at the back, I'll give you a rub down, a net of hay and a good long drink. Come to think of it, I could manage a bite and a pint of ale myself."

Thunder needed no urging, sensing the promise of a well earned break in the journey. Nathan was as good as his word, and tossing a coin to the stable lad, he tended first to the needs of his mount. Once Thunder was satisfied, Nathan chose a window seat in the inn from where he could see the stables. John Benham had given him, what he had called, an advance upon his future employ, enough to allow him the purchase of a tankard of good local ale, a wedge of lamb pie, and a little over.

On his return to the stable he found Thunder well rested and seemingly eager to be back on the road. The muscles in his broad back quivered in anticipation as Nathan settled the saddle in place and tightened the girth.

"All right, your Highness. I'm as willing as you are to get on our way." He swung into the saddle and cantered from the yard and up the hill into the open countryside.

Although Nathan felt confident that his earlier crimes as a smuggler would have been long forgotten, he nonetheless avoided the road to Chelmsford.

"No use in taking chances." He confided to Thunder. "The town fair bristles with the law in one way or another. If they see me riding a beauty like you, like as not I'd be stopped and questions asked. Once they start digging, no knowing what they might come up with, so if it's all the same to you, we'll give it a wide berth."

It was mid afternoon when Nathan caught sight of the river Crouch gleaming in the sun lit valley below. "We'll take a rest here. They're good folk at the farm. Kind, they were. They'll treat you right too. I reckon they'll be surprised to see me." He laughed aloud. "Especially when they see you. I'll have some explaining to do and no mistake."

The yard at Three Elms farm was empty as Nathan rode in through the open gate. He hailed the house and was rewarded with the welcome sight of the farmer's wife appearing, beaming at the door.

George Makepiece was summoned from the fields by a young farm hand, while Nathan sluiced his head at the pump. The farmer stopped dead when he caught sight of the thorough-bred drinking his fill at the stone trough. His eyes narrowed as Nathan stretched out his hand in greeting.

"That's a fine beast, boy. Where did you get him?"

"It's alright husband." His wife bustled forward. "I've been hearing all about the lad's adventures. The horse belongs to his master. He's on his way to his sister's wedding in Leigh."

"And your master knows that you are riding the beast?"

"He does, Sir. I have his blessing and that's the truth. What's more." He took John Benham's letter from his pocket and held it out to the Farmer." I've a note written in his own hand, saying I have the right to what he called temporary ownership."

George Makepiece took a moment to consider Nathan's assurance before waving away the piece of paper and smiling broadly. "I believe you, lad. Now best feed and water, what's 'is name?"

"Thunder, Sir."

"Aye, Thunder." He ran a calloused hand over the horse's

neck. "T'is a right and proper name for a noble 'orse like this. See to 'is needs, then we'll sit down to some vittels. I know the missus 'as a got a good pot on the stove."

Nathan passed a pleasant hour telling them about his good fortune and listening to the gossip which had come their way. Well fed and rested, both horse and rider were eager to continue their journey and bidding farewell to the farmer and his wife, Nathan set off at a lively trot over the bridge.

"Not far now, your Majesty." He bent low in the saddle as, at the touch of his heels Thunder willingly broke into a gallop. "Another nine or ten miles and we'll be home."

Dusk had begun to gather, spreading a grey veil over the fields flanking the road into Rayleigh. Horse and rider, taking a wide bend in the road, found themselves plunged into near darkness by the overhanging branches of an avenue of trees. The cathedral effect let in little light and what there was, threw shifting shadows across their path. Nathan was instantly alerted by his mount's reluctance to venture further. "What's wrong boy?" He bent over to smooth the trembling neck, allowing Thunder to slow to a trot. From the corner of his eye, Nathan thought he saw movement in the thick undergrowth, before two men sprang from the thick bushes beneath the trees. As one tried to grab at Thunder's bridle, the other clutched at Nathan's leg, doing his best to tumble him from the saddle. Neither was prepared for the reaction of the great black horse as it reared onto its hind legs and lashed out with murderous hooves. With a cry of pain one of the would be attackers fell to the ground, nursing his head, while the other backed away before taking to his heels. Nathan slid from the saddle as the injured man scrambled to his feet.

"Had enough?" Nathan raised his fist. "Or would you like some of this?"

"No! No!" The wretch whimpered, shielding his head with a ragged coated arm. "Don't let that devil near me! Let me go, Sir, I meant no 'arm."

"No harm? You meant to rob me." He peered down at the grovelling figure in disgust. "You look strong enough to find some honest work. If this is your only trade you'll find yourself shipped off to the colonies. Now get out of my sight!" The man got to his feet and shambled off into the night, hastened on his way by a loud snort from Thunder.

"Nathan climbed wearily back into the saddle, leaning to lay his head against the horse's thick mane. "Thank you your Majesty. You saved my life, or at least a beating from those two rogues." He laughed aloud. "I don't think they'll stop running for a few miles and it will be a long time before they try it on with anyone else on a horse."

His mount needed no urging to continue the journey but by the time they reached the town, both horse and rider were tired. Once clear of the scattering of houses, Nathan reined Thunder into a gentle trot. "No need for haste. Hadleigh is just beyond the next rise and by then Leigh will be in sight." The weary beast nodded his great head as if in understanding.

By the time they reached Leigh Church at the top of Horse Hill they were both all but spent. It was dark as they picked their way down the hill and over the last few yards to the door of the cottage where his life had begun.

An incoming tide rushed hissing across the pebble beach and seagulls, settling for the night, grunted and squabbled on the rooftops nearby. Nathan paused for a moment, his hand raised to rap on the cottage door. The last time he had been there, he had fallen, bleeding into his sister's arms. But now, he squared his shoulders, he had come home with his head held high.

CHAPTER THIRTY THREE

Tom had been far too excited for sleep. Throughout the day he had been underfoot, asking one question after another.

"So, what time is the wedding, Saffy?"

"Tom, I've told you a hundred times. 'Tis at noon on the morrow."

"And are the bells goin' to ring out?"

"So Jean-Pierre tells me." She smiled. "He says he's paid for the bellringers and for everything else."

"I like Jean-Pierre." The boy was suddenly serious. "Saffy..."

"Yes, Tom. What now?"

"Did 'e really mean it when 'e said I'm comin' to live with you up top?" He pointed in the general direction of the houses on the high ground above the village.

"Oh, Tom. You know he means it." She gathered the small child into her arms, sensing his insecurity. "Haven't you already seen our new house and your very own room?"

Tom nodded, searching her face for reassurance. "But why can't I come to the new 'ouse tomorrow with you and Jean-Pierre?"

"Because Poll wants you to stay with her and Gabriel for a few days. It'll be a sort of holiday." She turned away to hide her confusion, not knowing how to explain the need for her and Jean-Pierre to be alone for a while. "'Tis only for a few days until we get things straight."

"But...."

"No more of your buts, Tom." She set the child firmly on his feet. "You're staying with Poll and that's an end to it."

For the rest of the day the boy had wandered moodily around the cottage until in desperation she had sent him to play with his friends. "Stay close." She warned him. "And don't make me call you twice for supper. You'll need to be early to bed. You have a long day tomorrow."

Thankfully, the exercise and strong sea air took their toll and Tom returned ready to eat a good meal and soon after, to climb the stair to his bed.

With a sigh of relief, Saffron cleared away the remains of their meal before slumping onto the settle and closing her eyes. "Just a few minutes." She promised aloud.

She would have fallen asleep had it not been for the sudden urgent summons on the cottage door. Her eyes flew open as she scrambled to her feet to tear it open. A gasp of surprise escaped her as she saw Nathan grinning down at her. In a moment she was wrapped in her brother's warm embrace.

"Nathan, put me down. You'll break my ribs!" She was laughing and crying at the same time. "What are you doing here?"

He held her from him. "Why, little sister, I'm here to see you wed. And I've brought a friend." He stood to one side as Thunder's great head filled the open doorway.

Saffron, wide-eyed, reached a nervous hand to stroke the soft muzzle, "Where'd he come from? He's never yours Nathan, not a fine beast like this."

"No, and before you ask, I've not stolen him. My master gave me leave to ride him, so I could be here in time for your wedding. I'll put him in the lean-to in the yard. It's a fine warm night but he'll be needing food and water and a rub down before he'll settle."

"You sound like you know a lot about horses."

"I know a lot about other things too." He tapped his nose, winking at his sister. "There's a big world out there Saffron Clay, one you never dreamed of and one your big brother aims to be part of. Now, I'd best see to his majesty while you rustle up something for supper."

"There's only the remains of the stew Tom and me had."

"That'll do. I'll be back before you miss me." With a grin, he disappeared, leading the horse away into the darkness.

Grateful that Nathan's arrival had not woken Tom, she busied herself reheating the pot on the stove and laying a corner of the table in readiness for her brother's return. Her mind teemed with questions that needed answers, Nathan seemed so much older somehow. Far more of a man, than on that dreadful night when she had aided his escape from the excise men.

As he tucked into his food, he did his best, between mouthfuls, to fill in the gaps in his letters. "It's all down to Aunt Jane, I suppose. Mind you she's a hard taskmaster. Every night, don't matter how tired I am, she makes me study." He frowned. "I didn't realise at the time how it might make a difference to my future."

"What do you mean, a difference?"

"Well, see, its like this. I wrote and told you about Miss Charlotte, didn't I?"

"You did, Mother would have called her a brazen huzzey. You want to keep well out of her way."

"Well, that's just it. She cornered me and then told her father that I had sort of made advances."

"And I suppose he believed her."

"In a funny way I don't think he did. Of course he had to let me go. I couldn't go on working under the same roof."

"You mean he paid you off?" Saffron exploded with indignation. "That's hardly fair."

"Don't carry on, Saffy. You've not heard the best of it. I'm not a footman any more. I'm to take up a new position as a trainee at one of the Master's maltings. That's where they get the grain ready for turning into beer."

Saffron frowned. "That sounds alright I suppose. What about the pay?"

"'Tis a bit more than I earn as a footman and there's a cottage to go with it so my lovely Sarah and I can start planning our wedding."

"What's this Sarah like? Will she make you a good wife Nathan?"

"She's pretty and slim as a willow." Nathan stared dreamily into the fire. "And she's a good cook into the bargain. Best of all, she loves me the same as I love her. Don't you worry Saffy, when we're wed, I'll have everything I want. Now, what about this Jean-Pierre fellow you're planning to marry? Is he good enough? Don't forget I'm head of the family you know." He grinned wagging a finger at her. "I should have looked him over before you promised yourself."

"You weren't here to ask. Anyway, I don't need you to say yea or nay. I know my own mind. He's a fine man and will make a good and loving husband, that's all you need to know."

"Alright, Saffy, no need to bite my head off, I was only joshing. If you love him that's good enough for me." He yawned. "Is it alright if I get my head down now, I've been on the road since four this morning and I'm right tuckered out."

"I'm sorry, Nathan, I'm tired too and to tell the truth I'm worried that everything will go right on the morrow. Get some rest, we'll talk in the morning." She rose and planted an affectionate kiss on his cheek. When he had gone, she bolted the door and blew out the lamp.

"Thank you." She whispered. "Thank you for bringing Nathan home. Tomorrow the family will all be together again, I could ask for nothing more."

The following day dawned both bright and clear. Fingers

of sunshine crept between the curtains to wake Saffron to the realisation that her big day had arrived. She lay for a moment. Below in the kitchen, she could hear Tom's voice and Nathan's laughter. She smiled, relishing the few minutes of peace between waking and rising. Hugging to herself the knowledge that only a few hours remained before she would begin a new life as Mrs. Saffron Harding.

She threw back the covers and crossed to pour cold water from the jug into the basin, catching sight of her tousled appearance in the small mirror.

"It is as well Jean-Pierre can't see you now." She chuckled. "He would think he was marrying a wild woman." She stepped out of her night shift and ran fingers through her hair, turning one way and then the other. She let the tumble of curls fall into a cape around her slim shoulders, unashamedly brushing her hands over her firm young breasts and onto her flat belly. "Oh Jean-Pierre." She murmured. "I pray God I will not disappoint you." She shook herself back to reality, washing hurriedly and pulling on a faded print dress and apron. Time enough for wedding finery later in the morning.

Tom greeted her at the foot of the stair, his freckled faced flushed with excitement. "Saffy, Nathan's 'ere, did you know?" Saffron ran a hand through his fair hair.

"I did. He got here last night when you were asleep. Did he tell you he came on a horse?"

Tom nodded. "I seen 'im. 'E's called Thunder. I 'elped Nathan feed 'im. He took 'is food right out of my 'and." He held out a small hand palm uppermost. "'E didn't bite me, just sort of snuffled it up."

Nathan's roar of laughter brought a smile to Tom's face. "Snuffled it up. I like that! But he's a gentle beast, you're right there lad." He winked at Saffron. "If you want to go and talk to him, you can tell him he's off to a wedding today, he'd like that."

Saffron's agreement sent the happy child running into the back yard.

"Give us a minute to talk Saffy." Nathan motioned her to sit with him at the scrubbed table. "I feel bad that I wasn't here when Jonas died. Young Tom did his best to explain but there's more to it isn't there?"

Saffron glanced through the back door to where she could see Tom talking animatedly to the black horse. "A lot more Nathan." She paused, biting her lip.

"Too much to tell right now but Jonas had got caught up in smuggling. Like you, he wasn't caught, thank God, but it's why he got hurt. I covered it up, with the help of the Doctor. Poor Tom felt it most but of course I couldn't tell him the truth. Jonas was his father even though he never acted like it." She added bitterly. "Perhaps one day I'll find the right words."

Nathan reached to cover her slim hand with his own. "I'm sorry Saffy. Sorry you've had to bear the weight of it."

Impatiently, she withdrew her hand. "What's done is done. Now let's have no more sad talk. I'm to be wed in a few hours and I'd be glad if you would take the lad over to Poll's. His wedding shirt and britches are there and Gabriel has said he'll get him ready and to the church, so that's one less thing to worry about."

"He said he's to be the ring bearer. Right thrilled he is."

"Well, he did it at Poll's wedding, so he'll know what to do when the time comes."

"There's something else, Saffy. Gabriel came over this morning, before you were awake."

"What's wrong?" Saffy was instantly alarmed. "Is Poll alright?"

"No, it was nothing like that. He said that he was to give you away but as I made it here in time for the wedding he was happy to pass the honour over to me."

He shook his head. "Poll's got a good man there." He raised his head to grin at his sister. "So it'll be me handing you over to this Jean-Pierre."

Saffron smiled. "You're right, Gabrielle is one of the best. I asked him to give me away before I knew you would be able to be here. It's just like him to put things right. Now, off you go Nathan and tell Poll I'll expect her about an hour before I leave for the church."

Once Nathan had explained at some length to Tom why they could not take Thunder with them, they were gone, leaving behind a blessed silence. Jean-Pierre had made Saffron a gift of rose scented soap, sent down from London. Using it sparingly she washed and rinsed her hair until it squeaked clean. Standing at the open window, she separated the curled strands with practiced fingers, drying it in the onshore breeze. The tide had yet to make its way over the rippled mud, allowing the flocks of Brent Geese from the Arctic to make their annual arrival. After feeding greedily on the Leigh Marshes they would make their way to the Maplin Sands, their winter home.

She was jolted from her reverie by the sudden appearance at the window of her neighbour, Lizzy Smale. "I didn't mean to make you jump!" The woman laughed. "I just wanted to catch you before you left for the church. I made something for you." She held out a folded square of white linen. "I 'ope as 'ow you like it."

"Oh, Mrs.Smale, Its lovely!" Saffron shook out the small cloth and held it up to the light. "Its drawn thread work, isn't it. I remember Mother saying how hard it was to do." Impulsively, she leaned from the open window to throw her arms around the smiling woman. "Thank you, I shall treasure it forever. It will look grand on the table in the new house."

A frown flitted across her neighbour's face. "You won't forget us, will you Saffy? You moving up top and all."

"Forget you? How could I, you've been so good to us since Mother died. Besides, it won't make any difference where I live, I might be changing Clay to Harding but I'll still be Saffy, your friend." She added shyly. "And I'll be back most days, taking Tom to school and buying bread and such."

"Harding, that's 'is name is it? 'E looks to be a well set up fellow. Artist I've 'eard tell. Brings in a fair bit does it?"

Saffron chuckled. "He is, and it does. At least, when he sells one of his paintings. Don't worry, he can take good care of me."

"Your dear Mother would be glad to see you so 'appy, Saffy." She wiped a tear away with the corner of her apron. "I still miss 'er, you know. She were one of the best."

"She was, and I'd give the world to have here today. We all would." She dragged her mind back to change the subject. "Nathan's home. Did you see him?"

"I did, fine lad he's growed into." The woman straightened. "Well I'd best be off, see you in church!"

Saffron waved her goodbye just as Poll came hurrying into sight, her long hair flying in the breeze. Over her arm she carried a sheet wrapped bundle. Bursting through the cottage door she placed it carefully on the table.

"What ever have you got there Poll. And what's got you so excited?"

"Its your Jean-Pierre, that's what." She opened the sheeting to reveal a pale yellow dress. "'E says if I'm to walk with you to the altar as your Bride's maid then I should look special." Her eyes sparkled as she fingered the soft material. Gabriel says it's all right for me to wear it. If it's all right with you Saffy."

"Of course it is, and very thoughtful of Jean-Pierre." She held the dress against her sister's small frame. "I should think it will fit a treat. Have you tried it on yet?"

Poll shook her head. "Not 'till I'd asked you, Saffy." She hugged the dress to her. "There'll be some noses in the air when they see you in your white silk and me in this."

"Well, they'll have nothing to look at, we'll be that late. Now, get upstairs and let's see how you look. Then you can help me dress. Time's getting on and I've a mind to leave a few minutes early. I've got a call to make on the way."

Saffron would not be drawn further on the subject, promising that Poll would find out soon enough.

The yellow dress fitted perfectly, the gathered skirt falling discretely over the still early evidence of Poll's pregnancy. Saffron cut a piece from the overly long matching sash and tied it into the girl's hair. "There, you look like a princess. Now it's my turn."

She stripped off the cotton dress and shift, and taking the precious bar of soap, lathered and rinsed her body, rubbing it dry until her skin glowed. Poll helped her to wriggle into a clean lace edged fine cotton shift.

"I've seen that before, ain't I?" Poll stood back, head on one side.

"You have, it was Mother's. She wore it at her wedding and she put it away in the chest the next day. She showed it to us once, when you were little. She said it was put away specially for me to wear at my own wedding." She fingered the fine lace neckline. "I know its silly, but it makes me feel that she's here somehow."

"I know what you mean, Saffy. I'm sure she's lookin' down

on us right now. She'd be proud to see you, an' me an' Tom an' Nathan. All 'appy and 'ealthy and its all down to you Saffy." She hugged her sister to her. "Thank you." She whispered.

For a moment they stood in one another's arms until Saffy pushed Poll gently away. "Fetch my dress, Poll. I'll need a bit of help getting it over my head and there's a dozen buttons down the back that need fastening."

As the folds of white silk fell around her, Saffron slipped her arms into the long sleeves. Poll tugged the waist into place, muttering to herself, as she fumbled with the tiny buttons before standing back to admire the overall effect.

"Oh Saffy." She breathed. "All that's needed is some flowers an' a ribbon in your 'air."

"They are in the kitchen. Jean-Pierre sent them early this morning, before I was down. Nathan took them in. Could you run down and get them?"

Poll returned minutes later, her arms filled with deep pink roses, their heady scent filling the small bedroom. The stems of the bouquet were bound with satin ribbon, and on a small tray sat a bridal headdress, a circlet of matching rosebuds.

As the two sisters made their way down into the kitchen there was a gentle knocking on the door. The pony and trap, flower decked and beribboned had arrived.

The driver, who Saffron recognised as one of the young grooms from Leigh House, settled them both into the cush-ioned interior, before flicking his whip above the willing pony's head.

Saffron leaned forward, tapping the lad on the shoulder. "I want to stop on the way. I'll not be a moment. I'll tell you where."

The lad looked surprised. "You'll be late, Miss. Its no more than a few minutes to the hour."

"What I wish to do will cause no real delay. When you get to the burial plots I want you to stop."

The young groom shrugged his agreement and minutes later, reined the pony into the grass verge alongside the cluster of headstones. Gathering her skirts to avoid soiling them in the long grass, Saffron stepped from the trap.

"Shall I come too, Saffy?" Poll frowned, as her sister raised a staying hand.

"No, Poll. I won't be but a minute or two."

The graves lay said by side. Mary and Jack Clay, together in death as they had been in life. For a moment, Saffron stood head bowed. "I know you are both watching over me today." She began. "And I want you to know, Ma, and you too, Pa, that I'm marrying a good man who loves me as much as I love him. We're taking young Tom with us and we'll make sure he comes to no harm and gets his chances in this world. Nathan's got his life in order too. He got off to a bad start but he looks set to make a good future, thanks to Aunt Jane." She paused, lifting her head to the Autumn sun, which seemed to bathe her with it's blessing. "As for Poll, she's not had it easy but the good Lord sent along Gabriel to answer her needs, so you've no cause for worry." She pulled two roses from her bouquet and placed one on each grass-covered mound. "When I make my vows, I shall pray that the good Lord will make Jean-Pierre and me as happy as you were in life. God bless you both."

As the first notes of the organ rang through the clear air, Saffron turned her face first to the village below and then on, up to the houses beyond the square spire of Leigh church.

"God bless me and make me a fitting wife, whatever the future may hold, for today I begin a new life with the man I love."